THE FIRST TIME

Pace bent his head to apply his mouth to hers with a force that reflected his hunger.

She was soft and small. Pace felt the slight exhalation of Dora's breath against his lips when he claimed hers, but something kept driving him on. He expected resistance but instead received a tentative, questioning pressure of her lips in return. He wanted more.

Suddenly she shuddered and gave a soft cry, but her fingers curled more securely into his shirt. She was responding. She was answering his plea, molding her lips to his, allowing his invasion, moving her body closer into the curve of his. He couldn't believe it. Wouldn't believe it. He wanted all of her....

TALES OF LOVE AND DESIRE
BY PATRICIA RICE

TOPAZ HISTORICAL ROMANCES

Paper Moon   (406524—$5.99)
Paper Tiger   (406087—$5.99)
Paper Roses   (404696—$4.99)

ONYX HISTORICAL ROMANCES

Shelter From The Storm   (403584—$4.99)
Touched By Magic   (402987—$4.99)
Moon Dreams   (402324—$4.95)
The Devil's Lady   (403258—$4.99)

REGENCY ROMANCES

The Genuine Article   (182359—$3.99)
Mad Maria's Daughter   (170792—$3.99)

WAYWARD ANGEL

Patricia Rice

A TOPAZ BOOK

TOPAZ
Published by the Penguin Group
Penguin Books USA Inc., 375 Hudson Street,
New York, New York 10014, U.S.A.
Penguin Books Ltd, 27 Wrights Lane,
London W8 5TZ, England
Penguin Books Australia Ltd, Ringwood,
Victoria, Australia
Penguin Books Canada Ltd, 10 Alcorn Avenue,
Toronto, Ontario, Canada M4V 3B2
Penguin Books (N.Z.) Ltd, 182–190 Wairau Road,
Auckland 10, New Zealand

Penguin Books Ltd, Registered Offices:
Harmondsworth, Middlesex, England

First published by Topaz, an imprint of Dutton Signet,
a division of Penguin Books USA Inc.

First Printing, February, 1997
10 9 8 7 6 5 4 3 2

REGISTERED TRADEMARK—MARCA REGISTRADA

Printed in Canada

To the survivors:
May love and the power of God heal all wounds.

I would like to dedicate this book to my mother, who survived,
and to the Henwoods, whose acceptance gave her the family she needed.

Prologue

Matthew, Mark, Luke, and John,
The Bed be blest that I lie on.
Four angels to my bed,
Four angels round my head,
One to watch, and one to pray,
And two to bear my soul away.
—THOMAS ADY, *A Candle in the Dark* (1656)

November 1851

Alexandra Theodora Beaumont grasped the rim of the polished mahogany library ladder and attempted to unhook it from the ledge of Bible study volumes. Although she had just turned eight, her hands were too small and helpless for the Herculean task. With a moue of disgust, she glanced around the lamp-lit library for an alternative.

Her gaze alighting on the rich maroon leather of a high-backed wing chair near the shelves she wished to reach, she set her determined little chin and advanced upon her goal like a soldier marching off to war. The lamp's flickering flame cast shadows over the deep wine of her short velvet gown but shimmered on the gold-threaded embroidery of the bodice. The gold threads could not match the angelic halo of white-gold curls creating a nimbus around her elfin features. Despite the rich threads and halo, there was very little angelic about Lady Alexandra at the moment. She knew she approached forbidden territory, and she moved with extreme caution, testing the chair for the squeak of its springs before climbing up on it.

Even the extra couple of feet gained by standing on the leather seat did not give her the height necessary to reach the shelf just tantalizingly out of her reach. Gareth had told her that the shelf contained the angel books.

He had even pulled down a volume and showed her the
charming watercolors of golden angels in a blue sky.
And then he had laughed and shoved the book back in
its place—out of her reach. She hated her half brother
with every fiber of her being, but she wouldn't let him
defeat her. She might be ten years younger and small
for her age, but she could do anything he could.

With cautious patience, she eased the chair around so
the arm aligned with the bookcase. Then she scrambled
back into the seat again and stepped up on the arm. The
heavy old chair easily counterbalanced her slight weight.
Standing on tiptoes, she curled her fingers around the
first volume on the shelf.

The library door flew open with a thud that bounced
off the paneled walls, echoing in the high-ceilinged
room. The single lamp flame flickered, sending dancing
shadows of her precariously perched figure across the
shelves. Her fingers defiantly grasped the binding when
the expected bellow ripped through the quiet library.

"Father, she's at it again, just as I said!"

There wasn't any use in running. She could drop the
book, jump down, and look innocent, but it wouldn't
matter. She really didn't even know why Gareth went
to all the trouble of trapping her. He could tell their
father anything and be believed. Grasping the book
firmly, Alexandra pulled it off the shelf and hopped
down into the chair seat. She stood firmly on the floor
by the time her father had followed the sound of Gareth's voice and entered the room.

She clasped the volume to her chest, prepared to
argue her position when she heard the sound of her
mother's voice in the hall, and she cringed inwardly. Her
mother shouldn't be here. She was supposed to visit the
vicar. That meant the earl hadn't let her go after all.
That meant . . .

She wouldn't think about what it meant. She wouldn't
think about the whimpers and cries of pain coming from
her parents' chambers on the nights her father decided
her mother needed a lesson. It made her stomach hurt
just thinking about it. And now he had Alexandra's dis-
obedience to make him even more fierce with his justice.

She screwed up her inner courage, closed her eyes,

and tried praying fervently to God as her mother had told her to do, but God just wasn't there. Her father was. His large boots stormed across the beautiful Turkish carpet. His big hands wrapped around her slender arms as he jerked her from her feet. She didn't even register the roar of his words over her head or the pain of his fingers pinching into her flesh. She prayed hard and fast, praying for a miracle.

"George, she doesn't mean anything by it!" her mother pleaded. "Gareth teases her into it. You know he does. I'll spank her and send her to bed and she'll only have bread and water tomorrow. I promise."

One large hand casually lashed backwards, shoving his wife away as the other hand held his daughter dangling from the floor. Crying, his wife grabbed her husband's arm and clung.

"George, please. It's all my fault. I've cosseted her too much. I won't do it anymore. Punish me, George. She's much too little to understand."

Alexandra cringed and wept inside at these words, but she knew for her to say anything would only aggravate her father's ire. And raising his ire would mean even stronger retribution for her mother. She held still and tried making herself very small.

"She is weak, just as you are weak. It takes a strong love to provide guidance." The words boomed over her head. "I'll not have your interference, Matilda."

With his free hand, the earl grasped his wife's slender wrist, the one attached to the hand clutching his arm. In a single, simple twist from his powerful fingers, he produced a popping noise of damaged bones. Matilda's muffled cry of pain echoed through the thick air. The grip on his arm loosened as his victim grabbed her painwracked wrist.

"George, not tonight, please," Matilda whispered insistently, despite the pain. "You wished me to stay home so we could be together. I am here. Let Dora alone, and you can teach me to be strong. I'll have Carrie take Dora to her room."

Alexandra clenched her tiny hands into fists, squeezed her eyes shut, and prayed silently, ignoring the fiery pain in her shoulder. *Lord God, please do not punish my*

_mother for my sins. I will never touch the angel books
again. I promise, Lord God, just don't let him hurt my
mother again. Please, God, I will try to be good. If it
weren't a sin, I would drown myself in the river so she
never be punished again. Please, by all that is holy, amen._

It sounded reverent and holy as the vicar, and if there
truly was a God, surely He would hear and answer her
prayers. But as Alexandra had already suspected, God
didn't exist.

"Go to your room, woman. I'll be there directly."

His voice wasn't even a roar anymore. It was cold and
commanding, and a shiver went down Alexandra's spine.
She knew what that meant, and a tear squeezed beneath
her eyelid despite all her efforts to force it back.

Her mother knew, too. She slipped quietly from the
room. Further protest would only worsen the punishment for both of them.

Alexandra stoically followed at her father's heels as
he grasped her arm and led her toward the wide circular
stairway that was considered one of the architectural
wonders of this far corner of England. She lived in a
mansion far beyond the means of the fishermen and min-
ers here in Cornwall. They had no social equals here.
She had no playmates. The vicar and his wife were their
only friends, and the vicar relied on Lord Beaumont for
his living. If she couldn't call on God or her mother for
help, she could call on no one.

That night Alexandra got off lightly—physically. A
large man, with handsome black hair, flashing dark eyes,
and a sensuous mouth, Beaumont had the respect of his
peers and his lessers for not using his good looks to get
what he wanted. He was considered a religious family
man who treated his tenants sternly but fairly. He
wouldn't use his greater strength to deliberately harm
his only daughter. He merely made her stand in the corner on her toes with her nose pressed to an impossibly
high spot on the wall, then sent her nursemaid to see
that she stayed there. He paid the nursemaid well to
follow his orders.

Physically, the punishment was almost endurable. Alexandra was light and agile and she had grown an inch
or so since the last time he had used this punishment.

She didn't have to stand on the very edge of her toes to reach the mark. Weariness was her worst enemy, that, and the ache in her shoulder. The real punishment came later, as the house grew dark and silent, and the muffled sounds from the room below seemed to become the pounding of drums in her ears.

When her mother's piercing cry finally rang through the silence, Alexandra removed her nose from the spot and vomited the remains of her delicious duck dinner into the porcelain washbowl at her side. It wouldn't do to stain the expensive carpet and start the punishment all over again.

Later, in the early dawn hours when her mother entered the nursery and sent the maid away, Alexandra collapsed limply into her arms and listened with a child's dying hope to words she had heard a hundred times before.

"He doesn't really mean to hurt us, Dora. He's just much bigger and doesn't know his strength. He's so good, and he loves us so much, he just wants us to be good like him. We must try harder, Dora. Promise me, you'll try harder?"

April 1852

"Not a word, Dora. Don't say a word to anyone." Pulling her billowing cloak around her burgeoning stomach, Matilda caught her daughter's arm and hurried her up the gangplank to the hulking ship bobbing at the dock. Cosmetics could only partially disguise the vivid bruise on the side of her face.

Alexandra wanted to scratch at the coarse cotton irritating her skin, but one hand clung to her porcelain doll and the other clung to her mother, and she didn't dare release either.

She was frightened because her mother was frightened, but she was also curious, and she avidly drank in all the new and fascinating sights and sounds around her. Her father never let them come to the docks. He never let them off the estate. She had never seen Plymouth before. She had never seen the sea. She wanted to see it all at once, but she clung to her mother's hand instead. She knew without being told that her father would punish them harshly if he found them here. That's why they wore these coarse disguises.

"Wait here, Matilda, while I find your cabins and have the baggage transferred. You'll be safe with these nice people. They're Quakers. They won't harm you."

The man who had brought them to the docks was a stranger to Alexandra, but she liked his soft voice and pleasant smile. He seemed almost as worried and frightened as her mother though. Instinctively, she looked for good hiding places among the crates and barrels being loaded on deck.

"Michael is a good man. He'll take care of us," her mother whispered reassuringly for the third or fourth time as the stranger loped back down the plank. "He was my beau once, you know. I should have chosen him, but I loved your father more. I still love him. He just doesn't know his strength, Dora. We must look out for your baby brother or sister, mustn't we? I don't think Michael loves me anymore," she said sadly. "Maybe your father will welcome us back when the baby is born. I don't know what I shall do without him."

Alexandra could think of lots of things she could do if her father weren't there to stop her. She could see the sea more often, ride ponies, read angel books, play with the tenant children. When she had the chance, she would ask Michael if she could do these things now. If he said yes, she wouldn't go back to her father, no matter how much her mother loved him. Every time her father said he loved her, he hurt her. Love was vastly overrated in Alexandra's opinion.

They moved closer to the railing, watching the crowd milling about on the dock below. Her mother clenched Alexandra's hand too tight, but she didn't complain. She watched the road anxiously for the crested carriage that would signal her father's arrival. She wished Michael would hurry back and set this ship sailing.

Her mother flinched as a crate came loose from its rope and crashed to the deck with a noise like a gunshot. She pulled Alexandra closer in front of her and wrapped her arm protectively around her daughter's slender shoulders.

"He won't come," she whispered, as if reading Alexandra's thoughts. "He's in London. He'll never get here in time. Say good-bye to England, darling. Michael is taking us to America."

Alexandra thought that idea required singing and dancing with joy, but her mother openly wept. Maybe her father was right. Her mother was a weak woman. Maybe this man Michael could be strong for all of them.

She felt a little queasy from the rolling of the ship and the hot sun on her head and the constant fear when the dreaded finally occurred. With a terrible sense of the inevitable, Alexandra watched through sleepy eyes as her father's gleaming carriage clattered down the cobblestones with a scream of horses and cracking of whips. Behind her, her mother gave a moaning sob of despair.

Later, the scene came back as a sleep-induced nightmare, an unreality Alexandra never consciously remembered.

In her nightmares, she saw the stranger called Michael running for the ship. She saw her father, his black greatcoat flapping in the stiff breeze like giant bird's wings. She heard the sharp reports of more crates falling. Or perhaps they weren't crates. Red flowers erupted on Michael's clean white linen, and he fell backward to the accompaniment of disembodied screams.

Alexandra felt certain it was her mother screaming, but the sounds came from all around her, even from the gulls flying overhead. She tried squeezing between the crates and the rails, hiding herself from the screams, from the black wings and thunderous roars. She tried making herself small, invisible. Maybe if he didn't find her, it would all go away. She was the sinner. Let God cast her away.

No one stopped him. No one stood in the way of the great flapping wings and smoking pistol. No one dared interfere as a peer of the realm strode on deck demanding the return of his wife. Men hurried to clear his path. A wife belongs with her husband—Alexandra heard the voices whisper in her nightmare. *A wife belongs to her husband.*

He didn't even see Alexandra crouched among the
crates. With cold fury, the earl smashed the back of his
powerful hand against his wife's jaw. She stumbled backward, tripping over Alexandra's crouched body, slamming into the railing. Splintering wood caused a rippling
cry of alarm through the crowd.

In the next moment, Alexandra went airborne, her
mother flying free beside her, screaming "Dora!" in one
long, terrified wail. God had come for them at last.

God's cold hand reached for her through the splash
of icy waters over her head. Alexandra clung to her doll,
determined to take this beloved friend with her to the
new world.

The older man in the broad-brimmed hat and old-
fashioned collarless coat didn't hesitate as two feminine
figures went flying overboard into the filth of the harbor.
Flinging off coat and shoes, he leaped in after them,
ignoring the wild cries of the handsome, overwrought
earl on the deck.

Other men followed his example, leaping from dock
and deck. A rowboat full of sailors went out. Men
dived and swam and came up empty-handed. The earl
paced and cursed and cried. He swore eternal rewards.

The man in Quaker's homespun linen heard none of
them. Beneath the murky waters, he caught a glimpse
of the child's blue gown. His fingers caught in the cloth,
and he kicked upward, grasping hard and praying.

He broke through the water somewhere to the stern
of the boat where the current had carried them. Too far
from the dock to swim back, he grabbed a rope dangling
over the side of the ship, his fragile burden caught firmly
beneath his arm.

Another Friend pulled him aboard. Three more
Friends spirited them into a cabin where a woman took
charge, pumping at tiny lungs and frail ribs, breathing
into a rosebud mouth rapidly turning blue. Beside her,
the once expensive porcelain doll dripped seaweed from
its bedraggled velvet dress.

Holding hands, the group prayed as the woman
worked, as the sailors returned to their tasks, as the
ship's steam boiler heated and blew. On deck, a great

wail went up as the icy sea yielded a woman's body, and the earl hurried along the dock to claim her.

Only when the child choked and breathed again did the small group offer prayers of thanksgiving and think to send word to the child's grieving father.

The older woman, the one who had returned the child's breath, the one whose husband had brought the child out of the sea's cruel hands, looked up at the circle of concerned faces and said, "Go and seek him if thou must, but the Light has spoken. She belongs with us."

And so it would seem. By the time the message reached land and followed the weeping earl and the lifeless body of his wife to the nearest inn, the unsuspecting sea captain had ordered the ship to sail from the harbor with the tide.

The earl's demands that the ship be halted and his daughter returned went ignored by the authorities who came to take him away for questioning. His curses and vows of vengeance fell flat in the ears of officialdom.

When Alexandra woke, she was surrounded by a sea of quiet, concerned faces. These were strangers like none she had ever seen before. They wore no velvets or lace, gold nor jewels. She was afraid until the first one spoke.

"Thou must rest now, child. All will be well."

The soft singsong voice spoke like the angels of the Bible. She had died and gone to heaven. Not daring to say anything lest they know their mistake, Alexandra closed her eyes, and wrapping her tiny fingers around her doll's hand, she slept.

When next she woke, she was called Dora and given a new gown like that of the angel's. She didn't cry once. God hadn't forgotten her after all.

One

It is easy—terribly easy—to shake a man's faith in himself. To take advantage of that to break a man's spirit is devil's work.

—GEORGE BERNARD SHAW, *Candida* (1903)

July 1852 Kentucky

The spacious rooms resounded with the joyful airs of piano and violin in a rollicking reel. Hooped skirts in gay colors bounced and swung as young couples laughed and glided hand in hand through the formation. The family had pushed back the pocket doors between dining room and parlor to open up the rooms for reels and cotillions. The newly waxed floor gleamed in the light of chandeliers and oil lamps. The servants had carried the ornate mahogany dining table to the wide center hall, filling it with enormous platters of fruits, cold meats, and cheeses to feed the hungry crowd milling and gossiping while the young people danced. The old house rang with happiness and pleasure.

In the shadows, sixteen-year-old Payson Nicholls regarded the pageantry with cynicism. His gaze followed the actions of his older brother and his cronies as they flirted with the girls and slipped into the study for hasty drinks from flasks and decanters. Charlie's twenty-first birthday ball had just about reached its frivolous height. He crossed his arms over his chest and listened as Charlie sweet-talked his latest conquest.

"Sally Ann, you know you're the prettiest girl here tonight. I've been trying to catch up with you all evening, but you have so many beaux around I didn't think you'd have the time to speak with me."

The breathless Sally Ann gazed up in adoration at the handsome dark-haired young man holding her hand. "I swear, Charles Nicholls, you do know how to turn a girl's head. I've waited all evening for you to look at me, and you know it."

Charlie laughed and whispered something in her ear that Payson couldn't hear. Sally hit his brother's arm playfully with her fan, then allowed Charlie to head her toward the folding screen concealing the door into the kitchen gallery and the privacy of the dark night.

Sally's father intercepted their path, and Payson smiled to himself at the swiftness and accuracy of the older man's actions. Charlie instantly halted his progress to shake the other man's hand.

"Glad you could come tonight, sir. My father and I have talked about that new strain of tobacco you planted this year. It seems to be taking off well. Joe Mitchell and I are planning on picking up some acreage down the road here to try some experimental strains next year. We need to sit down and talk with you sometime. I was just taking Sally Ann here back to see the puppies that hound of ours whelped. Prettiest batch we ever did see. Maybe you'd like one for yourself, sir. The sire is that prize hound of Howard's. Could smell a rabbit at a hundred yards."

And a fugitive slave at the same distance, but Charlie politely omitted that fact, Pace noticed cynically. Sally Ann's father didn't approve of the local pastime of helping bounty hunters track runaways. With the Ohio River only a mile or two down the road, bounty hunting had become a lucrative trade. Charlie didn't do it for the money though. He did it for the sport.

Of course, Charlie hadn't planned on taking Sally Ann to see the puppies in the first place. Charlie just wanted the foolish female outside in the dark to see how far he could get with her. He and his cohorts kept score. Last Pace had heard, Charlie was down by one kiss and two feels.

The thought made him edgy. Most of the girls here tonight were older than Pace. He'd only bothered rigging himself out in this monkey suit so he could spy on Charlie. But the notion of what the older boys were doing

outside in the yard made Pace's unruly dick thicken and
stir uncomfortably. He had to keep his mind on the notion that Charlie intended celebrating his birthday in less
domestic ways than he presently exhibited. A stolen kiss
and a few drinks from his father's bourbon wouldn't suffice for Charlie this night.

Payson leaned against the back of the tobacco barn
and drew deeply of his hand-rolled cigarette. He'd shed
his fancy frock coat and tie and waited in shirt sleeves.
The musicians and guests had departed but a katydid
hummed a loud chorus in the old catalpa tree behind
the paddock, and an owl hooted from the barn loft. The
night sounded normal, but Pace kept his ears attuned
for changes. His father would no doubt beat him to a
pulp if he found him out here, but it wouldn't be the
first time and it wouldn't be the last. For some reason
known only to God, their temperaments had never
suited. He was quite fatalistic when it came to the differences between his father and himself.

He wasn't quite so casual about his father's attitudes
toward others. His shoulders stiffened as the night
breeze caught the sound of a woman's muffled sob in
the distance. He'd known his brother and his friends
were up to some devilment. He'd expected them to ride
out tonight. He had his horse saddled and waiting. But
it seemed they struck a little closer to home this time.
An awful gaping hole opened in his midsection at the
realization of what that meant, and for a brief moment,
Pace wished he'd brought his gun.

But he hadn't brought it for a reason: he'd known he
would kill someone if he had it in his hands.

Chances were good that he was the one who would
get killed, but that had never stopped him before. Everyone had to die sometime, and he pretty well figured he
would die sooner than most. He might as well go out
protecting those who couldn't protect themselves. It was
a singularly stupid thing to do, but it sure enough riled
his father and brother when he did it.

With resignation, Pace threw down the cigarette and
squashed it out with the heel of his boot. He hadn't yet
reached a man's size. Maybe he never would. He knew

the size of his enemy. It wouldn't hurt to take along a little self-protection. He grabbed the pitchfork in the stack of hay as he started at a run down the dirt path to the slave quarters.

He knew from the sickness in his stomach that he was really a coward, that he didn't want to do this at all. It would be a lot easier if he just walked down to the river and turned his back on what happened here in this straggly line of mud chink and timber cabins. But the tough filament of orneriness that his father had tried beating out of him more than once just wouldn't let go. The only friends he had in this world lived back here. The world might consider them animals, but animals could be kinder than humans.

By the time he made his way into the center of the slave quarters, he didn't hear sobs but heartbreaking wails of pain and anguish. Pace gritted his teeth and clenched his jaw. He was already too late. Damn, but he should have known. He'd failed again. He deserved the beating he would get this time.

He slammed open the plank door of Tessie's cabin, desperately avoiding looking too closely at the cornhusk bed in the corner. He concentrated all his savage attention on the heaving buttocks between himself and the young girl on the bed. A pitchfork might not be his chosen weapon, but it would suffice.

He lunged before the others in the room even knew he'd entered.

The man covering the young girl screamed as the tines pierced tender flesh. He rolled off, howling, still holding his wounds even as the others in the room grabbed Pace and slammed him backward against the wall. The girl in the bed scuttled into a corner, pulling a worn blanket over her nakedness as the room erupted in flying fists, kicking boots, and curses.

Pace wielded his weapon well for as long as he could hold it, but four men against one boy didn't make for fair odds. The pitchfork was heaved into the night, and he had only his hard-toed boots to maim and mangle soft parts until meaty hands hauled him from the wall and held him still while others aimed powerful blows at his face and belly.

The girl's screams pierced the air even more frantically than before. Pace slammed his elbows backward,
hitting Homer in his soft storekeeper's belly. His lithe
young body dodged sideways, allowing his brother's
blows to strike Homer more than himself, and in that
instant, he brought his boot up again in a kick he had
almost perfected. Charlie screamed in agony and bent
double.

By the time Carlson Nicholls arrived, Pace was little
more than a bruised and mangled mannequin in Homer's powerful arms. The big man roared for a halt, but
the fight had nearly reached its natural end. Carlson
gave his eldest son a look of disgust, then turned his
scorn to the boy slumped on the floor, barely breathing.

"By hell and damnation, boy, when you goin' to
learn? If that don't beat all, a boy of mine defendin' the
virtue of a nigger 'stead of stickin' it in where it belongs.
You ain't never had a gallup of sense and you never
will. Mama's boy, that's what you are. Ain't never goin'
to 'mount to nothin' a'tall. Get your be-hind outa here
and back to your mammy's skirts where you belong.
Lord a'mighty, I don't know where you came from, but
you ain't none of mine. Get your ass outa here, y'hear?"
Cursing and kicking at the pain-wracked body of the boy
on the floor, he forced Pace to crawl out of the cabin,
out of the way of his elders and betters. Then Carlson
turned and gave one last warning over his shoulder to
the hulking young men panting and rubbing bruised fists,
"Y'all keep it down out here, y'hear? You don't want
your mamas hearing what you been up to."

He walked out, leaving the young black girl to the
tender mercies of four furious young men.

Pace caught a rickety porch post and hauled himself
upright. Glaring at the big-bellied man who didn't claim
to be his father, he spat out, "You better run them out
of there before I come back with a gun."

"You ain't goin' nowhere, you stupid young pup, or
I'll make you stand in line and put it to her just like the
rest of 'em. It's time that girl's been of some use around
here. A little white blood will improve the breedin'
stock. It's about time you got your dick off and learned
what's it like to be a real man. Now get the hell out of

my sight before I take it into my head to whup the tar
out of you."

Since he was about to disgrace himself by emptying
the contents of his stomach, Pace hauled himself off the
porch and out of sight. Shame crawled under his skin,
shame and disgust and a festering hatred that he couldn't
control. He wouldn't ever amount to anything. He
couldn't even help those who counted on him for his
help. He could never look Tessie in the eyes again after
tonight. Damn, but she was only thirteen years old. She
wasn't even a woman yet. She was just a little bitty girl.
Bile roiled in his stomach and he spilled his guts into
the potato patch out behind the kitchen garden.

He'd learned not to cry many long years ago, and he
didn't cry now. He just let the hate build up inside him,
nourishing his rage, feeding his determination. He would
bring them down someday. He already had the basic
tools in his hands. He might not be tall and strong like
his brother. He might not have riches and power like
Homer and his ilk, but he knew how to hurt them where
it hurt the most—in their pockets.

By the time Joshua found him and carried him back
to his room, Pace's agile brain had already sketched the
outline of a plan. When the big black field hand laid him
down on his bed, Pace whispered, "Tell Tessie to be
ready tomorrow night. I'm going to get her out of here."

Joshua's battered face screwed up in a frown of worry.
"You ain't goin' nowheres for a while, Marster Pace.
Them ribs need bindin'. You lucky you ain't coughin'
blood."

"Tessie will be worse off than I am, and Charlie won't
leave her alone now. You want her to go through that
again tomorrow night?"

Joshua looked sick and turned his hulking back away.
"She ain't gonna be in fittin' condition to run. She'll
need her mammy. We cain't jist take her 'way like that."

Pace leaned wearily against the pillows. "It's your
choice, Josh. If you think you and Mammy can get away
too, then I'll take the lot of you, but it won't be easy.
My mother expects Mammy there with her all the time.
How will you get her out of the house?"

Josh's broad shoulders straightened. "I'll get her out.

You get Mammy and my little girl outa here, and I'll stay behind and keep them dogs away. See iffen I don't."

Pace nodded even though Josh couldn't see him. "All right. Tomorrow at midnight, down by the old cottonwood. If those dogs follow, we're all in big trouble and won't anyone get away for a long spell." When Joshua started for the door, Pace said with a catch in his throat, "I'm sorry, Josh."

The big man didn't turn around but bent his head and answered in a voice raw with unshed tears, "Ain't nothin' you coulda done, boy. Ain't nothin' none of us coulda done."

Pace clenched his fists and stared unseeingly at the ceiling long into the night. There had to be something someone could do, and it looked like it fell on him to do it.

He'd much rather cry and pretend it wasn't so.

Pace slipped out of the house early next morning before his mother could see the blackened circle around his eye and the swollen angry red of his jaw. He didn't have much interest in looking in the mirror himself. He didn't think he should expose his mother to it.

His ribs ached with such pain that he gasped for breath by the time he rode into town, but he'd made a promise, and he meant to keep it. He might not be good for much of anything, but he could at least keep a promise.

He rode the back alleys, avoiding Homer's store on the main street, skirting the mayor's house where another of Charlie's good old boys still resided. Joe Mitchell was twenty-four and still lived in his father's house. He didn't have much incentive to do elsewise. The elegant mansion with its fancy ironwork brought all the way from New Orleans was the finest house in town. It came provided with servants to do the housework and cook the meals. Joe's dead mother couldn't complain about the hours her son kept, and his father kept too busy with his own late hours to notice what his boy did. Pace had heard Charlie and his friends snickering over the women they'd sneaked into the mayor's mansion while the mayor was out politicking with the Frankfort big-

wigs. Joe had everything a man could want and didn't
lift a hand to earn any of it.

Pace didn't hold any bitterness on account of Joe's
having everything while he would have nothing. It was
a fact of life known since birth that Charlie would inherit
the farm and everything on it, and Pace would have to
make his own way in this world. He didn't find that
thought in the least dismaying. First chance he got, he
was going off to college to learn to be a lawyer, and
then he would be the one in Frankfort doing the politicking. It was about time someone around here heard
a little sense, and it sure enough wouldn't come from
their current backwoods mayor.

His reason for coming to town had nothing to do with
Joe or Charlie or Homer. Not this time, leastways. Pace
led his horse into the livery so no one could see it tied
up where it shouldn't be, then slipped off on foot down
still another alley.

The old man living in the last cabin at the very edge
of town was so old and bent and grizzled that even the
slave sellers didn't want him. He'd been given his freedom at his master's death, but that had been too late
for Uncle Jas to enjoy it. He scraped a living by barber-
ing those too poor for the town's main shop and fed his
soul with pursuits only a very few knew about.

Pace was one of those few. As he stepped onto the
old man's porch, Uncle Jas flung open the door and
hurried him in before anyone could see him.

"Young fool," the old man muttered, going back to
the crate holding his platter of ham and eggs. "Ain't no
call for you to be here when they's all up and about."
He gave Pace's battered face a shrewd look from beneath bristly white eyebrows. "Reckon you couldn't
make it last night."

Pace ignored his host's mutterings. "I've got two to
go tonight. Josh is taking care of our hounds. What
about Howard's?"

Jas shook his grizzled head and clucked disapprovingly. "You take too many from 'round here, and they's
gonna come lookin' for you. That ain't the whole point
at all, boy."

Pace clenched his fists in frustration. "I know it, but

I can't let them stay. Charlie and the boys raped Tessie last night. I can't let her stay and take more of that."

Clouded eyes looked sad as they stared out at nothing. "That's the way it is, boy. Tessie would get used to it, just like her mother did."

Pace nearly exploded with rage. "You mean you want her to stay here? Whose side are you on? They'll kill her!"

The old man clucked again and followed the young man pacing furiously up and down the narrow wooden floor with his clouded eyes. "She won't be the first, and she won't be the last. You learn that with age, boy. You cain't change the system one person at a time. You gets yo'self that fancy college learnin' and go up and meets the president, and you tell him what it's like out here. Make him change the laws. Then you'll be helpin' some. Right now, all we can do is help the little trickle that comes to us for help. And you hurtin' that trickle by bein' selfish and helpin' those you know best first."

Pace understood all that. He knew if slaves kept disappearing from his father's house that all eyes would turn to him and pretty soon they'd suspect anyone he had any dealings with. He'd tried being patient. He'd turned his eyes from more atrocities than he cared to admit. He couldn't turn away from Tessie.

"If you won't help me, I'll do it myself." He turned around to walk out, but the old man called him back.

"We'll get Tessie out, but you gonna hafta change your ways, boy. You gonna hafta be one of 'em. You gonna hafta find yo'self a little gal and you gonna hafta go with 'em when they go out huntin' them runaways and you gonna hafta bad-mouth niggers like ever'one else 'round here or you ain't gonna be no use to me anymore."

Pace felt the sickness fill his stomach again, but he clenched his fists and fought back the waves of nausea. He turned slowly to face the former slave and nodded slowly. "You just tell me what to do, and I'll do it."

Pace nodded off beneath the thick canopy of maples along the creek bank the afternoon after Tessie and Mammy disappeared across the river. He'd stayed out

all night helping row the boat and guiding them to the
first outpost on the Indiana side. He'd had his ribs
wrapped, but they still hurt worse than the seven rings
of hell. He hadn't had an ounce of sleep in forty-eight
hours, and exhaustion had taken its toll. He didn't have
the strength for going back to the house to get his hide
whipped off. Resting his head in his hands against the
grassy bank, he dozed. His fishing pole went ignored.

Gradually Pace became aware of a silvery tinkle of
sound humming in his ears, teasing at the back of his
mind as it came and went in some unfamiliar lilting form.
He brushed it off as he brushed off the gnats occasionally swarming around his face, but its persistence worried at his conscious mind and his sleepiness faded
slightly. The sound came closer, a singsong caress in his
ears. Nothing dangerous, just a curiosity that grasped his
attention and brought him more fully awake.

He opened his eyes and stared up into the mass of
leaves overhead. He could see nothing but thick green
shade and the silver shimmer of branches. He listened
closer. The sound came from his left, a sliver of song, a
tinkle of childish laughter. He smiled, remembering long
ago tales of angels and harps he'd heard in the nursery.
He sure as hell didn't believe in angels anymore, but the
careless innocence of the sound pleased his ear. He relaxed and waited for it to come closer.

The little brat must be crawling from tree branch to
tree branch. The sound shifted to almost directly overhead. If he looked close, he could almost see a flash of
blue that had nothing to do with sky.

"I shoot bluebirds that wake me up," he called out
loud, in his most menacing tones.

The silvery sound stopped, and he almost regretted
disturbing it. Then a maple seed whirligigged down, hitting his nose, and he grinned. "I do believe there must
be angels in my maple trees. Oh, woe, what will become
of me?"

Childish laughter floated in pure tones over his head.
Pace tried to figure which of the black children from the
slave quarters would dare explore this part of the farm,
but none of them came readily to mind. He had to de-
velop a new image of a white master like his brother,

but he couldn't bully children just yet. The image of
Tessie's once-innocent smile now sullen and shamed was
still too raw in his mind.

Two more seeds whirled idly downward, missing his
nose but landing on his chest. The laughter was quiet
again, tense, as if the child waited for his reaction. He
picked up one of the seeds and sent it whirling toward
the trickling creek. A shriek of delight accompanied his
trick, and he sent the other seed whirling in the same
direction. The delight turned into a fey tune sung in
accents totally foreign to him.

Pace struggled to make out the words, but they eluded
him. Puzzled, knowing none of the slaves could possibly
have made up such a song or sung it in such a manner,
he strained to see the creature perched above him. He
was rewarded with only another flash of blue and white
as she climbed higher. It had to be a she. Those were
very definitely pantalets, and no male voice could ever
make such a pleasant sound.

"I've heard of little angels breaking their legs by falling from trees," he warned. "You'd best get down here
before you fall."

"Angels fly." The sound drifted down to him much as
the seeds had done. Maybe he'd had too much sun and
too little sleep and he imagined this. Wouldn't his
brother get a laugh out of him talking to trees?

"Angels can fall," he replied firmly. "You'd better get
down out of there before I come up and get you."

Instant silence. Only the rustle of leaves in the breeze
replied. Or the rustle of leaves as one mischievous elf
scrambled from one tree to the next. The silvery song
came from his right now.

"I'm staying right here until you come down," he
warned, resting his head firmly in his hands and stretching his legs out toward the creek bank.

"Angels sing lullabies," the childish voice announced
in full round tones not of this world that he knew.

Pace grinned and closed his eyes now that she wasn't
in sight. "Bluebirds sing lullabies. Go ahead and sing,
little bluebird. I'll still catch you when you come down."

Unconcerned by his threat, she sang. Occasionally he
caught threads of her words, familiar sounds about rock-

ing horses and babies sleeping. So bluebirds and angels did speak some form of English, he decided sleepily.

When finally exhaustion overtook him and he slept, the slight figure in the upper branches pushed aside the leaves and daringly looked down.

He looked even more battered and bruised than her mama had after a quarrel with Papa.

With a soft sigh of sympathy, she scrambled down from the tree and quietly laid her newest treasure on his chest, between his crossed hands.

The blue feather remained snugly between his fingers as she scampered away, holding her bedraggled doll firmly in her arms.

Two

We hate some persons because we do not know them; and we will not know them because we hate them.

CHARLES CALEB COLTON, *Lacon* (1825)

December 1857

Dora adjusted her boots and reached for her gray wool cloak. Kentucky winters couldn't be any worse than Cornwall winters. They certainly couldn't be any wetter. She just remembered Cornwall as warmer and dryer, probably because she had never been allowed outside.

Six years had succeeded in dimming most of her memories, and she stayed too busy for wasting much time recovering them. She remembered them as mostly painful and not worth recovering. Papa John was the only father she wanted, and if Mother Elizabeth seemed a little harsher, a little more unbending than the sweet, frail woman she remembered, she didn't complain. She had come to understand that despite the Bible's promises, the meek wouldn't inherit the earth until the ugly stripped it bare.

Still and all, she understood her place in this new world to which her adopted parents had brought her. It was a simple enough task hiding behind shapeless gowns and concealing bonnets, speaking only when spoken to, going about her daily tasks without being told. The regimen, rather than confining, actually represented more freedom than she had ever known.

The simple dress meant she was no competition for the other girls in the county. It meant she attracted nothing more than a few taunting jeers from the boys. On the whole, people left her alone. It was truly amazing what one could do when one was virtually invisible. She had discovered she didn't have to hide in trees to go unseen.

She slipped out of the house with her egg basket and started down the road to town. The egg basket didn't hold any eggs at this time of year, but it made a convenient container for a collection of jams and jellies she had made this past summer. Mother Elizabeth had told her she could sell them and use the money however she wished. Dora could easily think of a dozen things she would like to buy, but she would start with small gifts for her adopted family. She remembered Christmas as a tremendous holiday. She couldn't quite let the meaning of it disappear even if her circumstances had changed drastically.

A large pot-bellied stove heated the mercantile. Dora toasted her toes by it while Billy John's wife, Sally, tallied the worth of the jams and jellies. She found it hard to believe that the Billy John whose finger she had once bitten in a childhood fracas was now married and running the store. The town had elected Joe Mitchell mayor after his daddy got sent to Frankfort last year as a representative. While she had only just turned fourteen, Pace's older brother and his friends had grown up and married and taken their places in the community. Sort of. Charlie hadn't married yet and hadn't taken over the running of the farm because his father stood in the way. But he had his hands in a little of everything that went on around here.

Growing up around Pace and his brother, Dora had always felt as old as they were, but she'd never grown up physically to match her mental maturity. She still had little or no chest to speak of, while Josie Ann—who was only two years older than she—not only had a full bosom but also a dozen beaux. Sometimes, just once in a while, Dora wished she could wear frilly pink gowns and hoops and giggle with the other girls, but then she would remember, and the wish would go away.

Once her toes warmed, Dora gravitated toward the yard goods. Her sewing wasn't of the best, but it was adequate. She fingered a soft gray wool, calculating the yardage needed and the cost. Mother Elizabeth hadn't had a new gown for Meeting in years. Dora didn't know how she could find the time or place to sew when her mother wouldn't notice, but she couldn't think of a more fitting gift.

A gust of wind blew her skirt sideways as the door flew open and two young women in full tarlatan skirts and oceans of crinolines swept in. Giggling and laughing as they approached the counter, they failed to see Dora in the far corner. People usually failed to see Dora.

"Did you hear?" one whispered to Billy John's wife. "They're auctioning off the McCoy property for nonpayment of taxes. Daddy says he'd like to acquire those acres himself, but he expects Joe Mitchell's daddy will buy it for him."

Sally's eyes grew wide. "I didn't hear that. I bet Billy John doesn't know. Tommy McCoy's his best friend. Whatever on earth are they going to do?"

Dora identified one of the newcomers as Josie Ann. She thought the other was one of Josie's many cousins, but she wasn't exactly certain. She didn't travel in Josie's circles, and since Josie had started courting, she didn't pay Dora much mind anymore.

Josie removed her flowered bonnet from her polished chestnut curls. Her voice held almost a thoughtful note when she spoke. "It doesn't seem quite right, does it? Tommy's folks have owned that land for as long as anyone can remember. I heard Tommy had to get himself a job on a riverboat."

Sally's reply was indignant. "Josephine Andrews! You know perfectly well why this happened. If Tommy's daddy hadn't harbored those runaways, they'd be fine right now. You can't steal another man's property and get away with it. That's what my daddy and Billy John say, and they have the right of it. The law says you have to pay when you steal. He got fined and sent to jail just like any other criminal. It's a shame the tobacco barn caught fire when Tommy worked so hard getting it all put up by himself, but that's God's way of punishing sinners."

That wasn't what Papa John had taught her, and that wasn't what Dora and a lot of other people believed, but she kept quiet. This was the first she'd heard about the McCoys losing their farm.

Josie Ann just shook her head. "I just can't believe Mr. McCoy would harbor fugitives. Just because he's too poor to own slaves of his own doesn't mean he has any sympathies with those abolitionists. And Tommy's always been one helping with the runaways."

Her cousin's reply was more shrill and decisive than Josie's hesitant comments. "We've lost thousands of dollars to those Yankees and their thievin'! Why, just last year Daddy invested *three thousand dollars* in some boys he meant to sell down in N' Awlins. When they up and ran away, Daddy wouldn't let us go shopping in Cincinnati like he promised because he didn't have no more cash until they got caught. When they found those niggers over in Evansville, those abolitionists claimed they weren't his! Abolitionists are thieves, that's what they are. It's a crime and a sin that they can't be punished more often. Why, if those slaves had been horses, those Yankees would have been hung on the spot. They have to be made an example of, and if Mr. McCoy is one of them, then he's lost just what it cost us. My daddy said it's those wretched Quakers across the river . . ."

Sally made a shushing noise and gestured toward Dora. All three feminine heads turned in her direction, but Dora merely drew out the length of wool she had decided on as if she hadn't heard a word. The Friends had taught her that anger wasn't Godly. She must feel sympathy for their ignorance.

Gathering up her cloak and basket and the bolt of wool, she started for the counter, nodding pleasantly at the now silent women. Josie Ann immediately smiled and started chattering about the upcoming Christmas ball while Dora spread her material out on the counter for measuring.

Only when she heard Pace's name mentioned did she pay attention again. She knew Pace had graduated from law school last June and now worked for a lawyer in Lexington. She hadn't known for certain he was home again. She'd felt his presence but that wasn't the same as knowing for certain. She'd been waiting for him. There were things he needed to know.

As Dora paid for her purchase, she heard the cheerful whistle of a cane flute outside, accompanied by the slow rattle of chains and the shuffle of a dozen pairs of feet. Her lips tightened and her heart lurched, but she calmly continued counting her money. Sally gave her an anxious look and then glanced back at the two girls drifting toward the store window.

Josie Ann quickly turned away from the sight outside, but her cousin continued watching with a triumphant smile.

"There's one lot that won't trouble us anymore. Sometimes, I think the preacher has the right of it. We ought to send them all back to Africa where they belong. Just look at them! Can you imagine what it would be like if the Yankees had their way and we had to live next door to those filthy darkies?"

Dora waited for Josie Ann or Sally to reply to this, but neither voiced an opinion. She was younger than all of them. They had no interest in her thoughts and wouldn't listen if she spoke them. She wished she could make them understand how ownership diminished people to objects and led to abuse, but she didn't imagine she was God. They would see what they wanted to see.

Still, Dora couldn't resist asking, "Is the Mitchell boy in that lot?"

Once she'd said it, she realized her foolishness. She'd allowed anger to get the better of her after all. All three girls stared at her as if she were a tree who had just learned to bark.

Josie Ann cleared her throat uncomfortably, then tried answering in a tone of reason. "Where would you get a foolish idea like that, Dora? People around here don't break up families. Why, Mr. Mitchell's had Fanny and her children all their lives. He wouldn't sell any of them."

Josie didn't make the mistake of saying that would be like selling off Mitchell's son, Joe. Except for the color of his skin, the slave Fanny's only son looked just like Joe, who looked just like his father. Dora had deliberately stirred up a hornet's nest by calling Fanny's son "the Mitchell boy." Everyone in town knew the young slave Roscoe was literally the congressman's boy, and not just by right of ownership.

Everyone in town didn't know that Joe had finally persuaded his father to sell Roscoe. Dora had heard her father discussing it last night. He was appalled that a man would sell his own son, but he couldn't do much about it. She didn't think Pace could do much either, but she had worse news for Pace than that. She needed to quit exhibiting her useless anger and go about her business.

She gathered up her package and basket and started for the door.

As she left, she heard Sally murmur, "That's not true what you said about keeping families together, Josie. Mr. Howard sells off all the slave children when they turn fifteen, unless he needs an extra hand. He says there's too many mouths to feed otherwise. He only has those few tobacco acres and the hogs."

Dora walked out on the last part of that conversation. She would like to know how those three rich girls justified Howard's breeding operation, but she felt a queasiness in her stomach at just the thought. She was only fourteen and knew nothing of having children, but she didn't want to imagine seeing every one of her babies sold off when they reached fifteen. She didn't want to imagine being sold off to a foreign land, either. Maybe, like her, they would be happier somewhere else, but she'd heard enough about what happened to slaves sold in the Deep South than to think that was the case.

As she hurried down the street, she avoided watching the coffle of slaves scuffling down the street toward the jail. The slave trader had just arrived, so he probably hadn't negotiated any new purchases yet. She didn't need to look for anyone she knew. But time was running out. If someone didn't act soon, it would be a miserable Christmas for at least two families that she knew of.

With unerring instinct, Dora hurried down a side alley and out toward the back of the town. She hadn't come this way since Pace had last been here this past summer. She stayed away from people in general and men in particular, but somehow, since that first day she'd seen

him, Pace had filled a part of her that was missing. She
always knew where to find him. God always told her.

She heard the voices coming from the old cabin and
slipped in the back door of a small, closed-in back porch,
separated from the main cabin by a narrow doorway.
She set her basket down on a shelf and stood in the
shadows, just out of sight of the men in the front room.

Even if she were tone deaf she would recognize Pace's
voice from the anger in it. He had so much anger and
bitterness built up inside him it amazed her that he could
sleep at night. But he was a grown man and she was still
a young girl. She couldn't do much about it. She waited.

"No! The pro-slavery men saw to that. The new constitution allows it and they've got it fixed so it would
take fifteen years to change that clause. The people of
this state may talk emancipation, but they're talking it
with their hands out. Look at what's going on! We're
turning into a state of slave traders. People are becoming
a bigger cash crop than tobacco. There's only one way
to put an end to it, and it's not by using the law."

A low soft voice made a reply vetoing any violence,
and Dora stirred restlessly. That would be David. He
and Pace might have the same goals, but a world of
difference existed in how they achieved them. But while
they argued, families were being torn apart.

Apparently Uncle Jas agreed. She heard his deep slow
voice ask if they had any more of that powder to lead
the dogs astray or if they wanted him to make some
more "hush puppies." Knowing "hush puppies" meant
a concoction laced with strychnine to kill the tracking
hounds, Dora grimaced and came out of the shadows.

"I can get the powder. How soon dost thou need it?"

Everyone looked up in surprise except Pace. He
merely leaned back in his chair and turned, including
her in the circle of his command. "You'd better go get
it now, before it turns dark. I don't suppose you can find
some more gunpowder, can you? If I buy any more,
they'll expect me to blow up the town, and David here
refuses to purchase the devil's weapons."

The young man in Quaker gray started to object, but
Dora ignored his argument. Holding out her hand, she

took the folded bills Pace gave her and left without another word.

After she left, the man in the broad-brimmed hat glared at the wealthy planter's son. "She's just a child! Thou mustn't mix her up in this."

Pace shrugged and went back to stuffing the dangerous canisters of gunpowder. "Did you hear her protest?"

The young black man attaching fuses to the canisters chuckled. "Payson done got hisself a girlfriend. That child attached to your heels like a shadow."

"Lay off, Jackson," Pace growled. "She's just a lonely kid. Let her be."

"Girls talk, boy," Uncle Jas warned. "She shouldn't be here."

Every man in that room knew that if Pace was there, Dora would be sooner or later. It had been that way since childhood. It was an embarrassment, but one he could deal with. He finished the canister and handed it to Jackson. "I'll take her home when she gets back. Don't worry about her talking. She doesn't do much of that."

"That's for sartin," Jackson grunted agreement. "It's downright spooky how that girl stands there and don' nobody know she even there. Reckon how long she was there for she said anythin'?"

Pace knew exactly how long she'd stood there. He'd felt the hairs on the back of his neck rise the moment she walked in the door. It amazed him that no one else knew when the devilish little fairy was around. And he'd lied about her not talking much, although everyone accepted it as gospel truth. Dora could talk a blue streak when she wanted. It just seemed he was the only recipient of her confidences. He wouldn't let that get about.

When she returned with her purchases—Pace didn't ask what lies she'd told to explain them—he pushed back his chair and reached for his hat. "I'll see you gentlemen later. I'll see Miss Smythe home now."

Dora made no acknowledgment of the other men in the room but flitted out the way she had come as if they weren't there. Pace shook his head in bemusement. He'd almost swear she wasn't a member of the female gender. He couldn't think of a woman who wouldn't have flirted, teased, asked ten dozen questions, or scolded him roundly upon finding him in this room with those other unsavory characters. Dora just accepted what was and went on, pursuing some unseen goal of her own.

"I've told you a dozen times before that you have no business going to Jas's place," he warned her when he caught up to her brisk pace. She was small, but she was fast.

"That slave trader from Nashville just arrived. Thy father is planning on selling Joshua, and Joe means to sell Roscoe. And I overheard him talking to Howard about selling the youngest girl out there, even though she's not yet fifteen." She shot him a sidewise glance. "It seems there's a large market in New Orleans for young slave girls with white features."

Pace ran his hand over his face and hid his grimace of despair. There wasn't any end to it. There would never be an end to it. And this innocent child had no business knowing what went on in New Orleans. Why in hell didn't her parents keep her home where she belonged?

He knew the answer to that last: because she was the spoiled child of their old age and they might as well try tying a hummingbird as to rein Dora in.

"Why would my father sell Joshua?" he made the mistake of asking. He couldn't think of any reason in the world that this child should know more than he did about his father's business, but he knew she would have an answer.

"He thinks Joshua helped those runaways last week, and that mayhap he helped with a lot of others around here. Thou must get him away, Pace."

"The whole damned world's gone crazy." Pace shoved his hands in his pockets and kicked up a dirt clod. "Everything that happens around here, they blame on the slaves. A fire at the McCoy's? Had to be fugitives. A hog slaughtered? Had to be one of the coloreds. You'd think white men never did anything wrong."

Dora answered calmly, "But Joshua did help them get across the river. The slaves have a whole network that goes clear to Lexington and probably farther. I imagine there's hundreds of them around here who know Joshua

will row them across the river if they can get free. And
did thou knowest they're auctioning off the McCoys'
farm?''

He did. And he knew what Joe meant to do with it
when he got his hands on it. Pace didn't like how quickly
those back taxes got called in, either. There was something mighty fishy about the whole thing falling together
the way it had. But he was only one man and he could
only fight so many battles at a time.

"I've got someone looking into it," was all the reply
he gave her.

She turned huge blue eyes up to him. "And the
others?"

Pace's jaw tightened. "Your father won't approve of
what I've got planned. Just tell him to make sure he's
with credible witnesses tomorrow night. I'll be at the
Christmas ball with the rest of the town. You'll hear
about it soon enough."

"Josie has a lot of beaux," she said simply.

With a considerably lighter air, Pace grinned. "None
of them as good as me." He stopped in front of the
small Smythe farmhouse and pointed at the front door.
"Now get yourself in there and don't set one dainty foot
out until day after tomorrow. Is that understood?"

Her bonnet fell backward and for one disconcerting
moment while he stared into the eyes of a child, Pace
saw the face of an angel.

Then her cloak flapped as she raised her arm in a
gesture of farewell, and she flew inside, out of sight.

He shook his head at the image of a halo of silver
curls burned into his eyelids. He would have to quit
drinking so much coffee and get a little more sleep before he really started seeing things.

Fingering a small blue feather in his pocket, he went
whistling back to town.

Three

And he dreamed, and behold a ladder set up on the earth, and the top of it reached to heaven; and behold the angels of God ascending and descending on it.

Genesis 28:12

December 1857

The hounds bayed and the night roared with the sound of pounding hooves. A dozen black fugitives lay panting, exhausted, beneath the huge thicket of briars overgrowing a forest of dead trees devastated by a storm years ago. Running down the road, followed by the hounds, meant certain capture. Staying here meant praying the dogs wouldn't catch their scent. No other hiding place existed between here and the river. They prayed the dogs would pass them by.

The first hound hit the wooden bridge over the flood-swollen creek. The hidden men held their breaths, sweat breaking out on their foreheads despite the winter cold and their lack of adequate clothing. The hound howled excitedly.

And then the night exploded into a crackle of gunfire and balls of flame, and the hound turned tail and ran, leaving the wooden bridge to burst into a roaring inferno.

The fugitives dashed from cover and darted down to the river where the boats waited for them.

Pace spread his wide hand across the small of Josie's slender back and swung her around in a wide circle, making her crinolines bell outward in a graceful swoop. She giggled in delight, and he smiled at her ebullience

He didn't know what it was like to be so easily pleased, but he liked seeing someone who did.

She was only sixteen and too young to court. He was just out of school and not ready for marriage. That was understood between them. There would be time for her to flirt and play while he built a career and saved some money. He couldn't offer her the kind of wealth some of her other suitors might possess, but he didn't worry about that. Josie had a timid soul, and the larger, more boisterous men scared her. Even Charlie with his handsome, gallant ways intimidated one so young. Pace had never quite gained his brother's height or practiced ways with women. He'd been laughed at enough times to know that. He would have the last laugh when everyone realized Josie would choose him just because of those things they thought so amusing.

Josie was an only child. Pace supposed eventually her father's farm would come to her, but he wasn't cut out for farming. He wouldn't mind the land and house, but he meant to live in Frankfort where the laws were made. With her quiet hospitality and easy manners, Josie would make an excellent politician's wife. He had it all worked out. He just needed to tell Josie.

When the waltz ended, he whispered in her ear and she giggled, hiding her smile behind her fan. The crowded ballroom buzzed with conversation, but in one of those sudden noiseless lulls that happened in the best of crowds, the sound of baying hounds intruded.

Several of the young men in the crowd looked up with interest. They were more at home on the backs of horses, following their hounds, than in tight coats and slick shoes on a dance floor. It took only the subsequent sound of the explosion to send them running for the front door.

Josie and her friends frowned as their beaux took to their heels and ran whooping into the night. The adults among them whispered and debated, and several of the older men eased out after the younger ones, muttering words about seeing that the young hotheads didn't get into trouble.

Pace grinned down at the budding young woman in

his arms. "Shall we dance, my lady? Or would you have
me run to the rescue with the others?"

Josie gave him a small, thoughtful frown, then flinging
aside whatever stray thought had caused her to wrinkle
her pretty forehead, she threw her arms around him
again. "Let us dance, sir. I'm certain any man who dares
brave a ballroom of disappointed women is more to be
admired than an entire flock of hotheaded sheep."

Pace danced her into the center of the ballroom, leading the crowd into resuming the festivities, making it
impossible for anyone to believe later that he had anything whatsoever to do with the successful escape of
thousands of dollars' worth of valuable slaves from an
irate trader.

"Mr. Smythe, you are getting too old for walking in a
winter rain. I'll not mince words with you. Your lungs
aren't as strong as they used to be. They've caught an
inflammation. You need to rest and drink lots of liquids
and keep warm until the inflammation goes away. If you
go outside again, it will be the same as suicide."

The doctor tucked his instruments back in his bag as
he scolded his patient in a stern voice. He turned to the
two anxious females hovering in the doorway behind
him and left instructions for nourishing broths and orders not to let the fire die down in the bedchamber. As
soon as the doctor walked out the front door, John
Smythe struggled for a sitting position and reached for
the pen and paper at his bedside.

"Papa, no!" Dora rushed in, taking the utensils away
from him. "Thou must rest. Lie back and close thy eyes
while Mama fixes the broth. If thou wishes something
done, let me do it for thee."

Coughing, John leaned back against the pillows, not
willingly, but because he was too weak for anything else.
"Thou must send to the Elders, ask that a strong young
man be sent to work for us. We will pay him what he
is worth. There is still much yet to be done."

Dora knew they had little money for wages. What
little they had went toward helping those who had nothing. She also knew she wasn't physically strong enough
to round up cows, keep them milked, mend the horses'

harness, and all the other labor involved in keeping a
farm running. Mama Elizabeth could do these things,
but Dora understood what Papa John left unsaid: his
wife was as old as he was. He wouldn't risk her health
too.

Dora penned the note as instructed, held it for her
adopted father to sign, and set off with heavy heart in
search of someone to carry it across the river.

She was frightened. She couldn't deny it. She had seen
enough illness and death while helping Mother Elizabeth
in her rounds of nursing. Papa John's gray pallor and
rattling cough were symptoms of a grave disease that
few ever survived, not in the cold of winter, not at his
age. All factors were against him. She felt the cold chill
of the winter wind clear to her bones as she tried imagining life without the kindly old man who had brought her
out of death. Tears filled her eyes at the thought of that
big breakfast table empty of his hearty laughter or gentle
questions. Her imagination failed beyond that. Papa
John shared the generous width of his heart and soul
with her. Without him, she would be nothing.

Her gaze focused inward and not on the people of
town as she hurried toward the livery and the man who
carried messages. She was slow to notice the small
groups of people gathered on corners, talking earnestly,
gesticulating emphatically. Not until someone shouted,
"There's one of them now!" did she even look up.

Dora's heart nearly stopped in her chest as every pair
of eyes on the street turned to stare at her. It fluttered
again in terror as she tried to imagine what she had
done. She could read accusation and condemnation in
their expressions, and the nightmares of her childhood
made her shake. She wasn't a good person. Everyone
must know that. Everyone must know that Papa John
was dying for her sins. It was all her fault. If she hadn't
left the gate open, the sheep would never have got loose,
and Papa John would never have fallen in the creek. If
he died, she was a murderess. The whole town knew it.

Consumed with guilt and mental anguish, Dora forced
her feet to continue on their path. She would do as told.
She would send the message. Maybe God would forgive
her if she did everything that she was told for a change.

She couldn't let Papa John die. He was good. She was bad. She should be the one to die.

"She was in the store buying gunpowder just the other day! She's one of them, I tell you! She blew up the bridge! Her and that Bible-toting family of hers. Let's show 'em what we think of Yankee abolitionists around here!"

A rotten apple came flying by Dora's nose, startling her so much that she stopped to follow its course. A squash that had turned soft on the vine smashed against her back. A broken piece of brick glanced off her bonnet, striking hard enough to draw pain. Giving a cry of surprise and holding her hand to her head, she looked around to see who did this, but women were quickly disappearing into stores and houses. Only men and rowdies remained on the street.

Feeling as much fear as guilt now, she hurried on her errand, hoping they would let her by. She hadn't heard about the bridge. She didn't know what had them riled. If she gave it thought, she might have guessed, but she wasn't thinking clearly any longer. She just wanted to run and cry and go home to the safety of her papa's arms, but she had to get the message to the livery first.

They waited at the alley for her. She recognized some of them, all boys not much older than she, some even younger. When they had a chance, they called her names, pulled at her bonnet, and tried to put snakes down her dress. Ignoring them usually worked, but this time they had a meanness to their torment, and she could see their older brothers gathered at the general store, making no show of stopping them. If she wasn't so terrified, she'd cry.

She froze like a doe caught in a lantern light. Her early years of terror had taught her the uselessness of fighting. Years of Quaker preaching had taught her violence didn't solve problems. Papa John would be terribly disappointed if she resorted to violence. She never wanted to disappoint him ever again. She knew no other escape, so she kept the rage and fear inside, where it hurt only herself.

"My daddy's dying. I have to send a message to the

Elders," Dora said with as much dignity as she could muster while she shivered.

"What's the matter? One of them niggers cut your daddy's throat for helping 'em? And what you been doin' with 'em while he's hidin' 'em, huh? What does a nigger-lovin' Quaker gal do with niggers when she's got 'em all to herself?" His laughter and those of the others crowding around her was lewd, but Dora had no understanding of their insinuations.

"Sammy, leave the girl alone." One of the idlers strolled in their direction, his fingers hitched in his pockets as he spat a stream of tobacco juice at the street. "Doc's been out there. Her old man's sick. How did he get sick, little girl? Blowing up bridges?"

Wide-eyed, Dora shook her head and tried shoving by Sam. She was too frightened to talk. People frightened her. Nothing she said was ever right anyway. She just wanted out of here.

She recognized the tall man asking her questions. Another of Josie's cousins, his father frequently traded in slaves. He'd probably lost money on some of those who escaped last night. She kept her eyes on the ground and tried easing around him.

He shoved her shoulder, pushing her backward. "Not so fast, little girl. Answer my questions. How did your daddy get sick? What was he doing last night when those niggers busted loose of the jail?"

She could turn around and go down another street, but they would only follow. She could turn and go home, but she'd promised to deliver the message. If the only way to do that was through this bully, then through this bully she must go.

Taking a deep gasp of air, Dora flung herself into the small space between the man and his young brother, hoping they would dodge out of her way. They didn't. The bigger one caught her by the shoulder and shoved. Stumbling on her long dress, she fell into the street. Dusting herself off carefully as she climbed back to her feet, she repeated the litany of "musts" to herself and again tried going around the two bigger males. This time, the younger one kicked her in the shins and pushed her backward.

Silently, Dora struggled determinedly to her feet to rush her attacker again, but the high whine of a whip whistling through the air and cracking as it struck stopped her from rising too swiftly. She caught her breath in dismay as the whip hit her larger assailant in the shoulder with a force sufficient to send him stumbling against the nearest wall.

"You want someone to pick on, Randolph? How about me?" Pace grinned menacingly as he came closer, coiling the leather of the whip. He looked the part of gladiator or worse. He was much bigger than she remembered, bigger and stronger, and exuding violence from every pore. "Or are you afraid you can only beat up little girls?"

Dora closed her eyes briefly, feeling the violence simmering beneath Pace's casual words. She knew they would fight, and this time, it would be her fault. Pace could go to hell because of her. She remembered the vicar preaching about hell. No matter how menacing he looked, she didn't want Pace going there, but she must get the message to the livery. And she knew well enough that she had no power against their violence. Fighting back a tear of terror, she cautiously stood. When the first punch flew, she took to her heels and escaped down the alley.

She shook all over and the words stuttered out of her mouth as she conveyed her message. The livery man caught the gist and took her coins, promising to get the letter across the river. He glanced at the alley where the fight had become a general ruckus and recommended she take another route.

Dora debated, her heart in her throat. She needed to get back to Papa John. She didn't have the size or strength necessary to stop a fight. She already ached from the earlier falls. She was a girl, and girls weren't supposed to fight. Violence begets violence. She was just as weak and helpless as her mother had been. She knew what the Bible meant when it said the sins of the fathers would fall on their sons. The same must apply to mothers and daughters. Her helplessness was daunting, more terrifying than the fight at the end of the alley. She had no defenses against their brutality.

But Pace had come to her rescue, and Pace would go to hell for murdering those boys. It would all be her fault. Horribly confused, torn between what she had been taught and what she had learned the hard way, Dora choked back tears and stalked determinedly back down the alley.

As usual, the odds were stacked against Pace. Because of his smaller size as a youth, he had learned to fight viciously, using hands and feet and teeth and every weapon at his disposal. He knew how to gouge eyes, throttle arteries, and kick where it hurt. He had grown considerably since then, and had muscles where the other men had fat. He had the strength of two men and the ferociousness of an army. It was pretty much concluded long ago that it took an army to fight Pace. So the idlers on the street felt justified in coming to Randolph's rescue.

Frozen inside with terror, Dora approached the melee without thought. If she thought about it, she knew she could do nothing. So her mind shut down and she moved woodenly, like the doll she had broken years ago while defending Pace in another such fracas. She grabbed the water pail hanging on the pump, and brought it down with a resounding clatter on one man's crown as he pounded Pace's head into the dirt.

She kicked another and threw dust in the eyes of a third. Pace came up swinging, flinging his closest assailant aside, slamming a fist into the stomach of the next, his dark hair falling in his eyes as he fought. Without a hitch in his movement, he grabbed Dora's arm and dragged her hurriedly out of the fracas and toward the main street.

No matter how furious the townspeople might be, they wouldn't allow the bullies behind them to blatantly attack a little girl in the middle of town in full view of everyone. Pace took a gasping breath and slowed his run as they reached the safety zone of the main road. He released Dora's skinny arm and kept up a brisk march, hating to leave a fight yet knowing he couldn't let the child walk home alone. He'd go back and finish later if they were still up to it.

"I told you to tell your father to stay in last night.

What happened?" Belligerence came easier than kindness. He'd never been taught anything else.

"The sheep got loose," Dora whispered. "It's all my fault. Papa John's going to die, and it's all my fault. I don't know why God punishes him because of me."

"You've got sheep dip for brains, you know that?" he answered with disgust. "If your father went out in the stinking cold and got himself wet chasing a few damned sheep, it's his own fault, not yours."

"I left the gate open," she pointed out, inexorably.

"Sheep aren't worth human lives. Your father should have stayed indoors. Better yet, he should have sat down at the general store whittling in full view of the entire town. He knew that. He's the one who chose differently." Pace knew he shouldn't take his anger out on her, but he'd not worked off a full head of steam yet. He was furious at leaving the fight to take a little girl home. He was furious at finding full-grown men terrorizing a child. He was furious at himself for dancing the night away while people's lives were in danger. He'd already got the report back from Jas. Dora's father hadn't been chasing sheep. He'd helped Joshua get away after Carlson had locked him up unexpectedly in the tool shed for fear he'd run before the trader came. Pace should have been the one wading that creek to rescue his friend, not some old man.

But he couldn't do a thing about any of it, and his helplessness fueled his fury. The girl beside him bit her lip and made no response to his angry words.

Good. Maybe if he made her mad enough, she'd leave him alone and stay out of his life. Maybe she'd even get smart and learn to stay home. He didn't mean to stay around here much anymore. He couldn't keep coming to her rescue every time she tangled with those cowards. He had better things to do.

Pace saw her to her door and didn't linger to hear her mother give her the ringing scold she deserved.

The next time Pace saw Dora, it was at her father's funeral, and tears streamed, unchecked, down her cheeks.

Four

But, soft: behold! lo, where it comes again! I'll cross
it, though it blast me——Stay, illusion
If thou hast any sound, or use a voice,
Speak to me.

SHAKESPEARE, *Hamlet*

May 1861

"Thou must rest. The weather is overwarm." The slender young girl in Quaker black held out the water bucket and dipper to the two young men plowing the cornfield. She spoke with a voice as soft and whispery as the frail spring breeze.

The white worker drank deeply from the dipper, shoving back the broad-brimmed hat from his sweat-soaked brow and enjoying the pleasure of cool water down his throat. The black worker waited until the other finished, then took his turn without hesitation. Despite the fact that one was slave and the other free, they had worked together long enough to know the etiquette of these delicate matters.

"What's happening up at the big house, Miss Dora?" Jackson wiped a cotton rag across his gleaming black forehead as he cooled off. What happened at the big house was always of interest to everyone in the county.

Since her adopted mother's death earlier in the year, Dora had been living in the Nicholls' house, ostensibly under the care of Pace's mother but more as unpaid servant. The shattering loss of both her adopted parents had left her too numb to care, but grief had a way of receding with time. She managed a tentative smile now.

"Spring cleaning. They're turning the place upside-down." A shadow passed across Dora's face as the suspicion of the real reason for the turmoil crossed her mind, but she didn't repeat the gossip. Instead, she asked, "It's not too late to set out the corn, is it? Dost thou think we'll have a crop?"

They both knew her concerns, for they were as involved in them as she. Since Papa John's death, David and Jackson had worked these fields on a sharecropping basis. The loss of a crop meant they wouldn't get paid for their hard labor, and Dora wouldn't have the money to pay the taxes on the land that had passed to her after her adopted mother's death. To Dora, it meant possibly losing the property. To David, it meant losing the cash he needed to buy a place of his own. To Jackson, it meant one year less before he could buy his freedom from the old man generous enough to allow him to earn his own way now that he was no longer needed at his owner's farm. The price of freedom came high.

"Thou mustn't, worry, Dora. The tobacco is strong, and thou still hast the hogs. This is good land. It will keep you comfortable."

A wry smile played across her face. "Would that I could say the same for Friend Harriet. I am here to carry the message, David: worldly goods do not make for comfort."

He laughed. The three of them had shared her jests about feather beds and velvet curtains she never slept behind because Harriet Nicholls called for her a dozen times a night. Sumptuous feasts were at her disposal, but she seldom sat down to eat them for leaping up to run to the invalid's room. Every idle dream of wealth and plenty the two men might have shared was diminished by the knowledge of the cost others paid for them in health and happiness. They felt no jealousy for the relative comfort in which Dora slept while they scraped by on the bare bones of existence.

David gave her a warm smile. "Thou wilt come of age this fall. With the crops in, thou wilt be a wealthy woman, Dora. Thou mayest do as thou pleases then."

She smiled back. When the crops came in, David would own a full share of them, and he would have the money he needed for his own farm. Between the two of them, they could sell this place and buy some very nice land David had his eye on over in Indiana. With the approval of the Elders, they could marry by Christmas.

Dora had never dreamed of marriage like other girls. In truth, she feared the idea and had not yet made the promises David desired. Still, marriage was the practical solution to her situation. She could not live in the farmhouse alone. She could not work the fields by herself. She could not live off the Nichollses forever. David was a kind and gentle man, soft-spoken and intelligent. He was built shorter and slighter than Pace, so she did not fear him as she feared other men. He was the brother she'd always wished she had. He would be the husband she would not have otherwise.

She had no foolish notions of love. Papa John and Mother Elizabeth had never proclaimed love for each other, but they went along very well together, just as she and David would do. She still had terrifying recollections of her real mother's "love" for the earl. If that was love, she would have no part of it. The Quakers were quite right in abhorring violent animal passions. She felt safe in their company. They were good, sensible people, and she tried very hard to be one of them. With her marriage to David, she would be fully accepted.

She still woke up in a panic at night over that incident after Mother Elizabeth's funeral. She had come back to the farmhouse to find Pace's father and a lawyer calmly going over Papa John's desk, searching for the legal documents determining her inheritance and ownership of the farm. They'd found the papers her adopted parents had kept in her mother's trunks, the ones with her real name on them. Carlson Nicholls had wanted to write to England right there and then to notify her relatives. Dora wasn't good at talking, but somehow she had persuaded those papers away from him that day. The memory still hung like a knife over her head every hour of the day and night. She doubted if the earl cared whether she was alive or dead, but she had no desire to find out. She never wanted to return to that house of her nightmares again.

Dora waved at the men as they returned to work, then started back for the big house. She had less than a mile to walk. Her feet just didn't fly over it as willingly today as they ought. The family expected Pace home any day now, and she would rather be elsewhere when he heard the news. They hadn't announced it yet, but they almost certainly would at the ball next week. Josie Andrews was marrying Pace's brother, Charles.

"Why, Josie, why? I thought we had an understanding. I'm running for the legislature in the next election. I thought you would stand by my side. What happened?" The anguished words were soft and barely heard over the chirping of the crickets and the croaking of frogs through the clear night air. The man in a gentleman's tailored frock coat ran his hand through his thick hair in blatant bewilderment, not looking at the slight woman in hooped skirts and sloping bare shoulders. The lights and the music from the party behind them scarcely reached this dark corner of the veranda.

"I couldn't wait any longer, Pace," she murmured, crossing and uncrossing her hands. "Today's my twentieth birthday. I expected to be married long before this. All my friends have babies already. You kept putting me off with first one promise, then another. And now there's all this talk of war and you're spending so much time arguing for the Union, you can't even write to me. I can't wait any longer. I don't think you want to get married, Pace. I think you're having too much fun up there in Frankfort trying to talk those silly men into joining the war. The worst of it is, you'll probably succeed, and then you'll go marching off to fight."

"War is inevitable, Josie," Pace growled irritably, running his hand through his hair again as he glared at the lighted ballroom behind her, looking everywhere but at her. "I told you I meant to run for office, not go to war."

"My friends and family are here, Pace. I want to stay here," Josie answered quietly.

He turned on her with an angry scowl. "You mean you want to live in a big house with servants. State it plainly, Josie. Charlie can give you a hell of a lot more than I can."

She clasped her fingers nervously, refusing to look at him. "Charlie isn't like you, Pace. He's not mad at the whole world. He's kind and thoughtful. He brings me flowers. He's helping my daddy now that he's down with the stroke. I put him off as long as I could, Pace. I just couldn't put him off any longer. There wasn't any reason to."

The man in the elegant coat gave a wild laugh that fit a jungle more than this civilized setting. He quit running his hand through his hair and gave her a savage grin that didn't reach his eyes. "Kind and thoughtful! Charlie! Josie Ann, you're going to pay for this, and I'm not the one who'll be setting the price. When you're sitting here in this big house, looking out over all the acres you and Charlie will own together, you just remember this night and what you said. I'll not stand here and try to persuade you different when your mind's made up. I'm not that kind of fool. But I wouldn't let my worst enemy walk into what you're walking into without some kind of warning."

Pace gripped his fingers into tight fists and nodded his head toward the windows spilling light. "You go back in there and listen to Charlie and my father. Really listen. Don't just look at their pretty faces. Then you watch what they do and how they behave when they think you're not looking. Just remember this, the apple never falls far from the tree. Maybe I am mad at the world. Maybe I pick my share of fights and lose more than my share. Maybe I am just as wild as you've accused those other men who courted you of being. I never tried hiding the fact that I didn't fall far from the tree, which is more than Charlie can say. But remember this, Josie Ann: I never in my life, *never* took my anger out on those less defenseless than myself."

He strode off into the darkness before Josie could recover from her shock and reply. Indignant, she stamped her little foot and returned to the party. Who did he think he was to brag about something so silly as that? If that was all he had to say for himself, then she was well rid of him.

Biting her lip, Dora backed away from the upstairs window. She hadn't meant to eavesdrop. She had just been listening to the music. The religion of her adopted parents forbade dancing, but she couldn't help the way it stirred her soul and made her restless and eager at the same time. She loved the lilting sound of the waltz in particular. She could listen to it all night. She had no desire to go downstairs and admire the elegant gowns and broad, black-clad backs dipping and swaying gracefully through the flower-bedecked ballroom. She found contentment just in hearing the music.

But she'd heard a great deal more than music by lingering on the porch above the veranda. She couldn't hear all the words. Pace's voice had been low and venomous. Josie hadn't said much. But she'd known the content anyway. And she heard the shattered emotions.

She turned back, inspecting the sleeping woman in the bed behind her. Harriet Nicholls had taken a sleeping draft before the ball started, saying the noise would disturb her otherwise. No one had offered to help her from her bed to dress and go downstairs to inspect the ballroom and greet the guests. No one had expected her to leave her room. And she'd made no attempt to do so. Dora wondered how long Pace's mother had been this way, but she had been taught the vulgarity of asking personal questions.

As far as she could see, there was nothing wrong with the woman but too much laudanum, too much medicinal whiskey, and inertia. Harriet couldn't sleep at night because she slept all day with the shades drawn. She couldn't leave her bed because she couldn't face the day without a strong dose of "medicine." By the time she was sufficiently anesthetized to get out of bed, she was too unstable on her feet to get down the stairs. So she called herself an invalid and stayed in bed.

Dora supposed Harriet might be inflicted with some pain the eye couldn't see. She knew it happened. Joints become stiff and painful and degenerated in some people for no known reason. Perhaps that was the case. She would give her the benefit of the doubt. But she couldn't think so charitably of the family who totally ignored her.

Only Pace bothered visiting his mother, and he came home so infrequently that he might as well not come at all. Carlson Nicholls acted as if his wife didn't exist. He kept his black mistress in a room near the kitchen so he didn't have to go out in the weather on a bad night.

Charles didn't go so far as to bring his women into the house, but he came in drunk and staggering at all hours of the night, and didn't seem to care that he might disturb the invalid's sleep. He never entered her room. He visited the grave of his late sister more often than he visited his still living mother. It was an extremely odd household.

But only Pace mattered to Dora at this moment. She had never questioned why this was so. She'd felt that way ever since the day she had found him battered and hurting beneath the maples. She felt his hurts as if they were her own, and he was hurting badly right now. She could feel his anguish all the way through her middle.

Checking once again on the sleeping woman, Dora reached for her bonnet and tied it beneath her chin. She recognized the total senselessness of her actions. She couldn't ease Pace's anguish. To him, she was still a child. He scarcely knew she existed. He was a lawyer now, with a partnership in Frankfort. With all of Kentucky at war with itself, Pace had found his element. He came and went on his own, without ever acknowledging her presence. He would probably head for the saloons in town now. It didn't matter. She didn't act on logic. She just knew she couldn't let him grieve alone. She would see that he had company first.

Of course, knowing Pace's penchant for taking his rage out on others, he would no doubt instigate a brawl before the night ended if he found male company. She'd heard he'd been shot in a fight over in Lexington. Rumors blamed a duel, but she didn't think Pace would have participated in one. She'd heard it said the new constitution forbade state representatives from taking office if they'd participated in a duel. Pace was too determined to get elected to risk his career on something so senseless. But she knew he carried a gun and wouldn't hesitate at shooting a man who aimed at him. His violence terrified her. Had he been anyone else, she would steer a wide path around him. But Pace had called her an angel and bought her candy sticks and surprisingly replaced her doll one day when she was really too old for dolls. It hadn't mattered. She'd kept the doll beside

her every night since. Pace was the only person in this
world who knew she really existed.

As she skimmed over the dew-dampened grass, Dora
thought possibly she made an unfair assessment. David
knew she existed, simply because he worked her farm
every day. He didn't look through her as so many people
did, but then, he was a Friend and used to her manners
and dress. She sometimes thought that was all David did
see: her land and her garb. Pace, on the other hand,
didn't see what she wore. He knew when she entered a
room without even looking at her. She was real to him.

The warm, clear spring night stirred her blood as Dora
raced down the lane toward the river. She didn't even
think about where she went. Her instincts for finding
Pace were unerring. She followed his invisible trail. Her
heart pattered erratically, but she didn't let that worry
her. Spring was like that. She could see it in the way the
lambs gamboled in the field and the colts threw back
their heads and whinnied for no reason at all. Life grew
thicker and more rampant in the spring. It made a body
do strange things.

Her body felt strange things now, but she was grateful
that she had a physical body at all. For a long while,
she'd had the fanciful notion that she really had died all
those years ago, and only this cloud that looked like her
walked on earth. That would explain why people never
noticed her. They couldn't see her. Only Pace could see
her. She didn't want to be a ghost, but she had felt
like one.

She felt like one now, a coalescence of gray air float-
ing on the breeze. If not for the pain she felt, she would
doubt her physical reality. And the pain wasn't even
hers, but Pace's. Strange, how God worked. He'd let her
die with her mother and brought her back as this odd
half-person and put her down in this strange country
where nobody saw her. Surely He had some purpose
that she would recognize someday.

The fishermen had left their cabins along the river
dark while they reeled in the fish that they sold to the
passing riverboats. She had learned how to call them,
how to set fire to turpentine balls and fling them over the
river so they would row into shore to see who needed

transporting across. She'd even done it once or twice when runaways came to her door expecting Papa John. David and Jackson took care of them now that they stayed in the farmhouse.

She wasn't looking for the fishermen tonight. She looked for Pace. She found him swigging on a bottle of bourbon, standing on the bank, staring out across the river. For once, he hadn't gone into town looking for a fight.

She'd rather not disturb him. She stood quietly in the shadows of the spindly willows on the shore, hands crossed in front of her. He had taken off his coat and the moonlit river silhouetted his broad shoulders. The wind plastered the fine linen of his shirt to his skin, delineating his manly form clearly. She had never really paid much attention to how men's bodies differed from women's other than to know that they were broader and stronger and taller. Seeing Pace's as she did now, she couldn't help but notice.

She had thought the frock coat made his waist look tapered and his shoulders wide, but she saw that was the shape of him: wide at the shoulders and narrow at the hip. It made her feel odd thinking of that. It made her feel odder still to notice how long and strong his legs seemed in their tight evening clothes.

His hair ruffled in the wind, blowing off his face as he tossed his head back and drank deeply from the bottle. She ought to stop him, but it wasn't her place. She would just watch and make certain he didn't hurt himself doing something foolish. Watching him turn to drink saddened her. Josie could have saved the man that Pace was meant to be, the man who helped little girls and gave them dolls, the man who fought for those who couldn't fight for themselves. Josie could have brought out the good in him. Instead, she had driven him to the dissolution he'd been taught from birth. Dora wanted to cry at the waste.

Pace took another drink with almost an air of defiance. That's when Dora realized he knew she stood there. Still, she didn't come forward. People called her his shadow. Perhaps she was, substanceless as she seemed.

"Dora, get the hell home," he finally said wearily, not turning his head to see her. He tossed the empty whiskey bottle far out into the current. "This isn't a place for little girls."

"I'll not fall from the tree," she said lightly, repeating the warning he had given her that first day. He was always warning her. She found it amusing when he was the one who took risks.

"I know. Angels fly." His voice was devoid of all emotion as he finally turned around, searching the night for her shadow. "Why aren't you back at the party, tapping your toe to the music?"

So he knew she listened. That didn't surprise her. "Why art thou not in town, slugging some poor brute in the face?"

He laughed at that, a wry laugh, but a laugh just the same. "I'll do that later. It takes more drink now than it did when I was younger to get my temper roused."

"I'm glad to hear that," she said simply.

"Go home, Dora. I'll be fine." She could tell he had found her now, a gray shadow blending into the trees. The white of her bonnet gave her away.

"I tried talking to Josie," she admitted, "but she doesn't listen to me very well. People seldom do. They think I'm a child."

"You are a child," he answered curtly. "Now get back to your bed where you belong."

He was a full-grown man, a lawyer on the verge of being an important person. She was seventeen, small for her age, and invisible. Dora understood his curtness, but she ignored it.

"Josie's parents told her marrying Charlie was the best thing to do. She was raised to listen to her parents, Pace."

He stood silent for a moment, hands in pockets while the wind off the river whistled around him, tumbling his hair into his face. Finally, he answered, "Maybe they're right. Maybe Charlie is the best thing for her. Maybe she's the best thing for him. I've heard it said a woman can be the making of a man. Maybe they're right. Maybe she's just what Charlie needs to settle down."

And maybe the moon was made of green cheese and

angels flew from trees. Dora didn't respond. She couldn't lie.

In drunken response to her silence, Pace regarded her with a leer. "Maybe when you grow up, I'll marry you, girl. When are you going to shed those dowdy clothes and become a butterfly?"

She understood the anguish that had drawn those words from him. He didn't really mean them. But still the pain of his cruelty cut through Dora like a fine-honed blade, making her more aware than ever of their differences. He was a worldly man, far beyond the ken of her sheltered upbringing.

With a sad nod, she whispered, "Good night, Friend Pace."

He watched her go, a diminutive gray sprite vanishing into the mists. For one brief moment Pace had the absurd notion of calling her back, holding the sprite in his arms, easing his aching heart with her closeness. Something intuitive told him she could take the pain away, as she had already eased it.

Common sense told him he was crazy.

Dora heard Pace crossed the river that night to join the Union army in Indiana. The Kentucky legislature's waffling back and forth between their Southern sympathies and their professed love of the Union led them to make no stand at all. Neutrality was not a concept Pace understood.

Five

Faith is to believe what you do not yet see; the reward for this faith is to see what you believe.

ST. AUGUSTINE, *Sermons* (5th c.)

December 1861

"Payson might be a burr under the saddle, but one thing he's not, and that's a fool." Charlie propped his boots on the embroidered ottoman and drew deeply on his cigar. "Someone has to show Lincoln a state's got rights and he can't steal a man's property, and I reckon those hotheads down South will do it, but I sure as hell don't want to be in their shoes when the shouting's all over. If we stand behind the Union, Kentucky will come out sitting pretty. Hell, Lincoln won't dare take away our slaves. He needs us too much."

Joe Mitchell put his hands behind his head and puffed a smoke circle at the ceiling. Removing the cigar from his mouth, he used it to gesture widely. "This war sure is wreaking havoc with the slave trade, though. I'll have to find a more profitable sideline. Land's always profitable. I'm thinking of building me a toll road to the rail line."

Homer sipped his bourbon and belched. "There's a good profit in smuggling corn to the rebs. They pay a damned sight more than the Yankees."

Charlie sucked on his cigar a little longer. "They keep making it tougher to get anything down South though. I don't relish getting my brain shot out trying to make a few dollars. I reckon since I'm the one with the fool brother in the army, I better start preaching a Yankee tune for a while. It's a damned sight easier to get tobacco down the river with a pass." He gave Joe a knowing look. "That is, until Joe gets his road built."

The other men frowned at this cynical betrayal of their southern sympathies. Then Joe pressed his fingertips together and slowly nodded. "That might work. Damned if that just mightn't work. Most of the State Guards have gone over to the rebs, so we ain't got any real protection around here. That hell-fired McCoy got himself appointed provost marshal with the Home Guards and is boot-lickin' the Yankees into a nice gravy train. I think I could get my pappy to see him kicked out on some charge or another." He grinned happily. "Ain't anyone around here gonna be sorry to see a shit-kicker replaced by one of us. That could make it a damn sight easier acquiring that land."

Charlie grinned as he followed Joe's train of thought. "I hadn't thought to go that far, but wouldn't that be a swat in the face for them feds!" He frowned briefly as he thought it through. "I'll have to get rid of most of the troops McCoy put together. They're nothing but a band of nigger-lovers."

Joe shrugged. "I'll help you. I owe that bastard one anyway." He glowered at Charlie. "And I owe that damned brother of yours one for helping him. If he hadn't brought that passel of lawyers down here, I could have had McCoy's land for next to nothing."

Charlie waved away the thought. "Wouldn't of done you any good the way things stand now. You just said yourself, the slave market is gonna be worthless. What would you do with a breeding operation now? Pace did you a favor. Besides, the McCoy place isn't in the same direction as the railroad."

The bourbon bottle sitting between them was already half empty and the night was still young. When Josie entered, her full skirts concealing the first stages of pregnancy, she frowned slightly at the smell of smoke and whiskey polluting her parlor, but she produced a polite demeanor as she spoke.

"I'll be going upstairs now, gentlemen. Is there anything else I can get for you?"

The men made a polite attempt at rising from their

seats as she entered, but they settled down quickly. Charles waved his cigar in her direction. "Go on up, honey, get your rest. We've got a lot to discuss tonight."

She nodded and swept from the room, her long skirts swishing rhythmically as she climbed the stairs. Dark shadows circled her eyes in her pale, unsmiling face, but she managed a look of polite interest as Dora stepped out of the invalid's room when she reached the upper hall.

"How is Mother Nicholls tonight?" Josie asked, keeping up the masquerade of concerned daughter-in-law and loving wife.

Dora made a wry moue and clasped her hands in front of her. "Restless."

For a moment, something flickered behind Josie's carefully blank eyes, and she reached out to touch Dora's clasped fingers. "I am grateful that you stay with her. Have you heard from David?"

Unhappiness pulled briefly at Dora's lips. "He is well. I think he is not happy working inside all day, but the income is regular and he will save money faster."

"Perhaps he is better off out of the farming business. It is so risky these days. You really should sell that property and go with him, Dora."

Dora's shoulders stiffened rebelliously. "It is all I have of my parents. I cannot. There was enough from the hogs and sheep to pay expenses. Next year will be better."

If the hounds didn't destroy any more of the sheep and if someone finally quit cutting the fence and letting the hogs into the woods. If locusts didn't destroy the corn and lightning didn't set the tobacco on fire. Or if someone didn't set fire to the tobacco when lightning didn't cooperate. They had a terrible lot of fires in this small area. It would seem the safest thing to grow around here was water.

She didn't let her bitterness and suspicion show. Josie had too many problems of her own. Dora found a happy thought. "How is the babe today? Still raising a ruckus?"

A brief smile touched Josie's lips as she covered her stomach with her hand. "He does not seem to like anything I feed him. He will be born hungry."

"Mother Elizabeth always recommended adding a little honey to milk and taking it warm. Shall I make thee some?"

Josie glanced nervously over her shoulder and shook her head. "No, best not. Not tonight. I promised Charlie I'd not go down there again. I'm trying hard to be the wife he expects, but thank you, anyway. I'll see you in the morning."

She scurried away, leaving Dora standing alone in the upstairs hall. Dora frowned at the familiar ring of Josie's words and the answering echo of loud male voices coming up the stairs. She had lived here long enough to grow accustomed to drunken men and loud voices and cigar smoke. She simply stayed out of the way, well aware they scarcely knew she existed. She had hoped that Josie's presence might civilize them to some degree, but they'd had their own way for much too long. It would take someone considerably stronger than gentle Josie to tame them now. It would probably also take a bullwhip and a shotgun.

Since she wasn't a likely person for that job, Dora chose to pace her room rather than go downstairs and find a book. Had she not been such a coward, she would have returned to her own house the day she turned eighteen, but now, a month later, she still stayed in this den of iniquity. The Elders were not pleased with her. They had tried to understand when she turned down Joe Mitchell's offer for her home. They knew the offer was a poor one, especially for the only home she knew. After losing so much money on the corn and tobacco, David could not make the proposal of marriage he had hoped to make, and she could not stay in the house alone. Others of their belief had offered a place in their homes, but she disliked staying with comparative strangers. They couldn't understand that. She hadn't known if she understood it herself. She didn't exactly enjoy the Nicholls household.

But the Elders didn't realize that. They thought she had fallen for worldly pleasures. Dora laughed to herself as she stared out over the bare trees from her window. She would give anything for the quiet emptiness of her own house right now. She would defy any one of them to stay in this household as long as she had and survive. Only her own peculiar abilities and background allowed her to remain at all. With Josie's marriage to Charlie, it had become even more impossible for her here, but if she believed in the Inner Light at all, she must believe she was meant to stay.

Without Papa John's guidance, she had to find her own way, but she knew he would tell her she did the right thing. She clung to that belief even as she heard the men below stumble out into the darkness, knowing they went out to make mischief, knowing what would happen when Charlie returned. No one told her these things. No one discussed it with her. She just knew it with an instinct bred from the first moment she'd heard her own mother scream out in the night.

She should get some rest while Friend Harriet slept, but Dora continued standing at the window, watching the night go by. The men had taken their horses and disappeared. Carlson Nicholls slept in the arms of his black mistress. The slaves had grown quiet in their quarters. Even Josie probably slept by now, albeit a restless sleep. The house lay silent, but still Dora stood, waiting.

Pace was coming. She had heard it discussed downstairs. She knew it with her mind. He had Christmas leave and he was coming home. But something else, something inside her, told her Pace was coming now.

Logically, she knew her foolishness. He could come home tonight or tomorrow or tomorrow night. It didn't matter. He would ride in, throw his bags down, say hello to his mother, and ride out again. He wouldn't spend much time in this house with Josie and Charlie. She doubted that he would even notice her. She should get into her nightgown and go to bed. She couldn't do a thing if he rode in tonight.

Instead, she tightened her boot laces and reached for a shawl. She could feel the tension building inside of her. Something was wrong. She didn't know where or how, but she knew it and responded without giving it much thought. Perhaps the Inner Light they spoke about in Meetings had something to do with these notions. If so, she should heed them, even if they made no sense.

She wasn't much prone to logic on the best of days, anyway.

A cry of pain escaped her lips as a sharp sensation shot through her ribs. It ached, but she leaped to her feet and tied the strings to her bonnet. She didn't feel her pain. She felt Pace's.

The certainty of that knowledge sent her fleeing down the stairs, grabbing her heavy cloak as she let herself out the side door to the stable. Harnessing a horse to the cart would be difficult, but she knew she must do it, just as she knew she needed her mother's black bag of medicines.

One of the bondsmen who slept in the barn sleepily helped her harness the horse without question. Apparently awaiting his master's return, he didn't complain of this extra service. Dora thanked him gratefully, but he merely wandered back to a stall and his slumbers.

She stopped at the empty farmhouse to find the bag, but the tension she experienced earlier reached the point of terrified anxiety. She couldn't separate Pace's emotions from her own. Of course, if she had any sense at all, she would admit that all the terror was her own and she imagined everything. But she wasn't in the mood for being sensible. Pace was injured.

She urged the cart down the lane at the fastest pace the horse could manage. No one noticed or cared. She had gone out this way before at a summons from some farmhouse where the women had remembered Mother Elizabeth's services. She didn't have as much experience or knowledge as her adopted mother had, but she had some use in nursing, and that was better than none.

She steered the cart east. If she'd thought about it, that would be the last direction she would take. The river and town were to the west and south. Those were the most likely places to find trouble. But she knew she must go east.

Of course, Pace's troops were probably stationed in Lexington or Cincinnati. He would come from the east in that case. Perhaps her instincts weren't so far wrong after all.

The pain in her side had dulled to a throb. The tension bothered her most, the feeling of something terribly

wrong. She urged the horse faster, praying she could get
there in time. Instinct might warn her, but she had no
reason to believe it would warn her in time.

If anyone saw her, they would think her crazed. Out
on a miserably cold December night, cloak flying behind
her as she yelled at the horse to hurry, fingers clenched
in fear on the reins, and no explanation whatever to
give. She almost convinced herself that she had lost her
mind. But the Light was stronger. Although in her case,
the word "light" was a misnomer. She saw only darkness. The cart careened down a narrower road at her
urging.

There, just ahead, in the gully beside the Butler's feed
lot. Dora reined the horse into a wagon road between
some trees and scampered down from the cart. The
clouds covered any sign of moon, and the sky appeared
pitch black. The trees from the fence row threw the lane
in deeper darkness. She could see nothing to confirm
her certainty that this was the place.

Somewhere in the distance a horse whinnied and a
hound bayed. A shiver shot down her spine. With a sinking feeling in her middle, Dora knew now what she
would find. Pace was incapable of doing anything so simple as coming home for the holidays for fun.

"I'm not going into those brambles, Pace Nicholls. Get
thyself out here before those hounds find thee."

A tall shadow unfolded itself stiffly from the weeds
filling the gully. His broad shoulders tilted slightly at an
uncertain angle, and Dora gave a small cry of alarm.
"You've been shot!" She didn't even notice the slip of
speech.

Pace didn't comment on it. He pulled another, much
slighter figure from the gully and shoved her toward the
road where Dora stood. "Get her out of here, Dora.
Hurry!"

Time shifted and tumbled abruptly while she froze.
Pace was hurt. He needed medical attention. She
couldn't leave him here for the hounds and the slave
catchers. The cart would barely hold two. She couldn't
leave the terrified black child clinging to her ragged
shawl and quivering alone in the roadway. If they caught

Pace in the cart with the child, they would throw him in jail and fine him heavily.

Pace's dark shadow had already disappeared into the shrubbery by the time Dora grabbed the child's hand and dragged her toward the cart. He could bleed to death. Frantic with terror, she didn't want to leave him. She didn't want to do this alone. She couldn't. They would find her. Pace would die. She couldn't let Pace die.

But because he'd told her to save the child, Dora covered the girl under the seat blanket on the floor and backed the horse and cart onto the road again. She spread her heavy wool skirt and petticoat wide to hide the lump in the blanket, keeping her feet off the child beneath them. And she switched the horse to a fast trot.

She bit her lip and shut off her thoughts as she drove the horse recklessly. Or she shut off her thoughts about such things as the gunshot in Pace's ribs and the baying hounds behind them and those other things beyond her control. Instead she focused on the best road to the river, whether or not anyone would be in the cabin on a cold night like this, if she could find any turpentine balls or if she should stop to make one. And then her mind would slip into the rut of wondering if she should hide the child at the farmhouse and go back to look for Pace.

Why had God seen fit to dump this responsibility on her frail shoulders? Surely He knew she wasn't fit. Surely He knew her weaknesses. She was only a woman. She didn't know what was right. Her experiences with the earl had taught her that. No matter what she did, it came out wrong. They would capture the child. Pace would die. She would end up in jail. Surely there must be someone else more fitting for this task. But Papa John had died and gone to heaven.

Resigned, Dora heard the horses pounding up the road behind her. She had known she couldn't escape them. Only one route led to the river from here. They would discover her sooner or later. She might be invisible most of the time, but the cart wasn't. And then they would have to notice her. No one else would roam these roads at this hour.

The horses reared and twisted as their riders brought them to a reckless halt, surrounding the cart. Dora looked up and scanned the bearded faces of the men, looking for some sign of someone she could trust. Charlie and Joe and the others weren't with them, but that didn't surprise her. They had found more lucrative mischief than chasing runaways these last years. Several of the men were strangers to her. They were probably bounty hunters. She doubted that the child beneath her feet came from around here. Pace had smuggled her from somewhere deeper in the state. These men were on the child's trail.

She said nothing. She only looked at them with curiosity from beneath her wide bonnet brim. She thought she recognized Billy John's younger brother, and one of the Howards with the hounds. The bounty hunters had found some locals to help them.

One of the men leaped into the narrow back of the cart. Too small to carry more than a sack of feed, the cart was obviously empty. Dora didn't have to pretend alarm as she glanced over her shoulder at him, then back to the large men keeping her from driving on.

"What are you doing out here at this hour, ma'am?" one of the younger men asked.

She glanced down at the black bag on the seat beside her. "There was a birthing this night. Might I ask what thou lookest for? I have no money."

Howard came forward and gave her a cursory glance. "We're looking for a nigger gal. Where're you hiding her?"

"If I were to hide her, I would not tell where," Dora answered calmly. "But as thou must see, I have nothing to hide. If thou wouldst tell me from which direction she comes, I would happily look for her, but I would not promise to give her over to thee. She must be cold and frightened by now."

Howard scowled and jerked his horse back so he could keep an eye on his dogs. "The hounds don't smell her. We lost her trail back at the Butlers'. Let's get back there."

"What about this Quaker? You know damned well

she has something to do with it or she wouldn't be out here on this road," one of the strangers shouted.

"She helped deliver my little sister last winter," the younger man answered. "She takes care of crazy old lady Nicholls. She wouldn't say boo to a fly. We've just taken the wrong road. Maybe they're not aiming for the river tonight."

Grudgingly, the band of men backed away and clattered back the way they came. The young man was the last to go. He tipped his hat politely and said, "Tell Pace he owes me one," before spurring his horse after the others.

Closing her eyes briefly to control her shaking, Dora urged the horses back to a trot. He'd known. Whoever that young man was, he'd known she harbored a fugitive, that Pace had brought her here. She could have been caught at any moment. They could have found Pace and had him arrested.

She murmured something reassuring to the child beneath her feet and continued toward the river.

By the time she delivered the girl to the fishing cabins, saw that she was filled with hot coffee before being ferried across the river, and turned the cart toward home, Dora had reached a state of utter panic. Pace remained out there in the cold night with a gunshot wound in his ribs and a pack of hounds on his trail. She could find him, but her presence would only lead those bounty hunters right to him. Could they do anything to him now that the child was gone?

By the time Dora returned the horse to the barn, the panic had dissipated. An odd calm had descended, and she carried her bag up the front stairs with firm decision. She knew what that meant. She hoped she knew what that meant. She sincerely did not wish to go back out into the night again.

She ignored the angry voices from the newlyweds' chambers. Josie objected to Charlie's drinking and hadn't learned yet to control her disappointment. Perhaps there was still hope for their marriage. The sounds emanating from that chamber by the time Dora reached Harriet's room didn't seem argumentative any longer.

Her stomach clenched nervously with ancient buried memories, but this was none of her affair.

Harriet tossed restlessly in laudanum-induced dreams. Dora settled her as best as she could, straightened her covers, filled her water glass, and when she lay still again, slipped back to her own room.

She uttered no gasp of surprise as the large figure loomed out of the darkness to move toward her when she opened the door.

Pace had made it home.

Six

It is not known precisely where angels dwell—
whether in the air, the void, or the planets. It has
not been God's pleasure that we should be informed
of their abode.

VOLTAIRE, "Angels," *Philosophical Dictionary* (1764)

"You really are an angel," Pace muttered, falling back
against the pillows on Dora's narrow bed. "How in hell
did you know we were out there?"

"God sent me," she answered simply, lighting a candle
and closing her curtains against the darkness outside.
Even as she said it, Dora knew he would take her words
as part of the standing jest between them. It didn't
matter.

Pace made a grunt that could have been a laugh and
began stripping off his shirt in the flickering light. "I
don't suppose you're carrying bourbon in that bag."

"No, I don't suppose I am." Dora poured water into
the basin and tried not to look too closely at the half-
naked man baring himself before her in the flickering
candlelight. She usually used her nursing skills on
women, not men, but the bloody gash marring his side
kept her mind focused.

"Just cover it up with something so it will stop bleeding. I'll see the doc in the morning." Pace winced as she
applied cold water to the wound.

He had already lost a lot of blood. His face was pale
against the dark auburn of his hair. This close, Dora
could see the whiskers sprouting from his jaw, visible
proof that he was a man and not the boy she first remembered. She turned her attention back to the bleeding. "Thou must have stitches," she murmured, probing
the gash.

He grimaced at her touch. "Careful, girl. The flesh is weak."

She laughed softly and reached for the needle and grain alcohol. "Let us hope it is also thin. I do not relish wrestling thread through tough hide."

Pace opened his eyes and gave her a mocking look as he sat back on the mattress and raised his hand to grasp the bars of the bed headboard, leaving his wounded side fully exposed and accessible to her ministrations. "God will guide you, I suppose. Why is it that He speaks to you but not to those who ought to hear a little hellfire and damnation?"

Dora bit her bottom lip as she applied the needle to his torn flesh. She felt his pain and tried not to clench her eyes closed against it. She wondered that he did not scream out. His muscles bulged with the effort of clinging to the bed. She mustn't think about muscles. Pace Nicholls had more than his fair share.

"I assume He speaks to those whose minds are open to Him," she answered more to keep him distracted than because she had any answer to his foolish question.

"That's a damned idiot way of doing things," Pace grumbled through clenched teeth. "If I were God, I'd scream fiery curses at the evildoers and leave the innocent alone."

Dora smiled at this conceit and tied off the thread. Blood still seeped, but the flow was slower. She reached for washrag and bandages. "If thou wert God, thou wouldst not limit thyself to curses. Lightning bolts would fly, and there would be precious few people left inhabiting the earth when thou wert done."

Pace managed a chuckle through his wince as she applied more alcohol. "It's daunting talking to someone who knows me too well. Did the girl make it across the river?"

"Thou wouldst not ask now if thou believest otherwise. I met the bounty hunters and one of the Howards, I think also Billy John's little brother. He said to tell thee that,"—she paused to recall the phrase—"thou owes him one.' "

"Damn." Pace lowered his arm as she applied the last of the bandages. "I don't want him knowing about you.

I'll convince him you were only out to save my worthless
hide and knew nothing about the girl."

"That would be a waste of time." Dora packed her
supplies back in her bag. Pace made no effort to don
his ruined shirt or cover himself in any way. She tried
very hard not to look at the way the band of muscles
rippled beneath the white bandage. She very definitely
did not want to see the way whorls of dark hair led
down from his navel to the waist of his trousers. These
were things of the body and not the mind or spirit. She
must hold herself above them. "I am suspect regardless
of my guilt or innocence."

The truth of that momentarily silenced him. He finally
reached for his shirt and tugged it over one arm, but he
didn't lift the arm on the wounded side. He draped it
over that shoulder. He looked at something beyond the
room and scarcely noticed Dora. "Don't you have
friends or relatives across the river?" he finally asked,
looking at her in the candlelight.

"Few." There was curtness to her murmur. Even after
ten years, she remained a stranger to most of the Quakers. Despite all her efforts, she knew she did not blend
in as she should. Or perhaps she was just as invisible
there as here, and they forgot to include her. "Thou
needst not worry. I will be fine."

Pace threw his legs over the side of the bed and waited
until the dizziness passed before attempting to stand.
When he stood, he towered more than a head over
Dora's slight figure. He looked down at her, searching
her face quizzically. "How can you be fine living in a
madhouse like this? You should have a life of your
own."

She supposed, if she'd stayed in Cornwall with the
earl, she would have a life of her own, of some sort. But
she had died, and now her life belonged to others. Pace
wasn't likely to understand that. She stepped out of his
way, leaving the path to the door open. "I am doing as
I am called to do," she informed him politely.

"That's a lot of"—he visibly sought a politer word
than his original choice—"nonsense, but I'll postpone
this argument until later, before I fall on my face."

Ignoring her look of concern, Pace strode to the door and walked out without looking back.

Dora clasped and unclasped her hands, hands that had touched his bare flesh. She could still feel the heat of him against her fingertips. She might be invisible, but her body was alive. She could still feel. It was a rather daunting knowledge.

Dora combed the invalid's fine hair into some semblance of neatness, gently chided her into eating some of her breakfast, and busied herself tidying the room while Harriet Nicholls ate. Pace's comment that she deserved a life of her own burned somewhere deep in her chest, but she didn't think about it. She could not imagine what other life she might have except that of wife to David, and it would be another year before they could consider that. With two armies gathering across state lines, she dare not even hope for that much.

As she carried the breakfast tray toward the back stairs, Dora heard the low roar of angry voices drifting up from below, and she cringed. She had hoped they would have sense enough to sleep late and stay out of each other's paths on this first day, but the Nicholls' men weren't known for either their sense or sensibility. She detested conflict, but she couldn't cower on the stairs all day.

Apparently Josie, at least, had kept out of the way. The morning sickness stayed with her even in her fourth month. Dora hoped the angry voices didn't carry behind the closed doors of the master chamber. Josie had enough to bear without her husband's family tearing her apart or crushing her with their various loyalties and angers.

"Don't give me that damned crap, Payson! Howard saw you. The authorities back in Lexington swear you were seen in the vicinity. If you wanted to keep your damned mistress, then you should have paid for her like any self-respecting man. It's theft, Payson! You're a thief and a liar and no better than you should be, just like I always said, despite all your fancy degrees. God, I can barely stand to see your face."

Dora winced as these words echoed up the stairway.

Words could abuse the soul just as sticks abused the body, and Carlson Nicholls wielded words like a whip. In his own intolerant way, he was right. Legally, helping slaves escape was still theft in this state, no matter what the federal authorities pretended. She wished she hadn't known the young girl was Pace's latest mistress; it made the sickness inside her roil a little stronger.

"I don't have to stand here and take this crap. I'm not a helpless child any longer. I don't need anything from you. I don't expect anything but abuse from you. I came back here to see if we could have some kind of truce for the holiday, but I'll just go up and say farewell to Mother and I'll get out of your hair. You won't have to look at my face again."

"That's it, break Mother's heart. Tell her we threw you out and then go back and enjoy your fancy pieces instead of standing up for yourself, like the coward you are." Charlie's sneering voice joined the argument.

"Look the hell who's talking! When did you last stop in to talk with her?" Outrage colored Pace's reply to this accusation. "You're no better—"

Dora entered the dining room, the breakfast tray still in her hands. "Thy voices carry," she reprimanded them quietly, drawing on her reserves of strength. She didn't enjoy entering this conflict. For her own sake, she wouldn't. For the sake of others, she had no choice. "Thy mother asks after thee, Payson. She would see thee now." She turned a flat, unreadable gaze to the handsome man lounging against the sideboard. "I do not believe Annie has seen to thy wife this morning. She must eat properly if she is to carry the child to term."

Her quiet words and presence effectively dampened the fires of fury raging through the room. Pace stalked out—although Dora wondered how he could even stand up this morning. Charlie went roaring off to the kitchen in search of the dilatory maid. Carlson Nicholls merely gave her a cold glare and returned to loading his breakfast plate with sausage.

Drained physically by the argument, Dora drifted back to the kitchen and out of the line of fire. Papa John had taught her that nonviolence would end the world's troubles, and sometimes it seemed as if he was right.

But stopping one fight didn't mean another one wouldn't soon break out. The war between father and sons was as difficult to elude as the current one between states. For some reason, men preferred anger and violence to love and reason.

Pace found her later, after she'd done her morning tasks and was walking toward the farm to see how her animals fared. He was riding, and his saddlebags looked full. Dora suspected he had never even unpacked. She didn't know how he'd hung on to the horse last night or how he stayed in the saddle this morning with that gash in his side, but despite her empathy for him, he still remained a mystery to her.

"It is almost Christmas," she murmured sadly as he stopped to ride beside her. "Thou shouldst be with family and friends."

The gold buttons of his blue uniform glittered in the faint sunlight. He removed his hat politely as he spoke, and the sun burnished his hair to copper. "That was my foolish notion, I agree. My regiment has orders to march on the first."

He did not elaborate. He did not need to. Dora knew what he meant. This might be the last time he ever saw his family. She had never seen a war, but she'd seen Pace fight. This time, he would do it with guns and bullets. She couldn't see how anyone could survive such a confrontation. She didn't want this to be the last time she ever saw him. She couldn't bear imagining him with blood flowing into unknown soil and his lively, all-seeing eyes closed forever. She kept her gaze on the dusty road ahead of her.

"I would thee did not have to go," she finally replied. "If thou must go to war, it should not be like this."

Pace walked his horse silently beside her for a way before answering. "It's not my choice, either, Dora. Sometimes, I wonder if all the world is crazed but me. They say that is a certain sign of insanity. Perhaps the world will fare better without me. Most certainly, my family will."

"Thou must have been hit in the head last night," she said scornfully. "Self-pity does not become thee. If thou wishes to stay, stay. The stitches in thy side should not be stretched until the wound begins to heal. Thou hast lost a great deal of blood and should rest. If thou canst not stay in thy father's house, then take mine. Jackson will be glad of the company."

Pace returned his hat to his head and his eyes focused on the horizon while he considered the offer. Dora all but held her breath as he scanned the rolling hills and barren trees. This was his home. She knew he loved it if he loved nothing else. She prayed love was a stronger emotion than anger.

"There are others I would say farewell to before I go," he finally responded. "I would not put you out of your home, though. Do you not use the farmhouse yourself?"

Dora closed her eyes briefly and gave a prayer of thanks before saying, "It is not safe for a woman alone. I stay with thy mother. I pay Jackson to stay and feed the animals. He had almost enough to buy his freedom if the tobacco had not burned. We are hoping for better next year."

Pace eased himself from his horse, favoring his injured side as he did so. When he stood beside her, he still leaned against the saddle for support. He studied her face briefly before concentrating his attention on hanging onto the horse and walking. "Tell Jackson to save his money. When the war is over, he'll be free without paying a cent for his freedom. He can use his savings to buy land."

Dora contemplated such a strange world where black men could buy land, then shook her head. "I cannot see thy father or his friends selling land to a black man. I cannot see Jackson living at peace with such neighbors. There is a woman he would marry, but she is not free, either, so he refuses to marry her for fear their children will one day be sold away from them. There is hate deep inside him, and he is surrounded by hate. I cannot see how it will work. War cannot change men's hearts."

"Their hearts may not change, but their laws must. You know as well as I do that it cannot go on like this forever. Once, there might have been a chance for peaceful change, but narrow minds prevented that chance and it's lost now. The war will not go away soon.

When it ends, Jackson will be a free man. He just must believe that a while longer. He is more fortunate than others. He can wait."

"The girl last night?" she asked quietly.

She felt Pace give her a quick glance, but her bonnet concealed her expression. He returned to looking straight ahead. "Her owner was from New Orleans. She meant to return her there. If she didn't leave now, she would never have another chance. She has just turned old enough to be sold to one of the brothels down there."

Dora cringed inside at such a fate. She had experienced having little freedom of choice, but she could not imagine having no choice at all, especially when the assigned fate was so ... She could not think of a word bad enough to describe the child's intended destiny.

"Violence is not the answer, but I cannot think what is," she finally admitted. "People are so very blind." She hadn't meant for the bitterness to show in her words, but the edge was there when they came out.

"Not all people are blind," Pace reminded her gently. "There are many others who believe as we do. I wish you would stay with your friends across the river. I thank you for your bravery last night, but it was a foolish risk to take. I would prefer that you seek the safety of your friends."

The simple compliment on her bravery warmed her, even though she knew the truth of her cowardice. Biting her bottom lip, Dora shook her head stubbornly. "I am of no use over there. I am needed here, so here I will stay."

They came in sight of the shabby farmhouse. There hadn't been funds for whitewash this past spring. Jackson and David had done what they could to mend the fences and barn roof, but they had other lives outside of this one and could spare little of their time for mending. The crops came first. And they were lost.

She could see Pace scanning the deterioration and forced her tongue to ask, "Wilt thou stay? It is not what thou art accustomed to."

Unexpectedly, he reached for her hand and clasped

her slender fingers in the largeness of his. "It looks like heaven to me. Isn't that where angels come from?"

Dora laughed and accompanied him down the lane. She hadn't laughed in a long time. It felt good. His hand around hers felt good.

She wouldn't think of anything else but the moment.

Lord Beaumont sat stiffly in the desk chair of his study, perusing the crude sheet of stationery on the desk before him. He had one hand on the prayer book beside him, whether in preparation to opening it or in a gesture of prayer was not evident. The door opening to admit his son Gareth interrupted his concentration.

"You cannot still be considering sending for the chit?" the tall young man asked in incredulity, seating himself without invitation in one of the high-backed leather chairs.

Grayer now but no less handsome than in his earlier years, the earl tapped his fingers indecisively on the cheap paper. "If it is truly her, I have an obligation to rescue her from those heathens. Alexandra is my daughter, my flesh and blood. I have had an investigator searching for her for years, and here she is served to me without request. God's hand is in this."

Gareth scowled. "Human hands are in this. Someone seeks to profit by a large reward. There is no proof that the chit is really Alexandra. There is no proof that she even survived except for the word of one of those pious old goats. Alexandra is dead. We all know it. Someone has obviously just found Matilda's old papers. They've set this all up, waited until they found someone the proper age and coloring, and now they're meaning to collect."

The earl kneaded his forehead with indecision. "I will send someone to investigate. I cannot ignore the possibility that she is alive."

Gareth slumped in his chair and crossed his arms over his chest. "There is a bloody civil war going on over there! At least wait until the bloodshed's done. It's not as if you've got the wealth to share. The damned funds crash saw to that."

The earl didn't seem to be listening. His gaze had

drifted to the mullioned window where a faint ray of sun peeked out from behind the heavy barrier of clouds. His fingers continued tapping against the ragged letter. He heard his son. His mind accepted the truth of what was said. It wasn't his mind to which he listened.

Seven

I hate and love. You ask, perhaps, how that can be?
I know not, but I feel the agony.

CATULLUS, *Poems* (1st c. B.C.)

May 1862

Stricken, Dora stared at David, still unbelieving. "But
thou canst not, David. War is the worst form of violence.
Peaceable solutions must be found. Thou canst not become a soldier."

David smiled at her sadly from beneath the broad
brim of his low-crowned hat. "Dost thou think I have
not heard all the arguments? I must follow my own
Light, Dora, and it tells me I must stand beside my beliefs. Slavery must end. Can we measure one wrong
against another, decide which is the greater sin, slavery
or war? If I do not fight, I am allowing slavery to
continue."

Dora tightened her lips in as much of a frown as her
delicate features allowed. "That is specious nonsense,
David. It is no better than Charlie saying he's taking
that provost's position for our own good. A wrong is a
wrong no matter how thou dost justify it. I know full
well Charlie benefits from that position, just as thou in-
tendeth to get away from the store and thy parents by
going off to war. Do not give me fairy tales as an
excuse."

Anger tinged David's reply. "If I speak in fairy tales,
then I am not the only one. Who dost thou think to fool
by living in the big house even when thou hath been
offered other homes? Hadst thou taken the Elders' offer,

they would have approved our marriage by now, and we could be living together on thy farm. What reason canst thou give for refusing their commands?"

"I need no reason! I am needed here. I would be a burden there. If thou didst truly wish to marry me, thou wouldst go against the Elders' rule as thou art doing now. Thy only interest in me is that dratted farm. Go off to war, then. Spill blood upon thy hands. Just do not think thou canst come home again and find everything still the same."

Dora picked up her basket and marched down the lane, turning her back on the frock-coated man standing beside his old horse. She heard him call her name, but tears streaked her cheeks, and she would not let him see them. She didn't even know if they were tears of self-pity, loss, or fear. She just knew she felt this great gaping emptiness, and only terror rushed in to fill it. Always, there had been this emptiness. She should be used to it by now. But each departure ripped the fabric of her existence a little wider.

She was sobbing and half-running by the time she reached the front yard of the big house. This wouldn't do. She couldn't let anyone see her like this. No one ever saw her like this. She would allow no one to see her pain. She must remain invisible. It was her only protection.

Stumbling to a halt beneath one of the big oaks, Dora wiped her face against her sleeve and took a deep breath. She shouldn't have left David like that. She should have been calm and gracious and applauded his noble actions. She had not behaved well at all. But considering she had wanted to stamp her feet and pound his chest and rage at the stupidity of men, perhaps she had found some kind of compromise by just bursting into tears.

If she could pull herself together, she could escape to her room and wash her face and work back into her usual routine. She had learned to wall off unfortunate emotions many long years ago. It took a little time to seal them off completely, but the sooner she began, the sooner it would be done. David was out of her life. She knew that as certainly as she knew that leaves grew on trees. She had left other lives behind and survived. She straightened her shoulders and set her lips and began the process of closing him out as she had walled off everyone else in her past.

The sound of a commotion in the back distracted Dora momentarily from her bleak thoughts. Following the noise, she trailed up the carriage drive, past the stables and kitchens, back toward the slave quarters. Screams and wails and raging voices told her the scene wouldn't be a pleasant one, and she had no business interfering. It didn't matter. Nothing mattered much at the moment.

"Marster Pace done tol' me I could! He tol' me he needed a boy. He tol' me them soldiers needs strong arms. I gots strong arms! I don' wanna be no houseboy no more."

The crack of a whip and a scream followed this outpouring of righteous rage. Dora hurried her steps. The only one who wielded a whip around here was Pace's father, and he didn't know when to stop.

"Damn you! You'll do what I tell you or I'll beat the tar out of your senseless hide. Do you know what happens to runaway niggers down in town? You ain't seein' half of what you'll get if those slave catchers find you!" The whip whined again.

In all probability, Carlson was correct. The slave catchers generally tied their victims up before beating them. Carlson preferred working out his rage by chasing them down. Dora didn't find much consolation in that difference. She cringed as she watched the whip lash through the young boy's shirt. Blood quickly welled in the gash left behind.

She recognized the boy as one who once served as Pace's manservant. The Union army didn't discourage Kentuckians from bringing their slaves with them, but Pace had left his behind. She wondered what had prompted the boy to join him now.

The screaming and arguing continued as Dora joined the circle of frightened black faces. Despite their relative isolation, word of the outside world traveled like wildfire through the slave quarters. They knew the Union soldiers didn't discourage runaways. They knew if they could find a federal regiment, they would find protection. But they were miles from Louisville and the nearest troops, and they feared what could happen between here and there. So far, none had been desperate enough to make the attempt. Until now, apparently.

The boy whimpered on the ground as Carlson swung the whip repeatedly. His aim was off as much as on, but blood streamed from a half-dozen cuts on the boy's back and arms. Dora quietly walked through the crowd and into the inner circle and bent over the child to examine his wounds. Her action effectively halted the progress of the whip.

The mask of hypocrisy always amazed her. Her bonnet and long skirt gave her a protection denied to any man. The fact that Carlson considered her a guest gave her even greater protection. No respectable gentleman would ever strike a woman, and to strike a guest was doubly reprehensible. That didn't mean Carlson wouldn't, but he managed to restrain himself in public.

"What in hell do you think you're doing, girl?" he cried in fury.

"The boy's arm needs suturing. He'll not have the use of it for a week as it is." Dora calmly turned to one of the women in the crowd. "Fetch my bag, wilt thou?"

"Dammit, Dora! I'm not done with him yet. Get out of my way. I'm teaching him a lesson he'll never forget." The whip cracked menacingly near but hit only dirt.

Dora ignored him and looked to one of the men. "Help me get him back to his bed. I'll need soap and warm water."

When the slaves hesitated to follow her command, she glanced up and saw Charlie hurrying down the steps from the house. Charlie represented another problem entirely. She didn't feel any relief when she saw Josie hurrying behind as fast as her unwieldy pregnancy would allow. Gentle Josie had developed a shrew's tongue these last months.

"What in hell's goin' on out here?" Charlie demanded as he strode up. Thirty-plus years and too much alcohol had softened his large frame, but he was still a powerful man. He glared down at Dora stooped in the dust, then turned a questioning gaze on his father.

"Just get the blasted girl out of my way so I can finish what I was doing," Carlson answered irritably. His temper was formidable when aroused, but died just as quickly. He'd already lost interest in the whipping, but his pride needed salvaging.

When Charlie moved to do as told, Josie caught his arm.

"You keep your hands off her! Dora, get that poor boy out of here."

Dora felt fear well up through the emptiness, just as it had all those long years ago. She wanted to run and hide and pretend this wasn't happening, but she knew better than to pray for help. What followed wouldn't be pretty. She had seen it once too many times. Charlie didn't like being thwarted. He didn't appreciate Josie's opinion on the treatment of servants. And he most certainly didn't like having their disagreements broadcast in public.

Shivering, Dora stood up and dusted herself off, momentarily distracting Charlie from the violence forming in his clenched fist. "I thought the boy belonged to Pace," she said carefully, forcing him to look at her and away from Josie. "I merely wanted to see that he wasn't damaged. Pardon my intrusion if I was wrong."

"It doesn't matter who he belongs to!" Josie cried. "You can't treat him like that. He's just a boy."

Dora cringed as Charlie swung his arm, carelessly shoving his wife out of the way. A gentleman might not strike a lady, but a wife belonged to a husband to do with as he wished. Another lesson Dora had learned a long time ago. She grabbed Josie's arm as, unbalanced, she staggered backward, but Josie had gone beyond reasoning now. Unlike Dora's mother, Josie hadn't learned to keep quiet. Recklessness replaced her usual timidity.

She pummeled her small fist into her husband's massive arm. "You push me around one more time like that again, you bully, and I'm going home to Mother! You can't treat me like one of your slaves. Pace warned me about you and I didn't listen! I'm listening now. You'll live to regret the day—"

Bringing Pace into this was not the wisest idea. With a growl of fury, Charlie swung around and slapped Josie

full across the mouth. She gasped and fell backward into
Dora's arms while the servants looked on, wide-eyed
and open-mouthed.

"And I'll not have a nagging bitch for wife! Get the
hell out of my sight before I take the whip to you too."
He grabbed the whip from his father's hand and turned
to apply it on the boy, but his intended victim had had
the sense to crawl out of range. One of the older men
now half-carried him back through the quarters. That
left only Josie to take his anger.

Dora hurriedly placed herself between the shocked
and trembling Josie and her irate husband while Carlson
attempted to soothe his son. With whispered words,
Dora got Josie moving in the direction of the house. By
all rights, she should go after the boy to sew up his more
serious wounds, but Josie was helpless in her pregnancy.
Memories of her own mother's helplessness haunted her.
If her mother had had friends to protect her, she might
be alive today. It seemed wisest to see Josie safe first.

"I'm going home," Josie wept as Dora led her up the
back steps. "Pace was right, I don't belong here. I
thought he was a gentleman!" she wailed brokenly as
they entered the house.

Dora assumed the last "he" meant Charlie, but anyone foolish enough to assume Charlie was a gentleman
didn't deserve an answer. As far as that mattered, the
word "gentleman" had become outmoded. If ever such
a creature existed, it was extinct now.

"He's your husband. Thou canst not leave. Thou must
learn to work around him," Dora suggested as they
started down the hall toward the stairs. Heaven only
knew, she had experience enough to know that leaving
didn't solve the problem. Charlie would just go after
Josie and beat her senseless. Wives didn't have any more
rights than slaves; they just usually didn't end up in jail
when they ran away.

"I'll tell Pace. Pace will know what to do," Josie said
firmly, straightening her shoulders and pulling from
Dora's hold.

Dora groaned inwardly at this stupidity. Maybe
smacking Josie was the right idea. Someone should
knock a little sense into her spoiled little head. In some

ways, Josie and Charlie were two of a kind. "What dost
thou think Pace can do? Thou art married to his brother.
Dost thou wish him to shoot Charlie? Thou dost carry
a child. He can't take thee with him, even if thou wished
to live in a tent and travel from battlefield to battlefield.
This is his home, remember? He has nowhere else to
take thee. Just what dost thou think he can do? Wave
a magic wand?"

Josie grabbed her skirts and stalked up the broad
staircase. "You're just jealous because Pace doesn't
know you're alive. He'll make Charlie stop hitting me."
She turned triumphantly and looked down at Dora.
"You didn't even know Pace was back in town, did you?
Well, he is. And before he goes, he'll make Charlie pay
for what he did."

Dora didn't follow her any farther. The gap inside her
grew a little more empty, and she took the black bag
the silent servant handed her without question, turning
back out the way she came. Pace was home. She should
have known it. The world exploded in chaos all around
her. Who else but Pace could be the cause?

She made her way back through the now silent yard.
Carlson and Charlie had disappeared about their chores
somewhere. The slaves had scattered. A mockingbird
sang its foolish head off at the top of the barn, but that
was the only joyful note heard on this lovely spring day.
Dora wondered where Pace was and what he was doing
here. She didn't think his regiment had been in that
dreadful battle at Shiloh last month. His name hadn't
been listed in the casualties. They would have heard
by now.

One of the house servants was trying to clean the open
wounds on the boy's back when Dora arrived. She respectfully stepped out of the way when Dora took over.

"Why didst thou not ask Mr. Payson to take thee with
him instead of running?" she asked the boy in puzzlement as she cleansed the gashes and pulled out her
thread to mend the worst.

"He wouldn't take me," the boy answered sullenly.
"He said I'd slow him up."

From the sounds of it, the army traveled slower than
molasses in January, but Dora didn't mention that fact.

Knowing Pace, he didn't travel with the army in any normal way. He was too impatient to take orders, too hotheaded to sit and wait with the enemy near. He belonged in the cavalry, but there hadn't been a regiment formed when he joined. The Union army had difficulty enough figuring out what to do with their rebellious Kentucky troops. She couldn't imagine what they would do with Pace.

"Thou must be patient. I will talk with him, but I make no promises. Friend Nicholls is right. If the slave catchers find thee, they'll beat thee far worse than this. The time is coming when thou wilt be free. That time is not now."

Even in his pain, the boy growled angrily. "I don' wanna wait until I'm old and gray."

Dora sighed. The boy had learned too well from Pace. "Let me talk to Friend Payson before thou doth anything rash."

A shadow blocked the sunlight pouring through the open doorway of the small cabin. Dora didn't need to look up or hear his words to know who the shadow preceded. Pace.

"What does my holy bluebird wish to talk to me about?" he asked gruffly, coming into the tiny, crowded room and filling it with his bulk.

Dora told herself that Pace was not a large man. He stood a head shorter than his brother and possessed half his weight. Yet his presence occupied the room so thoroughly that she thought she might suffocate. He cast a long shadow. Out of the corner of her eye she caught sight of his blue uniform and shining buttons. He was bare-headed, and the sun caught in his auburn hair. New crinkles had formed around his eyes from too much sun. Realizing she held her breath, she expelled it.

"This foolish young man," she answered sternly. "He thought to follow thee into war."

Pace gazed over her shoulder to the defiant youth in the bed. "Well, Solly, you've stirred up a fine hornet's nest. I hope you made your mama proud."

The boy glared at him but didn't say a word. Dora didn't blame him. She'd like to kick the man herself. She continued spreading salve on the less serious injuries.

"Dost thou think thy father might hire Solly out to me?' she asked carefully. "Jackson will have need of another worker."

She felt Pace's piercing gaze on the back of her head, but she didn't turn to meet it. Knowing Pace, he'd been the one who recruited David. He had probably known about David's decision before she did. At least he didn't have the hypocrisy to ask why she needed another worker.

"He'll still be a slave," he reminded her.

"Thou hast a better suggestion?" she snapped. Her patience had worn to fine threads this day. She had some difficulty in maintaining her cultivated calm.

"I can't take you with me, Solly," he said to the youth in the bed. "I don't stay in one place long and I travel fast. If I talk my father into hiring you out, will you stay and help Miss Dora? At least that way, you'll earn a little money until the time comes when you're legally free."

"Will I earn enough to buy my freedom if the rebs win?" the boy asked belligerently.

"The rebs aren't going to win," Pace answered firmly. "And even if you could buy your freedom now, you couldn't live free here. It's against the law. You'd have to move up North somewhere, and leave your mother behind. Is that what you want?"

The boy couldn't be much more than fourteen or fifteen. Dora knew he had a passel of younger brothers and sisters and a mother who worked too hard doing sewing for others as well as her own chores at the house. Money for his family was as important as his freedom. One didn't necessarily lead to another.

"How long's it gonna take to beat those rebs?" he demanded truculently.

Dora breathed a sigh of relief. He was beginning to see the sense of their words.

"Can't rightly say, Solly, but I expect Mr. Lincoln has plans. You've got some growing left to do. By the time you're ready to leave home, maybe you won't have to."

"All right." Sleep weighed at his eyes. "I'm no field hand, but I'll work for Miss Dora."

Dora closed up her bottle of salve and returned it to

her satchel. Carefully, avoiding brushing against Pace, she stood up and moved away from the bed. Even when she stepped out of his shadow, she could sense his presence. He smelled of his leather saddle and campfire smoke and something more elusive, something that was all male and all Pace.

The black woman hovering in the background smiled gratefully at Dora. Dora thought she was the boy's aunt, but she had difficulty telling family connections out here. It wasn't as if she'd been properly introduced.

"He will have to rest. Keep him from using that arm as much as possible until it begins to heal. I'll come back out to look at him again as soon as I can."

The woman nodded in understanding and Dora reluctantly stepped back into the sunlight, knowing Pace would follow.

"I must be losing my touch. I had to find you instead of the other way around," he said as they walked back across the yard.

"I did not expect thee, although I should have known to look for a black cloud when lightning strikes." He was making her nervous. Pace had never made her nervous before. She'd always felt comfortable in his presence as she had felt comfortable with no one else but her adopted parents. But this man in blue and gold was a stranger to her. She didn't like noticing his height or the muscular strength of his stride. She didn't like knowing he had a distinctive scent all his own, even out here in the fresh air. He wasn't wearing his gun or sword, but she could feel their presence just the same, and she didn't like that any better. He radiated violence.

"Well, that's fair welcome, I must say. I suppose I am to blame if my father has a temper made in Hades?" Pace exclaimed in irritation.

Dora swung around and glared at him. "One does not blame the clouds for the broken trees, either. David is gone. Solly is in pain. Josie is weeping her eyes out and will have a bruise to mark thy passing. And thy brother will no doubt find another poor dirt farmer to burn out to vent his rage. But I do not hold thee responsible. Thou wilt pass on as the cloud passes, leaving someone else to deal with the wreckage."

He stared at her incredulously. "What in hell would you have me do? Turn them all over my knees and beat sense into them?"

She turned and stalked away again. "Nothing. Thou needs do nothing. Go play thy war games. Shoot some poor misguided young men. Run thy horse up and down a few hills. Make thyself a hero. It is nothing to me."

Pace refused to follow her rampage. Remaining in the yard, he yelled after her as she stomped up the stairs, "Angels don't squawk!"

Muttering an undignified epithet, Dora slammed the door on him.

Eight

As the husband is, the wife is: thou are mated with a clown;
And the grossness of his nature will have weight to drag
 thee down.
He will hold thee, when his passion shall have spent its
 novel force,
Something better than his dog, a little dearer than his horse.

TENNYSON, *Locksley Hall* (1842)

Dora refused to go downstairs for supper. Mrs. Nicholls seldom ate much of the evening meal, and Dora simply finished up what she didn't eat rather than ask the servants to take on an extra task.

She'd heard Pace go to Josie's room earlier in the afternoon. She'd heard the furious outburst of argument later when Charlie came in. She closed out the argument that followed. The situation was hopeless, and all concerned knew it. Yelling wouldn't solve the problem.

She couldn't sit through the torture of that tense meal downstairs. She didn't know how they had any digestion left when they were swallowing all that bile. She would be glad when Pace left. At least when Josie stayed in her room, Charlie went about his business, and they didn't have to pretend they were one big happy family.

Dora straightened the covers on the invalid's bed. Harriet slept. She didn't have anything left to do in here. She was bored out of her mind. If Pace hadn't been home, she could have walked over to the farm and checked on Jackson's progress. The days grew longer and warmer. She would enjoy an evening stroll. She didn't know why she hid away in here just because Pace was home.

A little while later she heard a horse riding out, and she caught a glimpse of blue uniform through the trees when she glanced out the window. He was gone. Thank God.

She wouldn't contemplate why she felt relief at Pace's absence. He didn't look as if he had suffered the hardships of war. He probably loved every minute of it. A man like Pace belonged in the military. Maybe after the war ended he would go out West and fight Indians. Let him fight anywhere but here. She was tired of the violence.

She donned her bonnet and slipped down the front stairs. The light would hold a while yet. She could reach the farm and return before dark. She needed to tell Jackson about Solly.

Jackson wasn't happy about hiring an inexperienced boy in David's place, but he agreed they had little choice. Although Jackson didn't know of her ulterior motives, Dora thought Solly could use a man to take him in hand for a while, and Jackson was the best example she knew. Abolitionists might preach an end to slavery, but she didn't see many people thinking about what would happen to all the inexperienced, uneducated, naive negroes when it happened. They would be crucified unless they learned the ways of the real world. Jackson knew. He could teach Solly.

Satisfied she had done her limited best for the moment, Dora retraced her tracks up the lane to the big house. Darkness shadowed the lane, but she had little fear of the dark. One must fear dying to fear the dark. Dying didn't scare her. Living did.

She entered the front door and heard Charlie and Josie arguing in the upper hall without a thought to the invalid sleeping a few doors away. Dora didn't think she had it in her to face another conflict this day. She wanted to run and hide and not come out until everyone slept. She thought perhaps David was in the right. She should have left this place, married, and now she would have her own peaceful home. It would be achingly empty without David, but even emptiness sounded pleasant after this.

She still debated climbing the stairs and breaking up the fight or just sneaking around to the back when she heard the crack of Charlie's knuckle against the wall behind Josie. She had come to understand that Charlie unconsciously imitated his father's reactions to frustra-

tion, but that did not make the sound any more palat-
able. Josie's scream ended all thought. Dora reacted
instinctively, racing for the stairs as Charlie's cry of terror echoed downward. The horrifying sound of a heavy
weight hitting wooden treads made her feet fly faster.

Josie lay on the landing, screaming and crying and
holding her protruding abdomen while Charlie kneeled
over her, protesting his excuses helplessly.

At Dora's appearance, he turned his suave, handsome
face and terrified eyes up to her. "I didn't mean to scare
her! She fell. God help me, I didn't mean to hurt her!"

The voice of cynicism cried out to answer, but the
Smythes had taught her well these last years. Keeping
her expression carefully blank, Dora merely answered,
"Lift her gently and take her upstairs. It is likely the
child's time."

She didn't need to be a magician to know that. The
growing wetness and streaks of blood on Josie's skirts
warned her. Mother Elizabeth had allowed Dora to as-
sist in very few births before she died, but she had explained a great deal. Once the water broke, the child
had to be born or both mother and child would die.

Josie shrieked with hysteria as Charlie tried to lift her,
but she couldn't remain there and no one else could
carry her. Dora knelt beside her to make certain she
had suffered no other injury, whispered a few reassuring
words, and when Josie's cries settled to broken sobs, she
stepped away and allowed Charlie to try again.

She had to give him some credit. He looked devastated. He was a big man with more strength than he
realized, and Josie was very small in his arms. His actions hadn't been deliberate but made in the heat of the
moment. That didn't absolve him of the guilt of his inability to control his temper. The handsome lines of his
face looked crumpled and defeated now as he gently
carried his wife into their bedroom.

"Fetch Annie. Tell her I will need hot water and clean
linens. Then go and reassure thy mother. She will be
worried." Dora hastened to Josie's side once she lay on
the bed, cutting her off from her husband, sending Charlie from the room. All would go much easier if they did
not tear at each other now.

She heard Charlie's grunt of disbelief after her admonishment about his mother, but she didn't have time to worry over whether he heeded her words. Josie screamed as another contraction took over.

Annie came with the required articles. She lit the lamps, then helped Dora undress Josie and put her in a night shift. They placed thick pads of cotton under her, and she rested comfortably for a while. As Dora wiped her patient's forehead with a cool cloth, Josie grabbed her hand.

"Tell them to fetch my mama. I want my mama here."

Dora looked up at Annie, who nodded her understanding and quietly left the room. "She will be here in plenty of time," Dora said softly. "The first one needs lots of time."

As if to prove her wrong, Josie gave another low moan as her muscles contracted. She closed her eyes and clenched her fists and bit back a stronger cry until the pain went away, then she opened her eyes and glared up at Dora. "I'm going to kill him. Just see if I don't."

Dora didn't think it was her place to argue the point. Soothingly, she answered, "Thou wilt feel much better when the babe is in thy arms. Has thou thought of names?"

"Amy, for my mother," Josie answered decisively.

"And if it should be a son?"

"It won't be." Josie set her pretty face with determination. "I'm not having any boys. They're despicable creatures, every one."

Right now, Dora was in perfect accord with that feeling. She smiled and asked teasingly, "Even Pace?"

"Especially Pace. I hate him. I hate them all. I'm going home to Mama." Another contraction took over and Josie's declarations dissolved into incoherent curses.

Dora had a long time to wonder about a woman's plight as she watched the woman in the bed suffer through the hours of increasingly excruciating pain. She had never thought what it would be like to have a child herself. She'd always carried some vague image of presenting this gift of life to a loving husband someday, but reality sat on her doorstep now. Love hadn't created this child. Pain and humiliation and anger had created it. No loving scenes of tenderness and happiness would make this agony worthwhile. Only increasing hatred would mark its birth. Surely not all children were born into the world this way. Something more must exist or the human race would not continue.

A slamming door and loud voices warned more than Charlie waited below. She wondered what had happened to Josie's mother. She didn't know Mrs. Andrews very well. She didn't know how much of a help she might be. But Josie needed her right now.

Josie had given up on holding back her screams. She shrieked as another pain consumed her, and she sobbed when it passed. Dora looked up anxiously as the door opened. It was only Annie.

"Where is Mrs. Andrews?" she whispered so the woman in the bed wouldn't hear.

Annie shrugged. "The marster wouldn't call for her. Marster Pace done down there now. Maybe he'll go."

From the sound of rising voices, Dora doubted it. A crash of something breaking warned argument had swiftly deteriorated into fisticuffs. A third yell indicated the noise had brought Carlson out of his hideaway. She grimaced and returned to tending Josie through the next contraction.

When Josie lay panting and sweat-soaked again, Dora turned back to Annie. "Go down the back way and have one of the boys ride to the Andrewses. Surely one of them knows the way."

Annie looked uncertain, but the sound of a raging brawl below made her nod once. The men wouldn't have any idea what went on anytime soon. As she started to leave, Dora halted her.

"Wait a minute. Wipe Friend Josie's brow while I run across and look in on Friend Harriet. She'll be worrying."

Annie made the same disbelieving grunt that Charlie had made earlier, but Dora ignored her. She didn't have much time. Leaving Annie with Josie, she darted across the hall. From out here, the brawl echoed even louder. She distinctly heard Pace's voice shouting louder than all the rest. She winced as another thud and crash followed. She hurriedly let herself into the darkened chamber and closed the door.

"Have they killed each other yet?" The weakened voice came from the direction of the bed and sounded almost hopeful.

"Josie is having her baby." Dora slipped to the bedside to check the pitcher of water and straighten the invalid's covers. "I must be with her for a few hours until her mother comes."

"Amy Andrews is a useless bitch," Harriet murmured. "Just give me some of my medicine and don't worry about me."

"I'd worry less about thee if thou didst not take so much medicine," Dora said, not for the first time nor the last.

The invalid made an inelegant snort. "I suppose you would prefer I go downstairs and referee my charming husband and sons while they bash each other's heads in."

"A woman has a calming influence on hot tempers," Dora chided.

Harriet hiccuped slightly, then drank greedily of the cup given her. "I would prefer they killed each other," she replied when the cup was empty.

Dora couldn't say much to that. Seeing her patient settled down for the evening, she slipped back across the hall to Josie. This was going to be a long night.

The newest Nicholls didn't put in an appearance until four in the morning. Dora delivered her with Annie's assistance. Mrs. Andrews never arrived. The noise downstairs had apparently disintegrated into drunken slumbers. The infant squalled loud enough to wake all the devils in the house.

"Is it a girl?" Josie whispered wearily.

"Meet Friend Amy." Dora lay the swaddled infant beside Josie's head so she could inspect her. "She will look just like her mother when she grows up."

"I would rather she looked like you so men left her alone," Josie answered bitterly.

That was a hard blow to take on top of a day of hard blows. Biting back a rebellious remark, Dora returned to cleaning up. Maybe she wasn't invisible. Maybe she was just ugly. She hadn't thought about that. She'd never spent much time in front of mirrors. It wouldn't do to think about it now.

She heard a stirring below as the babe's squalls continued through her first bath. She supposed someone should tell the happy father of his child's birth. She wasn't in any hurry to do the honors, but she didn't see anyone else she could appoint in her place. It didn't seem quite appropriate sending poor Annie down to that saloon they called a parlor.

She delayed as long as she could. While Annie bathed the infant, Dora changed the bed linens and Josie's night shift. By the time both mother and child slept, they had returned the room to rights. There was nothing left to do but go down and make the announcement.

Annie and Dora exchanged glances. They could hear voices rumbling up the stairs. Argument could break out at any moment. It was now or never. Dora held out her arms for the bundled child. Annie surrendered her willingly.

"That child gonna need a mammy. I'll go get Della. She's nursin'."

Grateful that at least some of the initiative had been absorbed by someone else other than herself, Dora nodded. Then taking the tiny bundle, she slipped into the hall before she lost her nerve. She didn't even dare look at the child. She walled herself off from feeling anything for it too, knowing instinctively that it would be too easy to love, and that she couldn't bear seeing the child hurt. She must leave here soon, before she became attached.

All three men staggered to their feet when Dora entered the parlor. The rod in the velvet drapes over the bay window sagged on one side, leaving a puddle of material across the carpet. A broken bottle of bourbon saturated both velvet and carpet, and the room reeked of whiskey. A shattered lamp had sent crystals and broken glass across the polished wooden floor at the other end of the room. A framed photograph covered in glass had fallen from the mantel. The shards of its remains glittered in the light of a single candle.

Dora's gaze swept the room, then came to rest on the three sheepish men. Carlson didn't look too battered, just grumpy. Charlie had apparently taken the worst of it. His eye had blackened and one side of his face was bruised and swollen. Pace had a split lip and blood stained his white shirt. Dora didn't know what he'd done with his uniform coat. She tried not to look at the place where the shirt lay open at his throat, nor the way the hairs on his arm curled where he'd rolled up the sleeves. She bit her lip and held out the bundle in her arms.

"It's a girl. Josie said she was to be named Amy."

"I'll not name any child of mine—"

Pace slammed a fist into his brother's arm to shut him up. "How's Josie?"

"Sleeping." Dora knew her voice was more curt than necessary, but her precious calm had shattered this night and she hadn't the strength to mend it just yet. "She'll want to see her mother when she wakes," she reminded them, in case they had forgotten.

"I'll not give that meddling old woman—"

Dora thrust the sleeping infant into Charlie's arms. "Amy Andrews is the child's grandmother. Unless thou wishes to rouse thy mother to her duty, I'd suggest thou dost welcome thy mother-in-law to the task. A child needs a grandmother."

Pace grinned and gave a soft cheer as he peeked over his brother's arm at the squirming babe. "Better watch it, Charlie. You'll have a house full of women before you know it. Don't let that meek face fool you. Dora will chew your ear off if you don't behave."

That was the final straw. She'd been rejected, ignored, called ugly, and now named a shrew. If the good Lord had any more days like this one in store for her, she wished He'd just let her drown. Grabbing her skirt in both fists, she started for the door. "Annie is fetching a nursemaid. Good night."

"Wait a minute!" all three men screamed after her in varying degrees of panic and concern, waking the babe and sending her into howls.

Dora lifted her skirts and started up the stairs. Sometimes, vengeance didn't always belong to the Lord.

Nine

If a house be divided against itself, that house cannot stand.

Mark 3:25

May 1864

"Remember Tommy McCoy?"

Dora sat on the front step of her farmhouse carefully cutting the last of the seed potatoes so each piece had at least one eye. She nodded absently. "The federal troops arrested him last month, said he was aiding and abetting the Confederates. That poor family has more troubles. I don't know why Tommy is always the one who gets caught. Everyone around here is a southern sympathizer."

Jackson gave a grunt of disbelief and shook his head at her. "You cain't be as blind as you pretend. Joe Mitchell and Charlie been feuding with the McCoys ever since Tommy's papa called them a bunch of drunken asses and ran them off his property one night, way back before the war. I reckon they was sparkin' Tommy's sister at the time. They been tryin' to get even ever since."

Dora glanced up impatiently. "And?"

Jackson's black face split in a white grin at the surliness of her tone. "You sure are gettin' jumpity these days. Life in the big house still not a bowl of cream?"

"Amy's teething. Again. Friend Harriet complains night and day about the racket. Two more of the field hands disappeared, and their wives are worse than useless. They've been told soldiers' wives are free, so I guess their women will leave next. I don't even know if it's the truth or not, but that doesn't matter to them. I tried talking Josie into offering wages, but she looks at me as if I declared treason. And Friend Carlson has been so surly since Charlie joined the rebels, it's easier to get out of his way than talk to him."

Jackson dumped his basket of potatoes into a burlap sack for hauling to the field. "You want to move back here, just say the word. I can live out in the barn. I've been thinking of joining the army myself, breaking these chains once and for all."

Dora glared at him. "Don't thee dare! What good is freedom if thou art lying beneath the cold hard ground?"

His expression grew stubborn. "I could marry Liza and if the rumors are true, she would be free."

Dora sighed and threw her last potato into the basket. "Find the truth of the rumor first. Union soldiers are as apt to lie as any other men. What wert thou telling me of Tommy McCoy?"

"He's dead. The feds shot him."

Dora's head jerked up and she stared at him in alarm. "He was not a soldier. How can that be?"

"Confederate guerrillas raided the corn supplies last night. Tommy just got paroled. The feds hauled him back in and a few others with him and shot them as traitors. The general is gettin' fed up playing Catch Me If You Can with these damned rebels 'round here. We're supposed to be part of the Union, not workin' against it. He knows darned well it wasn't no reb soldier from down South come all the way up here to raid the supplies."

Dora stretched her cramped fingers and looked out over the lacy border of blooming deutzia edging the yard. The sky was so beautiful a blue it hurt to look at it. Spring breezes warmed the air and tickled along her neck. She could feel the earth burgeoning with new life: rosebuds had begun to swell and open, irises pushed their heads toward the sky, and honeysuckle vines bloomed in glorious profusion. And in the midst of all God's glory, men spilled the blood of other men into the ground.

Tears sprang to her eyes for no particularly good reason at all. She shook her head to rid herself of them.

Melancholy had haunted her this past week or more. She'd felt a fear, a helpless pressure that she couldn't explain. A baby's cries and an old woman's complaints wouldn't cause this pain around her heart. Only one thing could, and she was foolish to believe even that. Pace's letters were always infrequent and never to her. To believe any connection existed between them was to believe in angels and fairies. Perhaps she should seek a doctor and get a spring tonic. More likely, she should quit reading the newspapers. Since the first of May, the war had escalated on two fronts in an unprecedented surge of violence. She went cold inside each time she imagined the men she knew fighting in it.

"I wish it would all go away," she whispered, as much to herself as to Jackson.

"I wished that a few times myself," Jackson grunted. Then looking at a figure coming across the field, he continued, "And there's one I'd wish away now."

Dora glanced up to watch Solly's lanky adolescent lope across the plowed furrows. The youth grinned when he saw they'd spotted him. "He is but a boy, Jackson. Thou must be patient with him," she said consolingly. Solly was supposed to have been here earlier this morning to help with the potatoes.

Barefoot and in a muslin shirt nearly in tatters, he strode up like a Union captain in glittering uniform, saluting them as he stopped in front of them. "I'm goin' to join the army," he announced.

Dora stared at him, stricken.

Jackson cuffed him casually alongside his head. "You gettin' married, boy?"

Solly blinked and stared at him. " 'Course not. Why in hell would I do that?"

"Only reason I know of to go gettin' yourself killed for somethin' the white man shoulda done a long time ago. What'd the bluebellies ever do for you that you want to die for them? I taught you better, boy."

Dora lowered her eyes to the ground so neither man could see her laughter or surprise. Not ten minutes ago, Jackson had been the one claiming he would join the army. Now here he was, keeping a boy too young to know what he was doing from it—a boy he professed to

despise, no less. It had taken nearly two years, but
maybe Solly had started growing on the older man.

"I gets to be free if I join," Solly answered
suspiciously.

"You gets to be dead if you join. Why you think they
lookin' to take on niggers? 'Cause no white man in his
right head gonna do it, that's why. They all been shot
at and killed and tore up as much as they can take, and
they're startin' to think mebbe we ain't worth the trouble. Well, hell, they ain't worth it neither. Let them fight
their own wars. We got work to do." Jackson lifted the
hundred-pound bag of potatoes to his shoulder as if it
were feathers. Giving the boy another cuff, he started
for the field. "Come on, let's get these planted."

Dora prayed that would resolve the problem for a
little while longer. They'd been fighting for three years.
Surely this couldn't go on forever. There wouldn't be a
man left alive if they fought much more.

Thinking like that didn't help her state of mind. She
had to keep busy. She certainly had plenty enough to
keep her hands occupied. She just wished she had more
to keep her mind occupied.

Carlson Nicholls rode by her at a gallop, scarcely noticing Dora's slight figure as she walked along the grass
on the lane's edge. If she were any judge at all, she'd
say he looked fit to kill. But then, Pace's father always
looked like that these days. Ever since Charlie had given
up his lucrative provost marshal's position and joined
the Confederates, Carlson had been a man on the edge.

Dora knew Charlie and his so-called troops had harassed Unionists and others under the guise of upholding
the law, but the fun had gone out of the game the day
a local Yankee officer demanded he come up with real
charges against the people he threw in jail. Charlie had
quit shortly after that, and Lincoln's Emancipation Proclamation a year ago January had been the last straw.
Charlie had foamed at the mouth then just as his father
seemed to be doing now.

The situation hadn't improved once the Yankees
learned Charlie had turned traitor to their cause. As the
wife of a Confederate, Josie had even been threatened
with prison, but Carlson continued declaring his loyalty

and brought Pace's actions with the Union army forward
as a firm example. Dora could see the older man growing
a little more gray each day, and she could almost feel
sympathy for him if she thought concern for his sons
made him surly. Instead, she suspected his temper arose
from having to deal with the stubborn Yankee soldiers.

When Dora reached the big house, she found it a
whirlwind of activity. Annie ran up and down stairs carrying loads of petticoats and gowns. Della scolded little
Amy so loudly that the child's protests nearly drowned
in the vocal barrage. And Josie stood in the eye of the
storm, directing it.

"Good, Dora, there you are! Will you go tell the stable hands to have that wagon outside right now? I'll not
wait a minute more than necessary. Those trunks are
getting loaded or I'll know the reason why."

Dora was over twenty now. She'd survived in this
household for three years. She hadn't done it by running
her legs off every time someone barked. The Nicholls
family might incline toward thinking of her as an unpaid,
invisible servant, but she had carved out her own ideas
of her position in the family. She halted one of the maids
scurrying around with baskets of clothes and passed the
order on. The girl looked relieved for an excuse to escape the house.

"Has something happened?" Dora asked quietly,
watching the activity with a certain degree of anxiety.
This unexpected upheaval didn't ease the feeling of im-
pending disaster.

"That man has ordered me out of the house! He
claims it is all my fault that the Yankees are refusing to
pay him for those slaves they're taking. You'd think
those horrible old negroes were more important than his
son's wife and his granddaughter. I've never been so
insulted in my life! I'm leaving, and I'm never coming
back. These are the most ungrateful, pigheaded ..."

The tirade could go on for the rest of the day, Dora
figured. Once Josie got off the subject of her father-in-
law, she could launch into her ungrateful husband and
her useless mother-in-law. She'd heard the speech more
than once during this last year and a half. In actuality,
Josie had been delighted when Charlie rode out. She'd

played lady of the manor ever since. Carlson's edict meant she was reduced to returning home and playing dutiful daughter to her mother again.

Dora continued up the stairs to see how Harriet Nicholls was taking this latest excitement. With both of her sons out of the house and her husband too busy to be seen or heard, she had begun to improve slightly. The knowledge that Josie had produced a girl instead of a boy had also tickled the old lady, mostly because it so irritated the men.

Little Amy had escaped Della's scolding and hid now behind her grandmother's chair. Harriet winked when Dora entered the room.

"There's a little mouse in there. Better be careful where you step."

Dora's lips quirked upward slightly as the toddler scrunched down smaller behind the chair skirt. She had done her very best to stay away from the little girl, but she couldn't help the tug on her heart every time Amy crossed her path. She had her father's dark gold hair and her mother's pointed chin, but mostly she looked like a grubby elf. Della wasn't a particularly efficient nanny, and Josie had no clue as to how to make a child mind. Amy fairly well succeeded in doing anything she wanted, with her grandmother's cooperation.

"Well, I shall bring the cat up from the kitchen to catch the mouse," Dora responded casually. "Or dost thou think perhaps the mouse might be persuaded to go down to the kitchen with me to look for something to nibble on?"

Mrs. Nicholls nodded her capped head solemnly. The years had not been particularly kind to her. Her flesh had grown to flab and then wasted into heavy wrinkles. Her hair was thinning and had turned an unflattering iron gray. But the fact that she actually sat up in a chair marked the improvement she had made these last years. She wasn't big-boned like her husband. Pace had inherited his slighter stature from her. But she still wasn't a small woman. She made a commanding presence when she put her mind to it.

"Take the mouse away. I suspect she hasn't been fed

in all this commotion. Everything has certainly gone to hell in a handbasket around here lately."

Dora could agree with that, but not out loud. She crooked her finger at the interested child, and made a play of tiptoeing out of the room. Amy scampered to follow.

By the time Dora got mashed potatoes and new spring peas into the imp, Amy had succeeded in smearing not only herself, but Dora with the vegetables, pulled off Dora's cap and buried her sticky fingers in her hair, and wet herself and Dora's skirts completely through. She was sleepy and ready for a nap by the time Della found her and carried her off to the waiting wagon.

Dora ran her hands through her short curls and watched the wagon bearing Amy and Josie roll down the lane. She should be used to people leaving her life and never coming back. This aching pain and nagging loneliness should be second nature to her by now. But each leave-taking ripped still another hole in the fabric of her existence. Despite all her efforts to remain aloof, she would miss the golden-haired little imp and even Josie's scolding tongue.

When the wagon disappeared beyond the trees, Dora returned upstairs feeling as if she had no more substance than a dandelion seed blowing in the breeze. She had no purpose, no goal, no one to need her, no one to care if she disappeared into thin air. She might as well not exist for all it mattered to anyone.

She stopped in her room to clean the peas and potatoes from her face and change her damp gown. Catching a glimpse of her reflection in the small mirror over the washstand, she studied herself. With her cap off, she had no personality. Her face was small, her eyes too large, her lashes too dark for her light hair. Her hair was her only act of rebellion. Too fine and unmanageable to torture into ringlets, her hair wouldn't even lie down in a chignon. The huge bonnet she wore when she went out made long hair miserably hot. So she kept the mop cut and let it curl and wisp where it would. No one ever noticed. So much for rebellion.

Briefly, she wondered what she would look like if she

wore pretty blues and laces and maybe ribbons in her
hair instead of ugly grays and stiff round collars, but
what would it matter? No one would notice if she
walked down the stairs stark naked. She had cultivated
invisibility to a fine art. Now she must live with it. Even
if she suddenly did become visible, no one remained to
see her.

Unlike Pace, David wrote faithfully, but Dora had succeeded in walling herself off from any emotion gener-
ated by his letters. He tried to write cheerfully, but she
could read between the lines. He hated the war and the
violence and the senseless destruction. She wanted to
ache for him, to wish him home, to weep, but she
couldn't. He was out of her life now. Once people left
her, they never came back. She knew that as a matter
of fact. Perhaps the best thing she could do now was
leave this place. If she wasn't here, maybe Pace and
Charlie and David would come home alive. If she stayed,
she would never see them again. It was as simple as that.
Perhaps she should start thinking of where she should
go.

She supposed that kind of foolish thinking started silly
superstitions, but she couldn't help feeling as if she were
a curse waiting to happen. Perhaps she ought to volun-
teer as a nurse like Clara Barton. That way, the curse
could work either for the good or the bad. Either way,
whether her patients died, or got better and went home,
she would never see them again.

She wasn't so far gone as to not see the ridiculousness
of her notions, but that didn't make her feel a great deal
better. Maybe becoming a nurse was the best idea.

In a clean gown and cap, with her face freshly
scrubbed, she stepped into the invalid's room to see how
Harriet Nicholls fared.

Her patient was in bed and sound asleep. Finding a
folded newspaper lying on the covers, Dora picked it up
before it could fall to the floor. She hadn't seen today's
paper. She dreaded reading the newssheets. Grant's
march on Richmond, Sherman's advance on Atlanta,
and the list of Kentucky casualties filled the pages. Reading them was the scourge she lashed herself with to keep
herself from growing too comfortable.

She didn't read the blood-curdling paragraphs on the latest battle. Her gaze went directly to the list of casualties as if guided there. She didn't even have to look to find a familiar name under "Killed in Action."

David.

Ten

Be not forgetful to entertain strangers; for thereby
some have entertained angels unawares.

Hebrews 13:2

June 1864

The streak of a single tear dried in the dust on her face
as Dora rode beside the elderly frock-coated gentleman
on the wagon seat. Her wide-brimmed bonnet hid the
streak in shadow, and she sat stiff and straight, disguising
the heavy burden weighing on her shoulders. She should
have married David and made him stay home. He would
be alive today if she had followed the Elders' teachings
and not her own interpretations of the Light.

"Thou must know thee will be welcome with us,
Friend Dora," the man beside her said gently.

"I know, and I am grateful. If it were not for thee
and the others, I would feel lost and without anchor. I
must think what is best. Perhaps if I had been there,
I could have saved David. Perhaps if I go there now, I
can save the lives of others. Is that vanity?" Despite the
strength with which she held herself straight, her voice
was weak and whispery. Uncertainty was the bane of
her life. She had no confidence in herself to do what
was right.

"Not vanity, perhaps, but self-sacrifice, which is also
a sin. There is naught romantic about war and violence.
It is ugly and mean, and it makes men ugly and mean.
I have heard tales of the field hospitals. They are no
place for a sheltered young woman. And anywhere near
an army of violent young men away from the morals of

their homes and families is no place for a pretty woman. I admire thy need to help, but surely it can be done somewhere a little closer to home."

She could tell the Elder that she was invisible and not pretty, that men didn't notice her or know she existed, but he wouldn't understand. He lived in a community of Friends where their garb didn't stand out so that their personalities could. His quiet self-confidence and that of the others around him didn't allow for belief in invisibility. They were firm in their convictions that they led righteous lives and served the Lord. She was not certain of anything. She thought perhaps she never would be. She had worn velvets and lace and pretty colors until the age of eight. She had seen pretty colors and lace all around her ever since, but she lived in shadowy gray— part of the world but invisible.

She was too tired for thinking clearly. She hadn't slept in a week. This overwhelming sense of pain kept her awake, and her worries kept her tossing and turning. At times, she doubted her sanity. At times, she wondered if it wouldn't be best to sell the farm and go back to England and confront the life she'd escaped. Perhaps she had left something back there that she should have done, some part of her life that she had missed and needed to live through yet. The notion terrified her, but it nagged at her as much as the idea of following the army as a nurse.

It was nearing dusk when she climbed from the wagon and waved good-bye to the Elder who had taken her home from Meeting. She trailed into the Nichollses' empty, echoing house and wondered how she could have complained when the house had rocked with the noise of Amy's cries and Charlie's complaints and Josie's shrill tongue. At least there had been life here then. Now there was nothing.

Carlson had gone hunting for two young slaves who had disappeared last night. She didn't expect him back soon. Since the repeal of the Fugitive Slave Law, he couldn't call on the authorities if the boys escaped across the river. Kentucky law would still hold them as runaways, but she doubted if the boys were foolish enough to stay in Kentucky. Carlson would have to track them across the river and hunt them down by himself. He couldn't offer a bounty on them any longer, and the slave catchers were only interested in money. She didn't think he would find them, but he wouldn't give up easily, either.

She went back to the kitchen to check on supper, but she only found a pot of stew simmering on the stove. She didn't blame the servants for escaping the iron hand of authority every chance they got. But she had a feeling they thought the day would come when they could be this free all the time. She had news for them. No one was ever that free. Only the rich had options.

She filled two bowls and took them upstairs. Perhaps she could get Harriet Nicholls interested in household affairs again by telling her about the dismal collapse of authority around here. A little moral indignation went a long way sometimes.

Harriet had already fallen asleep by the time Dora reached the bedroom. Despite her improvement, she tired easily. Frowning at the bowl of stew, Dora set it on the bedside table and ate hers while looking out the window. She had hoped for a little companionship while she ate, at least.

When Harriet still slept an hour later, Dora took the bowls back downstairs. She couldn't remember the house ever being so empty. Admittedly, the Nichollses didn't have a host of relations always visiting like most of their friends and neighbors did, but there had always been noise and activity in the house. It seemed strange not even seeing a servant out and about.

She could hear music in the quarters. The balmy June evening hadn't reached the sweltering temperatures it would in a few weeks. Perhaps she could wander out there for a while. She didn't think they would mind if she just listened to the music. She didn't know if her invisibility extended to the slaves as well as their masters, but they seemed to accept her, perhaps because she nursed their ills and injuries.

Dora had just about decided to put her bonnet on and had reached the foot of the front stairs on the way to her room when she heard the sound of someone running up the drive. She probably shouldn't have heard a noise so subtle, but her nerves were on edge, and every peculiar sound caught her attention. Heart pounding, she looked out the front windows overlooking the porch.

Dusk made it difficult to discern little more than the long, loping figure running barefoot through the dirt, but she had no difficulty recognizing him. Solly. Solly never ran if he could shuffle, lag, or wander. Something was wrong.

Her first instinct made her glance at the night sky to see if the tobacco bed burned. She knew perfectly well that Charlie and his devious friends were capable of burning her out if they decided they needed her land for something. She felt certain they had been behind the earlier depredations. But Charlie was gone and the others had left her alone lately. They could find more fun out there now than burning out one tiny farmhouse and a few acres.

No fire illuminated the night sky. What then?

She stepped out on the porch, diverting Solly from running to the rear entrance. Catching sight of her, he ran across the front lawn and called, "Bring your medicine bag, Miss Dora, and come quick!"

She wanted to ask who and what and why, but she already knew. The pain she had suffered these last days told her. She should have known sooner, only with everything happening at once, she hadn't paid attention.

She ran upstairs and grabbed the bag and hurried back down again without her bonnet or cloak. The night was warm and she was in a hurry. She couldn't forgive herself for David's death. She'd never forgive herself if Pace died because she didn't get there soon enough.

Pace grimaced as the ground shifted beneath him. His head felt light and dislocated, but once he got it anchored, he thought he might be lying on a bed for a change. The agonizing pain in his arm and shoulder had become so much a part of him that he noticed minor things like the bed he lay on before surrendering to the agony. Only while leaving the hospital had he been in charge of his fate. Since then, invisible beings saw him moved from wagon to train to cart and now to wherever he was at the moment.

"Hot water, Jackson. Heat lots of hot water."

The voice whispered through Pace's head like wisps of thread pulling him back. He realized he'd allowed himself to float again. He'd done that with increasing regularity these last hours. When the pain grew intense enough, he could disengage his mind and float somewhere outside his body. The whispering voice called him back.

Gentle hands soothed his brow with cool fingers. He was conscious of the rough stubble of his face and the grime and stench of his clothes. He wanted to yell at her to get out, to get away from him, but he couldn't remember who he yelled at or why.

He felt his clothing stripped away. He couldn't tell if he screamed his anguish or if the sound was just inside his head. The cooling hands came back with warm, scented water, and the soft voice murmured admonishments when he struggled against her touch. Fiery knife edges cut through him when she reached his shattered arm, and he nearly threw her off the bed in his determination to withdraw.

"Leave it alone!" he yelled. Or he thought he yelled. "You can't take it!"

"I don't want it," she murmured unsympathetically, with a trace of humor. "I shouldn't think thou wouldst want it either, not this way. It's not of much use to thee in this condition."

Something in the way she said that shot right to his core, and Pace's eyes flew open.

He'd no doubt been delirious for days. He was probably delirious now. Lamplight shone through a halo of silver curls, casting delicate features in shadows. Still, he could see the bowed lips, the perfect pearl-like teeth, the insolent little nose, and the wide, long-lashed blue eyes of an angel. He wondered where she kept her wings.

Closing his eyes again, he managed to say coherently, "Angels don't belong in hell."

"If all the denizens are not beyond hope, then mayhap that is just where they do belong."

He wanted to laugh. His stubborn angel would do just that: go to hell to rescue the devil. But somewhere, he'd forgotten how to laugh. The only sound that came out now was a scream as she moved his arm to discover the extent of the damage.

"Thou hast seen the end of thy fighting for a while," she said somewhere in the gray haze above him. Pace couldn't tell if the words were sad or not. He was too busy clinging to consciousness.

"Don't take it off!" He repeated the warning he'd screamed with much stronger fury days or weeks ago, when he'd commanded his men to haul him out of the hospital and put him on the train.

"It's likely to rot off of its own accord and take thee with it," she answered bluntly.

"Then let me go." Pace knew what he said when he said that, although it took every last ounce of energy left in him to speak. He would prefer death over any other existence he could foresee now. He'd seen a four-teen-year-old drummer boy blown to tiny bits of scrap and bone. He'd watched a woman perish in an inferno of flame when she refused to leave her home and posses-sions. He'd seen his closest companions explode in blood and guts from bullets that had narrowly missed him. He'd watched wagon loads of arms and legs hauled from field hospitals to trenches for burial. He'd forgotten why he fought but had mercilessly continued killing rather than be killed. If death meant peace, then he was ready for it.

Dora watched with grief as Pace slipped into fevered unconsciousness. She shook her head as she studied the bloodied remains of gristle and bone that had once been his fine, strong arm. She was no doctor. She could do little here but clean and bind it. She glanced up at Jack-son hovering anxiously in a corner.

"Thou hadst best find a physician. There is nothing here I can do but make him comfortable."

"The doctor will amputate," Jackson answered slowly. "That's his right arm. He won't shoot or fight again with-out it."

"Is that all his life is worth?" she asked angrily. "May-hap he would be a great deal happier if he could not shoot or fight. Fetch a doctor."

Jackson went to do as told, leaving Dora sitting by

the bedside of the dying young soldier. If she could think of him like that, perhaps she would survive this latest tragedy. She could pretend she was Clara Barton and this man was a stranger to her. She could peel off the bloodied, filthy remains of his uniform and burn them without thinking about the wasted, fevered body uncovered. Strength still remained in the powerful muscles banding his chest and arm, but she'd seen him in full health. She knew the body lying here was but a caricature of his former self. How long had he lain in wagons and trains being transported up here? When had he last eaten? She shouldn't think those thoughts. She should pretend she didn't know what he had been.

As the fever deepened, Pace cursed and struggled against her touch. Dora bathed his forehead to cool him off, then washed the grime from the rest of him. Modesty dictated that she not wander below the folded sheet at his waist. She had never seen a naked man. Her patients were always women and children, or young boys with cuts and burns tended without disrobing. She never touched men. But he was covered in filth and stank worse than pigs in the barnyard. She couldn't leave him lying here like that.

Resolutely, still pretending she was Clara Barton, Dora took the washrag beneath the sheet and worked by sense of touch. If she did not look, perhaps it would not be sinful. She had seen baby boys, after all. She knew males were made differently.

Men were not boys. Dora flushed and pulled her hand away when she touched Pace's manly parts. He was much larger than she had imagined, had she ever tried imagining such a thing. Biting her lower lip, she forced herself to continue. He was unconscious. He was filthy. She was a nurse. She could do this.

It wasn't easy, but she eventually cleaned him to the best of her abilities without ever uncovering his lower torso. He'd stopped muttering in his sleep now. He lay so still she would have thought him dead had she not felt his heart beating against her fingertips. She watched the slow rise and fall of his bare chest with fascination. Soft dark hairs curled there, and her fingers ached to explore them. Had she lost her mind with this latest tragedy?

She couldn't imagine a life without Pace. That was certainly irrational. He was nothing to her, had never been anything to her. He'd made that clear upon more than one occasion. She was the one obsessed with him, and for no good reason. He had certainly never encouraged her. He'd just seen her when others hadn't, offered her a hand in friendship when no other would, given her a kind and courteous word upon occasion when she felt only scorn around her. And she had hooked her very existence upon this weak and ephemeral bond, even knowing the man behind the kindness lived in brutality and violence. She was mad.

The knowledge that Pace lay dying peeled her down to the very core. Childhood days of laughter disappeared. The music in her memories lost its tune. The precious doll still sleeping on her pillow didn't exist. Nothing had any importance. Without Pace, life would become meaningless. Life *was* meaningless. That discovery at a time like this shook her more than she cared to admit.

Why hadn't she seen it all along? Pace was just an excuse. Nearly thirty years of age, a well-known lawyer, an officer in the Union army, Pace lived a worldly existence far beyond anything she could imagine. And she pinned her dreams on a man like that? She lived a fairy tale just as David had said. She remembered a youth who talked to bluebirds and gave candy to little girls. That man—that dream—didn't exist. She was living in the past.

And this man lying here was very much of the present. She must grow up and face the facts. The boy of her dreams had become a dying stranger.

Jackson returned with a doctor from the army camped at the river. The man examined the shattered arm, shook his bearded head, and announced amputation was the only solution.

When he reached to draw the appropriate instruments from his bag, Dora stayed his hand. "That is not what he wants. He returned here because he trusts us to observe his wishes."

The doctor stared at her gray-clad figure in the weak lamplight. "Are you his wife?"

She hesitated. A Friend did not lie. A lie would give her strength, but she could not do it. She merely kept her hand on his arm, restraining him with her touch. "I am the sister he never had. He came to me for help. I cannot deny him."

"You have no authority in the matter. He's an officer in the army, and he will die if that arm isn't amputated. I will tell him you tried to stop me when he recovers, but this is for his own good."

Dora fought down a growing sense of panic. She didn't want Pace to die. She didn't want to make this decision. But Pace had trusted her. He didn't want to live without his arm. It seemed a foolish reason for dying, but she had no right to interfere. It was his decision. The doctor had no right to go against it.

"He will die if thou dost take his arm," she said quietly. She had no confidence in her powers of persuasion; she had no confidence in her argument at all. But Pace had made his desire clear. She must use that as her guide. "Tell me what I must do to treat it, and I shall make him as comfortable as I can, but I pray thee, do not take his arm."

The doctor looked uncomfortably from the small maid in Quaker gray to the dying man in the bed. He didn't understand the situation here. If not the man's wife, then she had no business here at all. But someone had cleaned the patient, treated and bound his wound, and he didn't think the terrified slave in the corner had done it. There was more here than met the eye. He paused indecisively. The man probably wouldn't live with or without the arm. Maybe he was a Quaker too. Maybe part of their religion involved keeping all their body parts. Who was he to say?

The doctor nodded. "If that's his choice, I won't argue. He probably wouldn't survive the amputation anyway. There isn't much more you can do for him than keep him clean and get some fluids into him. If the infection doesn't kill him, the fever probably will. It's just a matter of time."

Dora heard the death knell in his voice, and her eyes

burned dry as she shook his hand and offered payment for his services.

It was just a matter of time.

Cries of desperation rang through her soul, but her mask of calm stayed firmly in place. Pace would die, but she would remain God's puppet. She had no right to feel anything at all.

Eleven

I will despair, and be at enmity
With cozening hope; he is a flatterer,
A parasite, a keeper-back of death
SHAKESPEARE, *Richard II*

"Old Man Nicholls is at the door," Jackson said with
singular lack of respect as he entered the front bedroom.

Pale face nearly gray with weariness, Dora nodded
listlessly. The man beneath the covers didn't stir as she
applied cooling cloths to his forehead.

"Does that mean let him in?" Jackson asked impatiently. "He's frothing at the bit."

"Thou canst not keep him away," Dora said simply.
"Pace is his son."

"Yeah, I've seen him express his love and affection."
With a grimace of disdain, Jackson whirled around and
left the room.

Carlson Nicholls entered quietly, hat in hand. His
bulky body exuded sweat in the June heat, but heat
wasn't the only source of perspiration. He gripped his
hat brim tighter as he saw his youngest son lying white
and still against the sheets, his auburn hair a tangled
nest against the pillow.

"How is he?" he asked gruffly.

"The doctor says he's dying." Dora saw no reason for
mincing words. Jackson was right. This man had never
shown Pace an ounce of affection. She couldn't pretend otherwise.

"I'll send for another."

"It will do no good now. The matter is in God's
hands." Dora checked the bandage. The bleeding had
finally stopped now that Pace lay still. He couldn't afford

to lose much more blood. If only she could get some
fluids in him ...

"To hell with God! What favors has He ever done
me? I'll find a better doctor. I've friends in Frankfort
and Louisville. They'll find one who can make him better." Carlson's voice boomed with surety in the small
room.

Dora threw him an incredulous look. "Do that, sir.
And punch them if they don't tell thee what thou wishes
to hear. Pace would approve of that. He's that much like
thee, thou must realize."

Carlson stared at her as if just seeing her for the first
time. "My God, missy, don't you dare talk to me like
that! I've taken you in and fed you and clothed you like
you were one of my own, and now you bite the hand
that feeds you. I don't have to take that kind of sass
from you."

"It is not sass. It is fact. Thou and Pace and Charlie
all think the world can be punched into the shape thou
dost desire with a few blows. This is where such thinking
gets thee." She indicated the bed. "He wanted to be the
man thou wished for a son. I hope thou art proud of
him now."

Carlson looked as if he would explode. The red of his
face contrasted vividly with the pale gray of his eyebrows. He clenched his fists and filled his massive chest
with air. And then his gaze swerved from the slight figure in the chair to the still one in the bed, and the air
went out of him again.

"He's a damned bloody Yankee!" he cursed, then
stalked out of the room.

Dora thought she heard a slight snicker from the direction of the bed, but then Pace began to toss and
shove at his covers, and her hands were too full to contemplate her wishful thinking. If Carlson's curses had
returned the fire of life to Pace's blood, she could only
be grateful for the favor.

"You have to eat, Miss Dora." Jackson set a tray
down on the bedside table. His gaze flickered to the man
on the bed. Pace lay lifelessly beneath the covers, but
sweat poured down his brow. Dora alternately bathed

his face, then tried to restrain his thrashing when it began again. "How's he doing?"

"The infection doesn't seem to be spreading." Puzzlement as much as relief laced her words. "The doctor said either the infection or the fever would kill him. The fever seems to be winning." She glanced at the tray. "Where didst thou get that?"

Jackson shrugged. "Solly said they sent it down from the house. I didn't ask questions."

She nodded. "I wish I could find some way of getting water down his throat. If water on the outside cools him, it would do even better on his insides, I should think."

"We can do like we do with the horses when they don't want to take their medicine," Jackson offered.

Dora gazed up at him questioningly.

Jackson handed her the water glass, then sat on the opposite side of the bed, propping Pace upright with the pillows. Then pinching Pace's nose, he opened his mouth. "Pour a little in."

Dora dubiously spooned a few drops into Pace's mouth. Jackson closed his jaw, then stroked his throat. The muscles beneath his hand instinctively contracted. The water went down. He repeated the process, and Dora dropped a few more spoonfuls of water in.

It was a tedious procedure, and the patiently quickly tired of it. He thrashed again, endangering the bandages on his arm, and Dora called a halt. She hadn't slept more than a few hours in days, and she was weary to the point of exhaustion. She didn't have the strength to fight him.

"Eat, then get some sleep, Miss Dora. I'll look after him for a while."

"Thou art needed in the field, Jackson. I'm not useful for anything else. I'll get some rest. Thou mayest go now."

Although the house had plenty of room for the three of them, for propriety's sake, Jackson had taken to sleeping in the barn. Dora wasn't certain of the propriety of her nursing Pace, but she didn't care either. Someone must do it, and she didn't see anyone else rushing to offer.

Jackson left her with the tray, and she nibbled at the

contents when she could. She must maintain her strength
to do her job. If Pace died, it wouldn't be because she
hadn't done everything she could—except allow the doctor to amputate.

She hadn't even asked Carlson Nicholls if she had
made the right decision. The entire guilt would lay on
her shoulders. She wouldn't think of that now. She
would not think or feel anything. She had only one task.
She lifted the cooling sponge to Pace's forehead and
began to bathe him all over again.

Somewhere around midnight she must have finally
fallen asleep. The birds chirruped in the apple tree outside when Dora woke again. The faint gray light before
dawn filled the windows. Her eyes felt grainy and full of
sleep, but she forced them open. Without thinking, she
reached for the sponge. When her hand went to Pace's
forehead, she found him staring at her.

"Pace?" she whispered uncertainly. Perhaps she still
dreamed.

"Water." His voice was dry and croaked the word,
but she understood.

She tried lifting him carefully so he could sip at the
cup, but he was heavy. She cursed her weakness and
tucked pillows beneath his head. He drank eagerly, and
she had to pull the cup away before he made himself ill.

"More," he demanded.

"In a minute. It may come back up if thou takest too
much." She wiped his brow, then lit the lamp so she
could examine his arm.

He groaned when she touched the bandage, but he
didn't fight her as he had in his delirium. He didn't look
either. "It's still there," he croaked with an edge of
triumph.

"Thou ought to know. It must hurt like the very
flames of hell." She applied more powder to the open
wound. The torn muscles would never be the same. She
didn't think the bone broken in more than one place,
but the damage was too extensive to know for certain.
Her main concern at the moment was the angry red lines
trailing across the unharmed flesh. She thought perhaps
they were a little fainter today.

"It would still hurt if it wasn't there. I've heard them talk."

That didn't seem likely, but she had no way of knowing. She supposed Pace knew more than she about battlefield wounds. "Let's try the water again," was the only reply she gave him.

He slipped into a labored sleep not much later, but Dora allowed a small blister of hope to fester. It was an insidious thing, hope. It could grow and spread and take over, and then one day, it died, taking everything with it, leaving an abscess behind. She knew all about hope. She just didn't seem able to prevent it.

When the next day came and it appeared the infection in Pace's arm hadn't spread and the fever was down, Dora sent Jackson for the doctor again. The bone had apparently been set, but she knew nothing of keeping it in place. The constant bandaging and unbandaging to treat the wound and his thrashing about could have knocked something loose. She didn't want to imagine the pain that would ensue if it had set improperly and needed resetting. She hadn't worried about it when she thought he was dying, but hope had succeeded in making her think he might have a future.

After examining the patient, the doctor gave Dora a curious look, and left her to rebandage Pace's arm. He watched as she went through the ritual of applying Mother Elizabeth's healing powders, packing the wound with boiled lint, and pulling clean cotton tight to hold it closed. He shook his head and picked up the vial of powder.

"What in hell is in this?"

Dora was too terrified to tell him. A man of science would not think to use dried bread mold. It smacked of witchcraft, particularly when used by an uneducated woman. People didn't believe in witches anymore, but they still tended to be superstitious about the unknown. And Pace could still die. She would almost certainly be accused of killing him if she revealed such ingredients. And she had no scientific proof that the powder had anything to do with healing. She had just never seen it hurt the process.

"It belonged to my adopted mother," she answered

honestly. "She taught me to use it in open wounds. I don't know that it helps, but it has never seemed to harm."

The doctor sniffed and tasted the substance, then set it aside, still shaking his head. "Either that stuff works, or God has decided He doesn't want your patient just yet. I'm as likely to believe in one as the other."

Dora knew the hope in her eyes was painful to see, but she couldn't help turning them to the more knowledgeable man. "Will he live then?"

The man shrugged. "Hell if I know. You seem to have more answers than I do. But I'll tell you this, he won't ever use that arm. The muscles are shot to—" Realizing he was swearing in front of a lady, he bit back the most convenient word. "His muscles will never grow back the way they should, and that break may never heal properly. I doubt that he'll ever lift the arm he risked his neck to keep."

Dora didn't care. For one brief moment, she allowed herself to smile in relief. Pace might live. He might yet call her bluebird and laugh at her odd ways. He could go on to be a lawyer and a politician and make the government change the laws that kept an entire race enslaved. He might end the war once he returned to where he belonged, and fighting in the army wasn't what she had in mind. He didn't need an arm to fight in politics.

She saw the physician to the door, breathed deeply of the muggy June air, and returned to throw open the bedroom windows. It allowed the heat in, but the air needed freshening.

Pace recovered slowly. He slept restlessly, ate little, and said less. Until she moved the table to the left side of the bed, he would wake her in the night with his struggles to reach the water pitcher. He grew angry when she cut his food for him and grew angrier still when he couldn't cut it successfully for himself.

When he recovered enough to sit upright for extended periods of time, he ordered her out of the house.

Dora didn't know whether to laugh or rage at his foolishness. He couldn't even pull a shirt over his head by

himself so he sat there naked except for the sheet, and
he wanted her to leave?

"This is my house," she reminded him calmly.

"Then tell Jackson to get a wagon and carry me up
to my father's house," he demanded impatiently.

"Fine. I will do that. But I'll have thee remember I
live there too."

"Then go live there and leave me here!" He jerked
the sheet around his waist and hauled himself out of
bed, going to look out the window rather than at her.

"I see. Now that thou hast fully recovered, thou no
longer needeth my services. Very well. I will send Annie
down with clean bandages and thou mayest dress thy
wound thyself."

She walked out, leaving Pace scowling at the window.

She reappeared in the lane outside, and he watched
as she marched away with shoulders held straight and
proud. Her slender gray figure looked out of place
against the backdrop of verdant trees and grass. She had
worn her cap ever since that first night, and it concealed
the wealth of silver curls he knew existed beneath that
disguise—just as he knew a woman's graceful form resided beneath that shapeless garb. He had spent all these
past nights dreaming of that delightful form.

Slamming his good fist against the window frame, Pace
swung around so quickly that his head spun. Cursing, he
caught himself against the wall until the room tilted back
to normal. By the time he made it back to the bed, he
figured he would pass out, and rage filled him all over
again. His arm throbbed like all the hammers of hell,
and bound against his chest, it was useless. He couldn't
even stand upright for more than a few minutes at a
time. He felt like a parasite. He'd be damned if he lived
off Dora's patient generosity like the rest of his family
did. He wouldn't contemplate the other vile iniquities
that coiled and slithered through his evil mind.

When Dora returned that night with a tray full of
foods that were easily eaten by a one-armed invalid,
Pace flung it against the far wall.

Dora scooped the mashed potatoes back in the bowl
and slammed it back on the table beside him. "Thou
wilt clean up the soup thyself. I will not."

She stalked out of the room again, carefully leaving the door unslammed.

Pace hurled a curse after her for good measure, but he figured her holy ears didn't hear curses.

She returned five minutes later with a pitcher of cold lemonade. He was down on the floor picking up beans and pieces of ham from the floor with his one good hand. He glared at her and made no attempt to rise.

"Thou art a miserable, ungrateful wretch, but I will not allow thee to bully me," she informed him.

"Thou art a meddling, shameless bitch," he mocked from his position on the floor, "and thee will not bully me. I don't need a nursemaid."

"Thou needest a keeper! I have worked long hard hours to keep that arm of thine, and I will not see it rot off for thy lack of common sense. Thou mayest starve if thou dost wish, but I will tend that arm."

Giving up on the mess, Pace shoved the bowl away and leaned wearily against the wall. "I did not come back here to lay one more burden on your shoulders. Get back to the house, baby my mother, soothe Josie's ruffled feathers, and bounce Amy until she sleeps. Jackson can see to my arm."

Dora closed her eyes, apparently in an effort to gather the frazzled edges of her patience. "Josie and Amy left weeks ago. There is only thy mother, and she is much improved." She opened her eyes again. "Jackson has far less time than I to tend your wound. It has not rained in months, and he is digging irrigation ditches in hopes of saving part of the crop."

"Then send Odell or one of the men from the farm. I don't want you down here," he answered stubbornly. She looked as if she might kick him, and Pace tried not to flinch. He certainly wasn't in any position to dodge the blow. He reacted out of instinct, before remembering his avenging angel didn't strike that way.

"Odell joined the army last week. Those who haven't joined have run away. Thy father has only Solly left, and that is only because Jackson talked him out of leaving. He was helping Jackson until thy father refused to hire him out anymore. Now he will probably cross the river like the others."

Pace grimaced. "Then send one of the women. You can't keep coming here."

She gave him a curious look. "I have lived here these past weeks caring for thee. If it is my reputation thou seekest to protect, it is far too late for that and scarcely necessary. No one cares what I do or where I go."

He gave her a grim look and pushed from the floor. "*I* care. Now get the hell out of here."

She refused to move despite his most menacing expression. "I will tend thy arm first."

A bulldog with its teeth in a bone couldn't be more determined. Pace surrendered, and suffered all the torments of the damned while she leaned over him, her soft breasts brushing against his arm, her sweet scent filling his nostrils. He wanted to rip the ugly cap from her head and free her silver curls.

Who the hell was he fooling? He wanted to rip the bodice from her dress and grab her breasts. He wanted to lift her skirts and pull her on top of him. He wanted to jerk his guardian angel down off her cloud and make her as human as he was.

And he didn't have the damned strength to lift a soup bowl.

Twelve

It is hard to fight against impulsive desire; whatever it wants, it will buy at the cost of the soul.

HERACLITUS, *Fragments* (c. 500 B.C.)

July 1864

Lying in the muggy darkness, Pace tossed restlessly on the wrinkled sheets. He'd never learned to make a damned bed, but he wouldn't let Dora do it. He didn't want Dora anywhere around him. She made him itch. She made him think unthinkable thoughts.

My God, she was little more than a child. He'd gone without a woman too damned long to think of little Dora like that. He knew himself for a dissolute bastard, but he'd never sunk so low as to desire a child before. But she wasn't a child. He didn't know her age, but she sure the hell wasn't a child any longer. That knowledge frazzled all his brain functions.

He turned again, his body as restless as his thoughts. He couldn't settle his mind any more than he could settle the rebellious swelling in his groin. Dora was untouchable. He knew that. He'd never thought of her as human so much as an image of the one innocent perfect thing in his world. He'd have to find another woman to slake his lusts before he did something unforgivable. But the images of all the women he'd used before revolted him now. Only Dora's sweet scent and soft, lilting accents appealed.

He couldn't even begin to imagine pulling off those grim gray clothes of hers and sinking his carnal flesh into her. He thought of Dora as above all that. She probably didn't even have a body beneath those shapeless dresses. But his mind couldn't lie to his physical self. Dora had a body, a woman's body. He'd felt it. He never should have touched her.

Pace's thoughts chased themselves around and around uselessly as he tossed and turned. He heard almost with relief the muffled sound of hoofbeats coming down the lane. It must be past midnight, too late for casual visitors.

He'd figured out how to maneuver himself into trousers by now. It took him long painful moments to manage it. By the time he had his pants half-fastened, the hoofbeats had halted somewhere close by.

Pace could see the red flickering of a torch reflected through the windows when he reached the back room. His stomach clenched as he located his gun. His guardian angel had ingeniously packed the pistol away in a drawer, but he'd searched it out and found it some time ago. He tightened the fingers of his left hand around the grip. He'd never handled the weapon with his left hand, but at least the pistol was considerably more manageable than his rifle. He'd been laughed at when he purchased the newfangled Smith & Wesson, and he hadn't found it of much use for long-range shooting, but this wouldn't be long range. Checking the bullets silently, he let himself out the back door.

He'd seen the sight too many times for it to do more than raise his ire. The narrow-minded stupidity and bigotry of people never ceased to amaze him. But he had learned a long time ago that only cowards hid themselves in darkness and rode in gangs to terrorize victims too helpless for defending themselves. He didn't particularly consider himself a brave man, but he'd learned by now—despite his father's condemnations—that he wasn't a coward.

Finding a position with his back to the barn shed so no one could sneak up behind him, Pace lifted his pistol carefully and aimed before speaking. The light of the torch gave him a clear enough view of the silhouettes of men and horses. He didn't even care who they were. He could probably guess if he tried. Fury flew through him

as he saw Jackson led from the barn at the end of a
rope, but rage only made it easier for what he had to do.

Pace pointed the gun at the hooves of the pack of
horses and pulled the trigger. The shot rang out in the
silent night like a crack of thunder. The horses reared
and scattered as their riders cursed and fought to bring
them under control again.

"I'd suggest you let the man go, gentlemen, before
I hit something more valuable. My aim is a trifle off
these days."

Running down the lane in a panic at the sight of
torches near her house, Dora halted at the sound of
those cold words. Pace. Pace was not only out of bed
but with one good arm holding off a band of armed
men. The man was insane or suicidal.

She crept closer as one of the men replied.

"You just fired your round, Nicholls. How you gonna
put in more balls with a gimpy arm? Stay out of this. It
ain't none of your business anyhow. We're just gonna
teach the niggers around here a lesson. Or have you
gone soft on us since joining the bluebellies?"

"I need that man to work this land, and I don't cotton
to anyone taking him away. I suggest you folks drop that
rope before you learn about this newfangled Yankee
weapon. Like I said, I can't promise my aim's too good.
If I have to shoot the damned rope, I might end up
hitting something a little more personal. It'd be a
damned shame to geld a friend, wouldn't it?"

The men on horseback grumbled angrily between
themselves. The one holding the rope jerked it, bringing
Jackson to his knees. Had she been alone, Dora would
have just walked out among them and shamed them into
releasing their victim. As it was, she thought she'd best
stay out of Pace's sight until the last minute. While the
men fought among themselves, she slipped behind the
shed and came around Pace and Jackson from behind.

"You ought to geld that nigger," one of the men
shouted. "We cain't have niggers hanging around white
women, even if they are nigger-lovin' Quakers. It sets a
bad example."

"I don't think I'll aim for the rope, Howard, I think

I'll aim for your filthy tongue," Pace answered laconically.

Dora gasped and hastened to Jackson's side as Pace raised that nasty pistol of his. Jackson muttered, "Get out of here, Miss Dora," as she struggled with the bonds around his wrists, but she ignored the warning. She had his hands free before any of the men even noticed her presence.

"Hey, look! The bitch just freed the nigger! Hell, jerk that line and get him out here."

One of the men turned his horse for a better grip on the rope still wrapped around Jackson's neck. Another leaped from his mount to go after Dora.

This time, two shots rang out.

The man holding the rope lost his grip as his horse reared back and threw him with the first shot. The man approaching Dora let out a scream of agony with the second pistol crack, hitting the ground and grabbing his leg while emitting furious curses.

"You take one step closer to my woman and it won't be your damned ankle I'll hit next time," Pace warned, walking out from the shadows of the barn toward Jackson and Dora.

"What in hell are you firin' with, Nicholls?" Abandoning the game, one of the men still seated watched his progress with interest. "I ain't seen nothin' like it in my life."

"That's 'cause you're an ignorant hillbilly, Howard. The Yankees have a rifle even better than this piss-poor pistol, but I need both hands to blow your head off with a rifle. So I'll just stay close and blow it off point-blank for now. I wouldn't take any chances coming back if I were you, though."

Dora caught her breath as Pace grabbed her with his good arm and pulled her to his side, dangling the pistol from the hand in the sling as he talked. She stared at the smoking weapon with horror, but the hard pressure of Pace's arm possessively around her waist kept her speechless. That, and the reference to "his woman." She would tear him apart after these men left, but she didn't intend to try right now. She could barely keep her heart from fluttering up her throat.

Jackson had himself untangled from the rope and eased himself to his feet. Dora could sense the furious tension in him, but like herself, he kept his mouth shut. This was Pace's show. These were his people. He knew how to handle them.

"Hell, if she's your woman, you're welcome to her. But you sure oughtn't to let your hired help get so friendly with her. It leads to talk." The man apparently leading the group sawed backward on his horse's reins, turning it around. "Come on, boys. Lets get out of here. Mebbe we can find some of them guns over at the army camp. They sure would be mighty handy to have."

Pace continued holding Dora tight against him as they rode away. She didn't move from his side. She couldn't tell who held up whom at this point. Her knees wobbled, but Pace's weight sagged heavier and heavier against her. He should never have come out here like this. He was barely well enough to get out of bed. But he seemed immensely large and strong when she shifted to take more of the burden.

"Thou hadst best go back inside," she murmured once the marauders left.

"Are you planning on carrying me?" Pace asked sardonically. "Or do you want to watch me crawl?"

Silently, Jackson came up beside them and hauled Pace's good arm around his neck. Dora escaped, darting ahead of them to prepare the way. She felt warm all over. Her blood raced madly through her veins. She'd never felt this nervous before, even that time the slave catchers surrounded her. Crazy thoughts leapfrogged through her mind. She couldn't control them. Pace's arm around her had made an indelible impression, left a burning brand against her skin. Her thoughts kept going back to that moment, to the weight of him, the faint bay rum scent of him, the smoking pistol, the gruff rumble of his voice in her ear. Her teeth practically chattered, and then her thoughts would leap back to Jackson with his neck in a noose, and her stomach threatened to lose its contents.

She dashed in to straighten Pace's sheets. The bed was a wrinkled mess, and she hurriedly pulled the bottom sheet tight and smoothed it, then shook out the top cov-

ers and fluffed the pillows. She found the bottle of laudanum the doctor had left and poured a tiny portion into
the water glass. He needed to rest after overexerting
himself like this.

Pace caught her doing this last and lashed out irritably, "Don't give me any of that stuff! I'll not be lying
here in a stupor when those bastards come back."

Dora looked up in alarm. "Will they return?"

"Not tonight, Miss Dora, and they ain't gonna find me
iffen they did." Jackson carefully helped Pace to the bed,
then straightened once his burden was gone. "I'm gettin'
outa here now, while the gettin' is good."

"What about Liza?" Appalled, Dora could only stare
at him. Her mind had quit functioning entirely with this
last blow.

"I cain't do any more for her here than I can over
there." Jackson shrugged. "I'll just bide my time till I
can come get her."

"Don't be a fool, Jackson," Pace growled from the
bed as he sought a comfortable position. "They'll con-
fiscate everything you saved if you run now. You'll just
have to sleep in here until I can get over and talk to the
military commander. Maybe we can convince them your
owner is a true-blue Unionist. Then they'll pay him to
free you if you enlist and you can keep your savings.
They're paying good money for volunteers across the
river. You could probably double your savings."

"Thou art sending him off to be killed!" Dora protested. "What kind of friend art thou? We must find
another way."

"Get her out of here, Jack," Pace grumbled, leaning
back against the pillow and closing his eyes. "We don't
need any more of her nattering."

"Nattering!" Dora dodged Jackson and approached
the bed, jerking the pillow from under Pace's head to
plump it some more, then slamming it back in his arms
rather than touch him to put it back beneath his head.
"I do not natter! Thou canst not come in here and turn
my life upside-down and expect me to keep silent about
it. Thou toldest that man I was thy woman! What must
he think of me now? I will not be able to hold my head
up in town. I will have to explain myself in Meeting.

And now thou wouldst send Jackson off to be killed! Thou art a horrible, awful man, Payson Nicholls, and I would thee would tend thy own business."

"If he'd tended his own business, I'd be a dead man by now, Miss Dora," Jackson commented dryly.

"Thou wouldst not! I was on my way. And I would not have shot that poor misguided man to do it. Violence begets violence. Hast thou not seen example enough of it by now?"

Pace rubbed his aching head with his good hand and refused to open his eyes. "Out, Dora. Get out before I have Jackson carry you out. And, Jackson, take my rifle with you when you escort her home. To hell with the law."

Dora had never been so frustrated and furious in all her life. She wanted to scream and kick and throw things. But of course, she couldn't. As she had since childhood, she hid all her fury behind her usual placid demeanor, lifted her skirt and petticoat with fingers tight with tension, and swept from the room.

She was shaking by the time she reached the lane. She told herself it was merely the aftermath of what might have happened. The good, Christian man beside her could have died this night. She knew that evil existed in the world, but that did not make it any easier to encounter it. She kept her fingers clenched in her skirt and walked faster.

"I'm sorry to leave you in the lurch like this, Miss Dora," Jackson said from beside her, his long legs easily keeping up with her hasty retreat. "It looks to me like the crop's a loss anyways. Mebbe you ought to think of sellin'."

"I'd sell it to thee before I'd sell it to any of those miserable, thieving, good-for-nothing renegades around here. I'm keeping that land, Jackson, and there's nothing they can do to make me sell it."

Jackson was silent for a minute. His voice, when he spoke, was almost hollow with hopelessness. "They ain't much of a chance of me ever makin' a livin' from land 'round here, Miss Dora. I reckon once I go to be a soldier, I'll use my savin's to buy Liza free and take her 'cross the river. If I come back, I'll just hire out. I've got a strong back."

"Hast thou any people around here, Jackson?" Dora

calmed herself by turning her thoughts to Jackson's plight. Thinking of others made it much easier to forget herself.

"No, ma'am, not since my master sold my mama and little sister away. I don' know where they's at. I kept hopin' they could get away now with Mr. Lincoln declarin' them all free down there, but I ain't heard nothin'. Looks to me like most of them makin' their way up here ain't much better off than runaways anyhow."

"Unless the North wins and brings the Confederate states back into the Union, the Emancipation Proclamation isn't worth much, I'm afraid," Dora said sadly. "Jefferson Davis may as well announce all the slaves in the North are free, for all the good it does."

Jackson chuckled. "That's about right, I guess. Wouldn't it be something if the North wins and calls all us niggers free citizens and allows us to vote? I'm willin' to risk my neck for that, I guess."

Hope even infected the hopeless, Dora noted wryly. But she wasn't so naive as to believe the day Jackson dreamed of would come soon or easily. "Oh, I'd enjoy that real well, Jackson," she said with a trace of sarcasm. "I can picture that now, with thee and Solly and Odell going off to vote while I sit back at the house and wait to see who all the big strong men have decided to send to Frankfort to tax my little bit of land. Dost thou think if I joined the army they'd let me vote someday?"

Jackson laughed. They'd reached the foot of the porch stairs, and he halted there, leaning on Pace's rifle as he looked at her. "I'd a sight rather see you voting than Solly, but I daresay we'll all be watching from heaven before either of us sees any of that happen. You get on inside now, Miss Dora. Me and Pace will look out for each other."

"Oh, and a fine job thou wilt do of it, I'm certain. But if I find bugs in my larder, I'll make the both of thee scrub it on hands and knees."

"You can send Annie down to check on us once in a while." He remained at the foot of the stairs and watched as she went up them. When she was almost at the door, he called softly, "You deserve better than Mr. Pace, Miss Dora, but I'll look after him for you."

Dora pretended she didn't hear.

Thirteen

I have mark'ed
A thousand blushing apparitions start
Into her face; a thousand innocent shames
In angel whiteness bear away those blushes;
And in her eye there hath appear'd a fire,
To burn the errors that these princes hold
Against her maiden truth.

SHAKESPEARE, *Much Ado about Nothing*

July 1864

Pace tried sitting patiently in the chair beside his mother's bed, but his gaze kept drifting toward the window, then back to the door. His arm ached, but the pain was negligible compared to the way it had been before. The reason for that was around here someplace, but she avoided him.

"You should go over and see Josie and the baby," his mother admonished. "Perhaps you could make her see how foolish it is to stay over there when this is her home now. What would Charlie say if he came home and found his wife gone?"

Pace knew his mother fretted more over the fact that Charlie hadn't written than whether or not Josie stayed here, but he didn't correct her. "I'll ride over there this evening, Mama. I'll want to see my niece before I go, anyway."

"Go?" She looked alarmed. "Where are you going? You won't go too far with that arm like it is, will you?"

Pace stretched his injured muscles impatiently. He'd removed the sling and practiced moving it, but the arm wasn't cooperating particularly well. "My arm will be fine, Mama. It just needs a little exercise. Dora did a fine job on it."

He'd avoided her question, but she didn't notice. Now that her attention had turned to Dora, his mother's thoughts drifted in that direction. "I don't know what I would do without that girl. These darkies aren't worth anything anymore. I told your father we should sell them all, but he just wouldn't listen."

Unless things had changed drastically since his last visit, Pace didn't think his mother had talked to his father in years. He assumed the conversation referred to had taken place a decade ago. He could remember his parents arguing over the servants quite frequently back then. "There aren't many left to sell these days, Mama. And I don't know where we'd get hired help. Dora can't do it all on her own."

"Call her in here, will you? I want them to make dinner rolls for tonight. I'm sick to death of cornbread." Harriet Nicholls fussed absently with the covers, picking at imaginary threads and smoothing the sheets, not looking directly at her son.

"I'll tell them on the way out," he said soothingly. "There's no sense in making Dora run all the way up here just to tell her that."

"Dora always looks in on me this time of day," Harriet responded fretfully. "What can be keeping her?"

Pace had a good idea of the answer to that. Concluding his mother had had enough visiting for the day, he stood up and strode toward the door. "I'll find Dora on the way out, Mama. You just rest easy now and take care of yourself."

Her gaze momentarily diverted to her son standing in the doorway. "You're looking more and more like your granddaddy every day. Every bone in that man's body was mean," she declared.

"I know, Mama," Pace answered patiently. "You take care now."

He strode out, fuming with frustration and a nagging sense of something lacking. He'd never expected much from his mother and never received much, so he usually walked away from these visits with more of a sense of relief. He didn't know what was wrong with him now. Maybe he just felt his injury deserved a little more attention. That was plain damned foolishness, if so. He'd nearly had his head stove in before and his mother had never noticed.

Pace found Dora stirring the contents of a pot in the kitchen. He had the urge to fling something against the wall when he saw her there where the slaves belonged, but he curbed the impulse. He had promised himself he would display better control around her from now on. He was a grown man, an experienced lawyer, an officer in the army. He ought to show a little discipline around this snip of a girl.

"Mama is looking for you. You'd better go on up to her now. Where's the kitchen help? She's wanting dinner rolls instead of cornbread tonight."

Dora carefully cleaned off the wooden spoon on the edge of the pot, then laid it on an empty saucer. She wiped her hands on a towel before finally directing her gaze to him. "I'll take her some lemonade. I'm not too good with yeast rolls, but I'll try. Just don't complain if thou canst bounce them off the walls."

Pace shot her a look of annoyance. At times like these, he felt as if she hadn't changed in appearance since the first day he met her. She was like a tiny gray sparrow, all big eyes and ruffled feathers, nothing anyone would notice. But back then he'd seen flashes of color, moments of laughter and defiance and song. And now, somewhere under that dull plumage, he saw the body of a woman. Everything about her annoyed him.

"I didn't ask you to make rolls. We've still got some help around here, don't we? Just tell them to make the rolls. I probably won't be around to eat, so don't worry about me."

Her eyes widened with alarm. "Where wilt thou go? That arm is not strong enough to hold a horse yet. And Solly is out in the field. He can't drive thee."

Pace grimaced and headed for the door. "You're not my mother, Dora. I'll take care of myself."

He slammed the door after him. She wasn't his damned mother. He didn't need a mother right now. He needed a woman. He didn't suppose Josie would be so obliging as to accommodate him. In this mood, a little adultery wouldn't bother him greatly. He didn't know anyone around here anymore. Maybe he should go up to Louisville and find a whore. Wouldn't Dora pitch a fit if she thought he meant to try that? She would have a kitten just knowing he meant to take out one of the horses.

He'd managed to get Jackson signed up with the military across the river by the simple expedient of walking him down to the fishing shacks. The fishermen had rowed him over and back. But the Andrewses lived several miles in the other direction, and Pace didn't feel inclined to walk that distance in this heat. He would have to get back on a horse if he wanted to rejoin his regiment anytime soon. Today seemed as fine a day as any to do it.

He'd seen his father ride out earlier, so he didn't expect much interference from that direction. He'd avoided taking his meals up here just to avoid any confrontation. He'd gleaned enough information from Jackson and Dora and his brief forays into town to know that his father despised the Union soldiers who had taken control of the state. Accustomed to living on the wrong side of his father's beliefs, Pace could shrug it off. He just didn't relish disturbing the rest of the household by meeting his father head-on.

He persuaded his arm into throwing a saddle over one of the gentle mares. He cursed his lack of mobility when he attempted buckling the girth, but with a little practice he could manage it eventually. He hoped he could stretch the muscles before that became a necessity, but he wouldn't complain. He could be armless by now. Or dead.

By the time Pace had the mare ready, sweat dripped down his brow, and he would rather fling himself across a bed and collapse then put himself through the hell of visiting Josie. But he wouldn't surrender to weakness. The arm was mending. The time had come to get his strength back.

He should have known Dora would be in the yard when he rode the horse out of the barn. She had the ability to know where he was and what he was doing at the worst of times. Pace hoped he looked like he had control of the mare. Restive, the horse danced sideways, as if no one had exercised it in a while. It took everything Pace possessed to pull her up one-handed at the hedge so he could speak to Dora.

"I'm going to see Josie and the babe. Is there any message I need to pass on?" The mare pulled at the bit, and Pace gritted his teeth against the pain of hanging on. He refused to show Dora any display of weakness. She'd seen the worst of him already.

"Josie won't be there," she answered calmly, folding her hands in her apron. "She's visiting cousins in Cincinnati. I wish she hadn't left Amy and Della with her mother, but I suppose taking Della across the river would have been a mistake."

She may as well have hit him alongside the head with a split log. He'd gone to all this damned trouble just to see a woman who wasn't even there. Pace glared down at her. "Why didn't you tell me that earlier?"

"You didn't ask. Kiss Amy hello for me. I miss her." She turned around and walked back toward the house.

He would have to kill her. Sweat ran in his eyes. His arm felt as if it had been drawn out of its socket. And this damned horse was about to run away with him. And she just walked away as if it didn't matter one whit that he was killing himself.

Which was why she had done it, of course. Cursing, Pace let the mare go. As long as he'd gone to this much trouble, he might as well see his niece. He saw no sense in trying to figure out a woman like Dora. He'd told her to stay out of his business, so she had. He couldn't assign her the devious intention of making him suffer. He'd brought that on himself.

By the time he returned the horse to the stable that evening, Pace had gone beyond exhaustion. He didn't know how long it would take to recover his full strength, but he knew he couldn't wait any longer. He had to get back to the army where he belonged, and soon.

Sliding from the horse, he rested his head momentarily against the saddle, letting the pain of the day seep into the leather. When a soft voice spoke nearby, he didn't even jump. Somehow, he'd known Dora would be there.

"Thou must show me how to brush the mare down. Thy father has gone on to bed, and the boy who sleeps here is nowhere to be found."

Pace cursed silently to himself. Without raising his head, he replied bitterly, "Get out of here, Dora."

"Thou hast become quite a conversationalist," she answered, coming to stand beside him as she studied the bit in the horse's mouth. "How does this unfasten? Or do I remove the saddle first?"

If it was the last thing he did, he wouldn't let this little brat take care of his horse for him. Kneeling carefully on legs out of the practice of riding long hours, Pace unfastened the girth buckle. "I've arranged for someone to take me to the train station Saturday morning. I'd tell my mother good-bye, but I don't think she would comprehend it too well. Explain it to her after I've gone, will you?"

He didn't even glance at her stunned expression as she asked, "Thou meanest to return to thy practice in Frankfort?"

They both knew the train didn't go to Frankfort. Pace didn't look at her. "What practice? Our brilliant military commander is practically holding the state government hostage. Do you think any of them will even speak to a Union officer like me right now? I'm going back where I'll be useful. The army is closing in on Atlanta. We'll have the war all but won once we take that."

"Thou hast not the strength for that yet! What could a few bullets more or less matter now? It is suicide going back there like this."

He heard the fear in her voice but ignored it, even knowing Dora seldom showed her emotions. "Don't be ridiculous, Dora. Do you think the whole damned army is made of suicidal men? I'm an officer. I've left men back there who depend on me. It's not just a matter of the few bullets I can shoot. I can make a difference." Pace finally wrestled the saddle to the ground. Now he found the brush and comb and began to curry the horse.

"No, not yet," she whispered. Pace tried not to notice the haunted quality of her reply. It sent chills down his spine. She sounded as if she knew something he didn't. He refused to let her otherworldiness affect him.

"Thou canst not go yet," she protested vehemently a moment later. "Just a few days more. Surely if they have gone without thee all these weeks, they can wait a few days more."

He was too tired for this foolish argument. Dora hovered just out of his sight, but Pace could feel her as if she were attached to his side. She confused him. She ought to be laughing and singing as she had that first day he'd seen her. She shouldn't be standing here wringing her hands and worrying about a bastard like him. But the little bluebird was long gone, replaced by this anxious woman. Anxious female. He knew she wore no scent, but he could smell the freshness of her skin. She must have just washed. The idea of it made him go up in flames. She was female and he was a randy stallion. He'd better drive her out of here real soon.

"I'm leaving, Dora, and that's an end to it. Now get out of here before I get riled."

"Is there anything that can make thee stay just a few days more?" she whispered. "Anything at all?"

Pace snorted. She'd walked right into that one. "Yeah, a woman. I'm in real bad need of a woman right now, and unless you're offering, you'd better get out of my sight."

He felt her backing away, and he smiled grimly. He hadn't found anyone in town, but there would be plenty back in camp. Once he got a little relief, he'd get rid of these ridiculous notions. He just had to get this little witch out from underfoot until then.

"A w-woman shouldn't be so hard to find," she stuttered from somewhere behind him.

Damn, she was still here. Pace applied the brush more thoroughly to the mare. "I don't want any of those scrawny wenches in the quarters, if that's what you're meaning. There'll be women back in camp. Now get out, Dora. I'm not in the mood for this argument."

"Thou must stay," she whispered, terrified and determined at the same time. "There must be some way I can make thee stay. Just a few days. That's all."

This whole thing had gone on too long. It didn't even make any sense. What difference did a few days more or less make? He was too exhausted for reason.

Without a thought to what he did, Pace swung around, dropped the brush, and cornered Dora against the stall

wall. His arm protested like hell, but he had gone beyond caring. He had her trapped just where he wanted
her. She stared up at him as if he'd gone mad. Perhaps
he had. He didn't care.

"Yeah, you can make me stay. Just take me where
this leads."

And he bent his head to apply his mouth to hers. He
used a force that he should never have applied to any
but a camp whore but which reflected his hunger and
desperation clearly.

She was too soft and small. Pace felt like a bear maul-
ing a lamb. He felt the slight exhalation of Dora's breath
against his lips when he claimed hers, but something
kept driving him on. The punishing force of his kiss
forced her to respond. He expected screams. He received a tentative, questioning pressure of her lips in
return. Ruthlessly, he asked for more.

When her fingers curled fearfully in his shirt in reply,
Pace went wild. He shoved his hand into her hair and
tilted her head to meet him more fully. He bit her lip
and when she opened her mouth in surprise, he drove
his tongue inside. She shuddered and gave a soft cry,
but her fingers curled more securely into his shirt, and
he nearly lost it all.

She was responding. With inexperience and curiosity
and a touch of fear, admittedly, but she was answering
his plea, molding her lips to his, allowing his invasion,
moving her body closer into the curve of his. He couldn't
believe it. Wouldn't believe it. He wanted to scare her
away, drive her off.

God, she was so sweet! He hadn't thought such sweet
innocence still existed in this world. He ran his hand
down the slender curve of her spine and pressed his kiss
deeper. Her tongue shyly touched his in response, and
Pace felt the electricity of it shoot straight to his loins.
He knew it was wrong. He knew she had no notion
of his reactions. But he couldn't stop. His mouth felt
permanently sealed to hers and he feared he would stop
breathing if he moved away. He needed all of her.

Pace wrapped his good arm around Dora's back and
closed the distance between them. The exhaustion he
had suffered just moments before disappeared in the

rush of desire created by the slender burden in his arms. He groaned as she adjusted herself more comfortably against him. He could feel the brush of her breasts now, and he knew, if he didn't summon the strength from somewhere, he wouldn't stop with something so simple as a kiss.

With more restraint than he had ever managed in his self-indulgent life, Pace dropped his arms and shoved himself away from Dora. He glared down at her for a moment. His eyes felt like burning coals and he clenched his fingers into fists to keep from reaching for her again. The swelling in his groin surged frantically for the warm harbor it had almost found.

Dora practically cowered against the stall, her hands clasped anxiously at her breasts. He had pulled her cap askew, and even in the dim light of one lantern, he could discern the silver halo of her curls. She should consider herself fortunate that he'd only removed her cap.

"Get out, Dora. Get out now."

His voice was tight and grim, and he didn't try disguising the effort behind it.

She nodded once, slid cautiously around him, and hurried out of the barn.

Pace dug his fingers into the splintery stall, pounded his head against the wood, and groaned.

Fourteen

Tempt not a desperate man.
SHAKESPEARE, *Romeo and Juliet*

Late July 1864

Dora heard thunder in the relentlessly blue sky. The orchard of apple trees didn't relieve the heat and humidity engulfing her. Somewhere, a battle raged. She felt it in her bones, had felt it for days. She suffered the heat of flames, smelled the scorching stench of cannon shot, heard the rattle of muskets, all while she stood beneath the quiet rustling shade of the trees.

She didn't find the image odd. The Light came to her in mysterious ways. Others called it an inner reflection, an inner voice. She'd felt those, too, but when connected to Pace, the inner voice became colorful, insistent images. She supposed that was because Pace lived so much more fully than she. He experienced these things in reality. She absorbed them only vicariously, through him.

Of course, at the moment, he lay beneath the shade beside the creek and wasn't experiencing any of those things she felt. She wasn't God. She couldn't explain it. She just had the ominous notion that if Pace left on the morrow, he would join that terrible battle raging somewhere out of her sight, and he would never survive. She'd known it of a certainty last night when he'd pressed his mouth to hers.

She wondered briefly if Pace's brother fought in that faraway battle. She suspected he must. From all she'd heard, the Confederate troops had amassed on two fronts, and both of them were fighting fiercely. Charlie would be in the western front, just as Pace would be if he should return. The idea of the two brothers finally coming face to face on a battlefield with rifles in their hands was too abhorrent to hold long.

So she slipped through the cool shadows of the orchard into the breeze off the creek. She didn't think about what she did or where she went. She just knew she would find Pace here.

Drowsing in the shade, Pace felt the breeze cooling his brow and shifted to catch more of it. With a start, he realized he breathed the scent of more than new-mown hay and honeysuckle. It was a warm scent, an erotic one of female flesh and soap. He'd know that scent anywhere. It had haunted his dreams for weeks. He wasn't dreaming now.

His eyes flew open.

Dora lay there beside him, sound asleep. A tiny ray of sunshine crept through the leaves striking the silver tumble of her curls. He could reach out and touch the tempting satin of her cheek. Pace didn't think he'd ever been so close to her before, not even last night in the barn, when he'd so thoroughly kissed her. He hadn't seen her sweet innocence like this, in the full light of day. It wasn't the same at all.

He could clearly see the light cinnamon of her lashes where they brushed against her rounded cheek. Just the barest hint of rose coloring tinted her translucent complexion. In sleep, she looked relaxed and accessible, as if she would wake up smiling and welcoming at any moment. He wanted that welcoming smile with every ounce of his misbegotten soul.

He didn't dare touch her. He felt rough and crude in comparison to her delicate grace. His hands were cracked and calloused from ramming bullets into muskets, hauling on the reins of charging horses, carting dead bodies and digging graves. It would be obscene to lay even a finger on such pristine innocence.

That didn't keep him from looking. He'd never allowed himself the pleasure of looking at her so thoroughly before. He'd spent years denying her presence.

The time had finally come for meshing the reality of a human Dora with the ephemeral angel from his deprived childhood and warped imagination.

She was small. He had known that. Her shapeless gown had little to conceal. He could see the graceful curve of a firm breast beneath the thin cotton. She lay on her side, facing him, and his gaze drifted over the rounded slope of her hip to her slender waist. He could probably wrap his hands completely around her if he wanted. Her breasts would probably just fill his palms. Her legs would be just long enough to entwine with his.

Pace groaned and turned on his back to stare up at the leaves. He felt her stirring and knew he'd awakened her. Maybe he could convince himself that Dora and David had been lovers before David marched off to war. They'd courted for years. It was entirely possible. It gave him cause to wonder if that hadn't been the reason he'd persuaded David to do his duty and join the army. David hadn't taken much persuasion.

She'd come and laid herself down beside him for a reason. Maybe she needed the physical release of sex as much as he did. She certainly hadn't run away from him in the barn. He just didn't dare consider the inexperience of her kisses too closely if he meant to convince himself that his little Quaker was here for the reason he wanted her here.

"Go away, Dora," Pace muttered, covering his eyes with his good arm. The right one wouldn't lift that far.

"No, I don't think so," she replied thoughtfully. "Not this time."

The words ought to astound him, but nothing his fey angel did ever caused him surprise. She was as ever-changing and natural as the Kentucky weather. He could expect snow and rainbows if he waited. When one lived that way long enough, one came to expect the unexpected.

"You don't know what you're saying, bluebird. I'm not fit company right now."

"Thou saidst thou would stay if thou hadst a woman. I am a woman."

He'd known that was the reason for her presence. She had a way of flinging his careless words back in his face with a vengeance. The wondrous part was, that despite his cruelty and carelessness, she meant every word she said. He didn't have to look for ambiguities or hidden traps. He'd said he wanted a woman, and she offered herself. That was all there would be to it. Somewhere in that inscrutable little mind of hers, she thought she saved him from himself. God only knew, she might be right.

He didn't have much experience at resisting temptation. He was accustomed to having what he wanted, when he wanted it. And he definitely wanted this woman lying beside him, offering herself. He could see no barrier to stop him from having her.

But a silent war raged within him anyway. His mind knew Dora as a woman grown, capable of making her own decisions. His body wanted her. His body made no differentiation between painted women in red satin and this prim female in Quaker gray. There should be no impediment preventing him from reaching over and taking what he wanted. But something hitherto unknown and unused held him back. He thought it might be his conscience.

"I can't treat you like that," he protested feebly. Unexercised, his conscience was as weak as his arm. He didn't know how to wield it well.

"Thou didst last night," she pointed out.

"I was trying to teach you a lesson. You're a slow learner."

"No, I'm not. I'm very quick, actually. Thou doth not know me very well."

Pace wanted to laugh at her matter-of-factness. No, he didn't know her very well. He didn't want to know her very well. He just wanted the decadent pleasure of her body.

"If you stay here any longer, I'll know you extremely well," he warned with as much menace as he could summon. It hadn't worked on Dora as a child. He didn't hold out much hope of it happening now.

"I thought that was the point. Of course . . ."

Without looking at her, Pace could see Dora's little nose wrinkle and her bow lips purse up in thought. He waited breathlessly to see where her fascinating mind would wander.

"Perhaps this is not the appropriate time or place. Perhaps I should come to thee tonight, in the dark. Is that what thou prefers?"

Oh, damn. He couldn't win this one. One gimpy conscience couldn't stand up to heavy-round artillery fire from all sides. Pace turned on his side and stared down into Dora's face. The combination of innocent fear and fascinated admiration reflected there struck the final blow. He didn't want her afraid, and his soul begged for the admiration. She had discovered just the right combination to disable him.

"No, that isn't what I prefer," he muttered. Then before he could think better of it, Pace lowered his head and sampled the tempting fruit of her lips.

Dora closed her eyes to fully inhale the glorious wonder of Pace's warm breath moving across her lips. She'd thought maybe she had dreamed this wondrous touch. She could remember nothing in her life being so right, so real. No one had ever touched her like this. She had vague memories of a mother's hugs, her adopted parents stilted kisses, but those faint caresses were nothing akin to the passion surging between them now. She could feel life flowing from Pace into herself, feel the blood pumping through her veins, smell the scent of living as his mouth tugged more boldly at hers. She could reach out and wrap her fingers in Pace's hair, and he was real, not a porcelain doll, not a figment of her imagination. She could make him feel the pull of her fingers in his hair, the pressure of her lips. Pace was alive, as she had never been.

She couldn't get enough of such a heady nectar. She responded eagerly to his lips caressing her own, parted her mouth as he had taught her last night, and felt the thrill of Pace's breath and his life entwined with hers. They breathed each other's souls, and she whimpered with the joy of it.

Dora's hands took on minds of their own, caressing the thickness of Pace's hair, learning the powerful play of his muscles as he leaned over her. She sensed the greater weight he kept off of her, but she didn't fear it. She craved it. She needed the feel of him, all of him, to prove she was really and truly alive.

When Pace's hand found the buttons of her bodice, Dora's fingers rushed to help him. She needed the freedom of the breeze against her skin as much as she needed the brush of his fingers there. She hadn't known she needed it until he touched her, but the moment was so perfect that it could not have been any other way. Dora arched upward with feline satisfaction as Pace's rough hand curled around her breast.

The sudden sharp rush of desire shooting through her when he rubbed his thumb against her nipple caught her entirely by surprise, but she adapted quickly. The pleasure of this caress became something a little more urgent, more demanding. She didn't know how to react, but she trusted Pace to show her. She just pulled his mouth back to hers again and rejoiced in the plunge of his tongue into heated recesses while his fingers made her mindless.

Then his mouth moved to cover her breast and she gave a scream of sheer joy as life flooded through her and her body responded without thought. Her hands clung to his shoulders as he moved his knee between her legs, and the thundering tide found a direction.

"God, Dora, you're making me crazy," he muttered against her cheek as he pressed kisses along her jaw. "I'm not going to be able to stop without your help."

"Don't stop," she whispered into the breeze. "You're making me alive. I want to live, Pace. Help me."

He wasn't in any condition to hesitate, but her slip of tongue prodded that fragment of conscience into nagging him. In defense, Pace caught her hand and pressed it to the place in his trousers that strained for release. "This is what you're doing to me, Dora. Do you have any understanding of what I'll do to you if we keep this up?"

"No, not yet, but I want to learn." She pressed her hips upward, reaching instinctively for the place in him that ached. Her fingers curled tentatively around his hardness, and he groaned, bending his forehead to rest against hers.

"Just touch me, Dora. I'll try not to . . ." He couldn't complete the sentence when her eager fingers instantly sought his buttons.

He used his good arm to prop himself over her and

his right hand to hurriedly help her to unfasten his trousers. He was ready to explode. He'd been in the army three years now. He knew how to release his frustrations into the ground. That would be the best solution all the way around. But the act felt much sweeter with Dora lying beneath him, her lovely breasts exposed to his view. This was a thousand times better.

When her inexperienced fingers finally curled around him, he knew he couldn't do it any other way. With her caressing touch exploring his aching hardness intimately, Pace felt the hot rush of desire to his loins. The only alternative to using the ground was pulling up her skirts and plunging in right . . . *now*.

Pace groaned and rolled to one side spilling his seed into the grass beneath them. Dora's frightened fingers started to release him, but he caught her hand and held it there until the shuddering convulsions slowed. Then he lifted her fingers to his lips and kissed them.

"I haven't had a woman in so long, I've forgotten how to behave," he apologized, brushing a silver tendril from her cheek. "You deserve better than to be taken by a panting bull."

Wide blue eyes stared up at him with concern and bewilderment. "Is that all thou wanted? I didn't know . . ." She didn't have the language to explain what she didn't know.

Pace gave her a tender smile and brushed a kiss against her cheek. "That's not all I want. I want you. But this is your chance to escape unscathed. If we lie here like this any longer, I'm going to make love to you, and this time I'll wait until I'm where I want to be. Do you understand?"

He could tell from the bewilderment in her eyes that she didn't. It made him feel old and jaded. But when Pace brushed his lips against hers, and she responded eagerly, her innocent wantonness rushed through him. He didn't know if women could feel the ache of unrequited passion as forcefully as men, but Dora seemed ready to continue her lesson. He feared he couldn't satisfy her this first time. She had no experience and he wasn't in the habit of deflowering virgins. In this, they had something to learn together.

Dora didn't protest when he untied her skirt and bodice and pushed the wealth of material away. He helped her out of the long-sleeved top and then laid her chemise-clad body on the pile of skirts and petticoats. For the moment, he left her in her plain cotton undergarments.

Her skin had the translucency of fine porcelain. The only white women he'd taken to bed were expensive whores in the brothels of Lexington. They'd been older women with flabby flesh and coarse skin. Dora was as enchanting and fresh as a summer's day. Her flesh was firm and responsive to his every touch. Pace feared he would leave marks on her if he touched her too hard.

"You're perfect, Dora. I've never seen anyone so perfect." He leaned on his good arm and skimmed his other hand over the hills and valleys given to him alone to touch.

"I'm skinny and small," she pointed out prosaically.

"You're young and beautiful." He kissed her again, and felt the blood pulsing to his loins already. "You're enchanting and lovely. I don't want to ruin you."

The look she gave him had nothing shy in it as she rubbed her palm against his partially open shirt. "You can only do that by destroying yourself."

Her words were enigmatic, as they so often were. Pace disregarded them. He knew she lived in a fantasy world of her mind sometimes. What they did now had nothing to do with their minds.

He pulled his shirt off, rolling it up under her head for a pillow. He liked the way she studied him. He liked it even better knowing no other man had seen her like this. When her exploratory fingers found his nipples, he more than liked what she did. In return, he pushed the bodice of her chemise open and took her breast with his mouth.

Her eager cries quickly drew him to the brink again. Hastily, Pace discarded her cotton top and pulled her against him, teaching her the texture of flesh against flesh. Her kisses soon found his shoulders, and he shuddered with the flood of desire sweeping through him. She was so young and sweet, and he felt a million years old.

That didn't stop him from running his hand over the curve of her buttocks and pulling her against the aching hardness at his hips. His buttons were still unfastened, and he rubbed himself between her thighs. He hadn't divested her of her pantalets yet, but he knew she could feel his arousal. Her fingers dug into the skin of his back.

He fitted his hand between them finding the moist juncture of her legs, and he ran his fingers warningly against the open seam. "Now do you understand what I would do to you, Dora?"

She bit her lip and nodded as his finger parted the seam and rubbed insinuatingly at a part of her she had scarcely known existed. She thought she might explode in flames or boil away into steam from just this touch. The thought of what else he meant to do terrified her. But she knew. She had caught glimpses of that male part of him. Instinct gave her some notion of what happened next. She finally felt the first twinges of fear, but it was far too late for that. She meant to keep Pace here until he was safe. If that meant somehow taking his male parts inside herself, she would pay the price.

She loved his kisses. Dora returned to them eagerly, letting Pace blind her with their provocativeness. His tongue pressed smoothly between her lips, and she shuddered, understanding its subtle meaning now.

His hand caressed her breast into shivering anticipation, but he didn't move his kisses there. He kept her mouth occupied instead, making her breathless with need for more. She felt him unfastening her pantalets, but that wasn't any more intimate than his earlier touch. When he pulled the wisp of cotton off her legs and the breeze played against her bare flesh, she finally understood what she had done.

She had become part of the earth. Her body was one with the grass and the wind and the leaves up above. Completely bare and unmasked for the first time in her life, she offered her naked self to the one man who knew her from the inside out. Freedom and joy blossomed in that knowledge. She reached to pull Pace more completely over her.

What he did to her now was of little significance to what had already occurred. She invited him in with her

mouth and her hands and her legs. He accepted the offer
with alacrity. He touched her in her most private place
until he knew her better than herself, until she moist-
ened and opened to him, and then he spread her a little
farther, and accepted her invitation with a thrust that
left her gasping.

She hadn't understood it all then. This business of
being alive and part of the earth had other facets pre-
viously hidden from her. Layers upon layers of learning
lay ahead. Pace's body thrusting hot and hard inside of
her told her that.

The sensation of being filled by him overwhelmed her
in its variety. It hurt. But the pain brought incredible
pleasure. And then the pain disappeared and something
else replaced it, something she needed but didn't know
how to obtain. Dora rose to meet the pleasure/pain of
his sex, adjusted her hips to accommodate him, and felt
the wonder of Pace's moan of pleasure as he sank
deeper until he reached her womb.

She felt the perspiring heat, the cooling breeze, saw
shades of sunshine and shadow, and knew the total im-
mersion of their bodies into the living world. The thunder rumbled inside her now, marvelous, miraculous,
beyond her powers of understanding. And then Pace
touched her where they joined, and it all came together
in an explosion that drove them apart and into one at
the same time.

As his hot seed poured into her, Dora closed her eyes
and clasped Pace's back as if he were her only anchor
to the world.

Fifteen

Our doubts are traitors
And make us lose the good we oft might win
By fearing to attempt.

SHAKESPEARE, *Measure for Measure*

Pace didn't want to move. Nothing had felt more perfect in his life. Even the tormenting throb in his arm and the nagging protests of his conscience slipped into oblivion while he was positioned like this, buried in Dora's welcoming warmth, breathing her sweet scent. She was like satin beneath him. Such luxury came to him seldom.

But he was heavy and she was slight. As much as he would like believing he had died and gone to heaven in her arms, reality eventually intruded. With a groan, Pace rolled to one side. He didn't even have the strength to pull her with him.

He lay staring up at the tree leaves, listening to their rustle, trying to absorb some sense of what he had just done. He could feel Dora beside him, still and warm, her naked flesh a temptation to touch. If he looked down, he would see the evidence of her innocence smeared upon his loins. He'd never felt more of a bastard in his entire life.

When he didn't say anything, she started to rise, and he let her. He didn't know what else to do, what else to say. They had nothing in common. He could stay a few days more to appease her, he supposed, but no more than that. They had no future. He couldn't offer lies of love to Dora. He had no difficulty lying when the occasion warranted, but he didn't like lying to Dora. It would be akin to lying to God, he imagined. She would hear the truth no matter what his words said.

He heard her splashing in the dribble that remained of a creek. He tried to remember the drought killing her crops, but he could only think of how she must look naked and flushed with his lovemaking. Damn, but he was a selfish bastard.

When she knelt beside him with a wet cloth to cool his perspiring flesh, Pace finally allowed himself to look at her. She was all that he had imagined and more. Delicate dewdrops dampened the valley between pert, pink-tipped breasts. Moist silver curls clung to cheeks flushed with heat or embarrassment, he couldn't tell which. His gaze dropped to the narrow curve of her waist and the wide swell of her hips, finding the nest of pale brown between her thighs. His shaft hardened at the sight, and the deepening flush of her cheeks told him she had noticed.

"Aren't you wanted back at the house?" he asked bitterly. No one had ever offered him sympathy or affection before, and he didn't believe the offer now. She had her own motives for this seduction. He would send her back where she wanted to be. He didn't need her tender ministrations.

She did her frozen deer imitation, her hand stopping just above him, her wide eyes watching warily to see where he would strike next. "I thought I was wanted here," she finally answered softly, when he said nothing else.

"My arm is almost healed. It doesn't need your tender care anymore."

He had removed the bandages. Angry red scars inflamed the wasted flesh. He held the arm at an awkward angle to prevent the tearing pain in damaged muscle. Her fingers unconsciously traced the damage.

She finally raised her eyes to meet his gaze. "Thou wilt stay now?"

Damn, but he couldn't resist the appeal of those sky-blue eyes. Pace felt something twisting in his gut, and he pounded his conscience into submission. "You'll come to me tonight?"

She nodded shyly, the color flooding her cheeks again. "If thou wish."

He gave a sigh of relief and felt the knots of tension

ease from his neck as he relaxed against the sprawl of their clothes. "I'll come get you. You shouldn't walk around after dark by yourself."

She smiled. She actually smiled. It was like watching the sun come out at dawn. Pace felt it all the way to his groin. Had he the strength, he would roll her over and take her again. Considering the damage he had already inflicted, she should be grateful for his weakness.

"Didst thou think the fairies lit my way all these weeks?" she inquired teasingly.

This wasn't at all right. Dora knelt beside him, naked. He wore nothing more than she did. She should be ashamed, intimidated, embarrassed, anything but smiling and teasing. Pace felt a wild rush of something intoxicating in the freedom she allowed him, but he didn't know what to do with it. She defied the world as he knew it. He felt like a caged bird with its door suddenly flung open. He didn't know what to make of the change.

Pace pushed himself up on one elbow and felt his hair fall down in his face. He needed to get it cut. He rubbed his hand over his stubbly jaw. He hadn't even shaved this morning. He could see the abrasions on her tender breasts. Once his eyes focused there, he had difficulty raising them to meet her gaze. He should have known she would be so perfectly, delicately formed.

Her expression had turned slightly wary when he finally forced his gaze upward. Pace didn't want to know what she saw when she looked at him. He was too aware of the damaged mess of his arm, the ragged scar against his ribs, his hairy crudeness next to her smooth perfection. And his randy body made the evidence of his desire all too clear. It was a wonder she didn't run in terror.

"I won't force you," he said stiffly. "You've already sacrificed enough for no good reason."

Her wariness turned thoughtful as she caressed his stubbly jaw. "Is it so difficult to believe that this is what I wanted?"

"Yes," he answered curtly. "It is. I don't know what you think to accomplish, but I'm desperate enough to accept whatever you offer. Now get out of here before someone comes looking for you."

She drew away then, leaving her dampened chemise

for his use, drawing on her stiff cotton gown and petticoat without its protection. Pace tried not to watch her avidly, but he had difficulty tearing his gaze away knowing he might never have the opportunity again.

He hoped she hadn't caught the significance of what he'd just said. He could lie beneath these trees for the rest of the week and no one would come looking for *him*. He wasn't worth what she was throwing away. He just didn't want her realizing it quite yet.

Dora nearly dropped the soup tureen when Pace entered the dining room that evening. Garbed in evening dress as if this were a formal occasion, he wore his waistcoat buttoned, his frilled shirt neatly starched, and his narrow black tie tucked beneath his turned-down collar. He had apparently abandoned his uniform in deference to his father's opinions. He had shaved and had his hair cut. Something wary lingered behind the green of his eyes as he regarded the tableau in front of him, but Dora couldn't tear her gaze away from him. In frock coat and trousers, he looked every bit as magnificent as he did in uniform. The awkward angle of his damaged arm in no way detracted from his athletic frame. He looked every inch the gentleman he purported to be. She had difficulty believing such a man had ever looked at her.

Carlson Nicholls grunted at the sight of his son and took the tureen from Dora's hands. "Suppose this means you're marching back to war."

"I thought I would go over to the Andrewses' place tomorrow and bring Amy and Della back, if I might borrow the carriage." Pace spoke stiffly, scarcely looking at Dora.

"Good idea. Don't know why the fool woman took them away in the first place. They belong here. So does that damned wife of Charlie's. Tell them I said so." He looked up from his soup in irritation. "Why in hell you still standing there? Forgotten how to sit down?"

This time, Pace's gaze did turn to Dora. She was horribly conscious of her soiled apron and baggy gown, and she lifted the tureen to keep from looking at him.

"I'm waiting for Miss Smythe to take a seat," he answered with the same stiff arrogance as before.

Carlson snorted unpleasantly. "Then you'll wait until the mountains crumble unless you want to go whip some sense into those darkies' heads."

Dora finally found her tongue when the awkward silence grew. "Have a seat, Pace. I'll set an extra place for thee. The chicken is almost done. I'll take a tray up to thy mother and have Annie come down to serve thee in just a minute."

She knew Pace had no awareness of the deterioration of authority around here. He simply struggled to prove his identity as a gentleman, in her eyes as well as his own. She didn't know how to tell him that proof wasn't necessary. For all she knew, gentlemen were extinct creatures and probably useless in their own time. She gestured at a chair and went to the sideboard to fetch the china and silver.

He appeared noiselessly behind her, startling her with his nearness as he reached for the plates. She was altogether too aware of the man who had held her naked in his arms just hours ago. She knew his physical form intimately, the strength rippling beneath the elegant coat as he reached around her. His arm barely missed brushing against her breast, and she held her breath as their fingers touched when he took the plate away.

"I can set my own place and one for you. Go fetch Annie. Tell my mother if she wants to eat, she can come down and do so. I'll be happy to help her with the stairs if she needs it."

Dora didn't know why he went this far. With Pace, there was never an easy answer. She let him have the plates. She wouldn't surrender more.

"I'm sure thou and thy father have much to discuss," she murmured. "I will eat with thy mother as usual." She managed to tear herself away from him, wrapping her hands in her apron as she started for the door.

"You will damned well eat down here where you belong," Pace yelled after her. "It's time this damned family acted like one!"

Carlson gave his son a raised-eyebrow look and continued eating his soup. He'd abrogated his responsibilities as a family man a long time ago.

Dora could agree with Pace's sentiment, but she couldn't imagine how he would put his words into action. Silently, she left in the direction of his mother's room. It wouldn't hurt to try.

Harriet looked at her as if she were crazed when Dora expressed Pace's desire for a family dinner. "He wants me to go downstairs for the pleasure of listening to him and his father tear each other apart? No, thank you. I'll decline the invitation." She settled herself resolutely into the overstuffed chair beside her bed. "I'll go hungry first."

Dora had expected that response, but for Pace's sake, and to avoid conflict, she tried again. "Pace will be on his best behavior. And I'll remind him if he forgets. This means a lot to him. He will go back to war shortly. It would make things easier on the help if we all ate in one place. Perhaps thou couldst persuade some of the kitchen staff to work again. I am not good with servants."

Harriet tapped her toe and stared out the window. She'd not asked for her bottle of laudanum recently. She was awake more during the day. Dora thought sitting here doing nothing all day must bore her horribly. She needed to get out of this room. Perhaps Pace had offered the excuse she needed to break her self-imposed exile.

"Annie could fix thy hair," Dora suggested shyly. "Wouldn't thou like wearing one of those pretty dresses again?"

Harriet turned and gave her a shrewd look. "You're the one who ought to have her hair fixed and wear pretty dresses. You look like an old maid. You'll not catch my son's interest looking like that." Without a clearer reply, she gestured for Annie to fetch the silver-backed brush from the dresser.

Not daring to leave for fear Harriet would change her mind, Dora stayed to help choose a dress and locate undergarments. The styles were terribly outdated. Nothing fit. She had little talent for making adjustments in this kind of finery. Still, she found enough garments to dress Harriet fully. The older woman could no longer be called beautiful, and she could scarcely be called dignified with her sagging chins and overtight bodice waists, but she looked more human than she had in many years. Dora breathed a sigh of relief as Harriet swayed in unbuttoned shoes toward the door.

"Annie, go fetch my son. Dora, go get yourself fixed up. Servants don't eat in the dining room. You must look like a guest." She waved imperiously, dismissing her subjects as she shuffled carefully toward the hall for the first time in years.

Nervously, Dora escaped to her own room. Untying her apron, she reached for her best Meeting gown. Perhaps if she left the collar and apron off, she would look less like a servant. Mother Elizabeth would disapprove, as would the Elders, but making peace in this household seemed a more important task than maintaining her modest attire. Plain Dress had been intended to create equality, avert vanity, and avoid notice. By keeping to the styles of hundreds of years ago, they had forfeited that intent in Dora's mind. It was no sacrifice abandoning the disguising articles.

Dora heard Pace talking to his mother as he helped her down the hall. Considering what she had done with him this afternoon, her attire was the least of her sins. Her heart thumped in her throat and her stomach clenched as she listened to the low vibrations of his voice just outside her door. She found it hard to believe that she had done what she had with him. He was a man of the world, a well-respected lawyer in Frankfort, an experienced soldier. She was nothing, less than nothing. How could he see anything in her?

He didn't. She had to remind herself of that. She was nothing to him but a convenient vessel for his needs. She must remember that. She didn't consider what she had done a sacrifice because she had wanted it, but she had done it knowing it could have only one outcome. She would keep Pace from joining that battle, keep him alive to fight the legal battles that would follow this war, and watch his fight from the distance of hundreds of miles. He would never return here when the war ended. There was nothing for him here.

Armed with that knowledge, Dora combed her hair,

straightened her cap, and hurried to join the highly un-
usual party downstairs.

Pace frowned at the cap when she entered, but in
keeping with his unspoken promise, he said nothing argumentative. When Dora started for the door leading to
the kitchen, he just grabbed her arm and shoved a chair
under her.

Carlson had sat in the first chair he reached when he
came through the door, which wasn't the head of the
table. He glared at his empty soup bowl and ignored the
gray-haired woman taking the chair farthest from his.
Dora watched uneasily as he sipped at a mug of ale, but
he didn't seem much inclined to talk. Her gaze drifted
to Pace as Annie entered the room bearing a platter
of chicken.

Pace had taken a seat halfway between his parents and
directly across from Dora. He frowned but kept quiet as
Annie set the platter on the table without passing it.
Wordlessly, he helped himself from the platter when his
father passed it down to him. Dora didn't look at him
when he handed the chicken to her. She had sat at this
table before with him, but never after spending intimate
hours in his company. She didn't know what to do or
how to act.

"That gown is very becoming, Mother," Pace said for-
mally as he held the platter so she could choose from it.

"That's a lie, but I thank you for it," Harriet answered
stiffly. "Where is your uniform? Have you been
discharged?"

"I reenlisted in May. I'm having a new uniform made.
I will return to my regiment shortly."

Annie returned with potatoes and carrots, handing
them to Carlson first and walking out. She had been
trained as a ladies' maid and not a serving girl, but she
knew better. Dora felt the slave's resentment and hostility, but though she might sympathize, she had no power
to correct the situation. To even mention paying Annie
would throw Carlson into a rage not conducive to the
proposed peace of this dinner.

Carlson shoveled out some potatoes and pushed them
toward Dora. "Damned Yankees think they own us," he
muttered, *sotto voce.*

Pace pretended he didn't hear. Taking the bowl of vegetables from Dora, he said pleasantly, "I haven't thanked you for your care while I was ill, Miss Smythe. Is there something I can do for you to show my appreciation?"

Dora looked at him suspiciously. This was too much politeness for her taste, but she wouldn't say the first angry word. Pain had carved harsh lines around Pace's mouth, but she found something tender in the look of his eyes. She would respond to the good in him, and not his cynical provocativeness.

"Thou canst stay alive and come home safely," she murmured.

She heard his father make a disagreeable grunt at this reply, but Pace's gaze warmed slightly, and his mother interfered before anything else could be said.

"You could stay here and work the farm like you ought. That arm should get you a discharge." She dug into her potatoes with enthusiasm. Her "illness" had never diminished her appetite.

Pace stiffened, but his father replied before he could summon a polite answer.

"I don't need the likes of him around. I've still got a strong back and two good arms. I built this place by myself. I can keep it going by myself."

Dora could see Pace struggling to control his temper. She breathed easier when he answered with patience.

"I could help you find some hired hands. Solly doesn't make much of a field laborer. I was thinking of taking him with me."

Carlson slammed his fork against the table, sending a carrot flying into the air. "You'll damned well do nothing of the sort! That boy belongs to me, and don't you forget it! I'll not have anything to do with your Yankee abolitionist whimpering. Lincoln can't steal our property. It's against the Constitution! That's what this damned war is all about, upholding the Constitution. You and your blue-bellied friends won't change the way things are."

"Things have already changed," Pace pointed out reasonably. "Your slaves have gone and you won't get them back. You're going to have to hire help."

"And who in hell do you think I'm going to hire to do nigger work? Just tell me that, smartass. There ain't a self-respecting white man in this state that's goin' to work out in those fields. Your damned blue-bellied friends better start thinking about that before winter comes and they find their blue bellies empty."

Pace's temper began to show. "If the state of Kentucky hadn't made it unconstitutional for free black men to stay and hire themselves out, you and your friends wouldn't have to worry about getting your pristine hands dirty. Tell that to your mighty congressman next time he pats himself on the back for getting that heinous piece of stupidity locked into the Constitution for the next umpteen years."

"I'll not sit here and listen to that kind of guff from no son of mine!" Carlson roared, heaving himself upward. "Matt Mitchell is a damned good friend of mine and has a better head on his shoulders than you'll ever have. Why don't you get your Yankee hide out of here and back to those nigger-lovin' friends of yours where you belong? Lookin' at you makes me sick. You can't be any son of mine."

Pace leaped to his feet in fury, but his father was already on his way out the door. The look on his face made Dora's soul weep, but she had no magic powders for healing this festering wound. She hurried to take Harriet's arm when Pace's mother staggered to her feet.

"Well, I hope everyone enjoyed this happy homecoming. I think I'll rest now, Dora. Don't ask me to repeat this experience anytime soon.'

Dora didn't dare glance back at the look of despair lurking behind Pace's proud features. She led Harriet from the room and flinched as the front door slammed a few minutes later.

Sixteen

Being your slave, what should I do but tend
Upon the hours and times of your desire?

SHAKESPEARE, *Sonnets*

Dora didn't know how long it took to settle Harriet
down for the night. The old woman grumbled and complained the entire time she was undressed and returned
to her night shift and robe. She demanded her laudanum
for the first time in weeks, and raised a scene when told
they hadn't any. She chastised Annie for bringing water
too cold to wash in, then protested vehemently when a
steaming kettle was brought up to heat it.

Dora sighed wearily when she finally escaped the
room. She could endure the older woman's tantrums
well enough, but the thought of Pace sitting in that
empty farmhouse alone left her emotionally drained. She
feared he would pack his bags and go before she could
get there.

She didn't even take time to comb her hair or wash
her face before rushing out of the house into the growing
darkness. This late in July, daylight lingered still, but the
huge old trees lining the drive had already plunged the
path into darkness. Dora had no fear of the dark. Her
only thoughts were of Pace. She couldn't let him leave
yet.

She knew the night covered the acts of desperate men
in these uncertain times. Slaves escaping North from the
chaos of the South fled along these roads. Despite the
Emancipation Proclamation, Kentucky law still called
them fugitives. If caught, they could be thrown in jail
and sold to the highest bidder. Knowing that, the slaves

fought viciously for their freedom. There were plenty of greedy white men ready to deny them that freedom, and they haunted these roads as well, looking for prey. Violence followed in their trail.

Confederate raiders seldom made it this far north any longer, but their supporters did, and the Yankees patrolled to prevent their depredations. Anyone could be suspected of anything at any given time. The situation wasn't wholesome. A lone woman caught between two such bands had little chance of escaping unscathed. But Dora didn't even consider the consequences as she ran the mile down the road from the big house to her own home.

She didn't need to heed the consequences. Pace came running down the road to greet her as if he had watched for her, uncertain if he should expect her, afraid for her safety if he didn't watch. She threw herself into his open arms and felt giddy with joy as he swung her off her feet and around in circles.

She knew he had feared she wouldn't come. She could feel it in the piercing desperation of his kiss, the bone-crushing grasp of his arms. She clung to his neck and smothered him with reassurance. She knew he didn't believe what her kisses said, but it didn't matter. Nothing else mattered but that Pace Nicholls had actually waited for her, that at long last, he wanted her with him. For the first time in her life she felt the exhilaration of being needed, not just by anybody, but by this man she had adored since childhood.

The hunger she sensed in him was heady and terrifying at the same time. She didn't know if she had what it took to satisfy him. She was too young, too small, too inexperienced to be what he needed. But she allowed him to carry her into the house and into his bed without expressing any of those fears.

The fierceness of Pace's passion was equally terrifying, but Dora understood the bubbling rage inside him. It could easily spill over and burn her, she knew from past experience, but long ago she had given her trust to this man. She didn't know the whys and wherefores, and she wouldn't question now. Pace was a part of her that she had lost long ago. She needed him.

She gave a cry of surprise when he dispensed with her buttons by ripping them open, but her soul soared when he kneeled over her, and his mouth closed over her breast to suckle deeply. She fed his ravening hunger with her ardor, pulling at his shirt until she found his flesh, responding fiercely to the brutalizing passion of his kiss. Mindless now, she no longer considered right from wrong, peace versus violence. She only knew the heated brand of Pace's hands upon her, his mouth devouring her where his hands did not.

When Pace pulled up her skirt and ran his hands possessively over the curve of her buttocks, Dora knew this wouldn't be a gentle loving, but she had already given herself into his care and no longer concerned herself with how they got where they were going. She wanted him inside her again, pulsing with life, reaffirming their existence. She ached with the need for that consummation. She lifted herself eagerly from the mattress so he could remove her drawers, and she cried out with delight when he touched her there, sliding his fingers deep to prepare her.

When Pace opened her thighs wider and rammed into her with a passion bordering on violence, Dora gave a wild cry of startlement, but her body knew what she needed better than her mind. She responded instantly to his fierceness, digging her fingers into his back, meeting his hips with hers in a furious battle for power and release. She screamed with frustration as he gripped her buttocks and pulled her into him, then learned the exquisite pleasure of surrender as she wrapped her legs around him. His throaty cry of desire swept through her veins, and she finally succumbed to the waves of pleasure his possession induced. Triumph capped her desire when her contractions brought him to a shuddering release deep inside her body.

He didn't stop with just that one pleasuring. His kisses resumed immediately, a little less desperate, a little more gentle. These were even better than before, and Dora accepted them with joy. She'd never truly known physical pleasure before. She had always thought of her body as a troublesome vessel prone to pain and best disguised and forgotten. But Pace taught her that this nuisance of a physical self could have its usefulness. Her arms could hold him. Her lips could kiss him. Her breasts could tingle with his caress. And her thighs could part in access to that safe haven where they could be as one.

She lost track of time. She lost count of their couplings. She no doubt lost possession of her mind while caught in the trap of her senses. She only knew the man beside her in the bed owned her, body and soul, and she would never be the same again.

That didn't bother her too greatly. She had never expected to find true love. David had been the only man she had ever considered marrying, and she knew now that he would never have offered her what Pace gave her tonight. She didn't expect to find this happiness again. In truth, she had very little in the way of expectations. She had already died once. She knew she would die again. She would take what little comfort offered in between times.

Dora turned and drew her hand down the solid wall of Pace's chest, kissing the rounded muscle of his shoulder. His arm around her tightened, crushing her breasts against his ribs. They were entirely naked, their limbs entwined in impossible knots. His hair-roughened leg rubbed the smooth satin of her inner thigh. Dora could almost imagine she had died and gone to heaven, but she heard the early song of the mockingbird outside and knew the idyll had ended.

She was sore in a thousand places. She ached deep inside, and her muscles felt as if she had walked carrying a heavy burden all night. Knowing the source of the ache made her feel only pleasure, however. She nipped lightly at Pace's chest, then began to untangle herself.

"Don't go," he murmured, catching her arm in his fist, his fierce eyes closed now with satiation and weariness.

"I must." She escaped his hold but lingered a moment longer to run her hand daringly down his powerful chest and across his flat belly. "Thou wilt stay?"

"A few days only. I'll go get Amy for you."

He hadn't forgotten. She breathed a sigh of relief. She had tried very hard not to fall for the child, but she had missed her desperately these last months. She would enjoy hearing a child's laughter again. "Do not strain

thy arm," she warned prosaically, swinging her legs over
the side of the bed.

Pace laughed softly and finally opened his eyes to the
gray dawn to watch her pad naked about the room in
search of her clothes. "I have told you before that I do
not want a mother."

"I doubt thou knoweth what thou wants," Dora answered scornfully, wiggling into her chemise. "But I do
not think I would make thee a good mother."

She would make him a good wife were the words that
arose unspoken between them. But they were words of
the moment, not of the future. Pace would have his ele-
gantly gowned, beautiful hostess to further his political
ambitions. Dora would stay to tend her meager fields.
Their paths diverged too widely for them to ever meet
like this again in the future.

Pace climbed from the bed and naked, pulled her
slightly clad body against his. He kissed the nape of her
neck. "I don't need a mother. I need you in my bed."

She pulled from his arms and reached for her gown.
She didn't need reminding of what she already knew.
All he needed from her was her body. The knowledge
was demeaning as well as disillusioning, but she accepted
the fact that she had no other worth. The earl had taught
her worthlessness at an early age.

"I must get back before someone sees me. Wilt thou
stop for breakfast?"

"If thou wilt stop wearing that awful cap," Pace answered in amusement, eyes glittering in mockery as he
watched her try to button a gown he'd fairly ripped from
her the night before.

Dora gave him a swift look of disapproval. "Thou
needs not mock. I may be a fallen woman now, but I
needn't flaunt it."

Pace grabbed the cap from her hands and crushed it
between his long fingers. "I warned you even angels can
fall from trees. Now that you're down on the ground
with the rest of us, you don't need wings or halo. Leave
it off. Your hair is too pretty to cover up."

Dora's hand traveled restlessly to her crumpled curls.
"It is a mess. Mother Elizabeth would not approve. Give
me the cap, Pace."

He surrendered it reluctantly, watching her through cautious green eyes. "Why do you always call her Mother Elizabeth instead of just mother? Is that part of your religion?"

She tucked her wayward curls inside the cap by sense of touch, not daring to confront a mirror just yet. She shook her head at his ignorance. "She and Papa John were my adopted parents. They took me in when I was eight. I could not call them mother and father, so we worked out a substitute."

He padded around the room, uncovering his own clothes. "Your accent is not the same as David's." As if just realizing what he'd said, Pace straightened and turned to her apologetically. "I heard about David. I'm sorry."

She dismissed his false sympathy for what it was and focused her attention on the less painful. "David was from North Carolina. His parents could not continue abiding in a state that allowed slavery, so they moved to Indiana when he was very young. My adopted parents brought me from England. I had hoped I'd lost most of the accent by now."

Pace grinned as he pulled on his trousers. "Not by half. I thought you were from another world that first time I heard you. Where in England do you come from?"

He was treading too near the personal again. Dora didn't believe her father still looked for her, but she wouldn't risk revealing too much just in case. She shrugged and started for the door. "Does it matter? Will I see thee at breakfast?"

The distance between them became recognizable again: the lowly serving girl speaking to the master who had tumbled her. Pace gave a curt nod and turned away as she departed.

She had done it to herself. She had no reason to resent Pace for his attitude. It had always been thus between them. It was better for both of them if it stayed that way. They would suffer no confusing sentiments, no inconvenient misapprehensions about her place in the scheme of things. She would continue as before, and he would ride off into his glorious future.

But Dora could appreciate the little things he did for her while he stayed around. When Pace drove up the drive later that day with Amy and Della, she ran out to grab the little girl and give her a hug and kiss. Amy squealed with delight and babbled incoherently.

Pace grinned at the way Dora nodded solemnly and pretended to understand every single word. "I'm glad you understand her. I'd about decided she spoke Chinese."

Sticky fingers caught in her hair as Dora dared a glance at Pace. The lines of pain all but disappeared when he smiled like that. He was losing some of the craggy hollows of his illness, but she decided the newly-honed features that resulted were even more handsome than his boyish countenance of earlier. She tried not to notice the aching emptiness that knowledge caused.

"She is telling me her uncle is a terrible rascal who doesn't listen to a single word she says. The words are just as plain as can be. I don't know why thou canst not hear them."

Pace laughed as he helped Della down from the carriage. The matronly black woman hurried to take her charge from Dora's hands, scolding the child for wetting her panties, and hurrying her into the house—leaving Dora and Pace to face each other alone.

"I told the Andrewses that we hoped Josie would come back here when she returns." The laughter had left his face.

Dora nodded, hiding the pain that struck. Pace had loved Josie once. He still might. He and Josie would have made a much better couple than Josie and Charlie. That knowledge created just one more barrier between them. "I would like having Josie here again. It's just . . ." He frowned at her hesitation, and she hurried her explanation. "The soldiers know she is the wife of a rebel. They harass thy father, and his temper is not of the best. It is a difficult situation."

Pace climbed back into the carriage so he could take the horses to the stable. "I'll talk to the commanding officer, see what I can do." He gave her a sharp look. "They leave you alone, don't they?"

Dora smiled at that. "They scarcely know I exist. Go on with thee now. Dinner will be served shortly."

Pace left her standing there, a slight figure against the forbidding backdrop of the magnificently columned veranda. He had no reason to feel uneasy about Dora's welfare. Like a cat, she no doubt had nine lives. Or perhaps she was immortal like the angels. There was something completely untouchable about Dora that set her off from the rest of the world's population. He didn't understand why he was the only one who could slip behind that formidable barrier. He wondered if he actually had gone behind it, or if she had just erected a less visible one to keep him out.

Pace told himself it didn't matter. He waited outside the house that evening, whittling at a poplar branch while she finished her chores. Occasionally, he could see her flitting past the upper-story windows, alternately appeasing his mother or dawdling in the nursery. For such a little mouse, she certainly stayed busy. He almost resented the right of everyone else to her time but him.

She finally slipped out just after dusk. Pace pulled her into the concealing shadows of the nearest tree, circled her with his arms, and demanded a kiss. It was the least she could do to reward him for his patience.

She responded as eagerly and lovingly as he remembered. He relaxed slightly, not acknowledging the fear that the prior night had all been a dream.

"You smell like Amy," he murmured against her neck.

"Is that bad?"

"I suppose not. I'm just not used to having babies around. They make me nervous."

She laughed lightly as if his words had no effect on her. Pace hurried her down the road, trying to run away from what he had just said.

Babies weren't a part of his future. Surely no more than two or three nights in Dora's bed would be safe enough.

Seventeen

Farewell! God knows when we shall meet again.
I have a faint cold fear thrills through my veins,
That almost freezes up the heat of life.

SHAKESPEARE, *Romeo and Juliet*

Propping himself on one elbow, Pace looked down at the sleeping beauty beside him. Dark circles from lack of sleep colored the thin skin beneath Dora's eyes. He was responsible for that, he knew. He hadn't left her much time for sleeping these past three nights.

She'd brought him as close to heaven as he ever expected to get in his misbegotten life. He hated leaving. It would be so simple just to continue these lazy days of summer lying around all day and making love to a beautiful woman all night. But he had fully recovered now, or fully recovered as he could get. The damned arm still hurt like the very devil when he used it, but he refused to give in to the pain. He didn't have it in him to lie back and let nature take its course. He had things to do, places to be, people to see. He had to go.

As if sensing his restlessness, Dora opened her eyes sleepily and looked up at him through those blasted long lashes of hers. She had the face of a Botticelli angel when asleep, and the countenance of a wanton when looking at him like that. Pace felt his loins respond to the challenge, but it was almost dawn. He had to leave.

"Take me with thee," she whispered.

Nothing got past Dora. She knew what he would do before he did it. Pace shook his head and swung his legs over the side of the bed. "Don't be ridiculous."

She pushed herself upright, the sheet falling from her

bare breasts. "I could be a nurse. They need nurses. Don't leave me here."

The temptation she presented was too great. Scowling, Pace threw his weight over her, pressing her back into the soft down of the mattress. "I may have brought an angel down to earth, but I'll not lead her into hell. You'll stay here."

Holding himself over her, Pace kneeled between her legs and eased himself into her, knowing Dora's eyes followed all he did. In the dawn light she could see where his fully erect manhood entered her. She could see how easily he possessed her body. He wanted her to see, to know what he was, and what she was. She gave a breathless little cry when he pushed deeper. Her eyes widened as her gaze flew up to his face, and then her lashes fluttered closed again as she accepted his possession completely.

She was his. It didn't give Pace the satisfaction that he thought it would, but it was enough. He had one person in his life that he could count on. In a life fraught with uncertainties, he didn't need more, he told himself. Maybe someday he would let her go. But not just now.

Their lovemaking was fierce and bittersweet, knowing their parting could be forever. When they'd had their fill, Pace lay beside her long enough to let Dora drift back to sleep. Even if he survived the war, he didn't know if he would come back to claim her again. He had taken huge risks doing it this time. He shouldn't push his luck. Nothing good could ever come of what they had between them. He was better off walking away without looking back.

But when he left, he left his grandmother's gold ring on the pillow beside her.

The sun was well up when Dora woke again. Daylight streamed through the thin bedroom curtains. She knew before she opened her eyes that Pace had gone.

She tried blocking out the gaping emptiness ripping her insides. She refused to grieve. She had known their time together would only be temporary. But the habits of a lifetime failed her now. She couldn't control the waves of pain washing through her.

When she opened her eyes and saw the ring sparkling in the sunshine, she almost reached over and threw it across the room. She knew Pace well enough to know the ring didn't mean a thing. It wasn't a promise. It was a toy, a gesture appeasing his guilty conscience. She wouldn't even accuse him of offering payment. Pace wasn't that crude. He wanted to give her something and he had nothing else to give. The fool idiot thought it would make her feel better.

Nothing would ever make her feel better. She'd let him use her body over and over again, just for the sheer pleasure of it. She couldn't even convince herself anymore that she had done it to save his life. She sensed the danger had ended, if danger there had ever been. But it could have been over days ago and she wouldn't have admitted it. She had wanted him to stay, to bury himself inside her, to make her alive again.

Well, he had succeeded. She was alive and hurting so badly that she wished she had died. She didn't even know how to cry anymore. Her emotions were so stiff from disuse that she could only curl up and absorb the pain as if she had been physically battered.

He was gone.

Dora clutched the ring in her palm and wept silently, her entire body shaking with sobs. The bed smelled of him, but she would never know that scent again once she washed the linens. He would be truly gone then, gone from sight and sound and smell. She would never know his rough hands caressing her breasts again, never know the sound of his low voice murmuring sensual words in her ear, never catch the glint of sunlight in his auburn hair. He'd never put his arms around her or bruise her with his lips again.

She didn't know how she would endure the pain. It seared through her more surely than fire. Damn him for doing this to her. Damn herself for letting him.

She finally crept from the bed, feeling the ache between her legs where'd he taken her so roughly. She had never imagined what a man did to a woman until Pace had come along. It seemed incredible even now. She had wallowed in physical sensations for three fascinating nights. They might be all she ever had.

She had difficulty restoring herself to the wooden doll everyone expected of her. For the first time since she had donned Quaker gray, she hated the coarse material. She knew wealthy Quakers who wore silks and satins, but even that would not suffice for the way she felt now. She wanted to wear scarlet. She wanted to feel the wind on her skin. She wanted to immerse herself in the summer heat as if that would replace the warmth Pace had taken away.

She did nothing but dress and return to the big house in time for dinner, apologizing for her tardiness without further explanation. No one thought it the least odd that she had disappeared for an entire evening and half a day on the same day that Pace took his leave. Had she ever needed proof of her invisibility, she had it in that alone.

The next day's newspaper ran headline banners screaming the deaths of thousands in the battle for Atlanta.

Early December 1864

"Damn you yellow-bellied cutthroats, you can't take my horses! You've thieved everything else you can lay your hands on but I'll kill you before I'll let you take those damned horses! I raised every one of them myself and they're the finest stock in the state. I'm not lettin' any Yankee puke harness them to a wagon!"

Dora pressed a calming hand to her uneasy stomach as she heard these words bellowing through the center hall of the house. Carlson Nicholls had existed in a state of apoplexy ever since the army issued traveling passes to those remaining slave families on the farm, ostensibly so they could visit their soldier husbands and fathers. The women had snatched up the passes and took to coming and going as they pleased, even though most of the trains and riverboats wouldn't allow them on board for fear of reprisal. As long as they had those army passes in their hands, the women could visit neighboring farms whenever they took the notion. Carlson had wanted to whip them all. Hearing his furious yells, Dora feared going outside to see what catastrophe visited them now.

But his bellowing "damn hell" halted abruptly in mid-curse, followed by an alarmed shout from a strange voice, sending Dora racing down the hall to the veranda.

Carlson was on his knees, clutching his chest. His features had turned an unwholesome shade of gray, and he was gasping for breath. Three blue-coated soldiers stood around him, looking dismayed, while a fourth had run off to the water trough. They looked up with relief at Dora's appearance.

"Your father looks like he's been took real ill, miss. We'd best help him into the house."

Dora nodded agreement and opened the door wider so they could carry Carlson in. He fought them as best as he could, but he couldn't even stand on his own. He finally gave a gasp of sheer anguish and passed out.

"Jem, you'd better go for a doctor," one of the officers ordered. "He doesn't look real good. That's all we need is to have those rebel copperheads yelling we killed an old man."

Dora led them upstairs to a spare room. She didn't think it appropriate to take Carlson back to his mistress's room behind the kitchen. She knew one of the soldiers had run off at his officer's orders, but the other three managed to carry Carlson's heavy weight to the bed. When they had him settled and were removing his boots, she rested her hand on his temple, timing the pulse there. It wasn't strong.

"Jem's gone to get a doctor, miss. We're sorry about all this. We were just following orders." The blue-coated officer held his hat in his hands. He really did look apologetic.

It didn't matter. These past months since Pace had taught her to feel again had left her emotions in a chaotic uproar. Temper overcame fear now, and she spoke curtly. "I know, but thou canst not take all we have and expect us to survive the winter. Thou knoweth how much we lost when General Burbridge ordered us to sell the hogs. I know thou must eat, and the general feared the surplus would end up in rebel hands, but the prices were outright fraud. Thou hath barely left me enough to pay the taxes. Now thou wouldst steal the horses, when there is no way of replacing them. I cannot understand why we must be the ones to make these sacrifices. Art thy families giving up everything they own to pay for this war?"

She unfastened Carlson's waistcoat and cravat as she spoke, but she knew she had their attention. They shifted their heavy boots uneasily.

"We've been told this is a rebel household, miss. There aren't any rebels where we come from. Ohio is strongly behind the Union."

Dora checked Carlson's pulse again and scowled at the officer. "This man's son was severely wounded in the Union march on Atlanta. He is even now with General Sherman, possibly destroying the homes of family and friends. Thou must understand that thou art asking us to fight our own families when thou asketh us to destroy the South. All of Kentucky supported the Union until thou began treating us like captives. How can thee possibly understand how this man feels when he has given up everything he has for a war he never wanted?"

The young soldiers looked nervous and embarrassed and didn't dare meet her eyes. The older officer regarded her warily. "If this is a Union household, you will be adequately recompensed for the horses. The army needs them to travel on. We all must make sacrifices."

"Thou must leave us a horse to pull the cart. This is a house of invalids and infants. We must have access to town. Surely thou must see that."

"What I see is a virulent old man trying to hang on to his slaves as if they were animals he can own," the officer answered, finally getting angry. "Lincoln won't let us take the slaves away, but we have permission to take the animals. Kentuckians think they can have things both ways, but it doesn't work that way. It's time he gets used to it." He made a disparaging nod at the man breathing raggedly on the bed.

"He's a sick old man, and thou hath no right to speak that way." Dora would have said more, but her gaze caught on the anxious faces peering around the door from the hall. Amy came toddling into the room, looking up at the tall soldiers as if they were strange trees sprung up for her amusement. Della remained in the hallway, wringing her hands. Annie was there too, and several of the other women from the quarters eager for the entertainment of disaster. They managed to convey the spectrum of emotions from terrified to triumphant.

Dora knelt carefully to pick up the infant. Her back felt the strain of work these days, but she still had the strength for Amy. She kissed the little girl's cheek and tried to keep her voice pleasant.

"I would thee would leave now. We have no men to defend us here, and thy presence is disturbing. Friend Carlson's wife is an invalid and shouldn't be woken. If thou must take horses, I insist on payment. It should be easy confirming that Payson Nicholls is a Union officer. As thou canst see, I am scarcely a rebel. That leaves only one angry old man, and thou knoweth he has a right to anger. I want thy word of honor on this, sir."

The officer looked Dora's slight figure up and down, from the fists clenched silently in the child's gown to the determined set of her jaw beneath the simple muslin cap. She had no right to demand anything of him, but the fact that she dared to do so seemed to impress him. He didn't even know what her position was in the household, but he nodded agreement.

"All right, miss. We'll leave you a cart horse and pay you fair value for the animals we take. I hope Mr. Nicholls will be all right." He bowed and made a nasty retreat.

Dora wanted to collapse in a shivering heap, but someone had to be strong and she saw no one else to do it. She had no idea of the worth of the horses taken. She had to trust in the soldiers' honesty when they gave her the little pile of federal notes. They left just as the doctor arrived, and she escorted the physician upstairs. She watched in growing anxiety as he examined the patient and shook his head discouragingly. Although she had sent the servants away, Dora knew they lingered just out of sight. The general wail that ensued when the doctor finally spoke caused her to shut the door before she sat down and covered the gripping pain in her stomach with her fist.

"He could have another spell any minute now, and that one will carry him off. There isn't a thing you can do except keep him quiet and hope for the best. I'll bleed him, but it won't necessarily help."

Mother Elizabeth had disapproved of bleeding, but she had barely been more than a midwife. She hadn't dealt in cases as serious as this one. Dora closed her eyes and tried to calm her roiling stomach while the doctor performed his duty. She could hear the blood running in the bowl and felt she would certainly faint. She never fainted.

"There, that's done," the physician said with satisfaction. "Now maybe I better take a look at you."

Dora's eyes flew open to see to whom he was talking. When she saw that she was the only one in the room beside Carlson Nicholls, she turned wide eyes of puzzlement to the stout doctor. "I am fine. Bloodletting just makes me a little queasy."

He harrumphed and put his tools back in his bag. "I imagine everything has made you a little queasy these last few months. How far along are you? Four months? It's hard to say with a woman your size."

Dora stopped breathing. She didn't know what he tried to say. His words had nothing to do with her. But the whole time her mind denied it, her body screamed agreement. She'd been queasy for months. Her stomach had constant butterflies lately. She'd put on weight. She had difficulty buttoning some of her bodices. Those things couldn't mean anything, could they? Was she ill?

But she knew she wasn't. Even before the doctor uttered his next prosaic words, the truth finally dawned.

"When was your last menses? July?" At her anguished nod, he snapped his bag closed. "Well, that'll make it an April baby. Good time of the year. Not too hot, not too cold. You just make sure you get plenty of rest and drink lots of milk and you'll do fine. If you have any problems, just call for me." He glanced at the man in the bed. "You'd better make plans with the funeral home. I'll have them send someone out here if you want. There's no point in waiting until it's all over but the shouting. These things take time nowadays."

He left before Dora even had time to register his suggestions.

Carlson was dying.

She was going to have a baby.

She had always wondered how God knew to give babies only to married women.

Now she knew.

She had done what only married women should do.

Eighteen

The corruption of the age is made up by the particular contribution of every individual man; some con-
tribute treachery, others injustice, irreligion, tyranny,
avarice, cruelty, according to their power.

MONTAIGNE, "of Vanity," *Essays*

Carlson Nicholls had another attack that night and died
before he ever regained consciousness. His black mistress filled her pockets with every valuable she could
find and disappeared before dawn. Dora was left to call
the undertaker.

They waited three days to hold the funeral, sending
telegrams far and wide to scattered relatives. Josie Ann
arrived in time to attend. No word came from Pace.
They already knew Charlie couldn't come. He'd been
captured outside Atlanta and resided in a Yankee
prison camp.

Harriet Nicholls refused to attend. The December
weather was nasty, wet, and cold. She probably shouldn't
expose herself to it, but it made for a dismal turnout
when the only close relative attending was a daughter-
in-law. Dora felt sympathy for the angry old man, but
she could do naught else but pray for his immortal soul.
He had a lot of explaining to do when he reached those
pearly gates.

Dora had her own problems to cope with. Once the
house cleared of sympathetic neighbors that night, Josie
stayed behind to resume her rightful place as head of
the household, since Harriet refused the role. Now that
she knew the true cause of her thickening waist, Dora
dreaded the pending confrontation. Josie would almost
certainly be the first to notice.

Dora surreptitiously let out the seams of her gowns

so they hung on her loosely. She wore full aprons and didn't tie them tight. She felt immense. At night, before she donned her night shift, she ran her hand over her gently swelling belly and wondered at the magnitude of what she had done. She had allowed Pace to plant his seed in her, and now a child had taken fruit. She should have known that. She should have understood what they did. But Mother Elizabeth had neglected that part of her education, no doubt saving it for her wedding night.

So Dora stayed out of everyone's sight, delaying the inevitable.

Despite all their precautions, Harriet Nicholls came down with a pleurisy of the lungs and demanded around-the-clock care. Dora took on the burden gratefully, hiding herself away in the invalid's room, allowing others to carry up her meals. Josie brought Amy in once or twice a day to check on her mother-in-law, but she scarcely paid attention to Dora. Her mind was distracted by the thousand-and-one things that needed doing around the house and fields. She expressed her gratitude that Dora had taken one of them off her hands.

Pace didn't write. No one knew where he was or what he was doing. Furious at the burdens unexpectedly dropped on her shoulders, Josie wrote him a scathing letter and addressed it to his regiment. She received no reply. She should have expected none. The farm belonged to Charlie and was no concern of Pace's.

By mid-January, Harriet Nicholls had improved and the house was in such chaos that Dora felt she had no right to hide any longer. She suspected the old woman had already guessed her condition but prudently hadn't mentioned it. In only a matter of time, everyone would know. Well into her fifth month, she showed beneath all her loose skirts, if anyone cared enough to look. She could scarcely hide herself until April, and even if she could, she would have a difficult time hiding a squalling baby.

Dora briefly contemplated selling the farm and leaving town, but she was too much of a coward. If she couldn't gather enough courage to defy Pace's edict and become a nurse, she couldn't find enough to run away to a strange place where she knew no one and had no means of making a living. At least here she and the babe would have a roof over their heads and food in their mouths. It wasn't as if the scandal would ruin her nonexistent social life. She didn't think anyone in the Nicholls household would be cruel enough to put her out.

It took Josie a little while to actually notice the changes in Dora. Too many chores needed doing. They had to be in too many places at once. They spent little time in each other's company, particularly since Dora continued eating in the invalid's room as had become her habit. But one day Dora made the mistake of standing on a chair while repairing a minor rent in the heavy parlor draperies, and the bright light from the window silhouetted the shape of her figure. Josie walked in just as Dora reached to pull the final thread through the fabric.

"Dora!"

Josie's gasp nearly had Dora falling from the chair. She grabbed the drapery to steady herself and turned slowly to see what had taken Josie so aback. It didn't take long to discern the direction of Josie's gaze.

With a sigh of resignation, Dora snipped off the thread and climbed down from the chair. "I was in no danger of falling," she said dryly, responding to a caution she suspected hadn't been in Josie's cry. If Pace had been here, he would have warned her about climbing on chairs. But Pace wasn't here. She didn't know what she would do if they had word that Pace was returning. But they hadn't.

Josie looked at her uneasily, unable to broach the topic of unmarried pregnancy easily. A lady must express things delicately, but there wasn't anything delicate about Dora's condition. Cautiously, she asked, "Is David the daddy?"

That made an easy escape, but Dora had been taught not to lie. She had learned to evade the truth extremely well, however. That must be Pace's influence, or perhaps her early childhood. "David is dead," she stated flatly.

Josie gave a thoughtful nod, started to say something, then thinking better of it, just shrugged. "We'll need to look for a midwife. I'm not as talented as you." Then she twirled around and left the room.

It was a relief to finally have it out in the open. Dora went about her chores with a lighter step. She carried the child easily. The queasiness had disappeared, and she felt almost like her old self again, except for the growing movement of the child in her womb. Butterfly wings gradually became something a little stronger, but the miracle of that movement still kept her too astounded to complain. She had not only come alive again, she carried a new life within her. That knowledge terrified and thrilled her.

The only male left around the place, Solly was too easily distracted to go to town alone. Whenever they needed supplies, Josie went with him in the cart with the one horse they had left. Dora was relieved that Josie took over that burden. She had no desire to expose herself to the malicious gossip in town.

She had even given up going to Meeting. Finding transportation across the river had become too difficult long before her pregnancy had become noticeable. Now she no longer worried about explaining herself to the gentle people who had so generously taken her in. She was grateful for the new life they had given her, but she was grown now. She must find a life of her own.

But there came a day when Amy had a croupy cough, Josie was still recovering from a virulent cold, and they had no sulfur left in the house with which to complete a snuff plaster. Dora paced Amy's sickroom, alternately testing the child for fever and racking her brain for other remedies for the terrible cough. Emetics and purgatives were recommended, but she hated torturing the tiny child with such harsh treatment. She knew the snuff plaster would work, if she could just get the sulfur.

While Amy slept, Dora hurried into Josie's room to check on her recovering patient. Josie still had a hacking cough, a slight temperature, and congestion. She was improving, but not enough for venturing out into the chilly February wind. She simply had no choice. She would have to go into town herself.

Pulling a concealing cloak around her, Dora covered her head and bonnet with a hood, and borrowed a hand muff from Josie. Perhaps her invisibility would protect her. She need only go into the mercantile. On a blustery day like this, perhaps there wouldn't be too many people around.

Always eager to escape the narrow confines of the farm, Solly whistled and chattered as he drove the cart at a quick pace down the lane. Dora tried to find ease from her tension in his nonsense.

"Why hast thou stayed when all the others have left?" Dora asked him as they drew closer to town.

Solly grinned cheerfully. "I'se waiting for Marster Pace to come home. I figger I'se a free nigger right now, but I can't make no money out there with rascals just waitin' to get their hands on me and whup me back into the fields. So I'se gonna wait. Marster Pace gonna take care of me, and then I can take care of my fambly."

Dora shot him a curious look. "The farm belongs to Charles, Solly. He won't necessarily see things thy way."

Solly shrugged. "We'll see. Marster Charles ain't been home in a long time. He don' write. He might not come back. I'll wait."

A certain stubbornness prevailed behind some of Solly's immature beliefs, and Dora didn't argue with him. She was grateful that they had at least one man, or almost man, around to bear some of the burden.

She sent Solly to water the horses at the livery while she went into the mercantile. She didn't want the poor boy observing her disgrace if the town gossips started in on her as soon as she entered the store.

She found Billy John's wife behind the counter, idly knitting at a baby bonnet. Sally looked up in surprise when Dora entered, and hurried to greet her.

"It's been a coon's age since I've set eyes on you, Dora! Where've you been keepin' yourself?" Her voice lowered conspiratorially, and her eyes darted around the room to see if anyone listened. "What's Josie and Mizz Nicholls gonna do when they auction off the house? Go to live with you?"

Dora blinked rapidly, adjusting her eyes to the dim light of the store, trying to grasp the meaning of what Sally said. Cautiously, she asked, "Auction?"

Sally's face lit up like a lantern. "Haven't you heard? Billy John was fussin' on about it somethin' fierce the other night. He's certain Joe Mitchell and his daddy have got their fingers in it somehow, but we haven't got two pennies to scrape together right now, and he doesn't dare raise a ruckus against the mayor and his father. It's just like that time they tried to take Tommy McCoy's place. I'd've thought you all would have brought Pace home to take care of it by now."

Head spinning from this excess of information, or misinformation, Dora clasped her hands around the counter and sought the kernel of fact. "Are you saying they're planning on auctioning the Nichollses' place for back taxes?"

Sally nodded her head joyfully in understanding. "Isn't it awful? You'd think they'd give a poor widow woman a little while to get things together, wouldn't you?"

The child beneath her ribs did a somersault at the tension tautening Dora's muscles. "There must be some mistake. Friend Carlson always paid his bills promptly. We haven't seen any notices saying the taxes weren't paid. Wouldn't they have to send out notices?"

Sally's expression suddenly became sympathetic. "Are you still staying out there then? I thought Josie would look after the place now." She frowned slightly as she realized she'd been asked a question. "Well, I suppose they send out notices. I don't rightly know. Billy John takes care of all the paperwork."

"How did thee hear about the auction?" Dora asked patiently.

Sally brightened at being able to answer this question. "Billy John was over to the courthouse in the county seat yesterday, saw the bill posted. Said they were auctioning the place for nonpayment of taxes this afternoon. He sure would have liked to bid on it, but the taxes on a place like that are more than we make in a year. There's no tellin' how much it will go for."

Dora felt an ugly, sick feeling twisting in her stomach. This had all the evidence of Joe Mitchell's dirty dealings on it. She'd thought him a friend of Charlie's, but obviously friendship was worth sacrificing when a plum like this came available, especially when that friend was conveniently behind prison walls. She'd heard rumors of Joe buying up property around the county for little or noth-

ing. As mayor, he knew who owed what and when. And
with a district representative for father, he would have
the law on his side. No doubt they would declare the
notice of auction "lost" if anyone protested. By then,
the deed would be transferred and the opportunity lost.
She couldn't let that happen.

Dora bought the sulfur and hurried back to the cart.
Solly hadn't returned yet. That was all right. She needed
to talk to somebody, somebody on her side, or Pace's,
at least. She didn't trust Charlie's friends any farther
than she could throw them.

She hurried down the back alley praying the man she
sought still lived. It had been years since she had gone
down this road. She hoped Pace had kept in touch better
than she had.

The shack was a little more run-down than she remembered. No one had cut the autumn weeds, and they
brushed the split log sides with a dry rustle. But a lantern light glowed behind the yellowed paper window.
Someone lived there.

Uncle Jas's voice hadn't diminished with age as he
yelled for her to come in when she knocked. Hesitantly,
Dora pushed open the door and peered inside.

The old black man sat on a stool in front of the fire,
whittling at a piece of log. "Come in, chile, and close
that door. The draft is intolerable."

She slipped in and shut the door as firmly as it would
go. "I'm sorry to disturb thee, Uncle Jas."

"You ain't supposed to be here now any more than
you was when you was a chile. You don' never learn,
do you?" He shook his head, and when he looked up,
Dora could see that his eyes had grown white with disease. For all intents and purposes, Uncle Jas was blind.

She ignored his admonitions. "I need help. I don't
know where to get it."

He snorted and waved his carving knife. "So you
come to a blind old man? That's a lot of faith you
have, gal."

"Thou knowest everything that goes on around here,"
she answered accusingly. "Why didn't thee warn us of
this auction?"

Jas shrugged. "I don' owe Marster Charlie nothin'. Let him take care of his own."

"And what about Pace? That's his home too. It might not belong to him, but it's all he's got right now."

The old man's head nodded to his unspoken thoughts. "Still that way, is it? S'pose that chile is his, too?" When Dora stiffened, he just laughed. "Don't matter none to me. But I'd kindly like to see that boy Joe taken down a notch some. What do you think I can do?"

"Thou knowest Pace's friends, who to trust. If I can just keep Joe from that auction, I might halt it or do something to keep the place from being sold."

Jas looked at her shrewdly. "Wouldn't paying the taxes be easiest?"

"I thought of that. Today's Saturday. City Hall isn't open. I'd wager that notice never got posted until yesterday for just that reason. If Joe isn't there, I might persuade them to take the tax money at the courthouse."

"That's a long old ride to the courthouse. You could hurt that babe."

"I'm fine. I'm healthy. I can do it. I just can't let Joe get away with this. Someone must stop this nastiness. If we don't, he'll own the whole town."

Jas shrugged. "Far's I can see, he and his papa already does, but that ain't none of my concern. I cain't vote against the rascals. I cain't own property they can take. I ain't even supposed to live here like I do. But I'll do it this time, for Pace. He's a might wild, but his heart's always been in the right place. You go on now and get yourself over to the courthouse. I'll see what I can do about Joe."

"I thank thee," Dora whispered in relief before fleeing out the door and back up the alley.

Solly was loitering about the street, staring in shop windows when Dora returned to the main road. He looked up in surprise when she hailed him, but he was all seriousness when she ordered him to hurry home. She would send some of the smoked ham in the shed to Uncle Jas in return for his help. And a basket of jellies. If he could pull this off, she would see that he never worried about food again.

When they came in sight of the house, she ordered,

"Give the mare some grain when we get there, Solly, but don't unhitch her. We're going to the county seat just as soon as I can run in the house and come out again."

"Somethin' the matter, Miz Dora?"

"Something bad's the matter, Solly, and thou wilt have to help me stop it."

He stayed silent for the rest of the ride, concentrating on reaching the house as quickly as possible. He didn't ask questions and Dora didn't explain. They would have time enough for that later.

For now, she had to find enough money to pay the taxes.

Nineteen

There is no courage but in innocence;
No constancy, but in an honest cause.

THOMAS SOUTHERN, *Fate of Capua*

Dora clasped her chilled hands and the little bag of federal notes, hoarded gold, and receipts inside Josie's muff as the rude wooden cart rattled down the winter-ravaged road. She was shaking inside, but the jolting of the cart had little to do with it.

The Nichollses' place had become as much a home to her as her own small farm. It was Pace's birthplace, Amy's home. It still supported a half dozen slaves as well as Pace's mother. Furnishings carefully carried over the mountains from Virginia by earlier generations filled the rooms, along with the expensive china and carpets and other luxuries acquired in the years since then. It was a true home, a shelter for generations of family. It would be a sin to have all that destroyed by one greedy man. It would be a sin for Charlie and Pace to come home to nothing.

But the burden of saving an entire farm weighed heavier than Dora's shoulders could bear. She had searched Carlson's desk for tax receipts. She had found his small drawer of coins and added her own, along with the money from the horses. Still, she shook inside, knowing her inability to deal with problems as serious as this one. Assuming such responsibility terrified her. She had always had help, had always drifted into things without really taking on the responsibility of decision. The only things she had actually done on her own had all been wrong. The burden she carried inside her now was evidence enough of that. She was too ignorant to do the right thing. The men at the courthouse would eat her alive. Her nightmares reminded her too clearly of what happened when weak women like her mother took matters in their own hands. What made her think she could do any better?

But she simply could not just stand by and do nothing. She had done that for years, just letting things happen and following their course. She no longer had the luxury of assuming someone would take care of everything for her. She had no one left to turn to but herself. She knew better than anyone that Pace most likely wouldn't return, and Charlie couldn't. They had no one. And now she had a child to look out for. She must learn to be strong and go out into the world on her own.

Nervously, Dora twitched the gold band she had placed on her finger. She wasn't in the habit of wearing jewelry. She certainly wouldn't flaunt Pace's ring in front of his family. But she needed the support it gave her right now. She was not yet strong enough to go among strangers without this tiny symbol of Pace's protection. Even though she knew she stood alone, the ring felt right on her finger. A simple symbol couldn't hurt.

Solly slowed the cart and spoke warily, "They's somethin' goin' on up ahead, Miz Dora. Looks like trouble. Mebbe we ought to turn 'round and go 'nother way."

They traveled the main highway to the courthouse. Little better than frozen mud and ruts, this road was still the fastest, safest route, and she didn't have time for the bends and turnabouts of unknown lanes. She twisted at the bag inside the muff and strained to see the activity in the road beyond that stand of trees.

Masked highwaymen! Her heart jolted beneath her ribs, and the babe in her womb turned a dozen somersaults, causing her to catch her breath. There couldn't be more than three or four of them, all on horseback. In broad daylight! It didn't make sense.

She rested her hand on Solly's arm to slow him down. Whoever they were, they hadn't noticed the cart yet, hidden as it was behind a wooded bend in the road. Engrossed in their depredations, they didn't pay attention to what happened behind them.

Screams of fury came from somewhere beyond the circle of masked men. She couldn't see through the gaps between them. Their horses jostled each other, and Dora caught a glimpse of a pistol in the hand of one man as he struggled to keep his mount under control. She squeezed her hand tighter around Solly's arm in warning.

"You can't do this!" somebody screamed. "I've got business at the courthouse! You can't stop me. I'll have you all hung!"

Dora closed her eyes in fervent prayer as she recognized the voice. Joe Mitchell. It had to be Joe. She hadn't seen him around since Charlie left, but she'd been the object of his taunts enough in the past to know his voice without need of seeing him. She released Solly's arm and nodded. "It's all right. Keep going."

Solly gave her an incredulous look but did as told, his eyes wide with curiosity as the cart creaked and rattled into the bend.

Dora began singing loudly, alerting the men ahead of their presence in case their business entertained them too much to hear the cart and horse. By the time the cart came around the curve, only one horse and rider remained on the road. No sign of a mask or highwaymen remained, although the horseman had a rifle resting loosely across his saddle. Dora recognized Tommy McCoy's younger brother, Robert, and she stopped singing to give him a faint smile of greeting.

"Heading my way, Miss Smythe?" he called in response to her hello. "I'm going in for court day."

She nodded gravely. "I'd be happy of the company, Friend, if thou doth not mind the pace."

"I mind Pace well enough," he assured her ambiguously. The capital letter in "pace" was distinct in his emphasis. "There's rascals on this road often enough. A lady shouldn't travel alone. I'll be happy to keep you company."

They both knew what he had just done. The unbuckled rifle alone spoke of trouble. These were perilous times for man or woman. Dora tried behaving as if Robert's company had no significance, but she couldn't help saying with some concern, "I do not wish for thee to find trouble."

Had anyone overheard, they would find the conversation stilted but not inappropriate. Dora trusted Solly, but Robert didn't know him, and sometimes even the trees had ears. Even now, somewhere behind the flimsy stand of sassafras, sumac, and dead vines lining the road, masked men held their victim captive. It wouldn't do for any of them to know just how involved she might be with the incident.

"Trouble finds me more often than not," Robert replied carelessly. The cart had moved far enough down the road that he could speak a little louder without fear of his companions hearing. "I haven't much left to lose."

Dora glanced at him swiftly. He was younger than Pace by a few years, a slightly built man with a reddish mustache and hair already threatening to recede. But he held his shoulders straight and rode his horse with ease, exuding a degree of pride and male arrogance that brought a smile to her lips. She knew very little of Pace's friends, but she should have known they would match his arrogance.

"I was sorry to hear of thy brother," she finally answered, the smile slipping away. "He was not treated fairly."

Robert shrugged. "They drove him into thievery. He may not have committed the crime they hung him for, but he committed others. It was just a matter of time. Mostly I just want to see other criminals around here get the same treatment."

That was a perfectly innocuous statement that any law-abiding citizen might make, but Dora heard the tense undercurrent behind it. He held Joe Mitchell responsible for the McCoy family problems. Charlie's band of Home Guards had seen Tommy McCoy arrested. Neither Joe nor Charlie was precisely innocent of all wrongdoing; they were just a little more refined in their thievery and had never been caught. Dora understood that. But Robert's reply made her shiver.

"Thou canst not take the law into thy own hands," she admonished.

He gave her an amused look. "No? Seems to me that's

what's been happening for some time now, but it hasn't been me or mine responsible for it. Nor yours, either, from the sounds of it."

Dora heard the gentle reproof in his words and held her tongue. If she understood what had just happened here, Robert and his friends had stopped Joe Mitchell from reaching the courthouse for her. Spitefully, she hoped they had taken Joe's money as well as holding him hostage. Lately, she had found herself saying the things she had been taught but thinking of bitter, worldly things. Was this the result of daring the world on her own?

The conversation became desultory as they approached the crowded county seat. Court day always drew crowds. Solly dodged other farm carts laden with hay or winter greens or jars of canned goods. Robert helped him find a place to tie the horse on the back side of the court square, down a street, away from the line of horses and mules tied up by owners looking to trade or sell.

Dora's hands clenched even more nervously inside her muff as she realized the moment had come. Keeping one hand and her small bag of money inside the muff, she took Robert's offered hand with her other and climbed down from the cart. If he noticed her girth when the cloak swung outward, he said nothing. A gentleman wouldn't.

Setting her teeth and jutting her chin forward, she marched down the unpaved back street in the direction of the spire-topped courthouse. The clock in the tower donged three o'clock. What if they were too late?

Robert stayed at her side; Solly remained a step behind them. She found their presence vaguely reassuring, but she didn't think they knew where she should go any more than she did. Several farmers stepped out of her way as Robert guided her through the crowds standing and gossiping in the street, but nobody paid any particular attention to her. Nobody should. No one knew her here.

"The auction is usually held from the courthouse steps," Robert whispered near her ear. "We'll go around there."

Dora nodded in understanding. She had both hands inside her muff again, as if holding her own hand would help. Her heart pounded furiously, and she was thankful the weakness that had made her faint early in her pregnancy had passed. She needed all her faculties about her now.

An ominously empty circle opened in front of the courthouse steps once they fought their way through the crowds to get there. A small clump of men stood on one side, chewing and smoking, exchanging small talk. Wearing galluses and felt hats, they didn't seem very dangerous, but Dora kept a wary eye on them. Only these men stood near enough to the steps to follow the auction.

"Is there time for me to find the sheriff and pay the taxes?" she asked Robert nervously.

"I'd say not, Miss Dora," Robert replied resignedly, taking in the gathering group of men on the lawn. "That's the sheriff over there. They've already started."

Dora's eyes widened as he hurried her across the lawn toward the small group of men. She'd seen auctions before. They were loud and boisterous with much yelling of prices and persuasive selling. She didn't hear anything at all here.

"Two thousand dollars, boys, that's the price." A man wearing a black derby rocked back on his heels, waving a paper with one hand and gripping his suspender strap with the other. He didn't seem much interested in selling. His gaze drifted out across the crowd, seeing Dora and passing over her in search of something or someone more interesting.

"That's ridiculous, Harley," one of the listeners protested. "Nobody pays those kind of taxes."

The man in the derby shrugged. "Taxes ain't been paid for a while. Then there's interest and whatnot. Gotta cover costs, boys. These are hard times. I've got a couple of smaller places here. Want to look at them?"

While the men gathered around to look at the sheaf of papers he produced, Dora crept closer to the man Robert had indicated as sheriff. Hesitantly, while the others were distracted, she asked, "Sheriff?"

The man in the derby turned and glared at her. "This ain't no place for women. Can't you see I'm busy?"

Robert elbowed a man out of his way so he could stand beside her. "She's come to inquire about the Nicholls place. There's some mistake about the taxes. Mr. Nicholls passed away in December, but he always paid his bills on time."

The sheriff's bushy eyebrows drew upward as he looked down at Dora in her gray cloak and hood, then glared at Robert. "Well, I've got papers here that say he ain't. We don't auction off people's property without reason."

Timidly, still hiding behind Robert's bulk, Dora produced the little stack of papers she had found in Carlson's desk. "These look like receipts to me, sir. I don't see one for this year, but I looked and couldn't find a bill either. If thou couldst tell me how much is owed, I will make the payment."

The sheriff growled and grabbed the papers. The farmers shuffling through the other items up for auction lost interest in the small lots. Hearing the sounds of contention, they crowded a little closer. The sheriff elbowed a man peering over his shoulder, but everyone had already seen the distinctive receipts. He grudgingly handed them back to Dora.

"These look in order, ma'am," he said reluctantly. "I'll consult with the proper authorities, of course, but that don't take care of this year's taxes. I'm sorry for the widow, but the law's the law. She's got to sign the papers when she pays the bill. If she ain't here, then I've got no choice but to sell the place."

"I can pay the bill," Dora said quietly, her voice shaking. She sensed the sheriff's resistance while he waited for someone in authority to tell him what to do. She suspected that someone was Joe, mayor of the town where the bill would be collected. Joe wasn't going to arrive, but she didn't know if that would help her predicament.

"You ain't the widow, are you?" the sheriff asked belligerently.

"No, but Friend Carlson's son inherited. He's in—"

Robert interrupted. "He's fighting for the cause, Sher-

iff, and can't be here right now. This here's his wife.
She can sign your blamed papers. You ain't got no right
keeping women and children from their proper homes
while their husbands, sons, and fathers are fighting for
our constitutional rights. Just tell her how much it is,
and we'll be out of here."

Dora gasped at this outright lie. Josie was sick in bed
back home. She couldn't sign Josie's name. She certainly
couldn't sign Charlie's name. And Charlie wasn't fighting; he was rotting in a federal prison. And Pace certainly wasn't fighting for what these men stood for. But
the sheriff finally looked at her for the first time, seeing
her clearly. To her horror, she realized she rested the
hand with Pace's ring on it across her distended abdomen. Perhaps she had done it out of instinct, to protect
the child, but that instinct gave all these men the wrong
idea. She wasn't married. The ring didn't belong to her.
The babe had no name. How could she blurt such calum-
nies to a crowd of strangers?

The sheriff glanced nervously around, seeing no one
coming to his rescue. The farmers around him watched
expectantly, spitting their tobacco juice at the ground,
and waiting. The sheriff was an elected official. An incident like this could break him. He wavered, until one of
the older men finally said in a wry tone, "Looks to me
like if she's got the receipts, you ain't got a case, Harley.
Let her pay what's owed and let's get on with this."

The sheriff's belligerence collapsed like a balloon. He
made some hurried calculations on the bill and stated
an amount. Horrified at the number, Dora still started
drawing her bag of coins out, but the gray-haired
stranger grabbed the bill and looked it over.

"You cain't go collectin' interest on money that's been
paid, Harley. The lady don't owe half that amount." He
struck out a few more figures and came up with a new
total, handing it to Robert for inspection.

Dora had a suspicion that Robert couldn't make heads
or tails of the figures, but she let him nod importantly
over it before taking it from his fingers to look at it
herself. She studied the prior-year figures the sheriff had
crossed off, decided the new amount wasn't much different, checked her receipts to make certain they agreed,

then cautiously withdrew her bag of money. She was starting to learn a little about dealing with these people.

"The Yankees gave us these notes for the horses. Will they do?" she asked in a deliberately plaintive note. If she had these men on her side now, she darn well meant to hang on to the gold.

The sheriff frowned and started to protest, but Robert took the notes from her hand and counted them out. He shoved them in the sheriff's hand and demanded a receipt.

They had to go inside the courthouse for that. The men grumbled at the delay, but allowed as how the little lady ought to have a receipt. Dora shook all over again when they were inside and the sheriff produced a paper for her to sign, but she forced her fingers to the task. The only exception she took was to sign it "Mrs. Pace Nicholls" instead of with Charlie's name. She didn't know how that would affect the legalities of the transaction, but it looked to her like the law had been twisted so many ways by now that it wouldn't make much difference if it took another turn or two.

She almost collapsed in a heap when the sheriff rolled up the paper and handed it to her with the words, "Here's the deed, Mrs. Nicholls. Looks like you bought yourself a farm."

Twenty

Horror and doubt distract
His troubled thoughts, and from the bottom stir
The hell within him; for within him hell
He brings, and round about him, nor from hell
One step no more than from himself can fly
By change of place.

JOHN MILTON, Paradise Lost

"I can't take a deed," Dora whispered in horror as Robert hurried her out of the courthouse. "The farm belongs to Charlie."

"Not anymore," Robert chortled. "You just bought it at auction. Harley ain't too bright. He only knows one method of handling the transaction. Charlie didn't pay the taxes on time, so he sold the farm to you."

"That's not right!" Dora protested as Solly fell in step with them behind the courthouse. "I have to do something."

Robert shrugged. "You don't have to do anything right now. Mitchell can't get his hands on the property, and that was our main purpose in coming here. Whenever Charlie gets home, you can arrange something with him. Transferring a deed isn't any big deal. Let's just get out of here before the boys let Joe go."

That made sense. Leaving hurriedly without straightening out the mistake began to seem like the wisest thing to do. She wasn't particularly interested in crossing Joe Mitchell when he discovered what had happened. Of course, if Joe made too many inquiries, he might discover the false deed. Dora began to pray as she climbed into the cart.

"I signed Pace's name," she whispered miserably as Robert rode his horse up next to the cart to guide Solly into the traffic of passing horses and pedestrians.

Robert shrugged again. "Good. Let Pace settle it. I

apologize for not knowing the two of you got hitched,
but I wasn't around the last time Pace was in town. I
don't keep up with gossip much. How's he doing?"

She had never lied in her life, and now a sticky web
of deceit had her caught. She wasn't ready for the real
world yet. She needed Papa John's advice, but she already knew what he would say. She should never have
signed Pace's name.

"We haven't heard from him," she answered truth-
fully. "Thou needs not follow us if thou wishes to stay
for court day," she added for good measure. Her conscience was horrid enough company without adding another witness to her lie.

"It's not a good idea for a woman to travel alone. I
haven't got any money to buy anything with, anyhow."

Dora thought guiltily of the coins still in her purse.
"Could I pay thee for thy services today?" she asked
hesitantly. "I could never have done it without thee."

Robert grinned cheerfully. "I would gladly have paid
you for the entertainment. Joe will be a long time living
this one down, bested by a woman! Ask me to dinner
and tell Pace the score is even."

She would have to write Pace and warn him what she
had done. She didn't know if she could commit such sin
to a piece of paper. She would have time enough to
think of it when she got home.

But when she got home, she had dinner to fix and
Amy's cough to see to. Friend Harriet had had a restless
day and needed comforting. Dora meant to tell Josie,
but Josie had relatives visiting and wasn't interested in
business details. She stayed up entertaining Robert after
dinner, while Dora retired to the sickrooms.

Dora's bed seemed lonelier than ever when she retired
to it that night. She wished she could return to her own
house, sleep in the bed where she had slept with Pace,
but it wasn't safe there alone. She needed someone to
talk to, someone to tell her she had done the right thing,
but she couldn't silence her nagging conscience. A lie of
omission was still a lie, and her signature on that deed
was a forgery.

She couldn't change it now. The sheriff's men couldn't

throw them out. She would comfort herself with that thought.

Handsome dark hair fading to gray, the earl lay against the pillows, breathing heavily through lungs clogged by disease. The heavy velvet curtains draping his bed had frayed at the edges, just as much of the expensively decorated room showed signs of wear and age. The draperies pulled over the windows kept the sun from betraying too much of the decay.

"Find her," the ill man ordered from his bed, crumpling the old letter between his fingers as he thumped his fist against the covers. "Find her and bring her here."

The younger man paced restlessly across the once-elegant carpet. He had discarded his coat and cravat, and his linen shirt was improperly open at the throat. The sullen features of youth had coarsened with age. Thick pouting lips now looked more cruel than sensual. Hooded eyes turned with irritation to the man in the bed.

"Don't you think I'm trying? They're waging a bloody war over there. It takes weeks, months, to get messages through. The last one must have got lost somewhere. My investigator broke his damned leg getting on the boat. It's been one hellish problem after another."

"Go yourself," the invalid commanded hoarsely. "Go, and bring her back to me."

Like bloody hell, I would, Gareth thought vengefully, scowling as he slammed out of the room. If it weren't for the old lady's will, he wouldn't look at all. He just wanted to get his hands on the bitch long enough to pry the money away, then she could drown herself all over again.

Or maybe he would do it for her.

Gareth's agile mind immediately worked its way through several interesting possibilities.

Pace felt the heat of the sun boiling his uncapped hair as, stomach churning, he gazed down at the broken figure of the small boy at his feet. The child couldn't have been more than five or six. He would never see seven. Blood seeped from the crack in his skull.

His glance returned to the path of destruction he had already observed when he rode up. He had hoped to find the boy alive at first. Now he had little hope of finding any survivors. His stomach writhed with the horror of what he saw now, of what he had seen every day over these past weeks. War had turned men into animals.

His men stirred restlessly behind him, and Pace pressed himself to continue up the drive to a small farmhouse. Sherman was bent on destroying the symbols of wealth and slavery in his march across Georgia, but Sherman wasn't responsible for this. This lowly farmhouse held nothing of interest to an army on the move. It reminded Pace of Dora's home, two-stories of love and family with flowers outside the front door. They had no slaves here. No riches. Just a lone woman and her children, struggling to survive without the men in their family.

The woman lay in a bundle of worn cotton and twisted petticoats. Pace could tell by the way she lay sprawled across the grass that she hadn't died slowly or peacefully. The bloodthirsty animals running from Sherman's army had satisfied all their hungers here. Pace couldn't tell whether the attack came from deserters from his own side or the other. It scarcely mattered. Dead was dead, no matter who took that life.

He threw his coat over the fair face and cascade of golden hair and shivered. The cold February wind didn't cause his shiver. He thought of Dora living in her farmhouse alone. Charlie would no doubt return to the farm any day now. She wouldn't like staying in the same house with him. Pace didn't like the comparisons between what he saw now and what he'd left behind.

Pace finally retched and threw up the bilious contents of his stomach when he reached the old lady. No human being should suffer the degradations committed on her wrinkled old body. A person should be allowed some dignity after a lifetime of quiet living. He'd wager this gray-haired old woman had never harmed a soul in her life. Hundreds of thousands of people out there committed sins every day. Why hadn't they been subjected to this humiliation and agony?

The frozen look of horror on her face stayed with him long after his men had dug shallow graves and buried the bodies. Pace ordered crosses marking the graves in case some poor man should wander home and wonder where his women had gone. But chances were good that man would never return, as thousands would never return. This was the land of the dead.

Even though he walked through hell, Pace still didn't quit. He'd signed on to do a job, and he hadn't finished it. Lee still wreaked havoc in the East. Despite his damaged arm, Pace calculated he wasn't completely useless to the war. He would be if he went home.

Not until the day he took his rest beneath a pecan tree, closing his eyes as the young boy who usually rode beside him took a leak in the shrubbery, did Pace face his future and know his failure.

He heard them coming. That was the terrible part of it. If he'd fallen asleep, he could have excused his ineptitude, but he heard them. They were too far away for his pistol. He reached for his rifle, but he'd laid it on his right side and his arm wouldn't make the stretch. The first bullets rang out as he turned to grab the rifle with his left hand. The piercing scream of the young soldier who had trusted Pace to guard his back decimated whatever soul remained within him.

Somehow, Pace aimed the rifle and shot the bastards. The repeating action undoubtedly saved his life. There were four of them, and two lay dead before the rest of his troop came riding up. The men rode hard after the other two and brought them down, but Pace had gone beyond caring by then. The young soldier in the bushes died in his arm. His one arm. The useless one could scarcely hold the boy.

He had filed his request for discharge by the time the letter arrived.

Pace had read some of the earlier letters from home when they caught up with him. He'd received the telegram notifying him of his father's death, but he wasn't hypocrite enough to attend the funeral. His father had despised him in life; he had no reason to believe he would want him around in death. He'd held Josie's letter for a few days before opening it. He no longer felt any emotion for the girl he'd thought to marry, but she could still wreak havoc with his thoughts. When he eventually read the letter, her tirade was an anticlimax, and he threw it in the fire.

Dora's letter, on the other hand, frightened the hell out of him before he even opened it. Pace knew Dora well enough to know she wouldn't write unless it was important, not unless he wrote her first, and he hadn't. He didn't want to hear her admonishments for leaving a household of women alone and undefended. He'd heard of Charlie's imprisonment. It didn't matter anymore. Nothing mattered. Charlie would come home. Dora had her farm. They wouldn't need him. He didn't want to know any more than that. He didn't want to think she had any more than that to say to him. He wasn't the man she thought he was.

He eventually burned that letter without reading it. He was doing his damnedest to come to terms with the fact that he no longer had a home. His father was dead and the farm belonged to Charlie. He had no reason to rescue what wasn't his. He had a future of his own to carve out of the ruins of his life. The political situation in Kentucky had already made it plain no one would welcome a returning Union soldier with open arms. Any hopes of a political career had evaporated. The army wasn't precisely his choice, but he had possibilities with the army that he didn't have at home.

But the death of that boy soldier and his inability to react quickly in a dangerous situation put a period to Pace's army career, even if he hadn't lost the desire for it. Death and destruction had seared his soul until he had nothing left. He was worn out, burned out, and a hollow, rotten shell by the time the last letter arrived. He didn't much care what he found inside this new envelope.

The news that Charlie had died in prison didn't even touch him.

Pace calmly folded the letter and shoved it into his inside coat pocket where he had just tucked his discharge papers. He shook the hand of the officer who had handed it to him, walked out of the hotel in Nashville where the office was stationed, and headed for the nearest saloon.

He sat in one corner and quietly drank himself into a stupor all night. He woke the next morning beside a blowzy brunette who whispered sweet nothings in his ear and tried to earn her keep. Pace lay back against the pillow contemplating her oversize breasts with their flat dark nipples and couldn't find any desire in him. He'd gone without a woman since Dora. He should feel some physical reaction. He felt nothing.

The woman finally took herself off in a flurry of muttered imprecations which didn't improve any when she discovered he had next to nothing in the way of money. He'd sent the last of his pay home to the family of the boy who had died because of him.

Closing his eyes against the raging pain in his head, Pace allowed memories of Charlie to creep in. Charlie had always been there for as long as he could remember. Handsome, well-behaved, easygoing Charlie, the apple of his father's eye. The son who could do no wrong. The perfect son with the perfect wife. Josie was a widow now. Josie owned the farm.

Those thoughts didn't ease the raging pain. Pulling his clothes on, Pace staggered down the stairs and back into the bar. He could gamble his last few coins into a bottle of whiskey without too much trouble.

In the end, one of his men found him passed out in the street and poured him onto the next train going north. All the trains going north out of Nashville went to Kentucky.

Pace expressed his displeasure vehemently when the conductor woke him from a drunken stupor insisting they'd arrived at his station. He staggered off the train rather than argue. His only problem, when he stood on the wooden station platform and watched the train pull out, was that he didn't know where the hell he was.

He considered it a minute. Most of the effects of the whiskey had worn off. For the moment, he couldn't quite remember why he'd got drunk. The more pressing problem of his current location had his mind occupied.

He was out of uniform. The coat he wore was un-

pressed and stank. Pace rubbed his hand over his jaw
and concluded he had a three-days' growth at least. His
head pounded and his arm ached. He stuck his hands in
his pockets and came up empty.

A shout from behind him went ignored until it finally
sank in that they addressed him.

"Hey, mister! Is this yor'n?"

Pace turned and noted the horse before discovering
his interrogator. The horse was his, all right. Someone
had looked out for him. The last time he remembered
seeing the gelding, he had stabled it in Nashville. He
tried to remember putting it on a train, but the memory
failed him.

He staggered over and grabbed the animal's reins.
Gallant yanked his head up and down in greeting, then
shoved his nose at Pace's pockets, looking for a treat.
He found a grubby horehound and offered it while gri-
macing at the stationmaster.

"Yeah, he's mine. Where in hell am I?"

Discovering he had arrived at a station only twenty
miles from home didn't make him any happier. No
doubt some good-hearted soul had thought to take care
of him, but Pace would have liked it a lot better if they'd
just left him in the gutter. He didn't want to go back
there, to that house full of obligations that had never
belonged to him, weren't meant for him. Let Josie find
herself a new husband to take care of the place. He
wasn't inclined to oblige anymore, even if marrying Josie
meant that the house he called home would finally be
his.

But he found himself climbing on the horse and turning it in the direction of the farm. There just didn't seem
any way of avoiding it, and he didn't know anywhere
else to go.

He didn't allow himself to think as the horse ambled
down the road at its own pace. He had a pounding hang-
over, an empty stomach, empty pockets, and a useless
arm. If he thought about it, he'd realize he was dead
broke with a wrecked career and no home of his own.
Most of his family had died, his friends were probably
no better off than he, that is, if they lived at all.

He had proposed marriage to one of the women waiting for him and bedded the other. Thinking about Dora made him doubly uncomfortable. He'd done her wrong and he had no means of making it right. He'd sent her beau off to be killed, taken her innocence, and offered her nothing in return. He was a useless piece of wreckage. Dora deserved someone whole in body as well as spirit. He could offer her neither. The best thing he could do for her was stay the hell away. He might be cynical enough to offer Josie the wreckage of what he'd once been, but not Dora. Maybe he should turn this mount around and head for Lexington.

But he kept down the same road. He rode all night since he didn't have money for lodging. He stopped long enough to rest his mount and bathe briefly in a creek. March had just swept in, and the water was cold as hell. The sting took away some of the pain, but he was too tired and hungry to really appreciate the difference.

He was practically asleep in his saddle as dawn rose and his surroundings became increasingly familiar. Pace looked longingly at Dora's little farmhouse, but he couldn't tell if she lived there or not. He'd best not take chances. She would likely shoot him for a burglar if he came staggering through the door like this.

Not Dora, he corrected himself. She wouldn't have a gun. Remembering that, he smiled a little, but he kept on going. He needed the rest that little house offered, and he knew where she kept the key, but he couldn't do that to her. He had to confront her properly first.

Pace cut across the field rather than go up the lane. No one had laid out the tobacco bed. He saw no sign of spring plowing, but maybe it had been too wet. The sun shone now though, and the field seemed dry enough. Someone should be up and stirring, getting out the plow before the next spring storm arrived. These conditions didn't last forever this time of year.

As the house loomed closer, he only saw one figure out and about. A straggly trail of smoke came from the kitchen chimney, so perhaps someone else was up and just not visible. Pace strained his eyes to see who would hoe the kitchen garden this early in the morning, but the shape was unfamiliar.

The white bonnet was not.

Pace's gaze frantically swept the gray landscape, taking in the burgeoning tree buds, a scattering of daffodils, looking anywhere but at the cumbersome figure hoeing the garden. Awful curiosity drew his gaze back to those bulky skirts. His eyes rose again to take in the old-fashioned bonnet. He rode closer, his stomach suddenly clenching in violent knots.

The bonnet came up at the sound of his horse. Her fingers tightened around the hoe handle as she straightened when he rode through the back gate.

Dora.

Pace's gaze dropped to the full curve of her belly beneath the pristine white apron. Dora, pregnant. With child. His child. That awful certainty knotted beneath his breast.

He clenched the reins tighter and tried not to stare, but his attempt came too late. Her cold gaze warned she'd already noted his horror. Her expression wasn't any more welcoming than his when he dismounted.

Twenty-one

They have ty'd me to a stake; I cannot fly,
But bear-like, I must fight the course.

SHAKESPEARE, *Macbeth*

A cold wind seemed to blow right through him as Pace dismounted and walked toward Dora. The color had leeched from her face, and her features looked pale and lifeless beneath the enormous bonnet. Mud and grass stained her hands from pulling the more stubborn weeds. Beneath the mud, her fingernails were cracked and broken. Dora never had been one for a lady's graces. She'd never aspired to become a politician's wife.

This was the woman he had plowed and planted with his seed. Pace still hadn't recovered from the shock. Reluctantly, he dropped his gaze to the distended curve beneath her skirt, and he tried imagining his child growing there. His imagination failed him. He didn't feel alive enough to create anything.

His brain still didn't spin correctly. The first thing he said was "Mine," without a question mark after it, a statement of ownership. She didn't confirm or deny. She didn't need to. Dora had been a part of his life since childhood. Despite the gap between them, Pace knew her as well as he knew himself. Which wasn't saying much. He just knew the child could never belong to anyone else.

Since she wasn't speaking to him, either in anger or welcome, Pace ran a shaking hand through his hair and said, "I haven't eaten. Is there any breakfast left?"

With an enigmatic look, Dora returned to her hoeing. "In the kitchen," was her only reply.

Pace took himself off to the washhouse to clean up. He changed into wrinkled but clean clothes from his saddlebags. He found some biscuits and bacon keeping warm in the kitchen, although he saw no sign of a cook. With reluctance, he forced himself into the house to greet whatever remnants of the household remained. His mind, however, stayed on the problem of the woman in the garden beyond these walls.

His mother greeted him as if he'd never left, scolding him for wearing a wrinkled coat, complaining her breakfast was cold. Pace sat through her selfish diatribes without listening. His hands kept spinning his hat around and around while his thoughts whirled helplessly.

He knew what was required of him, what he was honor bound to do. Dora wasn't a lady of his own class like Josie, but she was an honest woman, and he had taken her to bed and given her his child. If she'd been a Negro slave or a loose white woman, he'd feel no obligation, but he had taken her innocence. He had no choice but to pay the consequences.

Only it was Dora who would really pay the consequences, no matter what he did. He would make a poor excuse for a husband. He owned nothing, had no future. He didn't even know how to operate her pitiful little farm for a profit. He doubted his ability to do any better at fatherhood than his own had. He had no example but his father to follow. He wouldn't wish that on any child. As a husband, he would no doubt be worse. At least his own father had land and the knowledge to build on it. He didn't even have that.

Despite the black spiral of his doubts, Pace knew he had no choice. He had to offer her the protection of his name, if nothing else. Dora wouldn't find any other suitors now, not after carrying a bastard. That alone destroyed any hopes she might have entertained of making a good match. Marriage wouldn't improve her situation by much, but if she was lucky, he would drop dead or get killed, and she could call herself a widow. Maybe he would just disappear from her life after the baby's birth, and she could call herself widow anyway.

That seemed a halfway reasonable solution. Pace rose

abruptly in the middle of one of his mother's complaints and started for the door.

He found Dora in the henhouse. She had washed her hands and covered herself with one of her blasted aprons. She carried a basket to gather the eggs in, but she'd only found a couple. For the first time since his arrival, Pace felt a wry sense of relief. If she started throwing things at him, she wouldn't have much ammunition.

"There's a preacher over in the county seat who will marry us, no questions asked. Can you travel that far?"

She looked up at him then, her fine blue eyes regarding him gravely. Pace wanted to wiggle with discomfort like a schoolboy caught chewing gum, but he managed to retain some sense of decorum. He would have liked to have done better than proposing in a henhouse, but now that he'd made the decision, he felt a sense of urgency to have it done with. He didn't know much about having babies, but this one looked as if it could arrive any minute.

"Thou needn't make such a sacrifice," Dora answered dryly. "Everyone assumes the child is David's."

He hadn't thought she would refuse him. Pace stared at her in confusion. She serenely returned to her egg-gathering as if that ended the subject. Anger began to take the place of wisdom. "The child is mine. I have the right to claim him."

She glanced up at him, as if in surprise to find him still there. To her credit, she merely replied, "I will not deny thee that right."

"Then you will allow me to give him my name," he said in satisfaction.

She shrugged as she straightened to look at him again. "Thou mayest call him anything thou wishes."

Pace gritted his teeth in frustration. "Legally. I want him to have my name legally. That means we must wed."

She was back to regarding him as if he were some strange species of animal. "That is foolish. Thou doth not wish to marry me. Josie is a widow now. It would be best for all if thou marries her and settles down. This place needs a man's hand."

Pace slammed his fist against the wooden wall, shaking

the flimsy building and sending the hens flapping and squawking in riotous cacophony across the floor. Dora dodged the panicked birds and eased toward the door, an uneasy expression he'd never seen before flitting across her face.

Annoyed at her look of fear, Pace grabbed Dora's arm and hauled her into the sunshine. "To hell with Josie. To hell with the damned land. That's my child, and I mean to claim it. If you can't travel, I'll fetch the preacher. Just get yourself gussied up and ready. I'm not having that babe born a bastard."

Finally, she seemed to take him seriously. She quit struggling against his hold, but her expression remained cold and wary as she studied his face. "Thou canst not mean that," she said slowly. "Thou hath a future that cannot include me. I cannot be a politician's wife. I doubt that I can be a lawyer's wife. Thou liveth in a different world. Thou mayest claim the child if it means so much to thee. I never wished to keep him from thee. Thou mayest adopt him, as Papa John adopted me. There is no need for us to marry and ruin thy career."

An overwhelming urge to weep swept over him. Pace turned his eyes up to the approaching gray clouds and fought against the bitter tears of despair stinging them, not knowing where they came from. Fighting the bleakness seeping through him at her words, he returned his gaze to Dora, forcing a blank expression, hiding the tearing agony of knowing even his guardian angel didn't want him.

He released her arm and shoved the awful bonnet from her hair. Silver curls gleamed in the sunlight. Blindly grasping for a last thread of salvation, Pace took a deep breath and answered without inflection, "I have no career. The voters would rather hang a Union man than see one in office. I can't see that changing anytime soon. I can put out a shingle and write wills and deeds, but the people around here aren't likely to forgive my politics. We'll probably starve on what I can make if I stay here. You're better off staying with Josie and my mother while I look for a place elsewhere. I would feel better if you carried my name under those circumstances. You are the innocent party. I don't want you exposed to scorn on my account. You have as much right to the name of Nicholls as Josie and my mother."

Pace could feel her studying him in that otherworldly way of hers. Sometimes, it made him feel like God looked directly through her eyes. It made him nervous and uncomfortable, for good reason. At the same time, Pace felt as if her judgment would see all sides, would see what he could not. He expected her to be fair, not human. It was an irrational expectation, he knew, but Dora hadn't failed him yet.

Her forehead wrinkled slightly in consternation as she took his words and processed them through whatever knowledge and information she possessed that might change or contradict his declarations. Pace could almost literally see when she recognized that he was not engaging in self-pity, that there was a decided modicum of truth in what he said. She glanced up at him with eyes filled with worry.

"Where would thee go?"

That wasn't the question he had expected. Sighing with frustration, running his hand through his already disheveled hair, Pace glanced nervously down at Dora's distended belly again before replying. He could swear he saw it shift as the child within moved, and he had the sudden urge to hold his hands against her to steady the movement. He resisted the urge, but his sense of immediacy escalated. That child was getting ready to be born, and he wanted no mistake about his ownership. His honor demanded it. He refused to acknowledge the possessive instincts suddenly flooding him. He'd never possessed anyone or anything before. He didn't need anyone or anything now. He just meant to do what was right.

"That doesn't matter now. What matters is getting you to the preacher as soon as possible. We can discuss details later. Can you travel or not?"

Pace doubted that Dora weighed even a hundred pounds on her own. The child must add another twenty pounds of excess burden. He didn't know how she carried it. Still, she seemed like a weightless bird poised for flight while she contemplated his question.

"I have no wish to marry," she stated flatly. "I have
no desire to be a man's possession."

Pace stared at her blankly, not comprehending her
argument. She might give birth at any minute. He could
literally see his child moving within her womb. What in
hell did possession have to do with anything? He would
throw her over his shoulder and haul her off to the
preacher if she didn't cease this unreasonableness. Perhaps it had something to do with her pregnancy. He
shook his lawyer's mind into action and tried desperately
for rationality.

"You are already mine," he stated as flatly as she had.
"You think I would allow another man to touch you
now? As long as you are here, within my reach, that
won't change. And you have already promised you won't
deny me the child. So unless you leave the child and go,
you cannot escape me. You are my wife in all but name,
Dora. The legal words will make no difference to what
is already between us."

He saw the flash of fear in her eyes, the frozen look
of a captured deer. That one brief glimpse nearly tore
him in two before it disappeared and he saw the calm
acceptance of his logic settle on her features.

He closed his eyes and gave a sigh of relief, ignoring
his own burgeoning doubts when she finally replied.

"I can travel. We needs must take the cart. The carriage horses are gone."

He swore a curse that made her flinch. When she
picked up her egg basket and turned back to the house,
Pace caught her arm in apology.

"I'm sorry. I've been around other men too long. Gallant has been trained to the traces. I'll hook him up to
the curricle. It has some springs, at least. I don't want
you jostled too much."

She looked surprised at his nervousness. "I am not an
eggshell. I will not break so easily. Didst thou wish for
me to press thy clothes before we go?"

No, he wanted the damned servants to do it, but he
understood now that there weren't any. No voices sing-
songed through the quarters. No laughter drifted from
the kitchen. No one called from the upstairs windows to
idlers lingering below. The unplowed field took on new

meaning. Pace clenched his jaw against a dozen questions and shook his head.

"I'll find something in my room. Wear something pretty, and leave that apron behind. A person only gets married once. We might as well try to do it right."

As if what they did was right, Pace thought later as he helped Dora into the curricle. He'd finally taken enough time to calculate that she was seven months gone with child. They would be married in a strange church, by an unknown preacher, without any friends or family around them. It certainly wasn't the wedding he had expected, but he couldn't provide better under the circumstances.

Dora wore a lacy cap to cover her curls instead of the concealing bonnet. Pace conceded this improvement and the probable necessity of keeping the March wind from blowing her hair to a frazzle. She had changed into a clean gown, one slightly less worn than the other, which warned him it was her best gown. Considering how difficult it must be for her to find something that fit, he admitted she probably couldn't do better. He couldn't even do much about it. He'd raided his father's small store of coins and found it too limited for wasting on new clothes.

When he took the seat beside her, she unfolded her fist and wordlessly handed him the gold ring he had given her. Pace glanced from Dora's expressionless face to the ring, then carefully tucked it into his coat pocket. The ring had been as close to a promise as he had ever made. Now he was carrying out that promise. He would find some way to take care of her. He just didn't know how yet.

They didn't talk much on the ride over. Despite the distant clouds the sun continued shining, but the wind was brisk and cool. Dora shivered inside her cloak, and Pace cursed his inability to even protect her from the weather. He really didn't want to know what Dora thought, and he appreciated her silence. She had probably hoped to marry in her own church, in whatever odd manner her religion accepted. He already realized they would not accept him, but she hadn't said a word about it.

The only words that came to his own mind were apologies, and they were fairly useless at this point. Even though Dora had been willing, he had taken her to his bed without any thought of the consequences. He was experienced. She hadn't been. Hell, she probably hadn't even known what could happen to her. This whole affair was entirely his responsibility. He shunned the thought of the shame she had endured these last months on his account, what she would have continued enduring if someone hadn't poured him onto the train going home. Now he knew what her letter must have contained. Apologies wouldn't begin to cover his actions. He accepted the blame. He would shoulder the responsibility of correcting it.

On an ordinary work day, the county seat quietly harbored only a few horses at the hitching post and a farm wagon half-loaded with supplies in front of the mercantile. Horse piles steamed on the macadam roadway as Pace steered his gelding to a place near the front of the courthouse. Dora clenched her hands nervously as she stared up at the imposing brick structure, but Pace ignored her nervousness. He had a duty to perform, and he meant to perform it correctly.

"I thought we were going to the preacher," she whispered as he reached to help her out of the carriage.

"I'll not have anyone questioning the legality of our marriage. I'll get a license first. Then we'll go and get the proper words said over our heads."

"I don't want to go in there," she murmured, pulling back from him. "The preacher is enough for me."

He didn't understand this reluctance any more than he had her earlier refusal, and he didn't have patience with it. "It's just a formality, Dora. We can go to the preacher first, if you prefer. But I still want the marriage recorded at the courthouse."

"Could you do it without me?"

He was so accustomed to her "thees" and "thous" that he always noticed when she didn't use them. She didn't use them when she was truly upset about something and trying to hide it.

"All right, let's go to the preacher first. He'll give us

a paper to sign, and I can come back here later and file it. Will that be all right?"

She nodded briefly without looking at him. He didn't have the time or patience for getting to the bottom of this little mystery. He walked her down the street toward the tree-lined residential area behind the courthouse square.

Conscious of her burden, Pace watched as Dora moved with careful grace instead of the awkward waddle of other women in her condition. By the time they reached the modest cottage of the preacher, he almost wished he had some way of carrying her burden for her. At the same time, he realized that in a few months, he *would* be able to carry the burden. The thought terrified him.

They were married in the preacher's tiny front room, with his wife and daughter as witnesses. Sunlight slipped through a crack in the heavy draperies, illuminating Dora's silver curls and translucent complexion. She looked more an angel than ever, if he didn't look at the rest of her. Pace discovered some difficulty in not looking at the rest of her. The small breasts he had once suckled had swollen to twice their usual size, and he was curious to see them bared. He would have that right shortly.

The thought suddenly made him randier than hell. He had a wife seven months gone with child and who probably hated his guts, but he was suddenly wondering how soon he could get her into bed. He was a bastard, through and through.

Pace slipped the gold band onto Dora's finger, repeated his vows without hearing them, and bent to brush a light kiss against his new wife's dry lips. The occasion certainly held nothing of the solemn or sacramental. He wasn't even surprised when the preacher presented him with the certificate to sign, and he could see the man had conveniently used 1864 instead of 1865 in the date. He counted himself lucky to have put some of his father's coins in his pockets. The man undoubtedly expected a sizable gratuity.

Dora didn't notice the discrepancy. Knowing her penchant for truthfulness, Pace offered up a prayer of gratitude. His major concern had been the child's legitimacy, but the nicety of pretending they had married first would be appreciated in the days and years to come. The truth would fade with time.

He made a decent contribution to the preacher's nest egg and carefully helped Dora back outside. They were married. She was his wife. Pace glanced down at her placid face with incredulity. He hadn't been home twenty-four hours, and he already wore the chains of a wife and child. How much lower could he sink?

Dora glanced up at him then, her all-seeing eyes looking right through him. He waited for her condemnation, but she merely gave him one of her small smiles, and murmured, "I thank thee, Pace. I believe I could learn to love a man like thee."

He felt as if she had knocked the ground out from under him.

Twenty-two

The hour of marriage ends the female reign!
And we give all we have to buy a chain;
Hire men to be our lords, who were our slaves;
And bribe our lovers to be perjur'ed knaves.

JOHN CROWN, *English Friar*

Dora didn't know why she said those words. Pace's stricken expression made her wish she could take them back. But they'd been said, as they must if she were honest. She knew better than to engage in dangerous emotions, but Pace had released them once. He could easily do so again. They could go on without her ever uttering the words again. Her burgeoning feelings for Pace had very little to do with the terrifying realities of marriage and probably a great deal to do with her relief that she no longer carried this burden alone.

She took Pace's arm, the one he always held a little bit crooked, and started back down the path to the courthouse square. "There are not many men who know what is right. There are even fewer who will act on it. Thou hast always been one of those noble few."

His expression eased as he took her words for gratitude. "I just did what any other man would have done in my place. I'm not a complete ass, Dora. I regret that you've had to suffer for my sins, but we'll put that behind us now. I'd rather not talk of it again."

She gave him a quick, shy smile. "I did not think that what we did made babies, Pace, or I might not have done it. The fault was as much mine as thine. I was willing to accept that."

"Dammit, Dora." He glared down at her. "I told you I didn't want to hear any more about it. I already feel lower than a snake's belly without your rubbing it in."

He was determined to punish himself. Well, let him. She had other things on her mind, like the sheriff back at the courthouse. She really didn't want him to know that she was just now marrying Pace. What would happen if the sheriff demanded his deed back? Or hadn't Pace received her letter?

She had difficulty broaching the subject. Pace had fallen into one of his black studies and barely knew she existed. When they reached the curricle, he helped her in without speaking. When she called his name, he just waved her away and hurried up the courthouse steps with their marriage certificate. She sat in the curricle, clasping her hands together, whether in nervousness or prayer she couldn't say.

He wasn't frowning any more than usual when he came back out again. Dora took that as a good sign, but when he asked if she'd like lunch at a restaurant, she shook her head no. She wanted to be as far away from here as possible, before the inevitable happened.

She just wasn't used to lying. She tried formulating the words to ask about the deed, but Pace kept interrupting her thought processes.

"Where are Josie and Amy?"

"They've been ill. Josie wanted out of the house as soon as Amy could travel. They're spending a few days with her parents." Dora bit her lip while thinking of a way to change the subject, but Pace followed his own train of thought.

"Why aren't the fields plowed? Don't we have anyone left?"

"Just Solly. He can't do everything. There's some of the women in the quarters, but they have small children, and they can't plow."

"What about hiring someone? Won't Josie do it?"

Dora shrugged. "Who would we hire? The president says the slaves are free. Kentucky says they're not. The laws haven't changed while thee were gone. A free black man cannot legally live in Kentucky. And there isn't a white man in the state who will do slave work. I would do it myself, but I cannot now. If this continues much longer, we'll all starve."

Pace cursed under his breath. "Why doesn't Josie sell

the damned place, then? That should give the lot of you something to live on for a while."

Dora sent him a questioning look. "It doesn't belong to Josie. Both Charlie and thy father designated thee as their heirs." She must not have explained herself very clearly in the letter, but he looked so astounded, she didn't have the heart to explain again that her name was the one on the deed.

"Me? They left me owner of that albatross? What in hell did they expect me to do with it? I don't know a blamed thing about farming."

Dora laughed at his astonishment. "Neither does Josie. I suspect they knew she would sell the place first chance she got." She stopped laughing and gave him a closer look. "I believe they thought thou wouldst more likely keep the farm in the family."

"Well, they thought wrong. I don't know a blamed thing about farming, and I'm not about to start anytime soon." He grew quiet for a minute, then sighed. "But I suppose I'll have to hire someone who does for a while. You and the others need somewhere to live until I can find a place for myself. And you'll need some kind of income. I don't know if the place will sell for enough to support all of you for any amount of time."

"I have my own place," Dora replied indignantly. "Thou needn't concern thyself over me."

He gave her a curt glance that took in her swollen abdomen. "Of course not. You'll no doubt go out and plow the fields and give birth in the shrubbery and go back to work when you're done. Don't be a fool, Dora. You're my wife now. I'll look after you, one way or another."

"I don't want to be looked after," she responded childishly. "I'm tired of people looking after me. I want to take care of myself for a change. Thou canst go thy own way and leave me to myself. I've been doing a fine job of it so far."

"Oh, yes, a fine job. And you're the one who just admitted you were too ignorant to know where babies came from. Well, there's a damned sight more you don't know about, and I don't intend to let you discover it the hard way. Somebody has to look out for innocents like you."

He was probably right, but that didn't keep Dora from resenting it. She shut up and glared at the road ahead. It hadn't quite seeped in yet that she was married, and he had the right to make these vast declarations. It soon would. Against all common sense, she had traded a name for her baby for the legal tyranny of marriage. Maybe she did need a keeper.

The clouds finally moved in at nightfall, bringing with them falling temperatures and the threat of rain. Or snow. Easter flowers bloomed beneath the oaks, and the redbuds were just swelling, but Kentucky weather didn't much attend to these signs of spring.

Dora grumbled as she drew on her heavy flannel nightgown. The north wind rattled the panes of her window, sending out a draft that nearly quenched her candle. This little room beside Harriet's had no fireplace or stove. She'd thought she'd seen an end to the cold winter chill of the room. She would have to put the heavy quilt back on the bed.

She tried not to wonder what Pace was doing right now. He'd grabbed a bite of lunch and ridden off to town as soon as they returned. He'd not even stopped to explain to his mother that they were officially married now. He'd left that to Dora. The old woman had taken the news remarkably well, although she'd apparently forgotten it not two minutes later. This late in Dora's pregnancy, the news was probably more of a denouement anyway.

But she'd seen Pace return earlier. He'd taken his horse to rub it down in the stable. He'd find Solly there, Dora knew. They were probably discussing what needed doing. Just because this was their wedding night, she didn't expect anything to change around here. It was not as if Pace had married her for any reason but her belly. And she knew already that made her repulsive.

She blew out the candle and crawled up under the covers. She still shivered. She wrapped her arms around herself for warmth, and for the first time that day, she wondered what it would be like to sleep with her hus-

band. Her husband. The words still sounded strange to
her ears. She hadn't intended to marry. She didn't feel
married. A piece of legal paper hadn't turned her life
upside-down yet. She had continued her daily routines
as usual. As little as Pace stayed around, he might as
well still be in the army for all the difference it made.
Or perhaps she could pretend they had returned to those
early days when she had been little more than a guest
in this house, and he studied law.

That thought didn't make her rest any easier. The
child in her womb kicked restlessly, and Dora sought a
more comfortable position. The bed creaked under her,
and she held her breath, hoping Harriet hadn't heard.
She would call for a drink of water or something if she
knew Dora could hear her. She really didn't want to get
out in the cold again.

The wind whistled and rattled the shingles. It was
going to snow. She could feel it. She turned her back on
the door, pretending she didn't listen for Pace's step on
the stairs. He had every right to stay out all night, drink
to dawn, whatever he chose to do. She had no claim on
him beyond his name. She would just be grateful if he
treated her as he always had, then she wouldn't fear the
dangers the word "wife" represented to her.

She'd almost convinced herself of that by the time the
bedroom door creaked open. She must have dozed off.
She hadn't heard him on the stairs. Why was he coming
in here?

She knew it was Pace. Somehow, she could sense the
height and weight of him, maybe even the density. Josie
was much smaller and lighter. The household only contained women except for Pace. The masculinity of the
intruder wasn't in doubt.

She could smell horse sweat, whiskey, and that distinctive male aroma that was just Pace. Dora pretended to
sleep, thinking he would go on to his own room. She
didn't know what he wanted, but she lacked the strength
to give him anything. The babe drained all her resources
despite her pretense otherwise. She didn't want him
knowing that. She didn't want him feeling any more bur-
dened than he did.

When she heard the rustle of his clothing, she stiff-

ened. Surely, he wouldn't? The bed was too small. The
room was next to his mother's. She was seven months'
pregnant! What did he think he could do under those
conditions?

Climb into the bed with her.

Icy hands touched her flannel-covered arm as he lowered his weight to the mattress. Dora started to protest,
but he already sprawled behind her, tucking his knees
up behind hers, warming his chest against her back. She
nearly choked on her protests when she finally realized
he was stark naked.

"What do you think . . ."

"It's freezing in here," he murmured against her hair.
"How do you stand it? Take off that gown so we can
get closer."

Take off her gown? Dora gave him an incredulous
look over her shoulder. She had a naked, hairy man in
her bed, and he was telling her to take off her clothes.
She didn't even dream of moments like this.

"I will not," she said. "It's cold. Besides, I cannot be
a wife to thee like this. It's impossible."

Pace nuzzled her ear. "Probably not, if we put our
minds to it, but all I'm interested in is getting warm.
Feel the heat? It's starting already. It will be better with
your gown off."

She felt heat all right. She was on fire. She still saw
no reason for taking her gown off and displaying her
ugliness. She could feel Pace's loins pressed against her
buttocks with the gown on. She blushed thoroughly at
the thought of how it would feel if she wore nothing.

"I can't," she whispered back fiercely. "What if thy
mother calls for me?"

"My God! Is she still dragging you out of bed, even
in this condition? I'll have a word or two with her about
that in the morning. Now let's get you out of this gown.
Annie can sleep in here tomorrow and listen for her.
For now, we'll make do."

He pulled the hem of her gown up around her hips
and waited patiently for her to lift herself. Dora couldn't
believe it. He embarrassed her right down to her toes.
But when he tugged, she lifted. In seconds, her gown lay
on the floor and his hands rested on her naked flesh.

"Better," he murmured, moving closer. "A man could come to like this real well."

Dora was appalled. She could feel Pace's hard-muscled thigh against hers. His hands roamed, gently exploring her belly first. He gave a grunt of surprise when the child kicked. His hand disappeared for a minute, then came back with a pillow. He tucked it beneath her protruding abdomen.

"Give the kid a place to lay his head. How's that?"

It was wonderful. The support took away some of the weight. Dora leaned a little closer into the curve of his body.

Pace immediately took advantage, raising his hand to stroke her breast. She gave a gasp of surprise, but he lingered.

"You're so soft and warm," he murmured sleepily. "I could hold you all night."

A minute later, she heard him snoring. The hand on her breast relaxed, but his heat continued to warm her.

As long as she didn't think of that long ridge of his masculinity pressed against her, she could relax too. Even in repose, he was large. She wouldn't think of what would happen when he awakened.

She had reason to remember that thought when she woke the next morning. The gray of dawn illumined the frosty windowpane, and drowsy with sleep and warmth, she snuggled deeper into the covers. She didn't know why she woke at first. It didn't take long to discover the cause.

Even though Pace still lightly snored, the male part of him stirred.

It felt odd, lying here in the comfort of her once lonely bed, feeling the child in her womb tossing restlessly on one side, and her husband coming to life behind her. Three in the bed was definitely a crowd, but she had been alone so long, she couldn't help lingering a while to sample the newness of the sensation.

She didn't linger long before Pace's nimble fingers began to stroke and feel. With a horrified "Pace!" Dora peeled back the covers.

He held her easily with the strength of one arm. "I

think it's possible," he murmured thoughtfully behind
her. "If you'll just . . .."

Dora nearly leaped from her skin when his hand pried
between her legs, caressing her and adjusting himself to
fit between.

"It's not decent!" she whispered in horror, horribly
conscious of her enormous size. "Let me go, Pace." Embarrassment drove even deeper as she realized a more
pressing urge than the man between her legs. "I can't,
Pace, please. I've got to get up. Please, thou must
leave now."

Something of the urgency in her voice must have finally penetrated. He lifted himself up on one arm and
peered down at her with uncertainty. "Am I hurting
you? What's wrong, Dora?"

She jerked the quilt over her nakedness and pulled it
loose of the bed so she could get up decently covered.
"I need to use the privy," she muttered through
clenched teeth, wishing him to the devil right now. She'd
never spoke of her private needs to anyone before. Now
she had a husband who would be intimate with every
one of them. She wasn't precisely grateful for that
knowledge.

"Like hell," he grumbled. "It snowed last night. Can't
you tell? Haven't you got a chamber pot in here?"

He scrambled out of the bed, unconscious of his nudity as he searched her washstand for the required article. When he produced it with a triumphant flourish, he
turned to see his red-faced wife standing beside the bed,
cowering behind all the blankets she could free from
the mattress.

Understanding dawned slowly. At first, he was more
intent on his first glimpse of his new wife without all the
primping and combing with which women usually
greeted the world. Dora's hair fell in a tangled mass of
silver curls across her brows and into her eyes, trailing
in tendrils along her throat. He didn't get much further
than that. The flush of embarrassment coloring her
cheeks and the wretchedness in the flash of her eyes
warned he'd overstayed his welcome.

Jerking on his trousers, Pace hastily departed.

Dora dropped the covers and grabbed the pot with a

sigh of relief. Her husband was an imposing man in his nakedness, even more so in an aroused state. But her physical need of the moment didn't match his. She relieved herself in the pot and thanked God a person could not actually die of embarrassment.

She tried not to think about Pace while she dressed, but she had some difficulty avoiding it while stumbling over his coat and picking up his drawers from the floor. They were knit drawers, and she knew full well how they looked stretched over his trim hips and muscled thighs. Hours on horseback must have given him legs like that. She didn't look at the opening in the drawers meant to accommodate his manhood. That was the main thing she tried not thinking about.

She would have to be a wife to him. She'd already given him that right when she had laid down with him last summer. He had made that right legal by marrying her. She no longer had full ownership of her own body. She belonged to her husband in every sense of the word.

What in the name of God had she done to herself?

Twenty-three

Anger may be foolish and absurd, and one may be irritated when in the wrong; but a man never feels outraged unless in some respect he is at bottom right.

VICTOR HUGO, "Fantine," *Les Miserables* (1862)

"Damn those Nichollses! Damn each and every one of them!" Finding the humidor empty, the gray-haired man flung it against the wall, narrowly missing the younger man sitting with his ankle crossed over his knee in the chair across from his desk. The speaker scarcely seemed aware of the near miss as he shuffled around in his desk drawer for a loose cigar. The stroke years earlier had left his fingers crippled and his motions awkward, which frustrated him even further. "I should have hired a lawyer before marrying my little girl off to one of those bastards. They can't do anything right."

The younger man calmly reached into an inside pocket and withdrew one of his cigarillos, handing it across the desk. "I don't imagine Charlie asked to die."

"But he could have named my daughter and granddaughter as heirs!" Ethan Andrews grabbed the cigarillo and crunched it between his teeth. "Who would have thought the bastard would leave it to Payson? That makes no sense a'tall!"

"It just puts a slight hitch in our plans, Ethan. Calm down, and don't make such a scene about it. We can work around it."

Ethan puffed the cigarillo furiously for a minute, then removed it from his mouth to glare at his visitor. "Sure you can. That relieves you from courting my daughter, doesn't it? People are beginning to wonder about you,

Joe. How old are you now? Thirty? Thirty-five? And no wife to show for those years? It don't look good."

Irritation briefly flickered across the wide mayoral brow, but Joe conquered it as he eventually conquered all things. "Josie ain't been a widow long enough, Ethan. You know that. I'll court her when the time's right, whether she owns the Nichollses' place or not. It ain't my fault she chose the wrong man the first time around. The problem at hand is that patch of land between that corner acreage of yours, the Nicholls place, and the Quaker land. We can't cut the road from here through there until we've got property rights. It would have made it a mite easier if Josie had inherited, then we could have gone around the Quaker land. Now we'll try a different route."

Ethan narrowed his eyes. "You'll not get away with that back taxes ploy this time, boy. Payson ain't anybody's fool. And he's married to the Quaker gal now."

"As if I didn't already know that. If it hadn't been for that fool girl getting over to the courthouse to sign that deed, we'd have been sitting pretty." Disgruntled at last, Joe glared at the old man puffing away on his last cigar.

"Charlie would have had your head if he'd come home and found you'd horned in on his farm," Ethan said calmly. "You played that one too damned close to the margin."

"I would have fixed it with Charlie. I just didn't have time to wait for him to get out of prison and get home. Now look where we are. This holds up construction for months. We've got to do something. With a little more capital, we could build a rail line instead of just a toll road."

Ethan wrinkled his forehead in thought. "I sure enough didn't figger on Pace coming home and marrying that little Quaker gal. Should've guessed it was his brat she's carrying, though. He had to do the honorable thing. It kind of relieved me to hear it when Josie told me last week. Josie's had her heart set on Pace since she was a young'un, and I feared she'd set her sights on him again. I guess she's probably smarter than that now."

Joe frowned and sat forward. "What do you mean, he

had to do the honorable thing? He hasn't been home since last summer. I figured that's when they married."

Ethan gave a short laugh and looked at his guest with sly triumph. "Shows you don't know everything, don't it? He may have plowed her last summer, but he just now got around to doing the honors."

Joe's eyes narrowed in thought. "That fool sheriff said she was married when she signed that damned deed. If she wasn't . . ."

The two men looked at each other. If Ethan's sagging mouth had been able to pucker, he would have whistled at the look on the younger man's face.

"Thou must eat, Pace. I have brought thee some dinner. I thought we—"

Pace made an absent gesture at the sycamore on the edge of the newly plowed field. "Just leave it over there. I'll get to it later."

Dora's lips tightened. "No, thou wilt not. It will be the same as yesterday. Thou wilt send it home with Solly and go hungry. There is more than enough for everybody, Pace. Thou wilt be skin and bones if thou doth not eat something soon."

"For God's sake, Dora, leave me alone!" Pace gave her a look of irritation as he lifted the hoe in his hand. "Go mother Amy. I'm busy."

"I can see that," Dora snapped back. "Thou and Solly hath stood here scratching thy heads and staring at the sky for a quarter of an hour now. Thou art very busy. Forgive me for intruding."

She couldn't properly march away with head held high as she would like. The newly plowed furrows made walking difficult, and her bulk made every step an adventure. From behind her, she heard Pace shout, "Dammit all, Dora, stay out of the field! You shouldn't be out of the house now."

She wouldn't be out of the house if he had the sense to come in for dinner, she grumbled to herself, but she wouldn't lower her dignity by shouting back at him. She saw no reason for arguing with a miserable pigheaded fool.

But she worried herself sick about him. He'd been

home for weeks now, long enough to get the largest field plowed and the tobacco set, but with each passing day he looked older and more fatigued, and he drifted farther away from her and his family. She sensed the wrongness, but she didn't know the cure.

Josie met her in the kitchen, glancing at Dora's empty hands. "Did he eat it?"

"I couldn't even get him to talk with me long enough to convince him," she answered wearily.

"He doesn't eat enough to keep a gnat alive." Josie worried at her bottom lip. "He's always out in that field. Does he ever sleep?"

That was a loaded question if Dora ever heard one. She washed her hands at the pump and smoothed the cool water over her face just to avoid answering. Pace had moved her into his larger room on the other end of the hall from his mother, but he spent little time there himself. Occasionally she would wake to find his dirty clothes lying on the floor and a hollow in the pillow beside her, so he apparently at least went to bed sometimes. She wasn't at all certain that he actually slept. Only a person who never slept could creep in and out of bed without her noticing.

"He is a grown man. I cannot tell him what to do," Dora finally answered, wiping her face on a towel.

"Someone must!" Josie paced the floor in agitation. "If he drops dead, all is lost. We can't possibly run this place without him."

Tired, irritated, worried more than she wished to admit, Dora replied angrily, "Thou art welcome to try and save him from himself if thou wishes."

Josie returned an angry glare. "Maybe I will. You may have trapped him, but he loved me first. It's killing him living like this."

Dora felt those words all the way to her heart. Josie could very well have the right of it. Pace's behavior made very little sense otherwise. He worked too hard. He didn't eat or sleep. He was killing himself by slow degrees. She didn't consider that the normal behavior of a happily married man expecting the birth of his first child.

"It was Pace's decision, not mine," Dora said with as

much dignity as she could muster. Then she walked out, leaving Josie to think what she wished.

She didn't know what to think herself. She was battered and confused inside, and more frightened than she could remember. Pace had always seemed so strong, so confident, so certain of where he went and why. And now he seemed as lost and aimless as she. With the weeks until the child's birth growing shorter, she needed reassurance, not uncertainty. But Pace could offer her nothing.

She found Annie in the upper hall, carrying the remains of Harriet's meal from her chamber. Since Pace had started paying her a small wage, Annie had become visibly more efficient. She couldn't overcome the habits of a lifetime of servitude overnight and so still kept her head bowed, and muttered in the presence of Josie and Pace, but she treated Dora more as an equal. After all, they had both been little more than servants in this household for some time.

"You're back soon," Annie said disapprovingly.

Dora didn't need that remark to rub in her inadequacy. "He's not a child. I can't make him eat."

Annie went on as if she hadn't heard the anger in Dora's reply. "Did you hear them militia done hung Uncle Jas last night? Old man like that couldn't harm no one. Someone ought to go after them with a pitchfork."

Dora closed her eyes and swayed slightly at this blow. Not Uncle Jas. She'd just sent him a ham last week. She knew better than anyone that the blind old Negro wasn't harmless, but he'd lived a long life and deserved to die in peace. What kind of fiends would find pleasure in hanging an old man who couldn't fight back?

"It will take more than pitchforks," Dora whispered. "But the devil ought to take their souls straight to hell."

Annie's coffee-colored face became a mask of concern. "You'd better take yourself off to bed, Miss Dora. You don't look too good. You go lie down now. You don't need to do nothin' else today."

There was plenty she needed to do, but Annie's words made sense at the moment. She didn't feel capable of doing anything. Dora nodded and entered the room that had been Pace's since boyhood.

She hadn't changed anything. Massive walnut furniture and midnight-blue draperies dominated the spacious chamber. A bootjack and a hat rack added more masculine touches. The only feminine detail indicating Dora's existence was a frail muslin cap hanging on one of the spare hooks of the hat rack. She had folded her few dresses carefully and tucked them out of sight in the bottom of the wardrobe. She had no perfumes or cosmetics to decorate the vanity the room didn't have. The only mirror was Pace's shaving mirror over the washbowl. Accustomed to invisibility, Dora didn't notice the lack.

Pace slipped into his room to change his filthy clothes. The slight lump of Dora's silhouette in the bed almost made him withdraw again. Dora never took naps.

In the dusky light he could see the silver halo of curls falling against her pale cheeks. His fingers itched to slide through their silkiness. He needed the touch of something soft and gentle, if only to remind him of the tough callus formed around his soul.

He drew closer, drinking in the sight he never dared observe when she was awake. Even carrying the bulk of his child, Dora was small. She looked much too fragile, too ethereal to carry a child. He wanted to pick her up and hold her and swear to her that he would take care of everything.

He still hadn't learned to lie to Dora. He tried hardening his heart and looking away, but the child within her moved, and he watched with fascination. His child. The child they had created together in those few halcyon days when he had pretended the world was Dora. It had been a stupid fool thing to do. He'd known it then. He suffered for it now, knowing he'd destroyed the one perfect thing in his life by doing so.

God, he had never wanted to hurt Dora. He would destroy himself before he would see Dora harmed.

But as it was, he was no good for her dead or alive. He could only stay out of her way and hope he didn't hurt her more.

Grabbing a clean shirt, he quietly left the room.

*   *   *

She slept until almost dusk. Waking to find the room cast in shadow, she hurriedly rose and dressed. Pace should have returned from the fields. She should have a hot meal ready. Some of the women from the quarters had agreed to cook for wages, but they needed a lot of supervising still. A diet of cornbread and beans couldn't improve anyone's digestion.

Dora worried what would happen when the small supply of coins in the desk dissipated, but she had more pressing concerns for the moment. She and Pace needed to talk.

She found him in the study where he had obviously been poring over the books. He had account ledgers scattered across the desk and stacks of papers covered in figures lying haphazardly all over the floor around the desk chair. Pace no longer sat in that chair but roamed around the room, hands in pockets, muttering to himself. He kicked idly at one of Amy's toys as Dora entered the room.

"I am sorry if I overslept. Hast thou eaten yet?"

"I had a sandwich. I'm fine. You'd better go eat something before Solly comes in and finishes it off." He didn't even look at her.

"Could we talk first?" she asked hesitantly.

Pace gave her an impatient glance. "About what?"

Now that he listened, Dora didn't know precisely what to say. She couldn't ask him directly why he didn't eat or sleep. She couldn't ask him if their marriage had been a major mistake and if he still loved Josie. All the things she really wanted to ask were forbidden. She contented herself with inquiring, "Will the army look for the men who killed Uncle Jas?"

Fury leaped instantly to his eyes, illuminating them from within like green fires. Just as quickly as the fury had appeared, it disappeared again. He regarded her with hostility. "Even the grand Union army doesn't have time for one blind old nigger. Go get something to eat, Dora. I'm not in the mood for small talk."

"Thou art never in the mood for anything," she said bitterly. "Thou doth nothing but sulk and hide and pretend the rest of us do not exist. Thou canst not make us go away by pretending we're not here."

He looked up and glared at her then. "For God's sake, Dora! What do you expect of me? Should I sit on the veranda, sip lemonade, and smoke cigars while keeping you ladies entertained? I've got this huge damned nuisance of a farm to run and nobody to run it with. I've got a blamed bad arm that makes everything I do useless. I've got a wife and a child to support and no damned means of supporting them! Should I shout hallelujahs?"

Dora cowered against the door, increasingly fearful of his ungoverned temper. Childhood memories of yelling and weeping crystallized into reality, and she reacted instinctively, not even knowing she did so. Pace was known for his volatile explosions. Logically she knew he had never subjected her to them. She still didn't like what she saw. She had seen the results of Charlie's violent temper and her father's before then. She just couldn't believe that Pace would deliberately take his rage out on her. Unlike Josie, she would remain calm and sensible. Perhaps that would cool him off.

"Thou couldst give thanks thou art alive," she answered reasonably, wincing when he shouted his reply.

"Who in hell says I'm grateful? What in hell have I got to be grateful about? I should thank God I'm a useless piece of nothing who's good for nothing but ruining young girls?"

He smacked his fist into his palm to accent his words, and Dora flinched but continued resolutely, "If that is the way thou feels, I absolve thee of all guilt. I do not regret this child. Thou art free to go anytime thou so desireth."

"Damn you, Dora, I . . ."

He swung his hand as if to strike. Dora instinctively dodged, emitting a shrill scream as she did so. Pace's fist slammed harmlessly against the wooden door, but he looked as shattered as she did when she edged away from him.

"You're my wife now, Dora, dammit. Don't look at me like that. I wasn't going to hit you."

His wife. His possession. To do with as he pleased. She had known. It just hadn't sunk in until now. The screaming. The yelling. And then the fist to the mouth.

Terrified, she continued backing away. The need to protect her child and a sense of self-preservation overruled anything else she might have felt. Unwittingly, she responded just as her mother always had. "I'll get out of your way."

Pace watched her disappear down the darkened hallway with a sick feeling in his gut. Dora's abject cowering made him want to hit something more than ever. He'd known himself as a worthless bastard. He hadn't realized he could go so far as to terrorize women, particularly a fragile wisp like Dora. The frustration boiling up inside him needed some outlet, but not Dora.

He didn't know what had made her turn tail and flee like that. She'd seen his outbursts before and ignored them. The fear in her eyes made him want to weep. He should never have taken his temper out on her. She had done nothing but offer him everything she had. He couldn't blame her if she couldn't fill the abysmal emptiness within him.

With a curse, Pace strode down the hall in the opposite direction and slammed out into the night.

"They say that Howard boy was so spooked, he ran buck naked into the woods to get away!"

Dora heard the glee in Solly's whispered voice as he spoke to his sister behind the kitchen. The child inside her womb rolled uneasily, and she really didn't want to hear more, but her weight made it impossible to escape fast enough.

"Was it really the haint of Uncle Jas?" the girl's voice whispered excitedly.

"The noose is still swingin' on his front stairs right now," Solly declared.

Dora worked her way through the walled gallery to the house, away from the voices. She didn't want to know what happened at the Howard house last night. Pace hadn't come home until the early morning hours. She had heard him come in. He hadn't come to bed.

She was afraid to ask where he'd been. She was afraid to say anything to him at all. The nightmare of her mother's death hadn't faded so much that she had forgotten, and the night of Amy's birth stayed with her as clear as if it had been yesterday. She might be stronger than her mother, but she didn't think she was as strong as Josie. Pace was her husband, father of her child. He had her tied in so many knots she didn't think she could escape. She didn't want to believe that she needed escape.

The little farmhouse at the end of the lane was seriously tempting, but Dora knew the futility of running away. Pace's pride wouldn't allow him to let her go. He would come after her.

She had no real reason to run, she told herself. Pace had never actually struck her. Only her cowardice made her imagine he would. But she knew as well as if he had told her that Pace had instigated whatever terrorism had occurred at the Howards' last night. And she had the ominous feeling that he wouldn't stop with terrorism. And sooner or later, they would clash over his methods. That had been coming for a long, long time. She must reserve her strength for that battle and avoid the smaller skirmishes.

Dora stayed out of his way all day and said nothing when Pace disappeared again that night and the next. She said nothing when she learned he came in at dawn to sleep on the sofa in the study. She refused to retreat to her bedroom as his mother had done, but Pace avoided Dora just as successfully as she avoided him.

Josie came back from a visit with her mother one day with news that Matt Howard had left the county, and Joe Mitchell had found a noose hanging from his veranda just that morning. Pace came in the back door as Josie imparted that information to Dora, and their gazes met briefly. He looked away first.

"I'm going over to the courthouse to conduct a little business. I'll be home late. Don't keep supper waiting." He stalked through the dining room in the direction of the hall.

"You might check our supply of rope," Dora called after him, maliciously. "We'll need a new clothesline soon."

He slammed the study door and Josie looked at her with curiosity, but Dora didn't care. She hated herself for her timidity. She hated herself for not confronting him directly. But most of all, she hated herself for not coming up with a better solution.

Someone must end the depredations of Joe Mitchell and his cohorts, but she didn't have a clue as to how to go about it. She just didn't think hanging nooses on their front porches and scaring the pants off them with make-believe ghosts was a very permanent solution.

She didn't like it any better when Pace came out of his study carrying a rifle and wearing his pistol in his belt.

Twenty-four

Revenge is a dish that should be eaten cold.
ENGLISH PROVERB

"That man done been touched by the debil, I swear he is," Annie muttered vehemently as she entered the dining room from the direction of the kitchen while Dora came in from the hall.

Dora didn't have to ask to what man she referred. Pace had always possessed a wild streak of the devil, and it grew wider with every passing day. She merely helped herself to a boiled egg from the buffet and settled her bulk into the nearest chair. "What has he done now?" she asked with resignation.

"You don' wanna know." Annie stalked across the room with her tray of food for the invalid.

Dora didn't figure she did want to know. Pace hadn't given in entirely to the bad side of him. He spent the better part of each day out in the fields with Solly, plowing, planting, and doing what he could with his injured arm and one horse. He tried very hard to be what he was not, but the pressure took its toll. He had scarcely been home for three nights in a row.

"Was anyone hurt?" Dora called after Annie's departing back.

Annie turned and glared over her shoulder. "The mayor's office done burned to the ground. At least Uncle Jas is dead and dey can't blame dat on him no more."

Josie came in them, and Annie escaped upstairs. She helped herself to some sausage and biscuits and sat across from Dora. "Billy John got himself shot last night," she said casually as she buttered her biscuit.

Why were they telling her this? Dora grimaced at her uneaten egg. It wasn't as if she could do anything about it. If Pace wanted to round up a bunch of violent vigilantes and burn and plunder and destroy, she couldn't do anything at all. She couldn't even know for certain that Pace caused the destruction. The fact that someone systematically harassed his old enemies didn't mean a thing. A lot of people hated the Mitchells and Howards. Maybe it was one of the McCoys. She didn't know how poor Billy John got dragged into this. He never had the money for slaves. He was friends with Joe Mitchell, but then, he was friends with the McCoys too. Billy John got along with just about everybody except Pace. Nobody got along with Pace.

"I'll wager Sally is worried to death," Josie continued. "Billy John isn't real strong. She's got those three babies to look after and can barely mind the store as it is. I don't know what she'll do now."

Dora's head came up and her eyes widened as a thought grabbed her and wouldn't let go. Pace would be beyond furious. She feared his violence and didn't wish it turned on her, but she had to take a stand of some sort. She wouldn't become her mother, shivering and shaking and catering to her husband's erratic whims. Besides, Sally had always been kind to her.

With a tone of determination, Dora announced, "I'll go in and take care of the store. Sally should be with her husband."

Josie crumbled her biscuit and stared at her. "That's the silliest thing you've ever said. Even if you could get into town, it isn't proper for you to show yourself like that."

Dora didn't consider these as reasonable objections, but her plan had other flaws. "I can't stand behind the counter long," she murmured, more to herself than Josie. "I wonder if they have a chair I could use."

"Dora Nicholls, you cannot work in a store! You're likely to give birth and have that baby fall out on its head while you're waiting on customers. This is ridiculous. You can't consider it."

"I'm very good with figures," Dora reminded her. "And the baby isn't due for weeks. I'll be fine. I just can't wait on customers very well."

"I'll tell Pace," Josie warned.

Dora shrugged. Pace would find out sooner or later. She rose and started for the door. Maybe she could find someone to help her hook up the carriage.

By the time she had donned her best cap and found her cloak, the carriage was waiting for her, and so was Josie. Dora raised questioning eyebrows at Josie's heavy gray polonaise.

"I'm going with you," she said defensively. "You can sit behind the counter and hide and do the figures while I wait on the customers."

Josie didn't possess a particular inclination for unselfish acts, but she was capable of helpfulness. Dora welcomed her suggestion, and they left together. She didn't know what Pace would think when he came back to the house at noon and found neither of them there, but she didn't intend to worry about what hadn't happened yet.

They found the store closed and shuttered and had to go around to the living quarters in back. Sally greeted their plan with tears and ushered them in the back way.

"I've been worried sick," she whispered as she hurried them through the humble kitchen and downstairs parlor. "We can't afford to close the store, but I just couldn't leave Billy John lying upstairs feverish and in pain. The doctor says he'll do just fine in a few days, but you know Billy John. He just isn't very strong. It could take a week or more. I've been out of my mind with worry."

The sounds of three young children playing in some upstairs room drifted down to them as they entered the storeroom. One toddler was already wailing, and Sally turned a worried expression to the ceiling, trying to judge the seriousness of the cry.

"Go on up," Dora reassured her. "I know the price of just about everything in here, and Josie can run up and ask if we have any questions. This will work out fine."

Sally gave Josie an uncertain look, but nodded agreement to Dora's assurances. She knew better than anyone how carefully Dora calculated every penny she spent in the store. She wasn't a rich woman like Josie. Dora knew the value of money. "All right. I don't know how I'll ever repay you, but I'll find a way." Her pale face grew a little tenser as she added, "Don't tell anyone that he's been shot. Just say he's down with a fever."

Everyone already knew he'd been shot. Josie wouldn't have heard of it if word hadn't already traveled all the way out to the country. But they nodded their understanding. They would maintain appearances one way or another.

Their first customer was one of the Howard sisters, Emma. She was married now and mother of two, but she still found time to keep up with everything that happened in town. She glanced at Dora doing some mending behind the counter, then turned in puzzlement to Josie dusting a shelf.

"What are you all doin' in here?"

"Helping Sally. Can we get you something?" Josie set aside her feather duster and tried for a prim and proper store-clerk look. The fact that her gray alpaca walking dress probably cost more than Sally's entire wardrobe didn't deter her.

"I need a card of silver buttons and some black thread." Emma turned to Dora who had picked up the sales slip pad. "I heard you and Pace got married, but I hadn't thought it's been that long." She looked pointedly at the rounded slope of Dora's belly beneath her skirts.

Dora calmly wrote up the sales ticket as Josie gathered the requested items. "It isn't as if Pace has been around much for anyone to tell." Lying didn't come easy for her. She hadn't exactly lied, but she hadn't spoke the direct truth either. Papa John would be upset with her.

Emma grunted. "He was obviously around long enough." She didn't even look at the card of buttons Josie handed her for inspection; she merely slipped it into her handbag. "I heard Billy John got shot last night. How's he doing?"

Josie smiled pleasantly. "Billy John just has a fever. He'll be fine shortly. Can we get you anything else?"

"I swear, Josephine Nicholls, I don't know what you think you're doing, but this isn't any place for you. And protecting Billy John is really the outside of enough. I suppose you'll tell me next that Pace Nicholls doesn't know anything about how that poor boy got hurt or how the mayor's office got burned either."

"That will be thirty-five cents, Emma. If thou hast questions for Pace, he's out plowing the cornfield today. Thou couldst stop and ask. His arm gives him some trouble still, so thou might find him a little surly, but I'm sure he'll gladly set the record straight." There were no lies in this. Dora really had no clue as to Pace's nocturnal activities or if he had anything to do with the mayor's house. She gave God's honest truth.

Emma gave her a sour look. "Well, it doesn't look like Pace Nicholls will run for any offices around here for a long time. He might as well learn farming. My husband says if the Yankees don't leave soon, we'll run them out on a rail. Pace best mind his back."

Dora could argue until she turned blue in the face, but it wouldn't do any good. Logic and emotion had little to do with each other, and Emma obviously wasn't strong on logic. Dora handed her the sales slip in exchange for the coins. "Thank thee, Emma."

The remainder of the day went little better. Word spread quickly, and every woman in town found reason to drop into the store to see the wealthy Josephine Nicholls working behind the counter and to hear about Dora's marriage to Pace. Everyone had an opinion on both subjects, and few were favorable. By the end of the day, Dora was exhausted and Josie looked as if she'd been beaten by a stick.

"I don't know how Sally puts up with it," Josie muttered as they climbed into the carriage. "She was always the prettiest girl in town. She could have done better than Billy John. Men! Honestly, I don't think they're worth it. Even Pace ought to be taken out and whipped. I don't think I'll ever marry again."

"Thou wouldst not have Amy?" Dora asked with curiosity.

"I wouldn't go through that agony again, I know that," Josie answered ominously. She gave Dora a quick look. "And we'd best find a midwife for you. I can tell you of a certainty that I'll be perfectly useless when your time comes."

Dora had spent many nights worrying about that, but she hadn't come up with the name of a suitable midwife yet. She didn't think she could send someone to the Union army doctor who had treated Pace, even if he were still there. She didn't know that with any certainty, either. It worried at her, but she had no solutions. the colored midwives she knew had all left the county by now. Other women relied on female relatives. Josie and Harriet were the closest female relatives she had, and both were utterly hopeless.

She let the question stand where it was. She couldn't do much about it.

Pace slammed through the house as soon as he heard the carriage returning. At the sight of the two weary women straggling in the front door, he exploded.

"Where in hell have you been? The damned cook fixed beans again and Amy's throwing a tantrum and—" Pace took a better look at Dora and slammed his fist into the wall. "Are you trying to kill yourself?"

She visibly shrank backward, away from him. She might as well have stabbed a knife through his heart. Pace had always considered Dora the one person in the world he could rely on through thick and thin, better or worse. And now he'd driven her away too. It was more than he could bear. With an expressive oath, Pace swung on his heel and disappeared out the back way.

His belly rumbled, his arm hurt like hell, and the rest of him didn't feel much better after all these days of heavy labor. But the burden of Dora's fear weighed heavier than any of these physical burdens. She shrank from his touch, looked at him through the eyes of a wounded doe, and made him feel like slime inside. He hadn't done a damned thing to deserve that.

He was doing what was right, what should have been done years ago. As he saddled his horse, Pace cataloged all the wrongs committed around here over the last decade or two. The list was innumerable. He held Joe Mitchell and his cohorts single-handedly responsible for tuning a quiet farming community into a hub of slave trade, a hotbed of rebellion against the Union, and a stinkhole of corruption. Not a dollar exchanged in this county didn't have Joe Mitchell's fingerprints on it. It didn't help Pace to remember his own brother had been smack in the middle of it all.

He knew black women around here who would never see their husbands or children again because of those evil practices. Children had died in the Mississippi fields after the traders had sold them away from their homes and loved ones. Female slaves had been forced into prostitution or become baby factories because Joe Mitchell worshiped the almighty dollar. He could see no excuse for what had happened to the souls of the people in this community once they learned the lucrativeness of slave trading. He couldn't save those lost lives, but he could exact punishment. Apparently the loss of the slave trade had turned their greedy mayor to other pursuits. Pace didn't intend to let Mitchell get away with any more corruption.

The April sun set relatively early. Pace rode his horse into the shadows of the trees along the river. He didn't notice the rosy hues of sunset. He didn't smell the fresh scents of newly green grass or notice the wealth of red-bud and dogwood blossoms overhead. His heart hardened against the warm rush of blood through his veins as he thought of Dora resting in their mutual bed, a bed he hadn't frequented in days. He had become what his father and the army had made of him—an unforgiving avenger.

The shadows had darkened into night by the time he rode up to the tiny farmhouse. He whistled, and a figure appeared in the briefly lit doorway. The door closed, and the figure slid into the shadows, appearing slightly later with a horse in tow.

"I don't give a damn about those darkies, Nicholls," the figure warned as he mounted the horse.

The "darkies" in question were chained to a wall in a miserable pen to keep them from escaping, but Pace didn't argue the point. He used whatever weapons came to hand, and this man was one of them.

"Homer has what's left of the mayor's records in his desk. If you want that fraudulent deed destroyed, you have to get hold of it before they take it to the courthouse. Letting those Negroes loose is the best distraction I can think of to get Homer out of the house."

"Even if I tear up the deed, he's bound to say the fire destroyed it, and that he's still rightful owner. He'll have witnesses."

"Relax, McCoy, I'm still a lawyer. I know what I'm doing. You made sure the original deed was registered at the courthouse, like I told you, didn't you?"

"It's there all right, for what good it's done me," Robert grumbled.

"Then you're protected and he's not. Mitchell may be a lying, conniving crook, but he never learned the law. His daddy can't protect him on this one. You've got a deed and he hasn't. That's all it's gonna take. You'll have your land back. Just don't let your mama go signing any more papers she can't read."

"I'd rather see the bastard swing. What's to keep him from doing something like that to all the widows in the county?"

"He'll swing all right. I'm just waiting for him to put his head in the noose. His daddy may be too powerful for the law to touch him, but we'll get him. It's just a matter of time."

The man on the horse beside him swore. "And look what else he'll do in that time. I say hang him now. The entire county will call us heroes."

Pace snorted. "Not likely. I'm a turncoat, remember? A Yankee and a nigger lover. I'm lucky they haven't showed up on my front porch with a noose."

Robert shifted uneasily in his saddle as they rode on. "Marrying Dora didn't help. You really believe in asking for trouble, don't you? If I were you, I'd get the hell out of this place before they fry you."

"I've got a little frying of my own to do before I'll consider that. That land belongs to my family, and I intend to see it stays that way."

As it wouldn't if Pace left it unprotected with only the women there. That much had already been proven. Only Dora's quick actions had saved it last time. Robert wondered if Pace knew that whole story. He was afraid to ask. Pace was a fuel keg with a lit wick. Robert wanted to be far away when he exploded.

Twenty-five

I am driven
Into a desperate strait and cannot steer
A middle course.
PHILIP MASSINGER, *The Great Duke of Florence*
(1635)

"No matter what happens, don't say a word," Pace warned as they tied their horses in the protection of the trees.

"I'm so scared, I couldn't say shit," Robert muttered. "This just ain't my kind of action."

Pace glared at him but said nothing further as they advanced on the outbuilding that his sources had already scouted. Inside that deteriorating gray-boarded shack lay a dozen slaves of various ages and genders, shackled to the walls. Some wore the welts of whips. All were malnourished and overworked. Homer meant to get all his fields planted even though he only had half the number of slaves he'd owned in previous years.

Robert stayed outside as guard while Pace let himself into the shack. Someone moaned. A scurrying rustle indicated he'd disturbed the rats. Then he felt the tension and knew they'd seen him. Not daring to light even a candle, he felt his way along the wall until he found the first chain bolted to the wall. The slave attached to the chain moved uneasily but didn't say a word as Pace ran his hands down the links to the padlock. Biting his lip as he positioned his awl in the center of the lock, Pace gave a prayer and swung a hammer onto the awl head with his left hand. His aim was anything but precise, and he muffled an oath as he hit his hand more squarely than the awl. The slave said nothing but waited patiently for him to try again.

Pace shattered the lock on the third try. The chains rattled to the ground, and the huge skeleton of a man rose up from the ground, taking the hammer from Pace's hand and moving silently to the next person. The whole room was awake now. A child cried, and someone hushed him. In the darkness, bodies shifted restlessly, eagerly, straining at their bonds to reach those moving freely between them. Impatience made them call out when a lock was overlooked. More hushing noises ensued.

Pace used the butt of his gun to hammer his awl into the next locks. The man he'd freed systematically smashed locks and jerked them apart with his fingers. Pace didn't want to be on the wrong side of that man's hands when he was angry. But he understood the fury with which the slave decimated the bonds. Some of these people were little more than skin and bones. At least one was little more than a child.

A woman darted out the door as soon as her chains fell away. Pace frowned and hoped she didn't give them away, but he didn't have time to stop her. Others immediately followed in her path. He couldn't blame them. Escape would be the first thing on his mind too. Kentuckians once spoke proudly of the loyalty of their "people." That day was long since gone. Resentment, fear, and hatred had taken its place.

The child cried out again, and a man cursed as he stumbled in the darkness. Robert whispered a warning for quiet from outside, but by then, it was too late.

Pace heard the shouts and knew the time had come. He'd known it would. He couldn't possibly keep a dozen people quiet until they all safely fled. He'd just hoped he could get them all free before the next part of his plan fell into place. With a solid blow to the lock he worked on, he freed one more. He didn't wait to see if the woman could rise on her own. He needed his good hand and his gun for something else now.

He slipped out of the cabin before he could check on who remained behind. Lantern light cut a swathe across the backyard from the door of the big house ahead. A porch light silhouetted Homer's pudgy physique with a rifle upraised in his hands. Homer couldn't hit the broad side of a barn, Pace knew, but he also recognized the rifle model. Leave it to Homer to have one of the hideously expensive new Winchesters.

Women went screaming into the night as the first shots fired into nothingness. A man came dashing from the overseer's house at the first sounds of gunfire, and Pace cursed his luck. He'd counted on Homer running for his horse and help, leaving the house empty. He hadn't counted on anyone getting hurt.

A man screamed as one of the wild shots found a mark. Still cursing, Pace raised his gun and aimed as carefully as he could with his left hand. The shot would have knocked the rifle from Homer's hands if his overseer hadn't taken that moment to enter the line of fire.

The overseer went spinning to the ground, screaming with Pace's first shot. He'd killed before, but not like this. Sickened, Pace looked for Robert but couldn't find him in the chaos erupting through the yard. If the boy had a lick of sense, he was inside the house, rifling the desk. He had to give Robert more time.

Pace's attention had wandered only a second, but Homer left the porch during that brief moment of inattention. He now ran across the yard, jamming more cartridges into his weapon. A woman grabbed a crying child and tried to run after the others, but she could barely stand on her own and the child caused her to stumble. Pace felt the sickness in his stomach as Homer raised his rifle to take aim. He hadn't wanted it to come to this. He lifted his gun again.

He didn't have time to fire. A skeletal shadow stepped out of the shadows, wrapped an arm around Homer's neck from behind, and jerked backward. Pace could hear the snap of his neck breaking all the way across the yard.

The sickness in Pace's stomach burned like fire, but he didn't have time for examining his emotions. This was war, pure and simple. He could only look after himself and his men. Homer was the enemy.

The slaves disappeared into the shrubbery and the wooded copse beyond. Skirting the groaning overseer, Pace dashed for the house and the desk containing the deeds to people's lives.

Robert was there, shoving thick stacks of paper into

his coat pockets, filling a gunnysack with the rest. They couldn't sort through them now. Pace helped him empty the desk.

Frightened female voices carried down from the upper story. Homer's mother and a maid, no doubt. Pace grabbed Robert's arm, nodded at the door, took the sack, and ran.

"Homer's dead and they don't know if his overseer's going to live." The words whispered back to Dora behind the counter although spoken to Josie. She pretended she didn't hear them. She couldn't tell if the speaker had intended for her to hear them or not. Surely everyone in town didn't suspect Pace.

"Where did slaves get guns?" Josie asked with true innocence.

"Someone helped them," the voice answered impatiently. "Someone went in there and got them free, and then they went hog wild. They'll murder us all in our beds now that they have a taste for killing."

Dora thought that was probably one of the more ridiculous statements she'd heard this morning. If she were an escaping slave, she'd head straight for the river. Hanging around to get revenge on the white man wouldn't enter her mind, particularly since the white men they most hated already lay dead or dying.

Josie's gasp of horror said she believed the woman's hysteria. The gasps and murmurs from the rest of the gossiping crowd gave evidence that she wasn't the only one. They would all go to their beds and shiver in horror tonight. Such a scandal was even juicier than reading a Gothic novel. It wasn't a climate highly inducive to intelligent reactions.

Dora kept her mouth shut. With luck, a few days of quiet would settle the rumors and all would return to normal. Without luck, someone would get their throat cut in the next few nights and the panic would turn into a witch hunt. Silently, she prayed for a thundering downpour to keep the populace behind closed doors these next nights.

She felt achy and wished she hadn't defied Pace and come into town again. The uncomfortable chair made her back cramp, and the child within her felt like a dead weight. She had the urge to get up and roam restlessly around the room, but the other women would have heart failure, no doubt. She shouldn't even be out in public like this.

So when the messenger burst through the front door, slamming it against the wall in his excitement, it just seemed like one more harbinger of doom. Dora winced against the pain the noise of his entrance produced, then listened with incredulity to his shouts.

"Lee surrendered! The Confederacy is dead! The war is over!"

The war is over. It didn't seem possible. David had died for this ignominious ending? Charlie had rotted in prison to prevent this feeble announcement? Men still died here in Kentucky. They still had slaves. What had changed to account for the deaths of hundreds of thousands of young men? Nothing that she could see. She had imagined bells of joy pealing overhead. She wanted fireworks and celebration.

Instead, the pain in her back struck a little stronger. It was too early for the babe. It must be gas. But Dora didn't feel like staying here anymore, listening to the wails of woe filling the room when it should echo with happiness and relief. The store would be a storm of controversy for the next few hours, maybe even days. She just didn't think she could manage it. Quietly, she slipped behind the curtains and into Sally's parlor. She would have someone take her home.

Pace still worked in the fields while Dora made her way up the stairs to her room. Annie had settled Harriet in for a nap and had gone down to the kitchen to supervise the cooking so they would have something besides beans tonight. Della had taken Amy out for a walk. As she carefully removed her gown to lie down, Dora worried about giving Della the responsibility for still another child. The woman was good with Amy, but not very attentive. How would she handle both an infant and a toddler?

She drifted off to sleep worrying over the question. By the time she woke, darkness shadowed the room. The pain in her back had shifted until it felt like a giant hand gripping her abdomen and squeezing. Dora gasped at the extent of it. When the pain receded, she carefully climbed from the bed, found a wrapper, and went in search of aid. The child had decided it wanted its freedom early. She should have known any child of Pace's would be rebellious from birth.

Annie wasn't in the invalid's room. Dora spoke a few careful words to Harriet who sat knitting in her rocking chair, then gently let herself out. She had almost made it down the front stairs when the pain struck again. She grasped the banister and held on, trying not to bend with the force of the cramp. She felt the wetness down her leg, and nearly cried. Childbirth shouldn't be like this. She wasn't supposed to be alone and scared. She wasn't supposed to be mortified at her inability to control her body.

Trembling with fear and embarrassment, she almost gave in to the urge to return to her room and change into a dry night shift. But she didn't think she had the strength for traversing the stairs again. She had to find help.

Dora eased her way through the dining hall, wrapping the robe around her and hoping it hid the stains. She could hear the sound of voices arguing in the kitchen, and she breathed a sigh of relief. She wasn't totally alone.

"If Miss Josie sent for Della, then it's her duty to go. That's no excuse for this slop. I thought Annie told you I didn't want to see these damned beans anymore!"

Pace. In the kitchen. Dora grabbed the wall and tried to keep her fears from flying off with her. She didn't know the man she claimed as husband. She knew the young boy. She knew the hurting young man. She couldn't understand the violent soldier. She didn't want to after what she'd heard today. One man was dead and another lay dying. She hated believing that Pace was responsible.

She couldn't worry about that now. Another pain enfolded her, and she dug her fingers into the wall for support. The pains came too close already. This damned child of Pace's was in a hurry. She should have known. What had she been thinking?

She must have groaned loud enough to override the argument in the kitchen. Before she straightened, Pace flew down the corridor, his tanned face paling at sight of her bent over and clutching her belly.

"Dora, my God! What are you doing down here? I thought you were sleeping."

He caught her when she sagged against him. The relief of having someone strong to cling to was such that Dora couldn't make herself straighten and walk away. She buried her face gratefully in his wide shoulder when he gathered her against him. Just for a minute. Just for this one little minute, she would let him carry some of this burden.

"It's the baby," Solly's mother said from behind them. "That baby's coming now. I'll heat up some water."

Wildly, Pace glanced around at the woman in the doorway, then down to Dora's drawn features. "Where's the midwife? Someone fetch the damned midwife."

No one answered his frantic cry. Only Solly's mother worked in the kitchen, and she had gone to boil water. Pace remembered Della and Josie had taken Amy over to the Andrewses' for the night. Annie had sashayed off on her own. Word had already reached the farm of Lee's surrender. A slave celebration would be in progress somewhere. There wouldn't be a servant left in the quarters.

Trying to stifle a growing panic, Pace carefully swung Dora into his arms. Despite the size of her belly, she didn't weigh anything. His bad arm scarcely ached as he held her. But he almost dropped her when he felt the moisture seeping through her gown. He wasn't ready for this.

"Dora, what do I do now?" he murmured as he carried her toward the stairs.

"Pray," she muttered in return.

Pray. Hell, he didn't even know what that meant. Prayer was for women. He only understood action. But the kind of action needed here wasn't the kind he understood.

He tried not to race up the stairs. Dora's fingers dug into his neck, and he could sense she held back her cries. He didn't want to jostle her any more than necessary.

He was cursing by the time they reached the top and he started down the hall.

"Blasphemy is not prayer," she reminded him as he carried her into their bedroom.

Their bedroom. He'd scarcely shared it with her these last weeks. He had harbored a tiny thread of hope those first days when he'd laid beside her and held her against him. He didn't know where that hope had gone. He supposed it had died in the tedious toil of the field and the shattered illusions of his nighttime depredations. He couldn't expect Dora to give him what he couldn't find for himself.

But at least she didn't fear him at the moment. That was something. They shut out the outer world when they entered this room. His entire world became this room and Dora and the babe making its entrance. And himself. Pace felt utterly useless and incapable of dealing with the magnitude of events.

"A dry gown," Dora ordered softly, resisting his effort to place her in the bed. "And pads. I would not ruin thy bed."

Gown. Pads. He didn't even know where to begin to look. He glanced hastily around. Her gray dress hung on a hook where she had placed it after taking it off. He didn't think she meant that. Still holding her in his arms, he demanded, "Where?"

"Put me down, Pace," she replied patiently. "Then look in the bottom drawer of the dresser. It was empty. I did not think thou wouldst mind my using it."

Dresser. He didn't want to put her down. She looked so frail he feared she would disappear if he let her go. But he couldn't get in the bottom drawer unless he put her down. Cursing again, he gently set her feet against the floorboards. She steadied herself on his shoulders, then carefully drew away. His arms felt empty, but she had given him an action he could comprehend. Hastily, he fell to the floor and ripped gowns from the drawer.

"Why in hell didn't you take one of the top drawers?" he cursed, shoving aside feminine garments and rags he didn't want to consider the use of. "You could have hurt yourself getting in this thing."

"It was good exercise," she answered with almost a note of amusement.

He gave her a look of irritation, then jerked out a plain white cotton gown. She should have ribbons and lace. He should fetch one of Josie's damned gowns. His wife shouldn't be reduced to rough cotton.

As if reading his mind, Dora nodded approvingly. "That one will do. It's old. I wouldn't wish to ruin a good one. The pads are in the chest. I've been saving old sheets for this."

Pads. He didn't want to consider the use of pads either. He suspected having babies meant lots of blood. He didn't want Dora bleeding for him. He damned well should have thought of that before he stuck himself inside her.

Pace began to sweat. This was all his fault. He'd gone and ruined the one good thing in his life. And now his carelessness would kill her. Dora wasn't meant for having babies. She was too small, too frail, too removed from this world to have babies. He should have married a big strapping girl like Sally, someone who could drop a baby a year without a qualm. He should never have taken Dora. Had he been out of his mind?

The answer to that question was yes, but it didn't help knowing that now.

Dora gave a slight scream and grabbed the bedpost.

She had taken her wrapper off. Pace could see the blood.

Events collided much too quickly. Inside his head, Pace screamed with her.

Twenty-six

A journey of a thousand miles must begin with a single step.

CHINESE PROVERB

"It's perfectly natural. I am fine, Pace."

Pace could feel the sweat pouring down his brow, but it was Dora's face he wiped. Somehow, he'd got the gown on her but couldn't button it. Perspiration shimmered between her breasts as well as on her face, but he didn't dare swipe that shadowy hollow. He should have known his child would arrive on one of the few warm nights of spring. He glanced longingly at the closed windows, but he was afraid of what he would let in if he opened them. He had no desire to drape the bed in mosquito netting at this point.

He could see Dora's face pull taut as the contraction started again. Pace strained with her, letting her dig her fingers into his palms as the pain crippled her and brought her near to screaming. Her agony terrified him. Surely giving birth shouldn't be this painful? Why in hell would women go through it? Something had to be wrong.

He'd sent Solly riding off for help. The only help he could rely on here was Solly's mother, but she had half a dozen children of her own to look after. She was industrious, but not the world's brightest person. She'd brought the hot water but hadn't told him what to do with it. He only had Dora's instructions, and he didn't see how she could remain coherent much longer.

"I've sent for Josie. You've only got just a little while longer to wait. It's going to be all right," he said when the contraction ended, more for his own benefit than Dora's.

Dora gave him a blissful look of amusement. "Josie won't come. Use the alcohol to clean your hands, Pace. Unless God sends down an angel, it's just you and me."

Pace didn't want to hear that. Stricken, he gazed at the large mound of her stomach. Surely it had doubled in size these last few minutes. How could he possibly get a baby out of there? What if something went wrong? Something would go wrong, he just knew it. His whole life had been wrong. Why should tonight be any different? Just the thought of losing Dora gave him the holy terrors. Dora had always been there. He had never realized how much he had depended on her presence, how much a part of him she had become. He couldn't tear her out now.

"Dora, I can't ... I don't know how ..."

This time, she nearly bent double with the pain. Pace grabbed her hands again, let her pull his arms half out of the sockets as she fought the pushing, straining motion. She was panting before it ended, and her clean gown was drenched in sweat.

"It's almost here, Pace. This one isn't going to wait. See if you can see its head."

He stared at her incredulously. She wanted him to ... ? She pulled her gown over her knees before arching her back in pain again. He would have to look.

Dora bit back her screams, but Pace could hear her choking gasps. They shot through him more painfully than screams. Clenching his jaw, he gingerly moved her gown back some more and adjusted her bent knees. He thought he saw something, but he wasn't sure. It still didn't seem possible. He was barely acquainted with this part of his wife. She had been shy and he had been careful with her. They'd scarcely known each other intimately for half a week. And now he was supposed to touch her in this manner as if she were just a mare giving birth.

That thought leveled some of the panic. He'd delivered foals. He could do this. If it just wasn't Dora weeping and moaning in this bed.

"Pace!" She cried urgently.

He came back around to the side of the bed and sponged her brow again. She grabbed his hand.

"Tie cloths to the bedposts. Give me something to hold besides your hands," she ordered.

In some dim way, that made sense. Pace hurried to find something suitable, grabbing up some of his best neckties and knotting them to the heavy posts so she could reach. She instantly wrapped them around her fingers and strained again.

This time, she couldn't hold back the scream. The sound pierced the hovering darkness, wailed through the halls, and shattered Pace into a quivering mass of nerve ends and tears. He hurried back to the end of the bed, hoping his damned child would make an appearance soon, before he was too distraught to think straight.

The bedroom door opened and his mother entered. Pace gave her a furious glance and returned to watching the slowly growing puddle of blood. He'd heard the expression of having his heart in his mouth. He was certain he chewed on his right now.

"Prop her up against the pillows so she's pushing down," Harriet said, opening the door to let in Ernestine, Solly's mother.

Dora didn't disagree. Pace didn't know if she was beyond hearing or not, but he attempted to do as told. Gently, he helped her in place. The next contraction came swiftly, and he hurried back to his assigned position, suddenly possessive of this duty. This time, when he looked, the baby's head had appeared, and his heart thudded erratically somewhere in the vicinity of his tonsils.

"Breathe slowly, child." Harriet took a place at Dora's side, wiping her neck and face with the sponge. "It's coming along just fine. Just a few more minutes now. Breathe with the pain, let it come."

Her agony was so much inside of him that Pace didn't hear Dora's screams so much as feel them ripping from his own lungs as the child pushed through the narrow opening and into his hands. He felt tears flooding his face, and his knees shook when the bloody infant filled his palms. Grief, joy, and terrible uncertainty paralyzed him. Wasn't it supposed to cry?

Ernestine matter-of-factly took the still body from his
hands, cleared its throat, turned it over, and gave it a
solid whack on the back. A choking cry built quickly
into a weak wail.

"Girl or boy?" his mother asked calmly, still wiping
Dora's face while unwinding her fingers from the ties.

He hadn't even noticed. Rubbing his face on his shirtsleeves, Pace tried to think, but it didn't matter. Hell, it
could be half girl and half boy for all he cared. He
looked anxiously at the growing puddle of blood and
asked, "What do I do now?"

"Cut the cord and tie it. Push on her belly a little
more to get rid of the afterbirth. She's going to be fine.
She did real well for a first one."

It looked to Pace like Dora had passed out and that
didn't sound good to him. All that blood didn't look any
better. But he comprehended orders when necessary,
and he preferred any action to none at all. He did as
told, all the while conscious of the wail of the infant
being bathed behind him. The child was meaningless to
him as yet. Dora was not. He didn't know how it had
happened, but Dora had become everything to him. He
knew beyond a shadow of a doubt that he would be
dead now if not for Dora, that she was the only reason
he remained among the living. He meant to do the same
for her, but he felt incompetent for the task.

Once the afterbirth was expelled, his mother took
over. Pace cleaned himself and went to sit beside his
wife, holding her hand, pleading silently for her to open
her eyes. She still breathed. He counted her breaths. He
felt her heartbeat through his fingertips. She was alive.
She had to be all right. If he didn't know himself better,
he would think he was praying.

"Dora," he called quietly. If she would just look at
him, he knew everything would be all right. He could
feel a hot burning sensation behind his eyelids, a sensation he hadn't felt since childhood. He wouldn't give in
to it now. "Dora?"

Her lashes flickered. The voice was too soft to be
Pace's. Pace yelled and railed and shouted. But there
had been a time . . .

The voice called her name again. She remembered

him whispering her name in her ear as his body covered hers. He had sounded like that then, loving, entreating, tender. It was wishful thinking to believe he sounded like that now. But she let the gentleness wash over her. She hurt. She ached all over. But that voice soothed the pains.

And then she heard the wails of an infant and her eyes flew open.

Pace sat there beside her. His linen shirt opened at the throat, revealing the sweat stains trickling down through the damp curling hair of his chest. She raised her eyes in embarrassment and met the green fires burning fiercely behind his gaze. She felt scorched, but the hand taking hers was gentle. Lines of strain marked the leathery skin around his mouth, and the crinkles around his eyes had deepened, but she saw something in the way he looked at her ...

"Thank God," Pace muttered fervently, bending to place a kiss on her forehead. "I've never been so scared in my life."

Dora widened her eyes slightly at this nonsense. He'd been in battle. He'd seen a great deal worse than childbirth. Why should something so natural scare him? She dismissed the idea instantly, too exhausted to give it careful consideration. "The child?"

By the time she asked, Ernestine had deposited the squalling bundle in Pace's arms. He looked at it with alarm until Dora giggled at his expression, then he set his square jaw and carefully explored the package he'd been handed.

"She's got the tiniest little fingers!" he exclaimed in amazement. "Are they supposed to be that small?"

"Give the babe to Dora, you imbecile," his mother ordered. "Of course they're supposed to be that small."

Dora knew Harriet's sharp words were not disapproval, but she saw Pace immediately stiffen. Not wishing to have any harshness ruin this moment, she pulled the blanket aside so she could see. The child had grown quiet in her father's arms. "What will you name her?" she asked softly, worshipfully, as tiny fingers curled into fists around Pace's large thumb.

"Me?" he asked, dumbfounded. "I don't know anything about naming babies. Don't you have a name picked out?"

The strong, competent man she had always known she could rely on looked as lost as a stallion in a parlor. But already he had learned to adjust his hold so he could support the baby's head and keep the blanket pulled around wiggling toes. He would learn quickly. Now, if she could just pray that the streak of violence would go away . . .

She wouldn't think about that. In answer to his question, Dora murmured, "Harriet Elizabeth."

A dead silence followed her reply. Before Pace could object, his mother snorted and answered, "I always hated the name Harriet. They'll call the poor little thing Harry half the time. If you're so foolish as to use my name, use Frances. That's my middle name. It's much prettier than Harriet."

Dora lifted her gaze to Pace, but he stared at his mother as if he'd never seen her before. Apparently coming to some decision, he nodded and carefully placed the infant in Dora's arms.

"Frances Elizabeth," he murmured. "Do I get to call her Frankie?"

He spoke so low only Dora could hear him. She shot him a glare, but the mischief dancing in his eyes so reminded her of the boy she had once known, that she couldn't deny him. She carefully shifted the bundle in her arms and touched his bearded jaw. "Thank you."

Pace looked startled, then a little pleased. "Maybe I should have been a doctor," he whispered back.

Dora managed a smile, but with the babe snuggled against her breast, she could no longer keep her eyes open. With the memory of the light in Pace's eyes warming her, she drifted off to sleep.

When Dora woke the next morning to infant cries, Pace had been replaced with Della, who showed her how to nurse the starving child. With no men in the quarters any longer, there were no nursing women either. Unlike Josie, Dora would nurse her own babe.

She slept the better part of the day away, aware that Josie stopped in for a while and that Harriet came and

went, but too exhausted to care about much else. She
knew Pace had returned to the fields. She'd had Della
pull back the draperies so she could see the sunshine.
Not until the shadows of evening filled the room did she
wonder if Pace would come.

To Dora's relief, he arrived with her supper tray. He
pulled the fried chicken apart so she wouldn't have to
balance the tray on her lap while cutting it. She noted
the mashed potatoes and gravy and remembering the
time she'd brought the same for him and he'd thrown it
at her, she lifted a questioning eyebrow in his direction.

"It's not beans," he warned her before she could say
a word. "It's the only thing I could think of to order
them to make. Be grateful."

"Unlike some people I know, I am always grateful,"
she admonished him. "But why did you order the menu?
Josie was here."

He returned his attention to his tray. "The news of
Lee's surrender has feelings riding pretty high. She
thought she'd stay with her parents for a little while,
maybe go up to Cincinnati and visit her cousin."

"It won't get better anytime soon, will it?" Dora
asked sadly.

Pace shook his head. "People don't forget easily, and
there're those who won't let them forget. General
Palmer is sending out squads of Negro soldiers now,
looking for slaves who haven't already volunteered. The
federal government says their families are free as soon
as they join, so they're joining right and left. A squad
went through town today."

Dora's head went up. "Solly?"

Pace nodded. "I told him he was already free, that he
could have the papers without joining up, but he liked
the uniforms and the promise of pay better than I can
give him, and with the war nearly over ..." He
shrugged.

"Ernestine and her children?"

"Where would they go? I gave her some things from
the attic to fix up her cabin, so she's content for the
moment just knowing she's free. But I have to come up
with funds to pay her."

"And feed and clothe her and the children," Dora

added. "Solly can't do it." She studied his face carefully. "Would it be better to sell the farm?"

Pace's lips closed in a grim line. "No."

They found more domestic subjects to discuss. They found it easier talking of the diaper cloth needed from the mercantile than asking how the neighbors reacted to the news that the South had lost. A new cradle mattress made an easier topic than the possible repercussions from the Union army against Southern sympathizers. And Dora didn't dare mention the question of Pace's night riding. Homer's death had not entirely faded from her mind. A man had died, and she knew in some way, Pace was responsible. She had difficulty imagining this man hovering over his daughter's cradle, reverently touching the tiny hands of his newborn infant, as the same man terrorizing the neighborhood with torches and nooses.

But she had seen both sides of Pace and knew the violence existed. She had married him knowing it. She just hadn't learned yet how to deal with it.

She only knew that if his violence ever turned against her child, she would be gone so far and so fast, that he would never find her again. She had discovered something inside her that gave her more strength than her mother had.

Oddly enough, she thought that strength came from Pace.

Twenty-seven

My grief lies all within,
And these external manners of laments
Are merely shadows to the unseen grief,
That swells with silence to the tortur'd soul
                    SHAKESPEARE, *Richard II*

Infant whimpers disturbed the silence of the darkened room. Dora dragged herself from thick clouds of sleep, wishing she had succumbed to the desire to keep Frances in the bed beside her. But foolishly, she had hoped Pace would join her there. He hadn't. The sheets in the place beside her were cold.

Before she could untangle the covers and force her aching body to sit, a noise in the corner of the room caught her attention. She hadn't expected anyone's help. The door hadn't opened. But someone whispered to the crying child.

Before she could wake enough to scream, a shadow stood beside her, handing her the thrashing, unhappy bundle.

"She's wet."

Pace. Dora stifled a giggle of relief. She took the soggy infant from his hands and reached for the stack of cloths beside the bed. He was here, not out riding through the night. Happiness soared through her, happiness she had no right to feel. "I didn't hear you come in."

"You were sleeping like a log. I didn't want to disturb you." He stepped back from the bed as she efficiently unwrapped the soaked diaper, cleaned the wailing child, and wrapped her up again.

"This is your bed. You're entitled to sleep in it." Dora tried to sound pragmatic, not terrified or questioning or any of those other things she felt. What was happening between them scared her. She feared she would do or say something wrong that would destroy these tentative feelings, drive him out into the night again, or worse yet, loose that barely buried violence. She wanted to make things right, but she didn't know how to go about it.

"You need your rest," he muttered, but he didn't move away as Dora unfastened her gown and guided her daughter's questing mouth to her breast.

Darkness cloaked any embarrassment she might have felt as the child sucked. Dora adjusted the pillow behind her and leaned back, enjoying the closeness of the moment. She had never felt close to anyone but Pace, and he had held her away from him for so long that she was ready and eager for any human touch. Having both Pace and the child at hand was heaven.

Carefully, she said, "You will not disturb me, Pace. Lie down and get some rest."

He hesitated, then made his way to the empty side of the bed, sitting on the edge to remove his boots. "I'll put the babe back in the cradle when you're done. You shouldn't be up and about yet, but I didn't dare disturb Annie. She has her hands full with my mother and everything else."

"I'm not an invalid. I can put her back to bed. Without Solly's help, you must be exhausted. Go to sleep, Pace."

She heard the rustling of his clothes and knew he surrendered to his exhaustion even as he protested. She wished she could see more in the darkness, but she satisfied herself with knowing he was here with her for a change. That should be enough for now.

"What happened to your 'thees' and 'thous'?" he asked with interest as he lowered his heavy weight to the bed.

More conscious of the size of Pace's shoulders and forearms as he propped himself beside her than on what she said, Dora considered his question. She didn't know the answer. "My Plain Speech?" she stalled, uselessly. He just waited for her reply. "Sometimes I forget. I was not born to it. Thou art a bad influence, I suppose."

She raised the babe to her shoulder to burp her, but she could tell she in no way distracted Pace's gaze. He rested on his side, propped on one elbow. She sensed his need to touch as strongly as she felt her own.

"The Smythes are gone. You no longer attend Meeting. None will know if you talk like the rest of us. What is the purpose of keeping it up?"

The infant exhaled a milky gasp. Dora rubbed her back a little longer, then set her to the other breast. She winced at the tug on her sore nipple, but the rush of pleasure that followed eased the pain. When Pace reached to stroke the soft dark down on the child's head, warmth flooded through her. This was the way it should be. This was what she wanted.

"Would it please thee if I stopped?" she asked with curiosity.

His fingers wandered briefly, stroking a baby-fine cheek, then measuring the texture against that of Dora's breast before reluctantly retreating. "I like the way you talk. Your voice is soothing. And it's the content of your words rather than the method of your speech that matters to me. I just thought it might make it easier for you if you didn't always have to remember to speak like the Quakers." He lay back against the pillow to stare at the ceiling.

That brief touch sufficiently exposed the fragility of her feelings. She wanted Pace desperately, as her husband, as her lover, as her best friend. She played games with the devil to want so much. But she ached with the need to be close to him, ached so much that she tried imagining he felt the same.

"I would find it just as difficult remembering not to use it," was all she said aloud.

"That makes sense." He turned a questioning gaze to her. "Would you like to attend Meeting again?"

"I can't." Matter-of-factly, she lifted the nearly sleeping infant to her shoulder one last time. "I married outside of Meeting, without the Elders' approval."

He muttered a pithy curse, then reached for the baby when Dora lowered her from her shoulder. "Well, there's one area in which I excel—wrecking lives." He swung his legs over the side of the bed and returned Frances to her cradle. When the baby uttered a protest, he stood there, rocking her until she settled again.

"Thou didst not wreck my life, Pace Nicholls." Dora sighed in comfort as she lay down and pulled the covers over her. "I made my own choices, and I do not regret them. Now come to bed."

He hesitated, then obeyed. Carefully, he made no move to touch her. "Then you're crazier than I ever thought you were."

Dryly, she said, "Thank thee," and turned her back on him.

Days later, Dora was up and about, but she hadn't yet dared descend the stairs. Harriet had ventured out of her own room to see the baby, but this day, Dora had returned the favor visiting her. The older woman looked more alert and younger than she had since Dora had known her, but she still seemed reluctant to leave the shelter of her room.

As Harriet watched Dora rock the fretting infant, she said petulantly, "I think it extremely selfish of Josie to take off with Della like that when she knew you would need her. How will you get anything done carrying a babe around?"

Privately, Dora rejoiced that she didn't have to leave her daughter with the careless Della, but she preferred soothing her mother-in-law rather than irritating her with unwanted opinions. She just smiled and patted the baby's back. "I'll find ways. I've been thinking. We had a good apple crop last fall, and those left in the barrels are getting wrinkled. If I cooked them down into sauce, do you think I could sell them in town? Then I'd have enough money to buy jam jars, and I could put up the strawberry crop and maybe even get some blackberries come summer. My jams always brought good money in town."

Harriet snorted and gave her a venomous look. "I suppose I should be happy you're not planning on working out in the tobacco field like a darky. I don't know what this world's coming to these days."

"It's changing, Harriet," Dora said softly. "And I can't make Pace bear the whole burden. He's paying Ernestine and her eldest to work the tobacco field. It's tiresome but not any harder than my kitchen garden, and they can use the money to buy their own clothes, I guess. But Pace won't see any cash until that tobacco gets sold. We've got to do something. It's for certain Joe Mitchell won't let the bank lend us any."

"That boy takes after his father. Pace will know where to find the money, I venture," Harriet said in a tone of gloom that expressed her apprehension as to the money's source.

Pace had already inquired into the disposal of the horses, Dora knew. When told the army had taken them, he hadn't inquired further. She should have told him right there and then that she used the funds for paying the taxes and remind him of the confusion that resulted, but he hadn't been in a reasonable frame of mind at the time. She felt as if she walked a tightrope whenever she was with him. He could be gentle and considerate when he wanted, but most of the time he walked around with a black cloud over his head that terrified her. He had stayed home every night since the baby's birth, but she had the feeling that meant the violence built inside him without outlet. She didn't want to provide the excuse for him to vent his rage.

A knocking at the front door followed by a familiar voice calling up the stairs shook Dora from her reverie. She lay Frances down in her basket so she could go to the hall and welcome their visitor.

"Sally! Come on up. What are you doing out here?" As the other woman approached, Dora saw the expression on her face, and her heart froze in horror. "What is it? Has something happened?"

"The telegram just came in. Lincoln's dead! He's been shot! What in heaven's name will become of us?"

Appalled, Dora didn't want to believe her. It seemed too ludicrous to comprehend. The war was over. The president had just been reelected and inaugurated weeks ago. Sally's news had no rhyme or reason. The immensity of such a disaster went beyond what she could contemplate. Only Lincoln's strength and vision had led the country through this disastrous war. They would need his maturity and intelligence to repair the chasm that had ripped the country apart. Leaderless, the country would fall into anarchy. There would be no peace.

That thought reverberated through her mind as Harriet and Sally exclaimed and worried themselves over the news. Dora tried to deny the echo of her thoughts. The frantic pounding of Pace's boots as he hit the veranda and raced through the open front door hammered the first nail into the coffin of her doubt. The high-pitched funereal wail of the black servants in the back nailed it tighter.

Frances woke and gave a cry of outrage as the bedroom door slammed open and Pace entered. Seeing Sally, he immediately yelled over the cacophony, "It's true? I just saw one of Howard's blacks . . ."

Sally nodded. "I saw the telegram from Washington. They shot him last night. He died early this morning."

Dora watched in mounting apprehension as the rage built behind Pace's eyes. His hands curled into fists, and his jaw tightened until she could see the muscle jump. She was afraid to pick Frances up. All eyes in the room turned to him.

And then something within Pace deflated. The rage died, his shoulders slumped, and he turned around and walked out without saying another word.

Tears stung Dora's eyes. This was worse than watching him pound walls. Torn between her daughter and her husband, Dora picked up the former, rocked her until she quieted, then handed her to Sally, who stood closest.

With some murmur of excuse, she left the room and went in search of Pace. She found him nailing a funeral wreath on the front door.

"I couldn't do this for Charlie," he explained calmly when she appeared beside him. "And Charlie wasn't here to do it for our father."

They hadn't had time for true mourning for either death. They had only been capable of surviving at the time. But now, seeing that black silk swaying in the breeze, watching Pace's lined face contort with grief, Dora opened the door on the vast emptiness and let the tears fall.

They mourned the death of a great man. In so doing, they mourned the deaths of all those who had died before him, because of him, and in spite of him. All those deaths and nothing left to show for it, no triumph, no celebration, no introspection on the injustice of it all, just tears and this dull, aching grief that matched the gray, drizzly day. Dora didn't dare turn to Pace for comfort, and that was the source of even further grief. His expression had hardened at the first sight of her tears. He turned away to drape bunting over the railing in his own private act of mourning.

The servants trailed through the house, begging scraps of cloth for their own miserable doors. Through the years of war, Lincoln had become a God to them, a beacon of hope. His death left them both confused and fearful. Dora knew she would have to explain the meaning of it to them sometime, but for now, she didn't understand it herself.

She was too exhausted by day's end to dress and go downstairs to eat, but she kept seeing that hollow look of pain in Pace's eyes. She didn't want him going out tonight. Perhaps if she went downstairs, he would stay home. It seemed a weak possibility, but she didn't know anything else to do.

Pace sat at the table alone, still dressed in his dirty work clothes. He looked up in surprise when Dora entered, then hurriedly stood and offered her a chair.

"What in hell are you doing up?" he asked in irritation.

"Keeping thee company?" she asked with a wry intonation that said she already knew his answer to that.

"Don't do it for my sake. I'm used to eating alone." He sat back down and returned to his meal while Ernestine's eldest child brought out another plate.

"Thou shouldst not have to eat alone. Thou couldst have come upstairs to eat with me."

"Don't preach, Dora. I'm not in the mood for listening."

"Thou art never in the mood for listening, so I shall listen for thee. Doth thou think the corn crop will be successful this year?"

"If I can keep the weeds out, we can keep the animals fed," he answered gloomily.

Dora made an inelegant noise vaguely resembling Harriet's impolite snorts. "Two horses, a mule, and three hogs are not hard to feed. Hast thou found that sow that escaped me last fall? Papa John always made money on his pigs."

"She's breeding. I've got her out in the pen. I always thought I'd make a great pig farmer." Pace speared a piece of meat with a vicious jab.

"If thou couldst sell one hog and hire a good worker, I can hold my own in a few weeks. Thou couldst go thy own way, then. I would not keep thee against thy will."

Her voice was stiff and unnatural, and Pace gave her a sharp look. "Obviously, your opinion of me is as high as everyone else's. I don't thank you for the offer."

Dora stared down at her plate. She didn't feel like eating. Her insides roiled in misery. She hadn't meant for dinner to go this way. But everything she said, he turned against her. She knotted her fingers in her lap and whispered, "Then what can I offer thee?"

"Nothing, Dora," he answered tiredly. "I don't want anything from you or anyone else. I just want to be left alone."

"I see." But she didn't. Scraping her chair back from the table, Dora wished she could understand what went through his head, but that gentle connection that had always existed between them had long since disappeared. She felt as if she floated helplessly in space, desperately grabbing for someone or something for support, and only finding air. She was drowning all over again, and this time, no one could save her.

As she started to leave, Pace shoved his chair back and stood up. "Dora, wait!"

She kept on going. She was tired of being everything to everybody. She was tired of reaching out and coming up empty-handed. She was just plain tired.

The gunshots and yells outside rang out just as she set foot on the stairs.

Twenty-eight

It is easy to fly into a passion—anybody can do
that—but to be angry with the right person to the
right extent and at the right time and with the right
object and in the right way—that is not easy, and it
is not everyone who can do it.

ARISTOTLE, *Nicomachean Ethics* (4th c. BC.)

"Dora, get upstairs!" Pace knocked his chair over as he
ran for the rifle in his study.

Dora looked from the man running for his weapons to
the front door. Exhaustion exploded into fury. Ignoring
Pace's command, she set her shoes in the direction of
the front door. She was sick and tired of being bullied.
She saw little difference between this nighttime terrorism and the earl's abuse. To survive, she must put a stop
to it.

"Payson Nicholls, get your damned hide out here!"
She didn't recognize the voice, but Dora didn't care. A
few people around here needed to learn some manners.

She heard Pace's scream of warning as she threw open
the front door, but she ignored that too. All her life she
had been bullied—by her brother, her father, her religion, the people of town. They'd told her what to do
and how to do it and punished her if she didn't do it to
suit them. She was tired of it. She wanted them to leave
her alone to make a life the way she thought best. She
wasn't precisely dumb. She knew how to survive. She
knew it wasn't by fighting people larger than her. But
she would do it anyway. She was tired of just surviving.

The men on their horses outside looked surprised
when Dora's petite figure emerged from the lamplight
shining through the front door. She could see their shock
and recognized the faces of one or two. She saw Randolph and his brother Sam. She remembered them shov-

ing her around in town when Papa John lay dying. She didn't recognize the man in front, but from his porcine appearance, she figured he was some cousin of Homer's. He looked more than half drunk. She glared at his unfastened waistcoat and gravy-stained neckcloth.

Putting her hands on her hips, she demanded, "What dost thee want? There are people sleeping here, and thy caterwauling will wake them."

The fact that Pace hadn't come from behind to shove her back inside surprised her. She had expected it, and she was prepared to fight him too. The fury boiling inside her was directed at him more than at these strangers. But he'd obviously kept the sense to stay out of her way.

"We want Pace, Dora. Call him out here, or is he such a coward he hides behind a woman's skirts?"

"Thy mother taught thee better than that, Randolph. If thou wishest to see Pace, then thou must knock at the door like a civilized human being. And thou must leave thy weapons on the outside. This is a genteel household and not a saloon."

"Randolph, go check the barn. Sam, you take the slave shacks. I'm going to rope that bastard up if it's the last thing I do."

Dora saw the shadow step from the corner of the veranda before the others did. She didn't fear these overgrown bullies, but she feared Pace and his temper. She knew he carried that deadly rifle of his. She knew every time he pulled that trigger, it took a piece of his soul. She knew it instinctively, seeing it clearly now as she hadn't before. He killed himself every time he aimed at others.

With a shriek of rage, she dashed down the steps and grabbed the riding crop from the porky one's drunken fingers. Then she slashed it down over his horse's rump until the sluggish animal reared and backed away despite his rider's screams and kicks.

"This is my house and my home and thou wilt not trespass! Be gone with thee before I am sorry that I did not let Pace riddle thy worthless skins."

Astonished by her attack, all three men clung to their nervous horses and stared down at her. A chuckle from the veranda swung their attention to the dark shadows behind the morning glory vines.

"Gentlemen, I have never seen my wife quite so angry and I've known her for a real long time. She's quite likely to burst a seam and do something she'll be sorry for in the morning if you don't move on out. You know how women are when they have young ones to protect. Not quite rational, you might say. So why don't you just skedaddle on out of here and sleep it off? If you've got a bone to pick with me, you can do it in the morning, when you're sober, in the company of the sheriff."

The fat one loosed a stream of invectives that brought a spurt of gunfire at his horse's hooves from Pace's weapon. The horse reared and bolted, and its rider slid to the ground with a solid thump.

Dora smacked the porch column with the riding whip and glared at Pace. "Stop that, Pace! I will not have thee shooting any more idiots. They are not worth the damage to thy soul." With the toe of her shoe, she jabbed urgently at the groaning man on the ground. "Get thyself out of here before I have thee trussed and delivered to the sheriff." She glared up at the other two men. "And thee too. Get him out of here. I'll not hear any more of this nonsense."

The men looked from Pace's powerful figure leaning idly against a column to the tiny irate woman standing boldly on the heels of their horses. Apparently deciding this resembled a scene from Bedlam more than a terrified household, they gathered up their drunken companion, threw him over his horse, and with a few muttered warnings of getting even, they departed.

Dora was still too furious to see straight. Giving her husband's lounging form a glare, she turned and stalked into the house, slamming the door after her. He followed, slamming the door after him. The windows shook with the double blows.

"Dora, get your ass the hell back down here before I have to come up and get it!" he yelled as she climbed the stairs.

She glared over the banister at him. "You cannot bully me any longer, Pace Nicholls! And if you lay one

miserable hand on me, I shall take this to you too!" She
waved her purloined riding crop.

Pace came to a sudden halt. He looked at her riding
crop. He looked at the rifle in his hand. Then he noted
the way his fingers had clenched into fists. When he
looked back at her, his face had filled with pain.

Quietly, he carried the rifle into his study and closed
the door.

Dora nearly cried. The sobs welling up inside her
threatened to tear her apart. All the furious energy that
had kept her going dissipated as if it had never been,
and she felt more tired than she had ever felt in her life.
And empty. She felt as if every ounce of her soul had
drained away, and she had no certainty it had been
worth the effort. She didn't think she had accomplished
anything but to make an enormous fool of herself.

She glanced at the closed study door, then wearily
turned up the stairs. She couldn't help Pace now. She
could barely help herself.

Violence begets violence, Papa John had said. It
seemed most likely that violence just killed the soul.

Pace listened to her walk away, then slowly returned
the rifle to its rack. He didn't understand what was happening. He'd never in his life meant to hurt Dora. He
wanted to protect her, to take care of her, to give her
all the things she wanted. But he'd be damned if he
knew what she wanted. He had never seen her act like
this before.

There had been those times as a little girl she'd come
racing to his defense, he supposed. She had been cute
and a little annoying. She'd grown up, however. She'd
become this quiet, modest little waif who talked in
hushed tones and never gave evidence of anger except
in an occasional disapproving glare. The wild person who
had raged and ranted at armed men tonight was not the
Dora he knew. Had childbirth changed her so?

But he found even his own reactions strange. Instead
of charging out there, dragging Dora back in the house,
and driving the bastards off at the end of his gun, he'd
let her rage. He'd almost admired the way she threw
herself at them, making them look the fools they were.

And she hadn't needed a gun to do it. He had been proud of her, until she walked off and turned her back on him.

He'd known why she'd turned her back on him. And he hadn't liked it. Pace put his boots up on the desk and stared at the guns hanging on the wall. He'd come a long way since fists and pitchforks were his only choice of weapons. He wasn't smaller than the other boys any longer. He could beat the tar out of them even with his crippled arm. But the war had taught him how to shoot, and how to shoot well. Returning to anything less effective seemed foolish. He had too much to accomplish around here to slack off now.

But he recognized the hunger in him for what it was. He wanted Dora's approval. She was the only person in this world who had ever looked at him with complete acceptance and approbation. He felt that shelter of approval deteriorating rapidly. It left him feeling naked and vulnerable. He didn't know how one little woman could do that to him, and he didn't think he liked the feeling.

He didn't need her. He could ride out of here tomorrow and make a life for himself anywhere he went. He was an educated man. Somewhere out there he could find a place that needed a gimpy-armed lawyer. He could even find other women. Women were easy. He knew more beautiful women than Dora, voluptuous, passionate women who could give him the sex he'd been deprived of all these months. Maybe that was half his problem. He needed a physical release Dora couldn't give him. But all he had to do was remember why Dora couldn't give him what he wanted, and he knew he couldn't leave.

He had a daughter now, a child he hadn't wanted and Dora certainly hadn't asked for, but his own flesh and blood just the same. He knew what not being wanted felt like. His father had made it painfully clear that he considered Pace an unpleasant surprise. He wouldn't allow any child of his to ever feel that way. Frances would have the home and loving parents he'd never had. Dora would show him how to do it.

It gave him something worth living for. Dora could

always find a better husband, but Frances could never have another real father, one who would love her just because she was his. He could do that. He *would* do that, just as soon as he figured out how to keep Dora from throwing things at him.

He heard his daughter's hungry cries and smiled to himself. He and Frances were in this together. Dora couldn't resist both of them at once.

As he climbed the stairs, Pace knew he wasn't doing Dora any favors. He would make a rotten husband. He had a bad temper, and he was a lousy farmer. But she had seen something worthwhile in him once. Perhaps he could make her see it again. And then maybe he could figure out what it was and go back to the path he'd lost somewhere along the line.

Dora looked up with surprise when he entered the bedroom, but if there was fear in her eyes, she hid it quickly. She didn't smile at him but returned her attention to the nursing infant. Pace felt a tug at his groin as his gaze fell to her breast. It had been a damned long time since he'd suckled there. The desire that hit him now shouldn't be so remarkable. He'd gone without a woman for nine long months. After Dora, he'd not had the desire for camp whores. The remarkable part was that he hadn't felt desire for any other woman except this one for a damned long time.

He didn't even know why he desired her. She was small and delicately made, scarcely the voluptuous type he'd preferred in the past. She had no coloring to speak of. Her hair was so fair as to be almost silver, and her cheeks were as translucent as his mother's best porcelain. But when she looked at him with those glorious blue eyes, he saw an angel, and he had no desire for anyone else. When given heaven, who would settle for second best?

He'd obviously stuffed his brain with too much poetry in school, and it came out now when he was tired. But he continued on his chosen course, sitting in the armchair to remove his boots, hanging his coat in the wardrobe. Dora had left the lamp on, and he knew she followed his movements, but neither of them spoke.

He waited until the child finished before approaching

the bed. He'd disposed of his shirt and wore only trousers for decency. He felt Dora's hesitation when he came to remove the infant from her arms, but she surrendered her burden without protest, allowing him to place Frances in the cradle. He kissed the squirming infant on the forehead, then lay her on her side and rocked her until she settled quietly. She would have his hair, he decided. He hoped she would have her mother's eyes.

When he came back to the bed, Dora hastily blew out the lamp. Pace smiled at her belated modesty, but he didn't chide her for it. He felt a trifle nervous himself, and for no significant reason that he could think of. He knew it was too soon after the child's birth to force himself upon her. He didn't know how soon he could take her in that way. She was too frail to bear the burden of too many children. He'd have to be careful with her. He wished he knew who to ask about these things, but Dora was the only person he knew who might have the answers. He didn't think it an appropriate conversation at the moment.

He left on his drawers so as not to alarm her unduly. He climbed into bed and felt her resisting the sagging of the mattress toward his heavier weight.

"I thank you for trying to protect me," he said gravely.

To Pace's surprise, Dora burst into tears and turned her back on him, burying her head in the pillow to muffle the sound.

He knew he was being facetious when he said it, but he hadn't expected such an emotional reaction. Actually, he'd hoped she would laugh. He hadn't heard Dora laugh in a long time. He supposed the blame for that lay with him too.

Cautiously, he tried touching her arm. She didn't pull away, but she didn't turn to him either. "I'm sorry, Dora. You just surprised me, that's all. I scarcely knew it was you out there."

"I didn't know myself," she wept. "I don't know who I am anymore. I feel awful inside. I hate those men and all the others like them. I'm tired of their threats and insults. I want to fight back. I want to. But I can't. I can't do anything. I'm so perfectly, awfully useless, and I don't know what to do about it."

She pounded her pillow until Pace thought the feathers would fly. He grabbed her fist and held it wrapped in his own. "Dora, if someone is threatening you, I want to know about it. We're in this together. You're not alone anymore. When you were little, you bashed your doll over the heads of my enemies. Give me the right to do the same to yours now."

She sniffled and allowed him to hold her, but she didn't turn to face him. "The whole world is a threat to me, and I'm tired of facing it. You can't help me, Pace. I've got to do it myself."

She still wore her hair short, but it had grown long enough to curl at her nape and form in wisps around her face. Pace smoothed them back with his large hand. "You felt safe with the Quakers, didn't you?"

She grew silent in thought, then answered, "Yes, I suppose. At least, I did not feel so alone with them, and they offered no harm."

A world where men and women spoke softly and never carried weapons was a world totally alien to the one Pace knew. He felt an odd longing for the peace such a world offered, but he knew he would never fit in. Obedience wasn't his strong suit. He had strong opinions and acted on them without need of consulting others. The Quakers would no doubt break their own rules to shoot him should he ever attempt to join their numbers. But Dora had found security with them, something she couldn't find with him. After tonight, he didn't think she needed that security as much as she thought she did. But he wasn't the one to correct her.

"Would it help ... Do you think you would like to attend church with me?" he asked cautiously.

That brought her around. She turned and stared at him through the darkness. "Thou never attended church in thy life, Pace Nicholls."

He shrugged lightly. "I was baptized in one once. My mother used to attend. Josie goes upon occasion. It might not be such a bad idea. You could get out and about more, meet people, make new friends. Then maybe you wouldn't feel so alone."

The thought frightened her. Pace could tell it from the way she stiffened beneath his touch. He couldn't blame her. The godly people in church despised him for the most part. She wouldn't find it easy facing those people who had mocked her speech and habits all these years. He didn't know why he had suggested it in the first place, except that he'd felt guilty at depriving her of the solace of her Meeting and friends across the river. It had been a bad idea. He'd look for other ways to make her accepted.

"Dost thou think ... Mayhap thy mother would go?"

Ahh, damn, now he'd done it. Now he would not only be stuck going to church, he would have to take his damned mother with him. He'd rather face a squadron of armed soldiers.

Twenty-nine

There are three modes of bearing the ills of life: by
indifference, by philosophy, and by religion
                    CHARLES CALEB COLTON *Lacon* (1825)

Easter services had already passed, and it was too soon
for Frances to go out the first Sunday after Pace made
his incredible offer. But on the second Sunday, Dora
made it clear that she would take him up on it.

She couldn't talk Harriet into getting dressed and appearing in public, but she dressed Frances in a long cotton gown adorned with eyelet and lace and a matching
bonnet and daringly made over an old gown of Josie's
for herself. She wouldn't have chosen jonquil yellow for
herself, but it was a far cry from the shades of gray she'd
worn these last years. Dora felt extraordinarily feminine
wearing the layers of old-fashioned petticoats Josie had
discarded. She felt even more so when she saw Pace
looking up at her with desire in his eyes when she descended the staircase.

"I've never seen you in anything like that," he murmured, catching her hand but standing back to admire
the effect. He spun her around to admire the satin bow,
then twirled her back again, poking inside the baby's
bonnet to admire his daughter's sleeping face. "You
both look beautiful."

Dora shifted nervously from one foot to the other. "I
feel foolish. Does the hat look all right? Thy ... your
mother says Josie will not mind if I wear it, but it looks
dreadfully expensive."

Eyes suddenly filled with compassion, Pace stroked
her cheek. "You look perfect, but you don't change for

my sake, Dora. You can wear your gray and say your
thees and thous all you like. I know you well enough to
see beyond them."

Dora hugged the infant in her arms. "But others don't.
Others see only what is on the surface. Plain Speech and
Plain Dress were meant to avoid the appearance of vanity and to equalize us, but they do not work in this new
world. If th ... if you must be a farmer, than I will be
a farmer's wife. I want us to be accepted here, Pace, if
not for our own sakes, then for our daughter's."

He couldn't argue against that. Pace lifted the sleeping
infant from Dora's arms and escorted them out to the
waiting carriage.

She had ironed the finely stitched pleats of Pace's
linen shirt herself the night before, and she admired the
effect beneath the high collar and necktie. His overlong
auburn hair was not fashionable, nor was his cleanly
shaven face, but Dora thought him the most handsome
man she'd ever met. She wanted to stroke the high taut
cheekbone he presented to her as he took up the reins.
She wanted to kiss that long, determined jaw. But she
merely took Frances into her arms and returned her gaze
to the road. She was little more than two weeks out of
childbed. She had no right thinking like that.

They arrived early, but people already waited on the
church steps and milled about the carriages. Dora felt
as if they all turned to stare when Pace pulled up, but
she refused to give in to her fears. She did this for
Frances.

And for Pace, but he wouldn't let her admit that. Pace
needed acceptance as much as she did. They didn't need
it from everyone. The good Lord only knew, there was
enough ignorance in these parts to make them more enemies than they could possibly count. But good people
lived here too, people Pace had helped, women whose
children Dora had helped birth or nurse. The whole
town couldn't despise them because of their beliefs.
Someone must hold out a hand of friendship.

It didn't look like it right now though. Dora held her
chin up as Pace helped her out of the carriage, but she
could almost hear the silence. No one called a friendly
greeting. No one came forward to comment on the

weather or their appearance. All eyes followed their paths as Pace led Dora across the street to the church. Whispers went on behind lifted hands. But no one said anything directly to them as they entered the cool darkness of the interior.

Dora knew she was crushing the fine cloth of Pace's coat as she held his arm, but she couldn't break her grip. She hesitated as her eyes adjusted to the dim light. This church was strange to her with its high decorated altar and fancy carved pews. The dust-moted silence reminded her of a long ago memory of a church with panels of stained glass, of her mother squeezing her hand and telling her to hush. She wasn't entirely alien to churches then. She had been born into one fancier than this. She could do this. God was God, no matter how he was worshipped.

Relaxing, she let Pace lead her to a pew. Several dark gowned old women hurried over to admire the baby, and Dora felt even better. Every mother wanted to show off her beautiful child. She basked in their "oohhs" and "aahhs." Frances squirmed restlessly but didn't wake.

More churchgoers filed in, and Dora felt Pace tense beside her. The old ladies hurried back to their bench. The church was no longer silent but filling with noise. Dora knew that the early arrivals would have already notified the others of their presence. She could feel curious glances sent their way, but everyone quickly took their seats. The time had passed for further talk.

It took a little while before she realized the benches all around them had filled but no one took the place beside them. She was so accustomed to standing alone, that the emptiness hadn't struck her, but Pace would have noticed. Pace belonged to this community as she never had. He should have been out on the steps exchanging gossip with the other men and straggling in late as they did now. But no one dared claim friendship with a man who had fought for the Yankees.

Biting her lower lip, Dora glanced over her shoulder to check the late arrivals. She saw Sally standing uncertainly in the rear of the church with her two oldest children. Billy John held the baby. He ignored the empty seats beside Pace and looked for others in the crowded room.

Sally's gaze met Dora's, swung to the stiff man at Dora's side, then without looking at her own husband, she marched down the aisle, dragging her children after her. She plumped her wide skirt and petticoats across the bench, settled the youngsters, then reached to take Frances and jiggle her for a smile.

Billy John stared after his wife in incredulity. As murmurs spread throughout the church, his big ears got red. The bench had room enough for just one more beside his wife. Or he could take a place on the other side of the church by himself. Scowling, he followed his wife up the aisle.

Pace's stiff stance didn't lessen any, but he nodded a greeting and was saved from saying anything by the preacher's arrival.

By the time the service ended and both women had taken turns quieting squirming infants and children, Pace showed signs of relaxing. It was next to impossible to remain formal and cold while wiping running noses and searching pockets for strings and keys to amuse bored toddlers. By the time the choir finished singing, Pace had one toddler over his shoulder and Billy John had the other. They practically ran out of the building ahead of the women with the infants.

Sally laughed at the sight and Dora managed a nervous smile. She knew the ordeal for her was just beginning, but Frances provided both shield and incentive. Feeling suddenly awkward in the multitude of unaccustomed petticoats, Dora idled down the aisle beside Sally.

Several of the women had stayed behind to admire the babies. They gossiped with Sally and looked at Dora with curiosity, but they said nothing overtly rude. Dora had done very little to disturb the townspeople in one direction or the other. They considered her Quaker beliefs odd, but they couldn't ignore her nursing skills. They struck an uneasy balance that allowed her to walk unscathed through the women.

Pace didn't fare so well. Even before she reached the church door, Dora could hear the raised voices outside and recognized one as her husband's. Moving a little faster, her silk skirt swishing down the church steps, she searched the crowd gathered outside for Pace's familiar gray top hat. She recognized the porcine creature confronting him at once. Holding Frances in one arm and lifting her skirt with the other, Dora hastened through the milling crowd. A path seemed to open miraculously before her.

"You're a damned murderer and a thief, Nicholls!" Sweat pouring down his round face beneath his silk hat, the big man shook his massive fist in Pace's face. "I'll see you hanged."

"You're a gut-crawling worm, Patterson. Where are those other two pieces of slime you dragged out to terrorize my family? If they had laws for animals, I'd haul you all into court."

The man called Patterson balled both hands into fists. "Why, you no-account nigger lover, I ought to "

Dora's breath caught in her lungs as a circle formed around the two men. She wouldn't let this happen the first time she came to town with Pace as his wife. Furious, she shoved her way through the circle.

"Stop this right now! This is the Lord's day. 'Tis ungodly to behave like this."

Pace and Patterson both turned to glare at her. Their hesitation gave time for Joe Mitchell to step into the ring and speak in placating tones.

"You're correct, Mrs. Nicholls. This is neither the time nor the place for this argument." He turned to Pace with a small frown on his handsome brow. "However, Pace, you do have a few things to answer for. A man is dead, and there's not only valuable property missing, but papers of some import to the citizens of this town. You're the only Yankee known in the vicinity who might have reason to free those slaves."

Dora watched Pace's jaw muscles tighten beneath sundarkened skin, but he visibly bit back his temper.

"You have any witnesses? I hear the overseer lived to talk."

Mitchell's frown grew a little deeper. "The overseer claimed a slave did it, but everyone knows damned well Homer kept those slaves chained."

Patterson shook his fist under Pace's nose again. "And everyone knows damned well who broke those chains."

Pace smacked the fist away. "Prove it in court, Patterson, otherwise get the hell out of my face."

"We'll take it to court if we have to, Payson," Joe yelled over Patterson's rumble of protest. "This is a law-abiding town and we can't allow damned roughnecks like you to run all over us."

That was the final insult coming from a man who had cheated and lied and stolen every waking minute of his life. Even Dora understood that. When Pace's hands knotted into fists and he yelled, "Get out of the way, Dora, go on to the carriage," she merely sighed with resignation and stepped between the two men. In a swift motion, she removed Pace's hat, holding it in the same hand as she held Frances while she held out her other. "I'd rather not have to get blood out of thy best coat, Pace Nicholls."

He didn't even look at her as he shrugged out of the tight coat and handed it over. The other man struggled to do the same. Pace could have landed a perfect blow while Patterson's arms were tied up in his coat sleeves, but he waited while Dora pushed back through the crowd.

"I'll be at Sally's," she warned him as she left. "It's too hot for Frances in the carriage."

She thought Pace's expression softened for just a moment as he glanced toward her and his daughter. There may have even been an apologetic gleam in his eye as he met her gaze. But then it disappeared and his fist aimed for Patterson's bulging stomach. Dora hurried out of the way as the crowd closed around the combatants and the yelling began.

She heard the preacher's carrying voice shouting over the noise of the crowd as he hurried into the fray, but Dora followed Sally into the mercantile and back to the cool interior of her parlor. She'd had more than enough attention for one day, and Frances was squirming in the first throes of hunger.

"Men! You'd think they'd find a better way of settling their differences." Sally threw herself down on the horsehair sofa and bounced her own whimpering infant in her arms.

"I've always thought so," Dora murmured politely, but after hearing the argument today, she didn't know what that better way would be. If Pace truly had freed those slaves, morally, he had done the correct thing by relieving their suffering. Perhaps even legally, under federal law, he might have been right, although she was less sure of that. She couldn't believe Pace personally responsible for the death of Homer, at least, she hoped not, but she couldn't find any justification in killing, under any circumstances. Two wrongs didn't make a right. The matter seemed hopelessly entangled, and both men had some right on their side. The law could never settle it to anyone's satisfaction.

But the appearance of Joe Mitchell on the scene had swayed Dora's feelings to Pace's side. If Joe Mitchell had anything to do with what had happened that night, then she knew Pace had done the right thing. Joe would find profit in his own mother's death if he could, and never leave a trace to prove it. She could understand Pace's frustration. She just wished he was busy punching Joe's nose right now instead of that other unfortunate man's.

The fact that she could feel that way horrified her, and Dora diverted Sally's thoughts as well as her own by unbuttoning her bodice to feed Frances. Gratefully, she took the shawl Sally offered and covered herself against any male intrusion.

The shouts and yells didn't last long. Sally checked out the front window to see what was happening and reported the crowd breaking up. She shooed her toddlers back upstairs and waited with Dora.

Frances hadn't quite finished nursing when they heard the sounds of two pairs of shoes stomping through the front entrance. Dora carefully adjusted the shawl and shrank back into the sofa as the parlor door opened.

She knew Pace stood there before she even looked up. Billy John stood behind him, and both men stopped politely in the doorway. Billy John made some noises about going upstairs to check on the kids and clattered out of the way. Pace remained patiently waiting for his wife to finish nursing his daughter.

Dust covered his newly pressed shirt, and one sleeve had pulled loose of the back seam. His hair fell in his face and blood smeared his cheek, but it didn't seem to be his own. She saw nothing of triumph in his eyes, only that dead blankness that had characterized his expression since he'd come home from the war. For a little while, Dora had thought it had gone away. She had been wrong.

"If you're almost done, I'll bring the carriage around," he said stiffly.

She nodded and watched him go, unable to hide her sadness. Sally tut-tutted but didn't say anything until Dora fastened her bodice and prepared to go. As she took the infant from her hands, Sally said, "There's something you ought to know, Dora."

Dora gave her a questioning look as she finished buttoning the bodice.

Sally handed Frances back to her. "Billy John says Joe Mitchell's got deeds on almost every property from the railroad station to the river."

Dora looked at her blankly.

Sally gave her a look of frustration. "Haven't you ever looked at a map? That property of yours and Pace's is right in the middle of that path."

It didn't make sense at the moment, but Dora figured it would when she had time to think about it. Right now, her only concern was driving that terrible look of pain from Pace's eyes.

Thirty

Vain are these dreams, and vain these hopes;
And yet 'tis these give birth
To each high purpose, generous deed,
That sanctifies our earth.
He who hath highest aim in view,
Must dream at first what he will do.

MISS LETITIA ELIZABETH LANDON

Dora had no nasty comments to make as they rode down the road toward home, but Pace accepted her silence as disapproval. He knew Dora wouldn't rant or nag, but her silences spoke for themselves. He knew he deserved her opinion of him, but he couldn't change into what she wanted either. She'd known what he was when she married him. She had his name and protection for the child. She shouldn't ask for or expect anything more.

The hell of it was, she wasn't asking for anything more. Dora never asked for anything. She just looked at him with those big blue eyes and either made him feel ten feet tall or lower than pond scum. Right now, the scum was winning. He'd rather she just yelled at him. He could deal with that.

He darted her a quick look in hopes of seeing an argument forming on her lips, but he just found that sad, faraway look in her eyes. His newly metamorphosed conscience stabbed him, and he turned his gaze back to the road.

Well, he had no intention of apologizing for something he couldn't have avoided. So he said nothing. When he halted the carriage in front of the house, he merely got out to help her down.

"I'm going around to check on the tobacco beds. I won't hold up dinner too long." Pace knew he sounded gruff. It was a defensive mechanism he couldn't turn off. He waited for Dora to look wounded or angry, but she

merely touched his jaw to check the swelling, then nodded and went up the stairs without his help. She may as
well have stabbed him in the gut.

He never knew what in hell to expect from her. Sometimes it was like living with three different women. Since
he already had Josie and his mother to contend with, as
well as a house full of female servants, he didn't need
three more in his wife. He never knew from one minute
to the next whether she would be terrified, angry, or
disappointed with him. He didn't want her to be any
of those.

Cursing to himself, Pace drove the carriage back to
the stables, unhooked the horse, brushed it down, and
threw it some grain, then wandered out to the tobacco
bed. He should have changed clothes, but there didn't
seem much point in it. Dora should have berated him
for tearing up the shirt she'd just so carefully laundered.
He didn't have many left. But she hadn't even seemed
to notice.

Hell, what difference did it make? They were his
shirts. This was his house. He wasted his own money,
no matter how much it felt like his father's and Charlie's.
She had no right to say anything. Dora wasn't dumb.
She knew that. He should give thanks he had a woman
who could keep her mouth shut.

But Dora had never used to keep her mouth shut
around him. He was the one person in the world she
used to talk to. Now who did she have? His mother?
Josie? Or did she just keep it all bottled up inside?

Like he did. That thought came from out of nowhere
and Pace dispensed it to the same place. Men didn't talk
about how they felt. They showed it in their actions.

He stopped outside the kitchen to wash up at the
pump before going in the house to put on a clean shirt
for Sunday dinner. In the warmth of the late April sun,
someone had opened the kitchen windows to the breeze.
As he bent over the basin, a familiar voice drifted
through those windows, and Pace nearly banged his head
on the pump as he straightened.

He slammed open the kitchen door, crossed the
kitchen in two strides, grabbed the new arrival by the

shirt front, and pounded him up against the wall. "Why the hell didn't you tell me you were back!"

Jackson grinned, caught Pace's chin in a broad hand, and shoved it back and upward until he forced Pace to drop him to save his neck. "You want me to leave a calling card at the front door?" he asked sarcastically.

Pace slapped Jackson's hand away. "You're a free man. You've got that right. What in hell are you doing back here?"

The grin disappeared and Jackson nodded at the laughing, chattering women. "Tell you later. Heard you got yourself hitched."

Pace's expression didn't change, but he pounded Jackson on the back and steered him toward the gallery to the house. "To Dora. She'll want to see you. Come on in and I'll call her down."

Jackson balked. "I cain't go in there. Things ain't changed that much. You want to talk, we can go outside."

Pace gave him a shove that nearly knocked the taller man over. "Shut up, Jackson. It's my house, and I'll invite anyone in I want to."

Jackson shut up, but his expression remained leery as he traversed the sunny gallery filled with geraniums and the overflow of dishes and pots and bowls from the kitchen. When he found himself in the elegant dining room with the polished mahogany table and chandelier, he stepped backward, almost tromping on Pace's toes.

"I don' belong in here," he muttered. "I'll go wait on the porch."

"You stayed in Dora's house," Pace reminded him, giving him another shove in the direction he wanted him to go. "Is there some reason you can't visit mine?"

Jackson eyed the expensive wool rugs skeptically, then sent his gaze over the crystal lamps dotting the polished tables as he entered the front parlor. "Dora didn't have all these gewgaws. You don' let your bulls in here, do you?"

Pace made a snort amazingly like his mother's. "You ever saw this place after Charlie and me got through with it? Don't ever walk through here barefoot. They can't get all the glass out."

Jackson seemed to accept that, but he refused to take a seat on one of the brocaded sofas while Pace called Dora downstairs. He stood there in the center of the elegant parlor, twisting his battered felt hat between his large black hands as he waited.

Pace watched as Jackson forgot his nervousness when Dora flew down the stairs to hug him and kiss his cheek. Pace figured it wasn't so much Jackson forgetting his nervousness as his being so astonished that he didn't know what hit him. In the jonquil Sunday dress and petticoats, with her hair curling all about her face, Dora was a far cry from the prim gray Quaker Jackson had last seen. Maybe married life wasn't as bad for her as it sometimes seemed.

"You're safe! You're alive! Praise be, Jackson, I've been so worried. They don't print anything about your regiment in the paper. I didn't know what to think." Dora practically danced with happiness as she grabbed his hand and led him to the sofa. Pace duly noted that Jackson sat without being told this time.

She hadn't danced and laughed like that when Pace came home, but then, he hadn't given her much reason to. Besides, Dora always seemed to know when he was alive and well or hurt and sick. She had known he was alive. She had known he deliberately pretended she didn't exist. He definitely hadn't deserved this kind of homecoming.

Still, Pace caught Dora's waist and held her possessively as he pulled her down on the loveseat across from Jackson. She looked at him with surprise, but Pace was intent on Jackson.

"Now tell me what you're doing back in this hellhole," he demanded. "You're a free man. This is not the place for a free black."

Jackson shrugged and twisted at his hat some more. "I got my discharge. I've got me some money. Liza's livin' across the river with some friends. It's time we made our home somewheres. And I thought maybe Miss Dor . . . your wife might be hirin'."

"I am still Dora to you," she said softly. "There are entirely too many Mrs. Nicholls around here, and I am unaccustomed to using titles as yet."

Pace relaxed and leaned back against the seat. He and Dora might have absolutely nothing else in common, but they both knew the difference between a man and an animal and skin color had little to do with either. That still didn't explain why Jackson had returned here.

"We're hiring, all right," Pace replied, "But you've got no business hiring yourself out when you could own your own farm if you went out West somewhere."

A mulish look rose in Jackson's eyes. "This is my home, and Liza's. She's got friends and relatives here. We got a baby coming, and she wants to be near her mama. I've got family that will come back here if they ever get out from down South. I mean to go lookin' for them first chance I get. I cain't do any of that if we run away out West somewheres. If you don' want me, I reckon I can look for someone else who will."

Pace talked right over Dora's reassurances. "You're a damn fool to want anything to do with this place. Stay across the river where you'll be safe. If anyone comes looking for you, we'll tell them where to find you."

"They got all the hands they need over there. It ain't like over here. They got just enough land to farm themselves, and they got their sons or a few hired hands to help. I know I'm takin' a risk comin' here, but you and Dora are likely the fairest I could work for."

"It could work, Pace," Dora said reassuringly beside him. "The army's saying everyone is free, even if the law doesn't. No one is arresting free blacks anymore. There's too many of them. Jackson is a soldier. The army will look out for its own. He and Liza could stay down at my place. I don't like it being empty." She hesitated, then offered tentatively, "Perhaps . . ." She threw a nervous glance to Jackson. "I once said I would rather sell to Jackson than any man around here. I haven't changed my mind any."

Jackson's expression remained stoic. Pace knew as well as Jackson the likelihood of anyone letting a former slave own land. They'd burn the house down before that happened. Neither man wanted to disillusion Dora, but both had reason to want what she wanted.

Pace eased the tension slightly by nodding. "All right. We'll talk about that later. First, we'd best get Jackson settled in with some story that will make it easy for people to accept him living down there."

Jackson relaxed and almost managed a smile. "That mean I'm hired?"

Pace gave him a scowl. "You never had a doubt, did you? What the hell do I know about farming? You're going to be mule, slave, and manager, all rolled into one. And you're not likely to see a damned cent until the crop comes in. You want the job, you've got it."

Jackson chuckled. "I ain't gonna be no mule. If I'm the one tellin' you what to do, that's your part. There's enough land out there for ten men. We got some fancy work to do." He looked at Dora. "Where's that boy, Solly? He ought to be useful right about now."

"The glitter of gold and brass buttons led him away. You weren't here to talk him out of it. At least the war's over so his mama doesn't have to worry about that."

"Stupid little fool," Jackson muttered, standing up. "White man's army will have him diggin' ditches. He ain't gonna learn nothin' that way. And he's probably fritterin' every penny on drink and women like all the others." He gave Dora an apologetic look. "Sorry, 'bout that. I didn't mean to talk like that in front of you."

Pace was reluctant to rise. He rather liked sitting here with his arm around Dora's shoulders like any normal married couple. The minute they got up from here, they'd go their separate ways again. He wondered briefly if that would ever change, but he could tell Jackson was eager to get back to his own wife with the news. Grudgingly, he stood up to shake his new employee's hand.

"Welcome back, Jackson," Dora murmured beside him as she rose to leave. "It will be good having thee with us again."

Both men stood and waited for her to depart. The moment she let, Jackson gave Pace a shrewd look.

"Liza and me can stay in one of them cabins out back. You and me both know what will happen if we stay down to the house."

Pace shoved his hands in his pockets and regarded the other man carefully. "If Dora's willing to sell, I'm willing to cut a deal. I need cash. You've got it squirreled away. We can set it up so you make a down payment and pay the land off over time. I'll give you a proper, witnessed deed that you can keep somewhere safe, bull I'll file the mortgage now. Nobody around here's got enough brains to check courthouse records for mortgages. A legal mortgage properly filed will give you proof of ownership should you ever need it. I'll put out word that Dora hired you back, and you're working the place for her. It's risky as hell, but it might work. Everyone's pretty well accepted that Dora was raised by the Quakers and doesn't think like they do. They won't like it, but they'll buy the story."

Jackson nodded slowly. "I'll talk to Liza. She already knows we're takin' a risk. I've got enough for a down payment. I'll farm Dora's place in the evenin's to get the cash to pay you the rest. I'll set enough aside for me and Liza to live on until the crops come in this year. We'll just have to agree on the price of Dora's land and what's fair wages for workin' your place."

Pace walked with him to the door. "I figure your wages will have to be a percentage of the crop. When the time comes, I'll have to take your crop in with mine. You know that, don't you? You'd better think hard before you agree to any of this. This town won't be ready for what we're proposing for another hundred years."

Jackson jammed his hat back on as he reached the veranda. "You don' think I been thinkin' of anythin' else every minute of every night and day since I left? I cain't worry myself into the ground no more. I got to reach and take what chances I'm offered. You're offerin'—I'm takin'."

"And I'm damned grateful. I learned to be a lawyer, not a farmer. I've been afraid to tell Dora I figured we couldn't hold out one year on what I know about farming. If I'm going in debt to buy seed corn, then I sure as hell would like to know it will come up and grow when I plant it."

Jackson grunted and started down the steps. "If you're lookin' for a sure thing in this business, you got the wrong career, boy. I'll see you soon as I get Liza settled in down to the house tomorrow."

Pace let the door close between them with a mixture of apprehension and hope. For the first time since he'd come home to find the entire burden of the farm dumped on his shoulders, he actually felt hope. It wouldn't last long, but he would nourish it while he could.

He took it upstairs with him that night, after all the house grew quiet. Dora had gone up to feed Frances half an hour earlier. She should be just about ready for bed. He had a need to somehow settle a few things between them. The differences between them loomed enormous, and he hadn't done much to bridge them. Maybe, somehow, they could start looking for some common ground.

He opened the bedroom door just as Dora slid the yellow gown off her shoulders. He caught his breath as lamplight gleamed like moonshine over silken skin. He'd never seen Dora wearing a corset before. She had her back partially turned toward him, but he could see enough. Her breasts were much fuller than he remembered, round and beckoning for release from their laces. He nearly groaned with the suddenness of his arousal.

He hadn't come in here for this, but the blood rushing from his brain to his groin washed away any memory of his original intentions. She wasn't two steps away from him, and Pace made those steps without conscious thought. He had his arms around her, pulling her back against him before she could register a protest.

"Have I ever told you how beautiful you are?" he murmured against her ear.

He could feel her head tilt back and knew those blue eyes looked at him with surprise.

"Thou needn't repeat untruths for my sake," she answered with a faint tone of puzzlement.

Pace held one arm firmly around her corseted waist although she made no effort to escape him. He ran his other hand through the fine curls around her face. "I don't lie when it's easier to keep silent. You look like an angel. Sometimes, you look so ethereal, I forget that you're real." His roving fingers slid downward, finding the flaps that opened so she might feed his daughter. He explored this new contraption with interest when she did nothing to keep his hand from straying.

"I am real. You are being foolish . . ." She gave a

gasp when he succeeded in freeing her breast. "Pace, we cannot. It is too soon."

He looked down at the tiny strawberry-crowned tip and sighed with regret. "I was afraid it might be. I haven't gone this long without a woman since I was a boy. I've about reached the state where I envy Frances."

He registered her shock and managed a slight grin as he met the question in her eyes. "I can't say my intent was to be faithful, Dora. It just happened that way." His gaze grew more serious as he continued studying her. He could offer her this, at least. "I made vows, Dora. I intend to keep them. I'll wait until you're ready."

Pace admired the slight flush across her cheeks as she registered his words. Some women would prefer that her husband find a mistress and relieve them of their wifely duties. If he knew nothing else about Dora, he knew that wouldn't be her preference. And he was glad. He'd never found real pleasure in paid liaisons, nor in the occasional encounter with women who just wished a night of sex. But he vividly remembered every minute he'd shared with Dora. He prayed she felt the same way. If the flush meant anything, he wasn't far wrong.

"I've been told it takes four to six weeks," she whispered in embarrassment, but she made no attempt to evade his exploring fingers as he loosened her corset completely.

He was hard and aching, and he could feel her breathing grow rapid as he toyed with her nipples. He made this difficult for both of them, but he needed this right now. He needed to know that she wanted him as much as he wanted her.

"What about babies? I want you fully recovered from this one before we make any more." He couldn't believe he was saying this. His first urge right now was to take her and to hell with the consequences. But his conscience seemed to be winning the inner war for a change.

"She said the chances are less when a woman is nursing."

That seemed preposterous to him. Ladies who didn't nurse but gave their children to slaves for nursing seldom had large broods of children. The colored nurses, however, usually had a dozen. But he didn't want to argue. Four to six weeks, and more than two were already gone. That was something he could count on.

"I'll wait. It might kill me, but it will be worth the waiting." Gently, reluctantly, Pace moved his hands from temptation to unlace her properly. "Jackson wants to buy your farm. I want to thank you for making the offer."

She gave a tiny shiver as he brushed her breasts again before removing the corset. "Papa John would have approved. I think he would have approved of you had he lived."

Pace smiled wryly behind her back as she pulled off her chemise. "He wouldn't have approved of what I did today."

"No. I cannot feel it is right either, but sometimes, I can see no other choice. It confuses me."

He shrugged out of his waistcoat and regarded her modestly turned back with some confusion. "You're not angry?"

"I am angry with Joe Mitchell. I am angry with that man for starting the argument in such a place. I am angry with myself for not knowing how to stop what happened. I am angry a great deal more than I ought. But I don't know what to do about it."

Pace's lips turned up in amusement as Dora pulled her night shift over her nakedness before unfastening the tapes of her petticoats. He'd never had a modest women before. He found himself rather liking the idea. "You need do nothing but look after Frances and this household. I might be crippled, but I can fight my own battles."

She turned and stared at him boldly even though he was removing his shirt. "Thou art not a cripple, Pace Nicholls. I will not hear thee say it no more than I'll hear it from any other. You are alive. Do you have any idea of what that means to me?"

She had tears in her eyes. Pace regarded them with astonishment. He couldn't remember anyone crying over him before. Except Dora. Something clicked into place, and he studied her cautiously. "You kept me from returning until the battle was over. Why?"

The tears glistened in the lamplight like dewdrops on

cornflowers. "You would have died there. Or met Charlie, which would have killed you as certainly."

He didn't think he wanted to hear this. "How could you know that? How could you even know when the battle would take place?" This conversation didn't make sense, even to him, but those days when he'd made love to Dora were engraved indelibly on his mind. He remembered clearly how he had returned to Atlanta only to find cold ashes. He knew of a certainty that she had given herself to him just to keep him from that battle. He didn't know how to react to that knowledge.

"I don't know," she whispered. "The same way I always knew where you were, how to find you. I just knew. And it's gone now. It's been gone since those days. Do you have any idea how much I suffered, not knowing where you were after you left here?"

He didn't know. He didn't want to know. The horror of what she said was still sinking in. In taking carnal knowledge of his childhood angel, he'd literally brought her down to earth.

Thirty-one

Love seeketh not itself to please,
Nor for itself hath any care,
But for another gives its ease,
And builds a Heaven in Hell's despair.
WILLIAM BLAKE, *The Clod and the Pebble*

They saw the carriage well enough in advance for everyone to hurriedly clean themselves up to greet the occupants. Pace politely helped Josie out when it arrived at the front steps, then unloaded the trunks while Dora greeted her warmly and took Amy into her arms.

It was mid-May, Frances was beginning to sleep through the night, and Dora almost felt human again, but she could never compete with Josie's healthy good looks and spectacular attire. Dora still wore her Quaker gray while doing her household duties. She still felt like a servant next to Josie's elegance.

After sending the carriage off, Pace bounded up the stairs to take Amy into his arms. The little girl squealed and clasped his neck happily, and Dora felt the knot of love in her insides squeeze a little tighter. Despite his faults, Pace was a good man. He was good with children. He seemed happier with them than with anything else in his life right now.

He looked at Josie with the politeness the occasion required, and Dora could find no other emotion hidden behind that careful facade. It could be wishful thinking on her part, but she let herself relax a fraction, until she turned and caught Josie's expression. Sadness and a hunger for something unavailable lingered there. It made Dora's stomach grind nervously.

"It's good seeing you again, Josie," Pace was saying. "Too many Yankees in Cincinnati?"

Josie managed a feeble smile. "Daddy says he needs me back here. I'm supposed to stay with him, but"—she finished brightly—"I left so much of my wardrobe here, I just couldn't leave it all behind. And I had to see my darling little niece, after all. Amy's done nothing but talk about-her all the way home."

Pace grinned and tickled Amy's stomach. "Want to see your new cousin, baby doll? She's saying your name already, you know." He carried her toward the stairs, more intent on the child's laughter at his foolishness than the tension between the two women left behind.

Josie's shoulders drooped as soon as he left the room. "I can't stay here. I thought I could, but I can't."

Dora wanted to shout her agreement. She wanted to yell in triumph that Josie had made the wrong choice and now she would suffer for it as Pace had suffered then. But she couldn't. She merely murmured sympathetically, "It's your home, too, Josie. Charlie would have wanted you to stay."

Josie gave her a sharp look. "Don't give me that humble Quaker nonsense, Dora. Pace didn't even look at me, but he wasn't paying much attention to you either. We're both in this together, whether we like it or not. I'll admit, you were smarter than me. You chose the right brother. But I know more than you do about men, and I can have him back if I put my mind to it. He adores Amy. He'll do anything for her."

Dora's gaze shot up to meet Josie's. "He has a daughter of his own now. There is no contest. What is it you want, Josie? I can see thou art unhappy."

"The 'thees' and 'thous' are slipping now, aren't they?" Josie said, a trifle maliciously. "Life in this place is like that. If not for you, I probably would have murdered Mother Nicholls in her bed. And if Charlie hadn't taken himself off to war, I might have murdered him too. It's hard to remain young and innocent when married to this family."

Josie's words harbored a grain of truth. Dora was afraid to agree with it. She gestured toward a seat. "Thou has best tell me what is on thy mind."

Josie took the seat and worried at her gloves. "My

father says it is time I consider marrying again. That's why he called me home."

She wore navy instead of heavy mourning, Dora noted. The choice wasn't exactly unseemly, but it did indicate a certain lack of respect for a young husband killed defending what he thought right. Dora couldn't precisely blame Josie for that. "Thou art young yet," she said cautiously. "Amy should have a father. Perhaps thy father is right."

"I don't wish to marry again," Josie answered, almost viciously. "I won't have another man knocking me around again. I won't do it. Daddy says he wants assurance that he has someone qualified to take over his land when he's gone. Why can't he hire someone? I don't want to be traded like a slave on the auction block."

Dora knit her fingers together and stared at her sister-in-law worriedly. "It is not easy finding someone to hire. Only ask Pace. And thy father is not well. He is worried about thee and thy mother when he passes away. I can see what he is saying." Unhappily, she added, "And I know what you mean, also."

Josie looked on the verge of tears as she looked past Dora to stare fixedly at the wall. "What can I do?"

Dora thought for a minute. "He cannot force you to marry," she said carefully.

"But if he died tomorrow, I couldn't run that place. It's his life. It means everything to him. You know how you feel about your father's farm."

Dora didn't mention that she'd gladly parted with the land for good cause. Pace had spread the word that Jackson was just tenant farming as before. "Does the farm mean more to your father than you do?" she asked quietly.

Josie stiffened, then considered. "I don't know. It might."

"If it does, then he is not worthy of your respect, and you needn't sacrifice yourself for him. People are more important than land, Josie." She continued in a more cautious tone, "Don't ignore your father's wishes, though. He could be right. A good man will not hurt you. He will love and worship you. But do not marry just to please your father." As Josie had before, Dora could have added, but refrained.

"You are right." Josie set her lips firmly. "You make it seem so easy." She finally turned her gaze back to Dora. "Thank you." Then she smiled and rose from her seat. "I still think I'll stay a few days. I left all those old gowns here. I must do something with them. And if Daddy wants me to start courting again, he'll have to buy me a whole new wardrobe. That will make the trouble worthwhile."

Dora followed after her, worrying at her bottom lip. "Josie, I . . ." She grimaced and forced herself to speak outright. "I took the liberty of using one of your old gowns, the yellow one. Harriet said you would not mind, that it was out of date. I could fix it back . . ."

Josie glanced over her shoulder as she swept up the stairs. "You would look horrible in yellow. Throw it out. I've got others much more suitable. I'll never fit in them again. And I've got the latest patterns. We can make them look like new." She grinned happily. "It will be just like the old days, planning wardrobes and talking about suitors. I just might enjoy this after all."

It might be just like Josie's "old days," but it certainly hadn't been Dora's experience. Still, she made no objection. She would be the kind of wife Pace deserved. Who better than Josie could tell her what that entailed?

Besides, the four weeks were up, and Pace had made no sign of taking his husbandly rights since that night two weeks ago. The jonquil dress must have done it that time. Maybe a newer and prettier one would work this time.

When Pace walked by Josie's bedroom a little while later, the two women were engrossed in a cascade of gowns and petticoats littering the bed and floors. He shook his head and kept on going. He should be grateful that he had a wife who didn't demand expensive new garments every time she turned around. From the looks of it, Charlie had spent every dime the farm had earned keeping Josie in clothes.

He didn't like thinking about that. He didn't like thinking about the empty stables and the three miserable hogs left in the pen. The army had stripped them of

everything but the chickens, and he supposed he should
be grateful for them. He knew farther south it was far
worse than that. Two armies had stripped entire planta-
tions of every living thing, including the men who had
run them. As Dora had once told him, at least he was
alive.

His bad arm ached constantly from the punishment he
gave it, but he couldn't let Jackson do all the work. He
could hoe a row as well as the next man. He just didn't
have to like it.

As he watched Solly's sister hoeing the tobacco patch,
it occurred to Pace that Josie hadn't brought Amy's
nurse back with her. He hadn't given Della any wages
before Josie left. He bet the woman had decided to take
a job in Cincinnati. Hell, he didn't have the money to
pay another servant anyway. Josie would have to look
after Amy herself.

But he sure would like it if someone could look after
Frances during the night so he could have some uninter-
rupted time with Dora. She fussed and fidgeted with the
baby all the time, getting up in the middle of night to
check on her even when she slept. Then she would look
so tired when she went to bed at night that he didn't
have the heart to wake her when he got upstairs. He
didn't think four weeks enough for Dora to recover, but
he would have liked a few kisses or hugs in the interim,
just enough to remember he was a man.

Hell, who was he fooling? He was so randy that he'd
go straight from kisses to the real thing. Dora wasn't the
problem. He was. He didn't know how to take her in
his arms and just give her a nice peck on the cheek once
in a while. He had no experience with that kind of thing.
His father certainly had never done such things. But
Pace kind of figured Dora would like that, and eventually, it might lead to something more.

But he didn't even know how to kiss his own wife: a
damned thing to admit but the truth. He must have been
out of his head that first time when he'd practically as-
saulted her in the barn. And the next time, she'd come
to him and practically offered herself. They'd never
courted. They'd never had time to ease into these things.

And now he expected to just hop into her bed and have his way with her whenever he felt like it.

That discussion about how she'd always known how to find him didn't make things easier. He still didn't know how to take it. He'd thought about it a lot of nights, lying there beside her while she slept. Dora had spoken the pure and honest truth as far as she knew it. She had always been able to find him. She had always appeared when the boys tried to beat the tar out of him. She'd found him the night Josie had announced her betrothal to Charlie, and the time the slave catchers had shot him. He remembered other times, too, times when she'd appeared where she shouldn't, all because of him. He'd never thought of how she'd done it. Now he couldn't stop thinking of it.

She had saved his damned life, and he'd showed his gratitude by taking her in a field and putting his child inside her. And then he'd gone off without a word, leaving her to deal with it all alone. If she was an angel, then he was the devil incarnate. No wonder they couldn't seem to connect anymore.

As he watched Jackson guide the mule through the far field, Pace wondered if Dora wouldn't be a hell of a lot better off if he got out of her life. He knew himself too well to think he could continue sleeping in her bed without eventually taking her. Then there would be more children. He didn't know if he could put her through that again. Even worse, he didn't know if he could feed and clothe the inevitable results of their coupling.

He wasn't good for much else. Jackson could plow the fields. If he could hire another hand, they wouldn't need Pace at all. He wanted Frances to have a father, but what the hell kind of a father would he be? One who would teach her to have tantrums and beat people up when she got mad?

It churned his stomach just thinking of it. He wished he could talk to Dora about it, but Dora had too good a heart to believe she would be better off without him. She would spout nonsense about this being his home, and she might even offer to leave rather than let him go. He didn't want that. He wanted to take care of her, to see that she had everything she deserved, and he wasn't doing much of a job of it this way.

He was thinking so hard, he stared at the carriage coming up the road for a full minute before he realized what he stared at. Not too many people in this area owned carriages. The roads were too rough to make them worth much. He knew every carriage and buggy for miles around, but he didn't know this one. Someone might have bought a new one, but this thing looked like it was on its last set of wheels. As a matter of fact, if he recollected rightly, they rented one like it at the train station.

The rails ran from Louisville to Nashville. He didn't know anyone coming from either place or anyplace in between, but that carriage was headed for their drive.

Shouting at Jackson, Pace loped back the way he had just come. If Josie had relatives arriving, he didn't want Dora meeting them alone.

He had waited too late to have time to put on a fresh shirt and tie. He bounded through the back door just as the carriage pulled up at the front. He could hear the women on the stairs speculating as to the identity of the new arrival. Amy gave a cry of distress somewhere on the upper floor. Pace could hear Josie's leather shoes clicking down the upper hallway after her daughter. He heard Dora opening the front door before he could traverse the dining room.

"We are here to see Mr. Carlson Nicholls," an arrogant, English-accented voice drawled loudly, as if talking to some deaf-and-dumb servant.

"I am sorry. He passed away more than two years ago," he heard Dora answer politely. "Might I help thee?"

Pace stood in the back of the hall now, studying the newcomers before making himself known. He didn't like the sound of their voices. He liked their looks even less. They wore high-crowned beaver hats and pearl stickpins in their cravats. The one had a spoiled, selfish set to his fat lips. The other was gray-haired and peered through his glass as if inspecting a particularly fascinating species of insect. Pace knew what would come next. He could halt it now, but some perverse reasoning allowed him to

let them stick their feet in their mouths. There were
some things from which Dora didn't need his protection.

"Then we wish to see the master of the house," the
one with the fruity voice and the gray hair replied. "We
don't care to be kept waiting out here. Let us in at once,
girl, and fetch your master."

Pace grinned, crossed his shirt-sleeved arms, and
leaned against the wall.

"I have no master but God," Dora informed him
curtly. "If thou wishest to enter, thou wilt state thy business first."

"By Gad, I'll not take this sort of insolence! Get out
of my way now, girl, before I have Smithers remove you.
I'll make myself known if you will not." The taller man
with the fat lips and narrowly spaced eyes pushed himself forward.

Pace was already lifting himself off the wall and heading toward the door with fists balled when the younger
man's eyes suddenly bulged as he glared at the small
figure in prim gray.

"Alexandra! My God, Alexandra! What have they
done to you?"

To Pace's complete shock, Dora literally slammed the
door into the man's nose and raced up the stairs.

Thirty-two

Angels and ministers of grace, defend us!
Be thou a spirit of health, or goblin damn'd,
Bring with thee airs from heaven, or blasts from hell,
Be thy intents wicked or charitable,
Thou com'st in such a questionable shape,
That I will speak to thee.

SHAKESPEARE, *Hamlet*

Pace had the passing notion that he'd best close the door on the floored visitor as if it would drop the lid on Pandora's box.

But the furious shouts of the older man and the prostrate figure groaning on the floor made him certain the problem wouldn't go away by itself. Josie's appearance on the stairs with a puzzled expression on her face finished the matter. She was already casting him curious glances and descending to examine the extent of the damage.

Throwing off his reluctance, Pace commanded Josie with a look to stay put while he strode through the hall. As the prostrate figure dragged himself up, holding his nose, Pace crossed his arms over his chest and blocked their entrance. He almost reveled in the fact that he wore only shirtsleeves and work pants still coated in field dirt. He wore old boots with his toe pushing out one side. He had to look worse than any peasant these elegant creatures had ever been forced to converse with. He almost grinned at their shock.

"May I be of some assistance, gentlemen?" Just for the hell of it, Pace used his best courtroom voice. Keeping the opposition unbalanced had always been one of his best ploys.

He couldn't tell if Dora's performance or his own was the major contributor to the fact that the two men stared at him wordlessly for a full minute before speaking. Apparently coming to some unspoken agreement, the older man stepped forward while the other dabbed at his nose with a handkerchief. Neither man removed his hat, Pace noted. He would have to teach them respect before he let them in.

"Excuse us, but I am Sir Archibald Smithers, solicitor for George Henry, third earl of Beaumont. This is his son, Gareth, Viscount Doran. We have a subject of most importance to discuss with the master of the household. Is he in?"

Pace still didn't like the man's tone. Nor did he like the looks of the snotty bastard with his bruised nose up in the air. That would be Gareth, he supposed. Gareth. Hell of a name for a man. He almost grinned at what he could make of that name, but Dora's reaction to these men still gnawed at his insides. They'd called her Alexandra. The snotty one seemed to know her. He didn't like that idea in the least. He didn't grin.

"I'm Payson Nicholls, and this is my property. My wife has taken objection to your disrespect and familiarity, so state your business quickly so you can leave." This went against all the rules of Southern hospitality. If his mother listened, she would rush down those stairs and box his ears in another minute or two. But Dora didn't run without reason. He wanted these men gone so he could go to her.

The two men looked disbelieving. They glanced at Pace's old work boots, then back to the elegance of the hall foyer behind him. Their gazes caught on Josie hovering in the background. The older man scowled.

"Mr. Nicholls, the subject we have to discuss is a delicate one requiring some explanation and privacy. We must insist that you let us in."

"I've told you, my wife doesn't like your looks. You'll spit it out here or be on your way." He was beginning to enjoy this. He'd been an officer in the army. He knew how to give orders and swing his weight around. But he'd never owned property before. He'd never held a position of authority where he could legally throw someone off his land. He really liked the idea of having that power over these two.

The gray-haired man looked suitably indignant. He

clutched his ebony cane in his gray-gloved hands and glared at the obstacle in his way. "If we must come back, it will be with the law at our sides. You cannot keep Lady Alexandra in a position of servitude any longer, not so long as I shall live, sir!"

The fun went out of the game. Pace stared at the older man, seeking the truth in his furious features. Maybe he was a candidate for an asylum, but it looked as if he would have to let him in to find out. Clenching his teeth, he stepped back from the doorway.

Josie drifted down, her gaze fastened with interest on both men—or perhaps more appropriately, on their expensive attire. Pace was forced to make introductions. "Josie, Sir Archibald Something or other, and his faithful sidekick, Gareth. Gentlemen, my sister-in-law, Josephine Nicholls."

Gareth scowled and ignored Josie's outstretched hand. The solicitor bowed over it respectfully. "Madam, a pleasure." He glanced reprovingly at Pace. "The viscount is properly addressed as Lord Doran."

Pace nodded his head impatiently at the parlor. "Whatever. I want to hear this cock-and-bull story. I don't have anything better to do today. Josie, will you get the gentlemen something to drink? They won't stay long."

Josie glared at him. "Pace, you are being unforgivably rude." She swept off in a trail of swishing silk and a cloud of French cologne.

The visitors took seats on the brocaded sofa, giving scant regard to the lovingly polished furniture hauled all the way across the mountains from Virginia. His ancestors had shipped some of it from England when this country was still a colony. To these men, the antiques were no doubt inconsequential trash. That didn't raise them any higher in Pace's estimation. This was his home, and he was proud of it. He hadn't fully realized that until now, when these snobs turned their noses up at what his family had worked so hard for generations to attain. He was damned proud of what his family had accomplished. He'd wager neither of these two could repeat the performance.

"Well, gentlemen, I'm waiting." Pace didn't take a

seat but leaned against the mantel, tapping his toe impatiently. "Tell me how I'm keeping your imaginary Lady Alexandra in servitude. You do realize the war is over and we don't have slaves any longer."

The viscount scowled, leaving the solicitor to answer. "As I said, I represent the earl of Beaumont. He received information from a certain Carlson Nicholls that he had reason to believe Lady Alexandra Theodora Beaumont resides in his household under the name of Dora Smythe. Due to the war and the clumsiness of our investigators sent to find the truth of the matter and other mishaps, we were unable to follow up that letter until now. We have come to take Lady Alexandra back to her rightful home."

Pace stared at them with incredulity, but the sinking feeling in his stomach told him the story was so wildly incredible it must contain elements of truth. Dora's accent mimicked this man's. She'd come from England. He had always considered her on a level well above her surroundings, but he had only acknowledged it by calling her an angel. He didn't have much acquaintance with English aristocracy, but he supposed an earl's daughter might have the characteristics of an angel to an ignorant ass like himself.

Worse yet, Dora had recognized these men.

But she hadn't run to them with open arms. Warily, Pace regarded his visitors. In their prissy clothing with their soft white faces and padded coats, they didn't appear dangerous. Dora had easily felled the big one. But Pace knew the legal ramifications of power. An earl would have plenty of power. They were dangerous all right.

"Have you proof of any of this?" he asked casually, accepting the mint julep Josie presented him even though he despised the stuff. At the moment, he welcomed a good belt of bourbon in any disguise.

The other men took their drinks and sipped them carefully, returning to their seats when Josie departed. She'd thrown Pace a look that meant she would thoroughly interrogate him later to pay for this, but Josie presented the least of his problems.

The viscount spoke for the first time, his tone harboring arrogance and impatience. "My sister was stolen from my father's arms by a band of lying, thieving religious fanatics when she was only eight years of age. I have a miniature of her here that will show she hasn't changed to any great degree over those years. Your maidservant is almost the image of her."

He held out a painted portrait in a gilded case. Pace took it gingerly, staring down into the blue eyes of the fairy child he remembered so clearly from his sixteenth summer. His stomach clenched with an immense wave of despair, but he concealed the pain as he handed the portrait back.

"The portrait resembles Dora, my wife, as a child. She has never mentioned anything about kidnapping. She was adopted by an elderly couple and reared in the Quaker religion. She seemed happy with them. I should think a Lady Alexandra would be quite vehement about returning to her real parents if your story were true."

The viscount's face grew mottled with anger at this slur to his honesty, but the solicitor interceded for him. "The matter should be quite simple, Mr. Nicholls. Call the girl down and let her tell us the truth."

Pace straightened and felt his jaw muscles tighten. "The 'girl' is my wife, gentlemen. I will ask her if she wishes to speak with you, but I will not order her to do anything she does not want to do."

"How do we know you will give us her honest reply? If she is held against her wishes, then we can't expect you to answer us honestly," the viscount sneered in retaliation to Pace's earlier insult.

He wanted to pound his fist into the other man's soft jaw, but he refrained with a control he hadn't realized he possessed. Glaring at them, Pace stalked toward the door. "That is your problem," he informed them as he walked out.

He didn't know what he would find when he went upstairs. He didn't want to believe a single word they said, but he couldn't think of any good reason for concocting such an insane story. There were too many truths in it, and Dora's reaction was the strongest one of all.

He found her sitting in the rocker in his mother's room, cradling Frances in her arms as she pushed the chair back and forth. His mother was up and dressed and gave him an icy look when he entered. Pace ignored her and turned to Dora. She wouldn't look at him. His insides turned to ashes, but he must go through with this.

"Are they telling the truth, Dora? Are you this Lady Alexandra they're spouting about?"

She smiled as Frances grabbed her finger and pulled on it. She stroked the infant's cheek, then looked up at Pace. He'd always thought she had the face of an angel, and he thought it even more so now when he feared she would be torn from him. The sunlight from the window gilded her curls and illuminated her translucent skin like some majestic painting of old. Her features were calm, her eyes steady as she gazed upon him.

"Lady Alexandra drowned with her mother a long time ago. She's dead, Pace. She has been for years. No one mourned her, no one cared. Tell them to go in peace, Pace, and leave us the same."

Hot tears burned his eyes. Pace wanted to weep for the child he remembered, the beautiful sprite who sang and cradled her doll and talked of angels and left brilliant blue feathers in the hands of a miserably abused boy. If anybody deserved love, an angelic child like that deserved it, with the complete worship and adoration of every human being who ever met her. The blunt statement that no one cared crippled him with anguish.

She was his heart, the only reason he still lived, and she sat here now, telling him nobody loved her. He didn't care how she phrased the words, the meaning was the same. Lady Alexandra or Dora Smythe, she had left England unloved and unmourned. He held those arrogant men below responsible for that. Fury welled inside him, but it was a strangely cold fury. It wouldn't escape in its usual manner.

Pace calmly crossed the room and kissed Dora's forehead. He carried the smile she gave him all the way down the stairs with him. A man would fight and die for a smile like that. He was ready to fight when he walked into that parlor.

"My wife informs me that Lady Alexandra drowned with her mother, gentlemen. I don't know about you, but I'll not question the lady's words. I'm sorry for your loss, but it appears to me that anyone who takes four-teen years to come looking for a missing child can't have any particular concern for her welfare. Now, if you will excuse me, I am a busy man."

With a sense of satisfaction at the fury in his visitors' faces, Pace turned and walked away, leaving them to find their own way out.

He shook with fury and some other emotion he didn't care to name by the time he reached the stable yard. He felt as if he'd just walked through the lion's den unscathed. He wanted to rage and weep and then run upstairs to take Dora in his arms and never let her go. He was clearly losing control, but Dora frequently did that to him. She was the only person in this world who could make him feel alive. He felt very much alive and ripping mad right now.

Pace waited until he saw the carriage leave, then returned to his field chores. He needed the physical labor to work off his raging emotions. He'd discovered that much in working these fields: the work made him too tired for indulging in tantrums. By the time they had the crop planted, he hadn't any fight left in him. He just wanted to go home to Dora, a hot bath, and a few explanations.

Josie was the one who greeted him, however. She halted him before he could even reach the hall. "Who were those men?" she demanded. "What did they want? Dora won't tell me anything. She's acting like they never existed."

Sweat dripped down his forehead and probably streaked through the dirt he felt encrusting his face. Pace rubbed a weary hand across his brow and considered shoving her out of the way. But despite popular opinion, he'd been raised a gentleman. "If Dora prefers not to mention their existence, then it behooves us to do the same. Get out of my way, Josie. I need a bath."

She stamped her foot but wisely moved aside when he reached a filthy hand out to catch her arm. "The first interesting men in this county in a coon's age, and you won't even tell me who they are! That's extremely unfair of you, Pace Nicholls!" she called after him.

Pace ignored her and continued up the stairs.

Dora had a bath waiting for him. She poured the last pail of hot water into the tub when he walked in. The rapport between them was so complete for this one brief moment, that Pace felt as if he didn't need to say a word. He unfastened his shirt with weary gratitude.

She didn't stay to help him, but then, he hadn't expected her to. He would have liked it, but he'd not yet introduced her to the pleasures of sensuality. She was still his modest little Quaker. He found it too incredible to believe that she might be a Lady Alexandra. Earl's daughters didn't fix baths for filthy bankrupt farmer husbands.

But he knew Sir What's-his-face and the bloody viscount would return. They didn't look like the kind of men who gave up easily. They also didn't look like the kind of men who would come traipsing all the way to the wilds of Kentucky looking for a long-lost female member of the family either. They wanted something, and that something had to be mighty important for them to come after it personally.

Josie sulked through supper, but Dora chattered pleasantly on inconsequential matters throughout the evening. Pace waited until both women had plenty of time to settle the children in their beds before going upstairs himself. He didn't know where Josie was, but he found Dora sitting quietly beside Frances's cradle, stroking a hand-colored illustration of angels in her Bible.

He checked to see that the infant slept, then he took the Bible from her hands and set it aside. Lifting her from the chair, he carried her to the bed, where he settled her on his lap and in his arms as he leaned against the headboard.

"They'll come back, Dora," he informed her calmly.

She sat stiffly for a moment, then gave up and leaned against his shoulder. "She really is dead, Pace. What can they do about it?"

He hugged her close, enjoying the subtle lavender scent of the sachet she kept with her gowns. Her silken curls brushed against his jaw, and he leaned his cheek against them. "I don't know until you tell me the story, angel. I should imagine earls have a lot of power in their own country, but it's a different story over here. That's why your brother brought along his fancified lawyer."

"He's not my brother," she said with the first trace of hostility she had shown. "He's my half brother. I would be happy to never see his face again."

Pace felt as if he trod on broken glass. He moved cautiously. "I can't say that I was enamored of his looks either. Why do you think he's come looking for you after all these years?" He didn't ask why she hadn't told him she was an earl's daughter. He didn't ask any of a half-dozen questions clamoring in his mind. He let her lead the way.

"Because he wants something," she answered without hesitation. "I doubt the years have changed him for the better."

That so closely concurred with his own conclusions that Pace couldn't argue. Carefully, he prodded, "How much do you remember? You were only a little girl when you left England."

Her fingers curled into his shirt beneath his open waistcoat. "I had nightmares for years. I remember the nightmares." She hesitated, then buried her face deeper into his shoulder. Her words came out muffled. "It's like remembering the scenes from a book you read long ago. I remember. I just don't know if I remember them right. I can feel them better than think them. They don't feel good, Pace."

He rubbed his hand up and down her spine, massaging her shoulders lightly. She was so slightly made. He could wrap his arm completely around her widest part and still have room left over. He tested that theory and found his hand brushing her breast. She didn't flinch from the touch, and he stroked there gently, idly, not pressing for more. He felt his arousal, but he knew he wouldn't do anything about it tonight.

"Children are often unhappy, Dora. Could you have just been lonely?"

She shook her head vigorously. "Oh, no. I remember much more than that. He killed Mama. He beat her and beat her until she ran away, and then he killed her. And I think he killed the man too. They didn't come back for me. No one came for me, except Papa John."

She seemed to have retreated to her childhood, to that terrible day she must be remembering. Pace felt her words like needles in his heart. He didn't want to understand, but he was afraid he understood all too well. He also thought he saw why Dora flinched every time he raised his hand near her.

"Who killed her? Gareth?"

"The earl," she stated flatly. "My father. I won't go back there, Pace. I'll die before I'll ever go back there. Alexandra *is* dead. Just tell them that."

"I did, and I will, but if there's murder involved, the authorities need to know about it. They may want you as a witness. You may be a danger to them. I think you'd better stick close to the house until they're gone."

She nodded and relaxed in his arms.

A moment later she arched against his hand and leaned back so she could see his eyes. The blue of hers had darkened to the purple of passion, and Pace felt as if he'd forgotten how to breathe when she whispered, "Will you make love to me tonight, Pace?"

Thirty-three

O lyric Love, half-angel and half-bird
And all a wonder and a wild desire.
ROBERT BROWNING, *The Ring and the Book*

The thickness in Pace's groin hardened until he felt his seams stretch. Dora sat sideways in his lap, and her thigh rubbed against him, taunting him further. She had her head tilted back so he could lean over and ravish her slender throat at will. The position pushed her breasts temptingly against the faded cotton of her gown. She hadn't covered herself completely after feeding Frances, and he could see the valley shadowed between her breasts. She was like a willow wand in his embrace, light and bendable at his choosing. A touch there—Pace's hand hovered near her breast—a kiss, here—his lips lowered to the corner of her mouth ...

Oh, God, he wanted it so badly. He could taste her. He did taste her. He allowed himself the one brief sweet sample of her lips. Then he jerked away, closing his eyes and holding himself stiff against temptation. It wasn't just his staff throbbing right now. Every inch of his skin was on fire to touch her. He ached inside his teeth—no doubt because he clenched them so hard. He dug his fingers into the thickness of her skirt and petticoat and held on tight until he had some measure of control.

Then he opened his eyes and found her staring up at him in confusion and embarrassment, and he wanted to crawl under a rock and burrow his head into the dirt. "No," he said, succinctly, because it was the only word he could get out just yet.

Dora tried to pull away, but Pace wouldn't let her go.

He wondered how much control it would take to keep
his hands off her if he undressed her. He wanted to at
least see her, to admire the ripe swells of her breasts,
the luxurious curve of her waist. More control than he
possessed, he realized when he couldn't take his fascinated gaze from the shadowed valley behind her bodice.

"What's wrong with me?" she whispered painfully.

"Nothing. You're perfect." He ground that much out
from between clenched teeth. He didn't think he could
do much more. He wasn't even sure he could concen-
trate long enough to voice explanation. He was in agony.
But he didn't want to let her go.

Perfect little eyebrows arched slightly. "And you're
not? Are you telling me you've been lying with loose
women and have caught—"

Pace choked on a laugh and covered her mouth with
his hand. "Don't, Dora. I'll rupture myself if I laugh
right now." He moved her carefully to the bed's edge,
not so far that he couldn't reach her, but away from the
center of his desire. He didn't think she was experienced
enough yet to notice the extent of his arousal, but Dora
was a quick student. It wouldn't take long.

"Then, why?"

She wouldn't let it go. Pace sighed and released her
long enough to shove his hair back out of his face. "I
don't think we should take any chances on making babies right now," he finally found the words to admit.

She sat silently beside him, digesting that piece of information. Her lashes were a light brown and her skin
was so white that it held him in fascination, but a flush
of pink still colored her cheeks. Pace didn't know if it
was from embarrassment or the same desire that had
him hot and panting right now. He just knew she was
beautiful and that she didn't buy his story for an instant.

"You didn't worry about making babies when you
should have," she spoke her thoughts out loud. "I've
told you it's not easy to make one now. You wanted to
a few weeks ago. Something's changed." She shot him a
direct look. "Gareth changed it."

He ground his fingers through his hair. "Look at him,
Dora! He was wearing more wealth on his back than I'll
make in this next year. You're a lady, dammit! How can

I keep asking you to do the drudgery of this house, drudgery my own mother won't do, and then compound the insult by filling you with babies we can't afford year after year? I'll not do that to you, Dora."

"I see." She slipped away from his side, crossing the room to blow out the lamp.

He could see her undressing in the moonlight from the window. She didn't wear corsets under her gray gowns. Once she hung up the gown and petticoat, she wore only a short chemise, drawers, and stockings. He wanted them to be silk for her. Someone like Dora deserved only silk against her skin. He could never buy it for her.

Pace sighed with gratification as she stripped off her remaining garments, and he could watch her silhouette move unfettered to the drawer where she kept her night shifts. She was rounder than he remembered, more womanly and less like a slender reed of a girl. He wondered if it were possible to die of want.

She climbed in beside him and asked, "Aren't you going to take your clothes off?"

"I don't think so," he decided, staring at the opposite wall through glazed eyes. "Nobility doesn't come easily to me."

She lay silent for a minute before replying quietly, "Gareth was born to it, but you have more nobility in your little finger than he'll ever know in his entire life."

Pace swung his legs over the side of the bed and stripped off the sadly rumpled coat he'd worn to dinner. "Don't make a hero of me, Dora. I'll fall flat on my face if you try."

"It's not drudgery to me, Pace," she whispered into the pillow as she turned on her side to watch him.

"That's because you don't know any better." He dropped his shirt on top of the coat and waistcoat over the chair back. "I'll bet you don't have any memory of scrubbing floors or washing baby diapers when you were Lady Alexandra."

He kept his back to her as he unfastened his trousers. Her voice drifted hauntingly to reach him anyway.

"I remember standing on the very tips of my toes with my nose pressed to a spot on the wall for hours past my bedtime, until my legs wobbled and my stomach hurt and I cried so hard I couldn't stop. My nurse paddled me when I couldn't stand any more."

"God *damn* them!" Pace flung his shoe at the wall and fell onto the bed beside her, dragging her into his arms and holding her through the thicknesses of bed-clothes. He buried his face in her hair and tried to block out the images she had given him, but his body shook with the rage of them. He knew she spoke of the least of the cruelties. He knew all too well that some subjects were too painful to ever put into words. He didn't want to picture what human monsters might do to the frail fairy child she once had been.

"It's all right," she soothed him, caressing his hair. "He didn't hurt me like he hurt my mother. I just want you to see that it's all over. I'm Dora now. I'm your wife. I like making jams and jellies. I like having a baby whose diapers I have to wash. And I don't have to scrub floors. We pay Ernestine to do that. And when you hold me, I feel like a lady. I'm right where I want to be, Pace."

Oh, God, You made me weak, Pace muttered to himself as he leaned over and pressed his mouth to Dora's. Her words spread like warm honey through his insides, but her lips set him on fire. She was everything he'd ever imagined and more. She soothed his wounds, supported his sagging pride when he needed it, and offered him the physical love he so craved. He would never get enough of her. He would die trying.

Carnal knowledge, that was the phrase, Pace thought incoherently as he parted her lips and immersed himself in the moist heat inside. He forgot the question when her tongue slid hesitantly over his. He groped beneath the blankets to find her breasts. He needed to touch her there. He needed to bring her to the painful peak of arousal he had already reached. He needed to bury himself so deep inside her he would never be free.

His fingers had just reached the moist juncture of her thighs when the thready cry of an infant intruded.

Pace cursed and spread his fingers over her heat, as if to hold her there until the cry quieted. Dora arched soundlessly against his palm, and he slipped a finger inside to ease her. The infant's cry grew louder.

He contemplated tearing off the rest of his clothes and driving into her right here and now, burying himself deep and not coming out until they were both drunk with satisfaction. He could do it. He could be quick. He was already full to bursting.

But his daughter's cries grew more pitiful. She hadn't woke at this hour for this past week or more. Something must be wrong. With a groan, he drew back so Dora could slide from the bed and rescue her. He didn't think he could stand on his own anytime soon.

Dora brought Frances back to bed with her and opened her gown. The babe gulped frantically for a few seconds, then gave another cry of distress. Pace watched as Dora put the infant over her shoulder and rubbed her back. Frances wailed even louder, arching her little spine with anger or pain. He couldn't tell which.

"What's wrong with her?" Worried, he leaned closer to better see the baby's face. It was screwed up in a tantrum wilder than anything he could ever remember throwing.

"Colic," Dora answered. "Her belly's all drawn up and tight." She lay the baby over her lap and rubbed her back that way. Frances squalled a while longer, then settled into a restless squirm with a gassy hiccup.

Pace buried his face in his pillow and felt the ache take over his body. "Hers isn't the only one," he complained.

"Would you like a tonic?" she asked innocently, still soothing infant whimpers.

Pace turned and gave her an evil look that she couldn't see. "I need a tonic all right, but it ain't the kind you drink."

His tone must have finally registered. She turned her worried look on him. "What would you have me do?"

"Just lie beside me and let me groan. I'll recover." Not anytime soon, he could tell her, but he didn't. She ought to feel something of the driving passion he felt. She would learn how it lingered until satisfied. But she was still recovering from childbirth. She probably didn't feel it as strong yet. He would only make things worse by encouraging her as he had tonight.

Dora finally got the child quieted and slipped beneath the covers with him. Pace could feel the brush of her night shift against his legs. He had only to pull up the hem and he'd be back where he'd been a little while ago.

Although she lay awake and willing beside him, Pace turned his head and shoved his hands under the pillow. For once in his life, he would do the right thing. He just had to figure out what the hell it was.

Dora admired the dark outline of Pace's broad shoulders against the pillow in the dawn's light. His auburn hair lay tousled and falling across his brow. The sheets had fallen back to cover only the lower part of him, and she had the urge to push them away from the narrow line of his hips, but she didn't have the courage to follow through.

Frances was already making waking-up noises in her cradle. She wouldn't have time to persuade Pace into changing his mind. She wasn't a natural-born seductress, but she knew Pace. Last night had given her some modicum of confidence. She could tempt him somehow, she knew. And she meant to. Not just because of how he made her feel, although the memory of last night burned sharp and clear and aching in her mind. That memory was a large measure of her desire. But she had to tempt Pace to hold him. She knew once the possibility of another baby had entered the picture, he would never let her go.

That was an utterly foolish and insane thing to believe after he'd left her last time, but Dora knew it with all confidence. She understood him. Or she understood enough to know that she was his wife now, his possession, and Pace had very few of those to claim his own. He might let her go under some misguided attempt to see her better cared for, but he would fight until death for any child of his. The idea of marriage as ownership had terrified her, but she thought perhaps it worked a little both ways. She owned some small piece of Pace, and that knowledge gave her the confidence she needed to protect what was hers.

Gently, she ran her fingers over the wide curve of his shoulder muscles to the broad expanse of his bronzed back, then trailed down the naked hollow of his spine. He stirred restlessly and started to turn over. Dora darted from the bed before he could reach for her.

She sat beside him and nursed Frances before he opened his eyes. She felt a tingle and knew he watched her. She had never given much thought to what it meant to be a woman, but Pace was so much a man that the contrast made her very aware of her femininity. She felt small and delicate right now with his shoulders looming beside her and his long hard legs stretching well beyond where hers ended.

He stayed silent so long that she feared his anger, but when she cast a quick glance in his direction, he watched gravely as Francis nursed. At Dora's glance, he looked up.

"The two of you scare me sometimes," he said without inflection, the green of his eyes muddied as he watched her. "Somehow, I've got to keep you in clothes and food and protect you for the rest of your lives. I've never had this much responsibility laid on me before."

Dora felt a place inside her tighten as she studied the lines of worry and pain around his lips. He held his right arm carefully, as if it pained him this morning. She bit her lip as she realized the burden she would dump on him should she put her plan into action. Perhaps she shouldn't . . . She didn't know which voice to listen to, whether she heard her own selfishness or God or worldly temptation speaking.

"I don't want to be a burden," she answered softly. "I want to help, if you'll just let me."

"That's not the way it's done," he responded gruffly, rolling over and throwing off the sheet as he stood up. "A man takes care of his family."

Dora felt a flare of anger. She didn't know where it came from, it just materialized. She watched as he jerked on his drawers with his back turned toward her. "And what does a woman do?" she demanded, trying not to admire the interesting aspect being covered.

He glared over his shoulder at her as he pulled on his

shirt. "Dress in pretty clothes and smile, I guess. How the hell should I know?"

The anger dissipated as quickly as it had appeared. Dora smiled at the interesting picture he painted. Of course he didn't know what women did. The only woman in his life had spent the better part of it lying in bed contemplating the ceiling. She would teach him differently, if he gave her enough time.

She wouldn't think about that. She had to believe that she was here to stay, and that Pace would stay with her. With that thought firmly in mind, she placed Frances over her shoulder and as she rubbed her tiny back, she daringly answered, "Thou hath found the wrong wife for that then. Shall I fetch Josie for thee?"

Pace gave her a scowl and reached for his pants. "She'd bankrupt me in a hurry. Now isn't the time to tease me, Dora. I'm not in the mood."

"I can see that," she said serenely. "Is it nobility or frustration that makes thee nasty in the mornings?"

He gave her a glare, grabbed his boots, and stalked out.

Dora wanted to laugh, but her own temerity scared her. She had actually dared say what she thought, and retribution had not followed. A vast horizon of possibilities loomed before her. Did she dare take a step forward all on her own?

Thirty-four

Outside show is a poor substitute for inner worth.
AESOP, "The Fox and the Mask," *Fables* (6th c. B.C.)

"The English gentlemen are staying with Joe Mitchell,"
Josie announced airily as she sauntered into the parlor.

"A man shall be judged by the company he keeps,"
Dora answered enigmatically as she took another stitch
in the seam of one of the gowns Josie had given her.
After all these years of wearing coarse gray cotton, she
was a trifle overwhelmed by the wealth of material be-
stowed upon her, but she intended to make the best of
it. She had plans, and these gowns would aid her in
them. If the Quakers no longer accepted her, then she
need no longer accept their principles. She wasn't so
certain she had ever accepted all of them, but some
made too much sense to give up. Gradually, she worked
her way through what she wished to keep and what she
must discard.

"Joe Mitchell is a gentleman," Josie replied, with a
slight scowl that warned against argument.

"Joe Mitchell is rich," Dora agreed, knowing Josie
wouldn't decipher the difference.

"Daddy has asked them all to dinner. I said I would
help Mama."

Dora knew perfectly well that Josie looked for reasons
why she shouldn't, but Dora had no intention of giving
them. As far as she was concerned, her past was dead,
and so were the people in it. She hoped their ghosts
would go away, but she knew they wouldn't until they

had whatever it was they wanted. Idly, she wondered if the local minister performed exorcisms.

"Dost thou wish to leave Amy here?" she asked calmly.

Josie clenched her fingers in her skirts and finally said with exasperation, "Quit playing the innocent, Dora Nicholls! You haven't survived in this household all these years without becoming as devious and conniving as the rest of them. You parade around with that meek and modest mask, but it doesn't fool me one second. If we're ever going to be friends, you're have to learn to talk to me."

Dora looked up in surprise at this outburst. "Are we going to be friends? Is that possible with Pace between us?"

Josie threw up her hands and walked the carpet. "Pace isn't between us. Pace lives in his own dratted world where men are men, and women are there to admire them. I'm not a complete fool. I've learned my lesson. I want a real gentleman, someone who will treat me like a lady. Pace doesn't even know I exist."

Dora bit back a smile at the irony of this conversation, but she wouldn't offer laughter at Josie's attempt at honesty. She just shook her head and bit off the thread she'd knotted. "You and Pace would have made a good pair. He would have loved pampering you and giving you everything your little heart desired in return for your smiles. But he can't do that now, so he'll have to put up with me."

Josie's eyes narrowed shrewdly. "He wanted you enough to bed you. I expect that's enough for any man when it comes right down to it. Help me, Dora. Tell me who these Englishmen are. They're not rude and uncouth like these country louts around here."

Dora met Josie's eyes squarely. "I have never seen the older man in my life. I know nothing about him."

Josie gave her an impatient look. "What about the younger one? He's more to my liking. He's supposed to be an English lord."

Dora hesitated. She would prefer to leave the past dead, but she could not lie. She would rather say nothing, but Josie made it plain she couldn't leave well enough alone. With a sigh, she answered, "He would be worse than Charlie. Stay away from him, Josie."

Josie didn't want to hear that, but she couldn't argue when she had asked for it. She eyed Dora with curiosity. "Will you give me reasons?"

"I was eight years old when I left England. How can I tell thee more?"

"Then you can't really know him now, can you?" Josie asked triumphantly.

"Skunks can't change their stripes, Josie. If you won't listen to me, then don't ask me. See for thyself."

"I shall. I think I should find it very interesting being called Lady Josephine." Josie started to leave the room until Dora called after her.

"You would be Lady Doran. Unless you have your own title, you must take your husband's."

It was a warning of sorts, but Josie chose not to hear it. Dora shook her head as Josie swept out. A man like Gareth would consider a woman nothing but a playtoy to treat as he wished. The nursery had been littered with Gareth's broken toys.

Dora twirled in front of the pier glass in Harriet's room as her mother-in-law looked on with satisfaction. Josie's refitted skirts swirled in soft blue waves around her legs, billowing with the flounced crinoline beneath it. The fitted bodice had scallops of blue silk at the daring low neckline, and Dora couldn't make herself look closely there. The tops of her breasts felt horribly exposed, but both Josie and Harriet had assured her that the décolletage was extremely modest. The sheered puff sleeves made her feel half naked, but those too were acceptable for evening. Still, Dora felt as if she understood why Quakers favored Plain Dress. She had never before thought of herself as an object of adornment.

But she did this for good cause. She must make Pace see her as his wife. If she must dress like Josie to accomplish that, then so be it. He wanted a woman he could set on a pedestal and cherish, so she would be that woman. If he needed a wanton in his bed, she could be that, too, and a lot more willingly than sitting on a pedestal. She blushed as she admitted that to herself. The woman in the mirror blushed with her.

" 'Tis a pity you haven't any hair," Harriet complained querulously. "I used to have such marvelous long hair. All the men admired it. At least you've got curls," she added generously.

Dora looked at the tousled mop of her hair with despair. She knew nothing about fixing hair. Hers wasn't long enough to pull into a neat chignon. She'd let it grow out lately, but it still just made a riotous cascade that barely touched her shoulders, and the sides were too short even for that. She'd wrapped a blue ribbon around her head to at least hold some of the waves out of her face since she didn't wear her cap, but she didn't think that she had accomplished much. The woman in the mirror didn't look very polished or sophisticated. She just looked young and very exposed.

"You look quite lovely, Dora," Harriet assured her, then ruined it by adding, "you ought to have a little more color."

Dora pinched her cheeks and bit her lips as Josie had shown her how to do. That made her a little pinker. She just thought it would look a trifle odd if she spent the evening biting and pinching herself. She turned to admire the huge satin sash at her back. That was a touch she could appreciate.

"I'm afraid this is the best I can do. Dost ... Do you think Pace will like it?"

"He'd not be a man if he didn't." Harriet listened to the sound of feet on the stairs. "He's coming up to change. Hurry, and you can slip downstairs after he goes in your room."

Dora leaned over and gave her sleeping daughter a kiss, gave Harriet a hurried hug, and left Amy playing happily with a doll. As the sound of boots disappeared into the bedroom, she dashed into the hall and down the stairs. If nothing else, she would shock or surprise Pace into noticing her.

She checked the dining room to make certain all the best china and silver were set out, then hurriedly gave Annie and Ernestine last-minute instructions. She'd promised them each a dress from Josie's discards for

cooking and serving this special meal. The outrageous
bribe so tickled the two women that they'd outdone
themselves. It would be worth every bolt of cloth.

Dora rushed back to the dining room to light the can-
dles, then arrayed herself on the sofa in the parlor, not
a moment too soon. She heard Pace pounding down the
stairs as she settled in. He would have a good appetite
after a day in the fields. She'd sent out a cold dinner
since they worked too far from the house to come home.
He'd be ready for a big meal tonight. She tried not to
laugh when she heard him hurrying for the dining room
where she usually set out the meal for him. Tonight, she
played the part of lady.

His gait as he returned down the hall was considerably
slower than when he'd hurried to the dining room. Since
he hadn't found her in either of the places he expected,
he was no doubt puzzled. Good. She meant to keep
him guessing.

Dora looked up from her embroidery as he stopped
in the doorway. She had pressed Pace's coat and waistcoat and left them hanging out so he'd wear them. He
hadn't bothered buttoning them, but she didn't mind.
He looked splendid just the way he was, with his white
linen starched and brilliant against the darkness of his
face, and the soft gray coat clinging to the breadth of
his shoulders. He gazed at her from beneath a hank of
hair falling across his brow. Her gaze dropped to where
his green silk waistcoat fell open, revealing the flat taut-
ness of his stomach. She saw nothing of Charlie or Gareth's softness in Pace. He was all hard muscle and sinew.
Her insides quivered at the thought.

He didn't say a word. He just stared at her with astonishment. She managed a tremulous smile. "Did you
have a good day?"

Pace's hand went surreptitiously to the buttons of his
waistcoat. He had one or two fastened by the time he
recovered himself enough to enter the room. Dora could
feel the heat rise in her skin as his gaze lingered on her
shoulders and a little lower. She remembered how he'd
touched her there last night, through her cotton gown.
It had been dark then. It wasn't now. The lamplight
surrounded her.

"I can't remember," he answered dryly. "Do you mind telling me what you think you're doing? Are we expecting company?"

He knew they weren't. She had set only two places at the table. Dora gazed at him through lowered lashes as she'd seen the other ladies do. "Just us. Josie is at her father's tonight. Would you like something to drink? Annie will call us when supper is ready."

He shoved his hands in his trouser pockets and rocked back on his heels. "By all means, let's have a drink. What will you fix for me, my lady?"

Since he was perfectly aware she knew nothing about alcohol, he had a right to his sarcasm, Dora supposed. But she knew a decanter sat on the table with glasses beside it. She merely rose and poured half a glass for him. He could tell her what the liquor was easier than the other way around.

He continued eying her skeptically as she settled on the sofa again. "Annie is fixing supper?"

"Annie and Ernestine," she replied serenely, although her insides shivered as he continued staring at her. "I've asked them to fry ham and fix sweet potatoes since you had a cold dinner today."

"I see." He continued rocking back and forth on his heels as he sipped his drink and watched her with a cautious eye. "You're going to make me ask, aren't you?"

She glanced up at him with surprise, then read his expression and smiled. "I am wearing a pretty gown and smiling. Isn't that what thee wished?"

"What I wish?" His gaze raked over the cerulean blue of her skirts and back to the tempting expanse of flesh above. "What I wish has absolutely nothing to do with pretty gowns. As a matter of fact, that gown is a hindrance to my deepest desires. But I won't ask you to take if off just yet. I think I'll need that ham first."

Oh, Lord, she remembered that look too well. Dora could almost smell the heated earth and fresh cut hay. She didn't think she could eat a bite of anything or even notice what was set before her. She didn't have time to worry about that. Annie called them for dinner.

Pace offered his arm and Dora took it as she had seen

the other ladies do. His arm was strong and hard beneath the deceptive pliancy of his coat. When he led her
to her seat, his fingers briefly brushed her bare shoulders
He'd shaved with that exotic-scented soap he'd told her
smelled like sandalwood from Australia, and she didn't
want him to move away. The knowledge that it would
be hours before she could feed Frances again and retire
to their bedroom gnawed at her insides. How could she
do to him what he was already doing to her?

She realized he did it deliberately after she put her
buttery biscuit down and Pace took her hand before she
could use the napkin. He took each finger into his mouth
separately, sucking on them gently, then tracing the path
of her palm with his lips before using his own napkin to
clean what remained of the butter from her fingers. She
didn't think she would ever use that hand again.

Dora stared at Pace mutely, at the way the candlelight
caught and gleamed in the auburn streaks of his hair,
the sensual tilt of his lips as he smiled at her, the glitter
of his eyes that told her he knew what she was doing
but he was better at it. She didn't need to seduce him.
He wanted what she did, at least in the physical sense.
Whether his stubbornness would allow either of them to
have it was another matter entirely.

"Who's taking care of Amy and Frances?" he asked
conversationally as she sipped at her water.

"Your mother is. She's promised to put Amy to bed,
but Frances will be hungry again before she'll sleep
through the night."

"You've planned this very well, my lady. Will you tell
me your motive before or after we go to bed?"

Dora blushed and stared down at her dinner plate.
"Must I have a motive? Thou didst state what thou
wished in a wife."

"Does that mean I'll come home to fried ham and
candlelight and bare shoulders every evening?"

She hadn't planned that far ahead, but she wouldn't
let him see that. "If that is what thou wishest." She
frowned slightly. "Though I think thou might grow a
little tired of ham."

He chuckled. "Give me the candlelight and bare

shoulders and I won't know what the hell I'm eating. You wasted whatever it cost to have them fix this meal."

She breathed a little easier. He wasn't angry. She gave him a sideways glance. He seemed to enjoy the food, but he was spending a lot of time looking at her and not at his plate. She squirmed a little in her chair. She liked knowing he paid attention to her.

"I will try that some night when we have beans," she answered lightly.

They bantered lightly through dessert. When Ernestine removed the last of the plates, Pace rose and held out his hand for Dora. "Shall we retire to the parlor for our coffee and brandy?"

She wasn't used to this idleness, but it was all for a good cause. She could make him see that she would be a good wife for him. She didn't know how she could prove that she wasn't a burden, but that would wait until another day. First, she would get herself settled firmly into his bed until no question remained of his leaving her or sending her away.

Pace sat beside her on the loveseat as Annie carried in the coffee tray. Dora had just started pouring the coffee when the knock came at the door. Worriedly, she set the pot down and watched as Annie answered it. Visitors at this time of night could not carry good news.

"The sheriff to see you, sir," Annie said politely from the doorway.

Dora's heart froze, and she stood up when Pace did. He had stayed home last night. He had stayed home every night since Frances was born. The sheriff couldn't want him for anything. Perhaps the sheriff needed Pace's help with something.

Annie showed him in and departed quietly. She no doubt listened from the dining room, but Dora didn't shut the parlor door. They had nothing to hide.

The sheriff didn't stand much taller than Pace, but he was built more on the design of a barrel compared to Pace's muscular grace. He took off his soiled derby and revealed his receding blond hair. His eyes widened at sight of Dora in her new elegance, but he merely nodded in her direction, then turned to Pace. "You might want to talk private, boy."

Dora felt the tension knotting Pace's muscles as he kept his fist clenched at his side. "I don't keep secrets from my wife, Sheriff," he informed the other man coldly.

"Reckon there ain't any way to keep this a secret anyhow. I just came out to give you fair warning. Joe Mitchell went over to the courthouse today. He said he's got evidence that your deed to this place is fraudulent. He's filing a claim and wants me to serve you with an eviction notice as soon as it's authorized. Knowing Joe, that won't be long."

Dora drew in a shocked gasp. It was the only sound made in the dead silence following the sheriff's words.

Thirty-five

Doubt of the reality of love ends by making us
doubt everything.
HENRI FREDERIC AMIEL, *Journal*, December 26, 1868

Pace checked on Amy while Dora fed Frances. Dora
could hear him in his mother's room, talking conversationally as if the whole world hadn't just exploded in
their faces. He couldn't get any further information out
of the sheriff, but Dora knew what was happening. She
had lied, and now Pace must pay for it.

She would suffer more for knowing how much her
family and friends would lose for her lies, but it was
unfair of God to punish them for her sin. It had just
been a small lie. The words of marriage had not yet
been said in church or Meeting, but she'd known them
in her heart. She'd known them that day she had given
herself to Pace. Had she been wiser, she would have
known them sooner than that. She had always belonged
to Pace. But now she would lose him through her sins.

Frances went directly to sleep as she often did this
time of night. Dora laid her in the cradle and rocked
her gently to make certain she slept soundly. She was
still bent over the task when Pace entered the room.

Nervously, she faced him, the words of confession on
her tongue. He merely began unfastening the remainder
of the tiny buttons down the front of her bodice.

"It is all my fault," she whispered at the floor as his
fingers worked briskly.

He hesitated a moment at these words, then returned
to his task. "You cannot carry the world's sins on your
shoulders, Dora. I'll go over to the courthouse tomorrow

and see what the bastard is up to. I don't want you worrying about it."

She jerked away so quickly he nearly tore the last hook from the silk before he could loosen his grip. She glared at him in the lamplight. Weariness shadowed his eyes, all the playful light of earlier gone. "I am not a simpleton, Pace Nicholls! Don't placate me. If I say it is my fault, then it is my fault. I forged the deed!"

Stunned, he stared at her for a moment. Then he swung her around and untied her sash. The bodice fell from her shoulders, but Dora clung to it.

"Explain, please," he commanded as he stepped back.

"I did. In that letter I sent you! Didn't you even read it?" Even as she protested, Dora realized he hadn't read it. Perhaps he'd never received it. She just knew Pace would never have neglected such a matter had he known. She knew that. She just hadn't wanted to confront him with her sins.

"I don't remember the letter."

She could see the flicker of the lie in his eyes, but she forgave him. That awful time wasn't so long ago that she hadn't forgotten. Still, he could have left her fully dressed instead of standing here clinging to her clothes while she explained. When he coolly took off his coat and waited for her reply, Dora shivered.

"Last winter, after thy father died, they posted the farm for auction for failure to pay taxes."

Pace cursed, flung his coat and waistcoat over a chair, then pulled Dora's bodice from her hands. His fingers expertly found the tapes fastening the crinoline and untied them. She still had the modesty of chemisette, corset, and camisole covering her bosom, but Pace was immoderately hasty about divesting her of her outer clothing. She feared the inner garments would go much more quickly.

Dora tried to put into words what happened that day, how Josie was ill and she had no time to do anything else, her lack of knowledge of the legal processes, but she didn't know how closely Pace listened. He had her crinoline and petticoat and skirts on the floor before he unfastened his shirt.

"You're telling me you went all the way to the county

seat in that old buggy when you were what? Six, seven, months gone with child? With no one to protect you but Solly? Were you out of your mind?"

"Robert was there," she said defensively, making no attempt to remove her other garments even as he began on his trouser buttons. "What other choice did I have? Wouldst thou rather I had let them throw thy family into the streets in the middle of winter?"

"It might have done the selfish lot of them good." Muttering at a button caught in a thread, he looked up to see her still dressed. With a curse, he jerked at her camisole ribbon and pulled it away from her corset so he could start on the laces.

Dora smacked his hand away. "Thou doth not mean that. I did what I had to do. Had I talked to thee, thou might have corrected the situation. Now it is too late."

"You're my wife. We have signed and recorded documents. The signature was not a forgery." Pace removed his hands but stared at her fixedly, waiting for her to unfasten the laces.

"I was not thy wife then!" Dora protested. "And Charlie was the true owner then."

"That's a matter we'll look into. We don't have Charlie's exact date of death, and we'll need to know when you signed the register. If that's all they have, then I can fix it."

She looked at him hopefully for just a second, then her face fell. "Gareth is staying with Joe. That won't be all they have."

She wasn't working at the laces fast enough. Pace shoved her hands aside and began on them himself. "Signing as my wife is all that's important. They can haggle over your legal name until they turn blue in the face. You did exactly what you should have."

"But I wasn't thy wife!" she cried. "Joe Mitchell wants this land to build his foolish road, and he'll do whatever he must to get it. How can you stop him?"

Pace stopped and stared down at her. "What road?"

Dora clutched nervously at the open corset. "Sally says he is grabbing all the property between the railroad and the river. He can have only one reason for that."

Pace swung away and pounded his fist into his palm.

"I should have seen it! Damn, I'll nail him directly to the courthouse wall. I'm going to skin him alive. I'll pull his entrails out and feed them to the hogs. Damn and blast that—"

Dora's silence warned him he went too far. He swung back to face her. "I can do this, Dora. I can bring Joe Mitchell to his knees. Will you believe me?"

He stood tall and somber in the middle of their bedroom floor, his shirt unbuttoned and open, his overlong hair falling across his brow. Behind the drawn features of the man she could still see the light and eagerness of the boy he had once been. The war had not killed that boy entirely then. She trusted the boy who tried to do right more than the large male creature whose physical potency overpowered her.

But knowing the one contained the other, she let her corset fall to the floor. She stood before him in skimpy chemisette and drawers and stockings. When Pace didn't reach for her, Dora went to him. His arms closed tightly around her, lifting her from the floor.

"Are you certain, Dora? You could be a rich lady and live in castles with dozens of servants at your beck and call. Will you regret that someday when you have babies crying and toddlers fighting and Annie packs up and walks out?"

"I made that decision a long time ago, Pace. It's foolish to ask it of me now." Dora wrapped her arms around his neck and lifted her mouth for his kiss and prayed that he would give it to her. She wanted him now, before the doubts built a wall between them.

Pace's mouth found Dora's and settled there gently, plucking lightly at first, then with a little more abandon as she crushed herself closer. She rubbed her breasts against his chest, and he groaned deep in his throat, pulling her tighter against him. She could feel his arousal brushing at the juncture of her legs where he held her, but the physical fears had dissipated with his touch. His tongue parted her lips, and she surrendered this gladly.

It had been so long, she'd nearly forgotten the sweet bliss of his kisses. Her senses filled with the man-scent of him, the hard crush of his arms around her, the taste of his brandy-flavored tongue. He hadn't taken time to shave before dinner, and she could feel the rough brush of his beard against her cheek. The sandpaper texture excited her as much as the way his fingers dug into the soft flesh of her buttocks through the thin muslin of her drawers.

"Please, Pace," she murmured as his kisses fled down her jaw to her throat. She didn't know for what she pled, but he seemed to understand. He lowered her feet to the floor again, and brushed aside her chemisette to cup her breast in his palm. She shuddered at the contact as flesh met flesh, and her knees nearly buckled.

"I won't stop with making love to you once," he warned gruffly, his lips vibrating against the tender skin of her throat. "I'm going to put myself inside you and stay there until dawn, I think. At least dawn. I might never get enough of you. You won't be able to stand when I'm finished. Are you sure you're ready?"

His whispered words made her knees fold. She had never been very good with words, but Pace said everything she could possibly say. She pulled his mouth back to hers and let him carry her to the bed. She could never have walked there on her own.

Drawers and chemisette dropped by the wayside, tugged by impatient fingers. Dora arched and gave a helpless cry when Pace lay beside her and slid down her body to kiss behind her knees as he drew off her stockings. When he didn't immediately return to her side but began kissing his way back up, stroking her inner thighs, licking at sensitive skin, she nearly screamed with helplessness.

His knowing hands reached the tips of her breasts before his mouth settled on her belly. She writhed with the need to dig her fingers into the hard strength of his arms, to bring him to her, to hold him, but she could do nothing. When he had her breasts full and aching with pleasure, sending trails of burning need to the place between her thighs, Pace leaned over and kissed her there. Dora exploded into shattering bits and pieces of sparkling light.

He drove into her then, not giving her time to think or react, just shoving deep inside until she arched and twisted and met his thrusts with a frantic rhythm that

had nothing to do with who she was or where they were
or anything but the animal need for mating.

Pace came quickly, filling her with the hot gush of his
seed as the spasms overtook them both. As he promised,
he didn't leave, but began the ritual all over again.

He kissed away her murmured protests. He filled his
hands with her breasts and spoke words of beauty to
them, words that caressed her as sensually as his fingers.
Dora had never felt so loved and cherished in all her
life, and she threw back her head and let him do as he
would. Pace made her alive as nothing or no one else in
this world could. She didn't know how she could make
him understand this, but she would try.

Every particle of her skin tingled, her stomach muscles
clenched, and her insides burned with the desire for life,
with the need for Pace. She stroked the strong arms
holding her, feeling the bulge of work-hardened muscle.
She smoothed her hands over the formidable curve of
his shoulders and down the taut planes of his chest. She
found his nipples and made him roar with her touch.
And she dug her fingers into the tight flesh of his buttocks as he drove deep inside her again.

They were one together, united and paired against the
world. Together, they could do anything. He promised
her that with his body, and she believed him. She took
him inside herself and held him there, and the wounds
of the past began to heal with this acceptance.

Dora slept on her side, and the rosy light of dawn
gave a pink tinge to the deep curve of her waist and hip
as Pace threw aside the sheet. The small of her back
was so slender, he could span it with his hand, but his
hand was more interested in spanning the heavy mound
of her exposed breast.

But he had ridden her hard last night. She needed the
sleep. Frances was just stirring. She would coo to herself
for a long while before she began her daily demands.
Dora deserved this moment of rest. Pace returned the
sheet to her shoulders and climbed from the bed.

He felt almost human again. For months, maybe even
years, he'd lived with a raging monster gnawing at his
insides. The monster was calm now, curled up and sleep-

ing in a cage that Dora had somehow helped him erect. He had a perversely stubborn wife, but at this moment, he was grateful for it. Her dogged determination had chased away all the doubts.

Pace had to keep from whistling as he shrugged into his shirt and coat. Even the ache in his arm seemed less today. Had Charlie or his father been here, they would have laughed to see Pace so satiated and content with just a good bedding. They would never have understood that the woman herself made him feel this way. He had a woman who wanted him and him alone. That on its own made him swell with pride. The knowledge that she had willingly forsaken riches for him added spice to the feeling. Knowing the depth of Dora's character and intelligence and that still she had chosen him made him almost heady with joy. Perhaps he had some value, after all, if Dora could want him. He needed that confirmation of his worth after all those years of his father's diminishing it.

They hadn't exchanged words of love. Pulling on his boots, Pace acknowledged that. They'd scarcely had time to learn each other's bodies. They would have time for the rest later. For all he knew, love was something poets had invented. He couldn't remember ever experiencing it himself. But he would give her those words because she deserved them. Maybe even tonight he would tell her.

Today, he had more important business.

He grabbed a biscuit and a piece of ham from the kitchen on his way out to the stable. He caught Jackson on the way to the field and gave him a hasty explanation of the sheriff's visit. The taut black skin over Jackson's jaw pulled tighter yet, but he nodded curtly and headed out to the fields on his own. Pace continued down the road.

He had Robert McCoy dragged out of bed. Once the other man had enough black coffee poured into him, Pace quickly gave him explanations and instructions. Robert pounded the table a few times in fury, but agreed without hesitation. Their politics might not agree, but their sense of justice did.

Pace rode away with the sack of deeds and papers

Robert had confiscated from Homer's desk. He'd only
had to scan them briefly to see the truth of Dora's sur-
mise. He would go through deed books and maps to be
certain. Some of the papers were only for small parcels
and not complete farms. Pace suspected greed and ease
of attainment dictated how much Joe and his cronies
went after. The only surprise he discovered was the signature of Josie's father as owner of several of the newly
acquired acres.

It began to make sense as he thought about it while
riding toward the courthouse. Ethan Andrews was a cautious man with his money. Joe Mitchell liked risks and
kept himself overextended. Joe always needed cash.
Ethan always had it. Ethan also had an unattached
daughter and Joe was a bachelor. Little by little, the
pieces clicked together. Pace didn't like the picture that
formed, and the arrival of Dora's half brother muddied
it, but he had a place to start. That was all he needed.

At the courthouse, he set the clerks to making copies
of records to be sealed and notarized while he dragged
out the deed books and settled in with a map of the
county. By the time the records were ready, he had his
own copy of the map drawn and the deeds in his possession marked in neat little plots that made a broken line
straight from the river to the train station in the next
county. His and Jackson's farms marked part of the broken spaces in the line. Pace sent his father and brother
prayers of thanks for the foresight in leaving the farm
to him rather than to Josie. He may have hated them at
times, but they weren't entirely stupid men. Or somewhere along the line they had begun to suspect Joe's
plans.

Joe Mitchell wasn't entirely stupid either, but he was
lazy and greedy and he made mistakes. He should have
recorded his ill-gotten deeds. It might have raised a huge
stink if anyone had realized how much land he'd acquired over the years, but no one could have done a
blessed thing about it once those deeds were properly
filed and recorded. There was damned well something
Pace could do about it now.

He stopped to file a petition in the judge's office. He
filed an appeal of the eviction notice and a countersuit.

He set a court date, then visited the newspaper office to
file a public notice. Pace was in his element. He knew
precisely what to do and went about it with efficiency
and organization. Joe Mitchell would regret the day he
went after somebody besides illiterate widows and or-
phans. And if he was taking the advice of the viscount's
expensive British solicitor, they would soon learn to
their sorrow that Kentucky law had absolutely no basis
in English common law. The men who founded this state
despised the British down to the very soles of their
shoes.

Pace realized how much he'd missed the mental chal-
lenges of law when he rode toward home with exhilaration winging through his veins. He could learn farming.
He could manage the physical labor even with his ruined
arm. He could damn well do anything he put his mind
to, but he liked law. He wanted to be a lawyer, not a
farmer. He wondered how Dora would feel about moving out West.

He didn't wonder for long. As he rode up the drive,
he saw the Andrewses' carriage waiting at the front
steps. He hitched his horse out front and took the stairs
two at a time. Josie used his carriage and not her father's. This wasn't Josie visiting.

He found them in the parlor: Dora wearing her simple
Quaker gray and the men wearing their elegant frock
coats, hats, and brocade vests. She looked so fragile in
front of them, so helpless and unprotected, that Pace's
heart turned over in his chest in some turmoil he didn't
try to interpret.

She didn't smile when he threw his hat down and
strode across the room to wrap his arm around her.

Before he could even turn to confront the elegant
strangers, she informed him, "My grandmother has apparently left me her fortune."

The gray-haired man in black worsted completed for
her, "With the provision that Lady Alice's solicitors approve her choice of husbands." A malevolent smile light-
ened his face. "I can assure you, Lady Alice's solicitors
will not approve of a country bumpkin. Shall we talk?"

Thirty-six

Dora stared out the darkened bedroom window. Pace had been gone for three nights now. She didn't know where he slept, but she suspected he slept at Jackson's. She tried to see the lights of the old farmhouse through the trees, but they were in full leaf at this time of year. She could see nothing but the twinkle of an occasional star above the canopy of leaves.

She couldn't complain that Pace had deserted her. He worked in the fields every day. He came to the house at dinner and supper to play with Amy and carry Frances around as if she were old enough to know what he said to her. Her heart wept every time she heard Pace talking to his daughter, telling her who his mother was, pointing out the stuffed doll he'd bought for her, showing her the honeysuckle blooming in the hedges. He was so very, very good with her. She hadn't expected that of a man who'd only known cruelty as a boy.

He didn't talk much to Dora. He avoided her so deliberately that she found it easier to stay out of his way. She would just listen to his voice in other rooms or drifting through open windows and catch a peek at him when she could. Her eyes felt swollen and red from crying most of the time anyway. She didn't want him to see her like this.

She thought she knew him so well, but she was learning that she didn't know anything at all. How could he so cruelly take her heart in his hand, dash it into the dirt, and walk on it while still playing with their daughter as if she was the most important part of his life? It didn't make sense. She didn't want it to make sense, because she feared what she might discover.

She'd tried telling him the money didn't mean anything. She'd tried telling him she didn't want it. She had talked reasonably, then resorted to yelling and shouting and slamming doors. Nothing got through to him. Nothing. He'd turned her off completely.

As much as she denied it, she understood his motives. He thought he would make it easier for her to return to England without him or Frances. He was showing her that he could take care of their daughter. She knew he could. She never had a doubt of that. But did he think her so shallow as to leave her heart and soul in this country while she returned to a stranger's cold abode for the dubious pleasures of earthly coin?

She could find no other logic in his actions. She didn't want to believe he thought her so shallow. She refused to believe it. But the fact remained, he didn't come to her bed or take her as wife.

She didn't know what had become of the eviction notice either. Pace had spent a long time talking to the solicitor after they'd thrown her out of the room. Maybe they'd reached an agreement. Maybe Gareth and the earl paid him to stay away and part of the bribe was that they would nullify the eviction. She could understand that a little better. Pace would do anything to save his father's land, to prevent his mother and daughter from being evicted from their home. She supposed he might give up a wife he didn't love to accomplish these things.

If that were the case, what choice did she have? If she stayed and persuaded him to keep her as wife, he would lose everything. He'd said he could take care of it, but perhaps the solicitor had told him something that made voiding the eviction impossible. She wished the damned man would talk to her. Surely they could find some way out of this mess without destroying their lives. Or maybe he thought their lives wouldn't be destroyed by ending their marriage.

That thought terrified Dora so much that she didn't

want to hear it from his mouth, so she kept away. She knew she would die if forced to leave Pace and Frances. But perhaps she wouldn't die in vain. Perhaps they would be happier without her.

Life went on. She was more aware of that than most people. This shell that she was would keep making the motions of living. She would get up and get dressed in the mornings, eat what was put before her, speak when spoken to. And if God would ever be so kind as to deliver her from that purgatory, she would die grateful. It behooved her to consider what was best for Pace and Frances.

When the next dawn arrived, Dora watched from the window as she fed Frances, but she didn't see Pace riding into the fields. That worried her. Even Frances sensed her tension, and the infant squirmed uncomfortably in her arms. Dora forced herself to relax by turning away from the window and pretending Pace went to the fields while she wasn't looking. Still, even after she put Frances down to sleep, her stomach churned uncomfortably.

She went through the motions of her daily chores without thinking, with her insides growing more tightly wound with each passing minute. Had she still felt that childhood connection with Pace, she would think that he suffered from some stomach ailment and she would hurry down to the farmhouse with her black bag of medicines.

She helped haul hot buckets of water for the laundry. She stood beside Ernestine and hung linens on the wash line. She stirred the stew they'd prepared for dinner and waited for Pace to come eat. When he didn't arrive at his usual time, the pain in her stomach grew worse. Something was happening. She knew it.

She wore her oldest gown and an apron splashed with lye when the Andrewses' carriage arrived out front. Annie came running outside to tell her. Dora didn't have time to do more than remove her apron and run her fingers through her hair as she ran into the house to meet the visitors. Maybe it was Josie. Maybe she knew what was happening. She'd stayed with her father all week. Josie always knew all the gossip.

It was Josie, but she had brought Gareth with her. Josie had let herself in without knocking, and they waited in the parlor. Dora took one look at her bulky half brother and felt the urge to flee, but she found herself rooted to the spot.

"Have you heard the good news?" Josie cried gleefully when she spotted Dora. "I'm going with you to England!"

Dora had no intention whatsoever of ever setting foot on England's shores again, but she didn't inform Josie of that yet. The news knocked her from her momentary paralysis and sent her mind spinning furiously as she eyed the smug expression on Gareth's countenance. Even though she hadn't seen it in more than a dozen years, she remembered that expression much too well.

She eyed him with curiosity as she spoke. "It was generous of Gareth to invite you. Is there a particular reason for taking such a long journey?"

Josie glanced at him nervously, but Gareth responded with complete aplomb. "Unlike you, I prefer seeking our father's approval before making some decisions. Mrs. Nicholls is very understanding."

Cold fury wrapped around Dora's heart as she looked from eager, simple Josie to her malevolent-minded brother. Josie's wealth was not great, but it was significant. Had the earl's wealth deteriorated so badly that his son now sought funds through a wife? And what would happen to Josie when her wealth evaporated? Would she conveniently fall into Plymouth harbor?

Dora had no intention of finding out. If Josie was too naive to protect herself and Pace too busy to notice what happened, then someone else must step in. Dora smiled, but the pair in front of her didn't notice the emptiness of the expression. Once she had suffered helplessly, believing love meant pain. She knew better now. Pace and the Smythes had taught her that loving someone meant doing whatever necessary to keep them from hurt. Gareth wasn't here out of love. She would prove it.

"How very delightful." She stepped into the room, gesturing for Josie to take a seat. But Dora remained standing, just out of Gareth's reach. She cocked her head and eyed his fleshy face with interest. "We've not had time to talk, Gareth. Did Father ever remarry? Or have you sought and buried any wives these past years?"

His full, pouting lips tightened visibly. "Your mother's wanton behavior nearly destroyed him. He never fully recovered from the scandal. I have been in no hurry to find myself hitched to another such as she."

"Yes, attempting to save her unborn child from brutality was no doubt wanton beyond reason. It's a pity they don't hang earls. How do you plan to get rid of me if I should return to England? Or do you think to beat me into keeping my lips sealed?" Dora kept her voice pleasantly unconcerned, as if they discussed the wine served at dinner.

Gareth's face took on an unhealthy flush. "You always were a devilish brat. Had I a choice, I'd leave you here, but Father insists that I bring you home. I'd suggest you polish your manners if you mean to live among society when you get there."

"Ahh!" Dora's expression showed enlightenment. "That is how you will do it. You will have me locked away and claim guardianship over my wealth. I knew there had to be something in it for you. You're a foul, evil villain, Gareth Beaumont, and I will see you in hell before I follow you anywhere."

She had gauged his temper perfectly. The steam already boiled from his ears before she threw the insult. She meant to step away before his hand came flying toward her, but he was much faster than she realized. Gareth's fist caught Dora on the jaw and sent her crashing sideways into the lamp and table in the front window.

Josie screeched and loosed a stream of invectives at Gareth, mixed with terrified questions of concern for Dora as she fell to her knees beside her. Dora pushed herself up on one elbow, put her hand to her jaw, and shook her head to stop the spinning stars. Her gaze met Josie's directly. "Show Lord Doran out, will you?"

The crash and screech brought Annie and Ernestine running in from the back rooms and Harriet to the top of the stairs. Gareth looked like a trapped grizzly amid all the feminine skirts. Apologies fell from his lips, but Harriet had grabbed the iron poker from the ancient fireplace in her room and wielded it now as she limped down the stairs. In her billowing nightgown, she looked like some vengeful gray ghost. Gareth blanched and backed toward the front door.

"It was an accident," he pleaded. "I never meant to hurt her. She fell like that on purpose, just to make it seem worse than it was."

Josie gestured at Ernestine. "Fetch me the sword from the study," she ordered.

Ernestine ran to do as told.

"This is preposterous," Gareth protested. "She's my sister. We've always quarreled. I'll make it up to her, if that's what you want. I assure you, she's not nearly as seriously hurt as she pretends. Dora was always an actress."

Harriet had reached the bottom of the stairs with the poker by the time Ernestine came running up with Pace's huge military saber. Josie gripped the handle and hefted it carefully, deliberately pointing it in Gareth's face.

"I would suggest you depart at once, Lord Doran. I have heard all those excuses before, although admittedly, yours are even more demeaning than my late husband's. I think, in my best opinion, that if it's all right for a huge man to hit a tiny woman, then it ought to be perfectly all right for a woman to take the nose off a man. What do you think Mother Nicholls?"

Dora had brought herself to her feet. She clung now to the door frame, holding her jaw as the two women advanced on Gareth, driving him backwards, stumbling, out the door. She wanted to laugh. She wanted to crow with relief. She wanted to hug them both for discovering there was strength in numbers and that nothing justified abuse. But her jaw hurt too much to do more than watch with approval as they slammed and bolted the door in Gareth's face.

Josephine swung around and dropped the sword as she regarded Dora's rapidly swelling jaw. She burst into tears and leaned against the door for support. Harriet found herself in the awkward position of choosing which daughter-in-law to comfort first.

"It's all right, Mother Nicholls," Dora said, using Josie's name for her for the first time. "It's just a bruise. I'll see if there's any ice left in the icehouse."

"He could have broken your neck!" Josie wept brokenly. "I thought he was a gentleman!"

"You thought Charlie was a gentleman," Harriet snorted ungently. "You don't think too well, girl. You'd better come upstairs and lie down a spell." She glared at Dora. "And you too. I don't believe in heroics. You're a damned fool, and you'd be a sight better off without my son. Get yourself rested and throw him out if he comes crawling back here."

Josie straightened and rubbed hastily at her eyes. "Pace! He's over at the courthouse now. They're having a big trial. He's suing Joe Mitchell over some illegal deeds or something. I heard Lord Doran and his solicitor talking. They've made some kind of deal with Pace and my father. I don't understand all of it, but Pace will give up his claim to the farm and let my father claim it in my name. Then he's supposed to turn around and sell it back to Pace for a dollar or something once you return to England. I don't know what one has to do with the other, but—"

She halted as Dora brushed past them all, pulling herself up the stairs, stumbling and running, holding her jaw and her skirts and the railing in some frantic race to the top. Josie and Harriet exchanged glances, then took off after her.

Thirty-seven

I am one, my liege,
Whom the vile blows and buffets of the world
Have so incens'd, that I am reckless what
I do to spite the world.

SHAKESPEARE, *Macbeth*

"You're out of your mind," Josie protested as Dora pulled the yards of gray silk skirt, embroidered petticoats, and crinolines into the carriage and settled them around her. With a little more experience at managing the bulk of her attire, Josie hurried to climb in beside her. "What can you possibly accomplish?"

"I don't know." Dora sat back and gave Jackson a nod when he turned his head questioningly. She didn't have to explain herself to Jackson. He'd come running when she'd called and took up the reins of the carriage as if born to them. Dora had a feeling that he'd argued with Pace all along, and that he was on her side. She just hoped she knew what her side was.

"You're going to walk into that courthouse and make a spectacle of yourself and you don't even know what you'll do when you get there?" Josie exclaimed in horror. "Dora Nicholls, you're insane!"

"Yes, I think I am. It's better than being dead, however. I won't be a ghost everyone ignores any longer. I will not let Pace throw everything away like that. I won't."

"But he won't be throwing it away!" Josie protested. "Daddy will sell it back to him."

Dora gave her a disgusted look, then turned to watch the passing scenery. Jackson let the horses have their heads. They'd no doubt bounce through the roof of the carriage before they reached the courthouse.

She tried to think, tried to plan what she meant to do, but her brain had quit working. Her jaw and head ached unmercifully from Gareth's blow, but that pain was as nothing to the pain in her heart. Pace was throwing her away. He had gone into that courthouse to tell the judge and everyone who cared to listen that they hadn't been married when she signed that deed, and then he meant to let Gareth's fancy lawyer prove their marriage wasn't valid because she'd not used her proper name. She knew it. She'd known it all along. He would let her go out of some stupid sense of duty, believing himself inadequate and an unfit husband for a wealthy Lady Alexandra. She'd curse Pace if it weren't for the fact that she knew his father had done this to him, stripped him of his confidence and self-esteem so that he couldn't see his own worth any longer, as her own father had tried to do to her. She'd been luckier than Pace. The Smythes had rescued her. Now she would rescue Pace.

Somehow, she would show Pace that he was a better man than any man in this county, maybe the entire state, maybe the whole world for all she knew. He was better than foolish titles or earthly coin. Even if he couldn't love her, she would fare better with him than left alone. And she would spend her life showing him that she was better for him than any other woman alive.

The horses couldn't go fast enough. Even as she slammed into the side of the carriage and nearly fell from the seat, Dora mentally urged Jackson to hurry. The case could be over already. She didn't have any idea how long these things took. She couldn't bear the thought that she would arrive too late. Surely God wouldn't do that to her, not after bringing her all this way. She had to get there in time.

Josie had given up protesting and grimly clung to the hand grip to keep from being thrown off the cushioned bench. She looked as if she might throw up, but Dora was grateful to have her by her side. Remembering Josie waving a sword in Gareth's face gave her great pleasure. Had it not been for her Quaker teaching, she would feel regret that Josie hadn't taken the bastard's nose off. She supposed the earl's violent influences in her were stronger than Papa John's reasoning.

Jackson didn't even attempt looking for a place to park the carriage when they reached the courthouse. Wagons and buggies and carriages filled the street, along with bustling crowds of people. He merely drove the horse through the center of the mob and stopped when he reached the front of the courthouse, holding on to the horse while Josie and Dora let themselves out.

Dora turned to thank him, but Jackson hurriedly waved her away.

"Get yourself in there, Miz Dora, and do it quick before Pace makes an ass of hisself."

His words confirmed her fears. Dora nodded and hurried to comply, lifting her skirts and nearly running for the courthouse steps. Such an unseemly pace had men dodging sideways to avoid the swinging wire of her crinoline. Josie followed in her path, keeping up a mumbled tirade on what ladies should and should not do.

Dora's shoes clattered down the wooden hall. The stale cigar stench soaked into the walls made her gag, and she tried not to identify the odors of unemptied spittoons and urine rising from the stairwell to the basement. The courthouse was a man's world. Even the stink told her that. She didn't need the stares of passersby to confirm it.

She heard the loud and angry voices bouncing from the room on the far right. She would find Pace where the argument roared loudest. She was glad he had found a way of channeling his love for argument and controversy into constructive arenas, but she would wring his neck for dragging her into it. He could tear Joe Mitchell into little pieces all he wanted, but she wouldn't let him sacrifice her in the process.

Dora didn't even attempt to be quiet as she threw open the huge double doors of the courtroom. She meant to make an impression. All her life she'd hid from the eyes of the public, but she had no intention of remaining invisible any longer. The time had come to make herself known. The doors slammed against the walls and every head in the room turned to stare at her.

Pace stopped in mid-speech as his modest little Quaker wife strode up the aisle, her gray silk skirt swinging in a wide arc revealing the exquisitely embroidered

pink stitching of the petticoat beneath. She wore a hat
with pink roses and a swaying gray feather that swooped
over her cornsilk curls in back. She was corseted so tight
she looked as if she might snap in two at any minute,
but she kept her bosom primly covered beneath a line
of jet buttons that revealed every damned curve. He
would throttle her just for appearing in public like that.
That thought came before he saw the hideous blue-black
bruise spreading across her delicate white jaw.

Rage roared through him. Fury clenched his fists into
battering rams. His gaze swept the room, searching for
the fancified English solicitor who had observed the pro-
ceedings. As he'd thought, the man was whispering furiously to Dora's bulky brother. The latter had arrived
late, but Pace had ignored him until now. He wasn't
ignoring him any longer. Too many memories came
sweeping back. He remembered every flinch, every hint
of fear. Dora's childhood nightmares took on new and
very frightening reality. How blind could one man be?

Throwing down the law book he held in his hand,
Pace glared at Dora. "Gareth?" he demanded, without
needing to expand the question.

"And what do you care?" she retaliated. "You're
about to tell all these men that we're not married. Do
you think that hurts any less?"

Pace slammed to a halt as if stopped by a physical
blow. He stared at her angelic face, marred by a brutish
hand until swollen nearly beyond recognition. A blow
like that could have killed the dainty woman standing
here proudly in front of these staring strangers. And she
was telling him what he did hurt even more.

He stared at her, feeling the fury drain out of him at
the enormity of what she said. He didn't think she could
mean it. He offered her freedom and wealth. She didn't
have to go with her ignoble brother. She could go anywhere she wanted. She could go back to the Quakers if
she so desired. She didn't have to saddle herself with a
miserable failure like himself. She just hadn't thought
this through clearly.

But staring into the incredible blue of Dora's fearless
gaze, Pace knew he was the one who hadn't thought
clearly. He'd seen an opportunity to right old wrongs

and grabbed it. He had thought he would give his angel her wings back, but instead he was ripping them off and throwing them away. Why could he see that now and not before?

It didn't matter. Flashing a fierce grin at her, Pace turned and strode across the courtroom before Gareth and his solicitor could make their hasty escape. Rob McCoy and a few of his friends moved into the side aisle, blocking that exit. Without a care to the judge pounding his gavel and calling for order, Pace grabbed Gareth's coat front, rammed the larger man up against the wall, and slammed his fist into his brother-in-law's soft gut.

Gareth didn't even offer a fight. He slid down the wall and landed on the floor with a loud "oomph," followed by an ominous gagging noise. Pace turned around and walked away as several men grabbed the English lord and dragged him from the room. His solicitor remained behind, watching Pace with interest as he returned to the front of the courtroom.

Someone had offered Dora a front-row seat. She sat beside Josie now, gripping Josie's hand with a fierceness Pace didn't wish to interpret. He'd never thought of Josie and Dora as friends, but that wasn't his major concern of the moment. Turning to face the furious judge, Pace spoke calmly.

"I apologize wholeheartedly for the disturbance, Your Honor. There are some things a man just has to do, and one of them is showing mighty English lords that they can't backhand our women." Pace let the roar of approval from his audience drown the room while he turned to locate Joe Mitchell. His grin this time was malevolent. "And another one of those things men have to do is show would-be tyrants that this is a country of free men who won't kneel to wealth and position, who won't let their families be trampled for greed and ambition. I'm here to tell you right now, Judge, that our esteemed mayor, Joseph Mitchell, has put his wealth and greed in the way of free men for too long now, and I'm here to prove it."

With the crowd's roar of approval, Pace returned to the case he'd been presenting. He'd stacked the audience in his favor by spreading the word to all the landowners Joe had tricked and misled over the years. They were out for blood and hanging on his every word. He didn't need their support to win this case, but he would prove something to Joe and Ethan Andrews and any of the other men who thought they could steal from the weak and trample the helpless. And now he would show Dora that she needn't regret her decision, because when he finished here, she would be stuck with a poor farmer of a husband for the rest of her life.

As he presented his evidence and worked through his witnesses, Pace remained constantly aware of Dora's intent gaze at his back. Everything he said and did, he presented for her approval. Admittedly, he'd resorted to violence with Gareth, but he couldn't help that. He would always act first and think later when it came to Dora. But he wanted to show her he'd learned a more effective means of handling his disputes than violence. If he could give her nothing else, he could give her a husband she didn't have to fear.

When Joe's attorney brought up the forged deed to the Nichollses' farm, Pace was ready for him. He hadn't meant to argue this one. He'd meant to surrender it and the next point that Mitchell's defense would present, thanks to Gareth and his solicitor. He'd thought he would help Dora in doing so. He'd hoped to give her a better life than he could afford. But he would fight now. He hoped she was ready for the result.

Pace gave the other attorney a look from beneath uplifted eyebrows at the man's declaration that Pace and Dora hadn't been married at the time she'd signed his name to the deed. Then with calm insouciance, Pace removed a sheet of paper from the stack on his table and carefully presented it to the judge on his bench.

"My wife signed that deed in January of this year, Your Honor. We have a child born in April. A man is justified in calling out anyone who would suggest that we were not married while she carried my child. But I'm a reasonable man, Your Honor. I'll present our marriage certificate as evidence of our legal status. Ask any man in here and he'll tell you that Dora and I have always been childhood sweethearts. I just waited until she was of an age to know her own mind before making her my own."

Pace brazenly presented the backdated marriage certificate. Had Mitchell known he would do this, he could have called the preacher as witness. But Joe had expected Pace to cave in and it was too late now. He had filed the certificate at the courthouse with last year's date. No one needed to know anything else. Pace just couldn't turn and face Dora right away. She didn't like these little necessary lies, although all the rest was true. He couldn't help it if he'd been a little slow in realizing how much he needed her.

Joe threw a tantrum, but his attorney quickly stepped forward to drown him out with the presentation of copies of Carlson Nicholls's will leaving the entire estate to Charlie. With a glance of triumph at Pace, he declared that Dora had no legal right to sign the deed since Pace was not the owner at that time.

The courtroom grew hushed. Pace could see Dora nervously twining her fingers together, but he'd known all his opponents' arguments in advance. He didn't enter a courtroom unprepared. Retrieving another paper from his dwindling stack, he added that to the growing one in front of the judge.

"I took the liberty of wiring the military authorities in charge of the prison camp where my brother died, Your Honor. The defendant could have had the decency to wait until my brother was dead a little longer before attempting to steal his widow's home, but the fact remains, Charlie died the week prior to Joe Mitchell's efforts to auction off my home."

The other attorney immediately objected to this prejudicial declaration, but the judge, irritated enough by the earlier histrionics, just ordered him to shut up. Pace's opponent retreated to his table where he triumphantly removed several formal documents from his stack of papers.

"I have here the copy of a birth certificate for one Lady Alexandra Theodora Beaumont and signed statements from both her brother and her father's solicitor to the effect that Dora Smythe Nicholls is said person. If Your Honor will take notice of the signatures on both deed and marriage certificate, he will note they are signed under the alias Dora Smythe, and not under her true name, thereby making both marriage and deed null and void."

Pace heard the gasp going around the courtroom. He'd hoped to protect Dora from this little bit of nastiness, but he had come prepared for it just the same. Picking up his law book, he proceeded to the bench and began to quote letter and verse of the official acts of Kentucky's assembly declaring themselves herewith dissolved of all acts of English common law and independent as to the construction of their own constitution and liberties.

As the crowd rustled and coughed while waiting for him to make his point, Pace slammed the book shut and faced the judge firmly. "Your Honor, the legal redress under which these men seek to nullify my marriage is based entirely on English common law and acts of their Parliament. There is no place within the Kentucky statutes stating that my wife could not take the name of her adopted parents instead of carrying the despised name of her mother's murderer!"

The courtroom burst into shouts of triumph and gasps of horror. The earl's solicitor raised a hand covering his eyes and offered no objection. Pace couldn't tell if the older man expressed mortification at the appalling theatrics of a country courtroom or conceded the point. He didn't care. The judge pounded his gavel and overturned Mitchell's appeal. The marriage and the deed would stand as is.

Pace turned around in time to catch Dora as she flew into his arms. This was neither the time nor the place to indulge his joy but he couldn't resist the sweet victory of her kiss. He smoothed her poor, battered face and held her as close as her skirts would allow.

Behind him, the judge coughed and declared a fifteen-minute recess.

Thirty-eight

Let me not to the marriage of true minds
Admit impediments. Love is not love
Which alters when it alteration finds,
Or bends with the remover to remove:
O no; it is an ever-fixed mark.

SHAKESPEARE, *Sonnets (116)*

"Hallelujah, you did it, Nicholls!" Robert McCoy came racing down the courthouse steps to pound Pace on the back. The milling crowd gathering on the courthouse lawn looked up at Robert's yell. As if in concert, people suddenly surged in the direction of the courthouse steps until a human barricade formed at the bottom and spilled upward.

Pace determinedly held Dora's waist as he answered Robert while keeping a wary eye on the crowd. Crowds easily became mobs in these uncertain times. He didn't want Dora caught in the middle. He caught sight of Jackson's black face lingering beneath the elm tree on the lawn and felt a modicum of relief. He had one friend in the crowd at least, should he need to call on someone for help.

"I haven't done anything yet," Pace answered stoically. "It's up to the original owners of those parcels to file suit now. All I did was prove that Mitchell is an unscrupulous crook. Seems everyone should have known that."

Dora gripped her skirts as they gradually eased down the stairs. Pace sensed her nervousness, but he hadn't seen any overt signs of hostility. This crowd seemed more ready for a Sunday gossip than a hanging. He should have experience enough to know the difference by now.

A scarecrow of a man in red galluses and a patched

workshirt called out, "Does this mean I can get my bottom pasture back, Pace?"

Pace turned in the man's direction. "Get yourself a good lawyer, Amos, and prove Mitchell obtained it under false pretenses or with fraud. The judge has to look at each case individually. I just opened it up for the law to take a look at it."

The man shrugged his narrow shoulders diffidently beneath the suspenders. "Reckon you could take the job? Seems like you made a pretty good case in there today."

A murmur rumbled through the crowd. Heads nodded. Beside him, Dora looked up at him expectantly, her sky-blue eyes watching him with all the admiration and approval he had ever desired from her. Pace choked on the emotion welling up inside of him as he looked down into those trusting, adoring eyes. A chaos of sensation paralyzed his usually easy tongue. He didn't deserve what he saw in her eyes, but he craved it with every ounce of his soul.

He finally ripped his gaze away and nodded briefly at his inquirer. "All right, Amos, I'll come out and look at what you've got tomorrow evening, if that's all right."

A clamor rose from the crowd, demanding his attention, throwing out questions, asking his opinions. Pace acknowledged only the joy rising from the woman beside him. He hugged her waist and gave her a grin of triumph as he tugged her downward and into the clamoring mob. It was a heady feeling, knowing these people who had despised his politics now needed his talents. He wanted to savor it for a while. Mostly, though, Pace wanted to celebrate his triumph by taking Dora home and into his bed. Not every day did a woman whistle away a fortune in return for what little he could offer.

"Somebody ought to lynch Mitchell!" A voice screamed from the back of the mob.

On every side people complained bitterly of the way the mayor's smooth words and cheap promises or his blackmail, lies, and threats had robbed them and their families. Another shout rose in agreement with the first. Fists shook in the air as the crowd suddenly realized Joe Mitchell had not yet left the building. The shifting winds of violence found a new direction.

The crush of people pushed toward the steps, flowing upward. Caught in the middle, Pace held Dora and glanced hastily back at the courthouse. He saw no sign of Joe Mitchell and his attorney, but Josie came out the door on the arm of the gray-haired Englishman. Pace didn't know what had become of Dora's brother. He didn't care. The crowd had turned ugly. He just wanted Dora out of there.

He turned back to where he'd seen Jackson standing last and breathed easier when he saw the tall black man shoving through the crowd toward them. Catching Dora's shoulders, Pace whispered in her ear, "Get over to Jackson. I've got to stop this."

She nodded and slipped quickly between two farmers. A path of sorts opened for her, and Pace saw her safely in Jackson's care before he took the courthouse steps two at a time. When he ran ahead of the crowd, he turned and waved his arms to draw their attention. The men in front of him halted and shouted at the people behind them. Gradually, the surging anger quieted until Pace could shout above their complaints.

"Killing isn't the answer! We've had enough killing around here. If you want to get rid of Joe Mitchell, then impeach him. Go to the council and demand his withdrawal from office. You're the ones who voted him in. Be men and admit you were wrong. Take responsibility for correcting your mistake by voting him out. Let the world see that we aren't ignorant savages but intelligent, civilized men who uphold the Constitution and want justice done. That's what our laws are for. Let's use them to get rid of the greedy vultures who would feed off our carcasses if we let them!"

A roar of approval rang through the crowd. Dora stepped back into the shade of the old elm where Jackson had led her, Pace's words ringing clearly in her ears even from this distance. He looked magnificent out there with his waistcoat undone and his fingers hooked in his trouser band, controlling the crowd with the simple expedient of his voice. He had a marvelous voice, a commanding one. She had never seen him in quite this way before, and her heart ached seeing him like this now.

She turned hesitantly to Jackson. "He was born to be a politician, wasn't he?"

"Reckon so. He sure can swing them words around, cain't he?"

"Maybe I should have let him go," she whispered softly, more to herself than the man beside her.

Jackson made a grunt of outrage. "Maybe you should've told me to put a bullet through his haid, then. That man's been madder than a rabid fox for days. I thought I'se gonna have to put him out of his misery soon enough. You give up that notion real quick, missy. That man needs you, whether he admits it or not."

"I'm not a politician's wife," Dora reminded him, watching with admiration as Pace worked his way back down the steps, shaking hands, pounding backs, and roaring with laughter at some joke someone told him. The crippled muscles of his right arm worked well enough when he used them for this.

"I never heerd that Lincoln's wife was much either, but he managed. Some men can stand alone when they meet the world. Reckon Pace is one of 'em. He ain't done nothin' else but face the world alone. But he sure is a might easier to live with when he's got someone keeping him on the straight and narrow. That's your job."

"My job," Dora echoed in growing wonderment, staring at the handsome man working his way steadily through the crowd in her direction. She could feel his gaze on her even as he shook the hand of someone pouring their troubles into his ear. Her job. A smile curved her lips as she realized she really did have a place in this world—as Pace's wife. Jackson was right. Any woman could give Pace children and feed him meals. Only she could calm his rages, soothe his fears, and give him joy. She knew that with a certainty that came from deep inside her, that spilled over and filled her as she stepped out from the shade to meet him. The love in his eyes confirmed it when she walked into his arms.

Pace swallowed her up in his hug. Not releasing her, he looked over her shoulder at Jackson. "Take Gallant. I'll drive Dora home."

"Josie?" she asked breathlessly, clinging to his shirt

frills. She wanted what he wanted right this moment, but she couldn't desert her friend.

Pace glanced back up the courthouse steps where Josie flirted vivaciously with the solicitor while walking toward the Andrewses' carriage. "She's found herself a beau. She'll be fine."

Dora followed the direction of his glance and frowned slightly, but Josie's choice in men wasn't her concern any longer. She looked up to Pace. "Let's go then," she murmured.

He didn't need convincing. They reached the carriage and rattled down the road within minutes, leaving the town and the crowds well behind. Dora breathed a sigh of relief as familiar cedars and sassafras whipped by.

"I'll never be a town person," she said idly, apropos of nothing.

"You don't need to be," Pace agreed without question. "You can stay home and make jams and jellies and applesauce if that's what you want."

She thought about it a minute. "Yes, that's what I want. And I'd like to learn to ride. The county doesn't have a midwife, and some of these roads aren't fit for carriages."

Pace gave her a grin. "Got mighty big plans, have we? What happens if the farm goes broke? You planning on supporting us with the ham hocks you'll get in return for your services?"

She gave him an indignant glare. "I can do just as well as Mother Elizabeth, you just wait and see." She turned her gaze ahead and away from him. "Besides, thou wilt be a wonderful lawyer. We can use the payments from Jackson to buy a little place of our own if thou must sell."

He shook his head and gave her a look of wonderment. "You really mean that, don't you? You don't care if I can dress you in satins or lace or not. Fancy gewgaws don't mean a blamed thing to you, do they?"

"Of course not! Have I ever said otherwise?" She gave him a look of surprise.

He continued shaking his head. "I don't know where you come from, Alexandra Theodora, but it certainly isn't from that fancy family of your brother's. The fairies must have left you.''

A smile turned the corners of her mouth. "Angels. They thought a devil like you needed all the help he could get.''

Pace caught her shoulders with one arm and drew her closer, pressing a kiss to her hair as he guided the horse with his other hand. "Thank them for me, will you? They couldn't have found anyone more perfect.''

Dora glanced at him anxiously, but he seemed content and satisfied even though she could never be the elegant, beautiful hostess he once expected for wife. He was eight years older than she, a man of the world, but the lines of worry and pain around his eyes had miraculously disappeared while they talked. He looked a twenty-year-old boy again, ready to take on the world.

She gave a sigh of contentment and caught him glancing with interest as her breasts rose and fell with the motion. She tingled all over at the look, and heat flooded her cheeks. Pace gave her added color a knowing look.

"It's a mite warm out here. Why don't you unfasten some of those fancy buttons? No one will see you.''

Momentarily shocked at the suggestion, Dora's hand flew to the row of jet buttons down her bodice. Then when she glanced up at Pace and saw the glitter of desire in his eyes, she felt the same rush of physical longing that he displayed. It startled her, but there was nothing unpleasant about it. Slowly, holding his gaze with hers, she unbuttoned her gown.

No one but the birds in the trees could see them. The musty scent of sun-warmed cedars surrounded them. No clouds threatened the sky as she fingered open one button after another, then daringly untied her chemisette so the sun could find the flesh rising above her corset. She felt filled to bursting, but it wasn't her need to feed Frances that she noticed.

"I'll not make it all the way back to the house,'' Pace warned in a husky voice that made her tremble.

Dora glanced at his lap and saw the swelling evidence of his desire surging against the thin nankeen of his trousers. Shocking even herself, she reached over to unfasten his shirt studs.

The heat of his skin beneath the linen and the pounding of his heart beneath her hand held her in such fascination that she scarcely noticed when Pace wheeled the carriage off the road and into a stand of trees. A breeze off the river lifted curls from her face, but she used his momentary distraction to work on his trouser buttons, not caring where the carriage stopped.

When Pace grabbed the carriage blanket and swung her into his arms, Dora flung her arms around his neck and felt her breasts swell high above her corset. From Pace's glazed expression, she gathered he had noticed too. She wiggled in delight that she could make him forget everything and look at her. Every doubt as to her visibility faded. She knew herself to be very much visible in her husband's eyes.

She was even more visible minutes later after he stripped her clothing off and kneeled over her, filling his palms with her breasts. Pace wore only his unbuttoned trousers, and Dora could scarcely tear her gaze from the overwhelming expanse of chest filling her field of vision in the broad light of day. When he bent to twine his tongue with hers, she lost herself in the sensations of heated flesh and raging desire. Nothing else mattered but this man who held her, pressing his solid body into hers.

He made no excuses or apologies as he stripped off his trousers and parted her knees so he could kneel between them. Like some warrior god, he hovered over her, his dark hair glistening with red in the dappled sunlight beneath the trees, his bronzed chest gleaming golden. His eyes radiated male satisfaction and triumph as he looked down at her, and Dora felt pride sweep through her in company with desire. She was his, and she wrapped her arms around his neck to prove it.

She was more than ready when he came into her. She gasped as his hard thrust reached deep inside her. Dora lifted herself to hold him, and Pace groaned with pleasure, then repeated the motion faster and harder until she bucked mindlessly to his rhythm, surrendering herself totally to his needs. She cried out as the explosions overtook her, then wept in happiness as he gave himself up to her, filling her with the heated liquid of his loins.

She welcomed the knowledge that from this, a child could grow. She wanted to bear him a son to keep their daughter company.

"I love you," she whispered, threading her fingers through the thickness of his hair as he lay on top of her, their perspiring skin sticking and sliding together.

Pace kissed her cheek, then the corner of her eye as he dug his fingers into her curls. "I've said those words to other women, Dora," he murmured regretfully, "but I never knew what they meant until now. Are you sure you can love a cold, jaded bastard like me?"

Dora smiled and ran her fingers over the muscles guarding his rib cage. He stiffened in more places than one, and she circled her hips suggestively near his. "Cold? That isn't a word I'd use to describe you. Passionate, maybe, in anger as well as love, but never cold." She swept her hand down his side to his hips and confirmed her words when his male hardness pushed against her again.

Pace brushed her face with kisses and fingered the delicate outline of her jaw. "If I am passionate, it is because you have taught me to use my passions wisely. I don't know how you learned such goodness, but I love you for it. Will you ever forgive my stupidity in not seeing it sooner?"

She rubbed her fingers over his sandpaper jaw and smiled at the familiar texture. "We will be here forever if we list our various stupidities. I should return to Frances."

He glanced down at the fullness of her breasts, then kissed them lightly. "Thank you for giving me my daughter. I would never have known how wonderful it is to be a father if you hadn't shown me."

Dora laughed and struggled to sit up when he rolled off her. Pulling on her chemisette, she kept an interested gaze on her husband's blatant male nudity. She had never known how beautiful a body could be until she'd seen Pace's.

"You can experience the wonder of fatherhood by changing her diaper when we get home. And when she is old enough to defy you, you may experience the wonder of learning how to discipline her. If she grows up anything like you, it should be an edifying experience."

Pace made a wry face. "I think I'll open an office in town and leave you to deal with the little witch then. The wonders of fatherhood should extend only to hugs and kisses."

Dora's laughter rivaled the songs of the birds in the trees overhead.

Epilogue

Stone walls do not a prison make
Nor iron bars a cage;
Minds innocent and quiet take
That for an hermitage;
If I have freedom in my love,
And in my soul am free;
Angels alone, that soar above,
Enjoy such liberty.

RICHARD LOVELACE (1618–1658)
"To Althea, from Prison"

"You know damn well you'll make a better mayor than that greedy bastard, Mitchell," Billy John declared loyally, pounding Pace on the back as they stood on the veranda steps in the warm November sunshine. The weather promised good voter turnout.

"I haven't won yet," Pace answered dryly, staring out over the emerald expanse of lawn that he was just realizing truly belonged to him. The election seemed less real than the rich Kentucky soil beneath that expanse of lawn.

"You'll win." Robert McCoy leaned against a column and blew a smoke ring. "You got Mitchell out of office, won a lot of people some decent money, and you haven't ticked anybody off lately. Joe's daddy bootlicked the federals too long for him to come back and make himself mayor again. He should have stayed in Frankfort."

"Maybe you ought to run for his seat next election," Billy John suggested as he went down the stairs to his horse.

"And get myself hung by all the rebs in this county? Not a chance. I don't have the ambition to fight those battles anymore. I've got enough to do right here at home." Pace threw a quick look down the hall behind him. The day was unseasonably warm, and Dora had

opened all the doors and windows to air the house out.
He hoped to catch a glimpse of her as she efficiently
went from task to task, but she hid somewhere in the
depths of the interior, out of sight. He didn't often have
the opportunity to hang around the house in the daytime
to watch her at work.

"You'll get a good price for that tobacco," McCoy
reassured him. "I don't know how you kept the danged
grasshoppers out of your patch. They ate mine plumb to
the ground. That hailstorm damaged so many fields east
of here that good tobacco will bring a pretty price. You
must have a guardian angel looking out for you."

Pace grinned as his own personal guardian angel
darted across the hallway in a swirl of heavenly blue.
She was learning to dress for unexpected visitors. She
didn't even notice him as she hurried up the stairs carrying—Pace squinted to make sure he was seeing correctly—a crimping iron?

Billy John caught his horse's reins and called up to
the other two men, "Polls will be closing. You goin' in
to keep an eye on the count?"

Distracted by the sight of Dora with a totally unneces-
sary piece of feminine equipment, Pace didn't even turn
around to reply. "I'll be down later. Keep an eye on
things for me."

Noticing Pace's distraction, Robert grinned, hitched
his jeans up, and started down the stairs, too. "We'll go
in and keep them in line for you. Want us to crack a
few heads if there's any sign Mitchell is cheating?"

"Whatever." Pace already moved toward the open
doorway.

Robert chuckled and threw himself in the saddle as
the town's favored candidate for mayor wandered off
after a swinging skirt. It looked like one more hotheaded
idiot had fallen under the spell of a pretty face. Despite
his Yankee politics, Pace Nicholls just might make a fair
mayor one day.

Later that evening, Dora glanced out the bedroom
window at the sight of flickering light. Her heart nearly
stopped pounding in her chest as she recognized the flare
of torches against the night sky and saw the mob surging

up the drive. She glanced hurriedly in the direction of
Jackson's farmhouse, but no lights glimmered there.
That meant the mob had left Jackson alone and had
come directly up the drive after Pace.

Feeling a scream welling inside her and not wishing
to terrify her sleeping daughter, she kept it stifled until
she hit the stairs. Then frantically screeching "Pace!"
she raced down the steps, holding her skirts high to keep
from tripping.

He immediately emerged from the study. In his shirtsleeves with a law book in his hand, he caught sight of
Dora's panicked expression and dashed down the hall
to grab her.

"A mob!" she gasped. "With torches! Oh, Pace, what
can we do?"

He blinked in disbelief, then smiled slowly. "A mob?"
His grin grew a little wider. "We'll go meet them."

It was Dora's turn to blink in disbelief. Looking at
him as if he'd finally taken leave of his senses, she tried
tugging away from his encompassing arm, but he was
too strong. He hauled her toward the door, grabbing up
a lantern left burning in the foyer for visitors.

The front lawn filled with horses and wagons and people. When Pace threw open the door, a ragged cheer
went up, followed by a louder, more boisterous one.
Pandemonium ensued as men stomped and whistled
when Dora peered hesitantly around Pace to glimpse the
cause of their excitement.

"Speech! Speech!" A voice sounding suspiciously like
Robert McCoy's yelled from the crowd's center.

Pace stepped out on the veranda, pulling Dora with
him. Relaxing as she realized what the mob represented,
Dora glanced expectantly over her shoulder. Mother Nicholls had warned her they would have company if Pace
won. She hadn't warned her the company would be half
the town.

Pace was wielding his compelling rhetoric well by the
time Dora caught sight of the person she waited for.
Slipping from Pace's arm, she stepped backward and gestured for the hesitant figure inside to come forward.

Pace turned immediately to see where Dora had gone.
His eyes widened in disbelief as his mother leaned on a

cane and hobbled toward him. She had her hair crimped
in curls around her face and wore a gown long out of
style, but she was walking out of the house for the first
time in decades. Proudly, Dora stood to one side so Harriet could approach her son.

The crowd grew quiet as she stood in front of the
town's newly elected mayor. Every person there knew
Harriet Nicholls came from one of the community's oldest and most respected families. They also knew her as
an invalid too ill to appear in public. Gossip had given
her illness many names, but none seemed applicable now
as she reached to hug her much taller son.

"I'm proud of you, Payson," she whispered brokenly
as he kissed her cheek. "I couldn't ask for a finer son.
You favor my daddy more every day. He was a fine,
upstanding man. Just ask anybody."

Dora blinked back tears as Pace hugged his mother
in full view of half the town. The election hadn't mattered to Dora one way or the other, until now. If it took
an election to bring mother and son together, then she
was thankful for it, no matter what followed. When Pace
held out his hand to her, she grabbed it and stood on
her toes to kiss his cheek. His face was as wet as hers
as he hugged them both.

The crowd cheered some more, then whistled and
stomped as Jackson came around the corner of the
house rolling a keg of beer. Behind him, Ernestine and
Annie carried trays of mugs. They hadn't held an old-
fashioned barbecue on these lawns for years, but nobody
had forgotten the basics. Yelling in triumph and merriment, the crowd turned from the touching display on the
veranda to the more important business of partying.

In all the commotion, the arrival of a new carriage
went unnoticed. As Amy came running down the stairs
in her night dress crying "An' Dora, An' Dora" to see
what the excitement was about, Dora scooped her up to
carry her back in the house. Only Pace's low whistle of
surprise halted her.

Pace had kept Dora informed when her half brother
and the solicitor left town. As long as they left her alone,
she hadn't much concerned herself with their where-
abouts. Josie had sulked for a while, but once she started

receiving thick vellum letters with wax seals on them, she returned to smiling. After Dora ascertained the letters had nothing to do with Gareth, she lost interest. If Josie wanted to correspond with a gray-haired old man who called himself Sir Something-or-Other, that was her concern. The solicitor had seemed relatively harmless, particularly half a world away.

But he wasn't half a world away. He was here now, driving up the lane, with Josie by his side. They had both rigged themselves out in all their finery, Josie in the latest winter fashion of fur-trimmed pelisse and muff even though the temperature remained mild, and Sir Archibald in top hat and frock coat. Dora stared at them in disbelief, while Pace stepped forward to shield her from anything untoward.

Holding a bouncing Amy who now shouted "Mama! Mama!" Dora waited for the explanation for this unexpected arrival. Harriet stood stolidly beside her, leaning on her cane and looking the part of grand matriarch in the evening dusk. The newcomers hurried up the stairs, smiling broadly. Surely they couldn't mean harm.

Sir Archibald held out his hand to Pace. "Congratulations, young man. I knew you would succeed in any endeavor you chose to undertake."

Pace reluctantly accepted the older man's hand and gave it a brief shake. "I thank you, I think."

Josie smacked him lightly with her muff. "Don't be such a goose, Pace. Archie is here with good news. Pretend you haven't turned into a surly Yankee and invite us in."

Archie? Dora exchanged a glance with Pace, then surrendered Amy to her mother and led the way inside. Engrossed in free beer, the crowd outside scarcely noticed their departure.

In the front parlor, Pace helped his mother into a seat while Dora offered their guest a drink from the decanter. Sir Archibald accepted it, then took a place beside Josie after Dora settled into a chair near the fireplace.

When everyone looked at the solicitor expectantly, he harrumphed a bit, swirled his drink, glanced at Josie, then settled his gaze on Dora. "Lady Alexandra, I took the liberty of inquiring of your husband the circumstances by which you were transported to this country. He corroborated a tale I had already heard from other sources in Cornwall. If you don't mind, I would like you to repeat what you remember as carefully as you can."

"I'd rather not." One of the Quaker ways that Dora had decided to continue was the refusal to acknowledge titles. She would not call this man "sir" anything. "It was a long time ago and isn't relevant to anything in the present."

The solicitor looked solemn. "I'm afraid it is, my dear. You see, your father was never convicted of any crime in the deaths of two people that day. He was held in custody for a while, but witnesses were too terrified to come forward. Only the Friend who remained behind to report that you lived would stand as witness, and a Quaker's testimony won't stand in court because they consider it an insult to swear to their truthfulness. It may be impossible bringing your father to trial after all these years, but your corroboration of the story will give the courts evidence preventing him from claiming any authority over your mother's affairs."

Dora hesitated until Josie intruded. "For land's sake, Dora! He's just asking you to tell what you remember. He isn't asking you to stand up in court. Men who brutalize women should be publicly whipped, but this is the next best thing."

That was true. If her testimony would in any way prevent her father or Gareth from ever hurting another woman, then she had a duty to give it. Haltingly, Dora repeated what she had told Pace, carefully emphasizing that much of that day was more nightmare than concrete memory

Sir Archibald nodded, took a few notes on paper he withdrew from his pocket, asked a few questions, then carefully tucked the document away. "I regret that you had to carry that nightmare with you all these years, Lady Alexandra. I also regret that I believed your father's explanation of events and dismissed the charges of the young man who declared you alive. Recent occurrences have opened my eyes. I have offered the earl my resignation, and I fear he will have great difficulty finding another solicitor or barrister to represent him once your tale becomes public knowledge, as it most certainly will if I have anything to say about it."

Dora clasped her hands in her skirt and stared at the floor. She didn't notice as Josie slipped from the room to put her sleepy daughter to bed. "I suppose I should despise him for all he's done, but I cannot help thinking that all turned out for the best. This is where I belong. I could never go back there."

Pace came to stand behind her, placing a reassuring hand on her shoulder. The solicitor nodded approvingly.

"That's as it should be. You won't be called upon to return to England if you have no desire to do so. I would just like you to know that your testimony today has saved another woman from suffering as your mother did. My sister was prepared to accept the earl's offer until Gareth asked my help in locating you. Until then, I'd understood you had died with your mother. The change in story concerned me, particularly when I realized the earl had suffered financial reverses. I have always considered him a devout and Christian man, one who did not succumb to the temptations and licentiousness so frequently indulged in by men of his wealth and upbringing. I never had reason to question his word. His denial of your existence until you stood to inherit a substantial fortune led me to question his credibility. I have already made my sister aware of my doubts and she has agreed to wait for my decision. I will notify her immediately that the earl is not a suitable husband. All of England will know that as soon as I return."

Dora looked up to meet the man's cool, gray eyes. She nodded imperceptibly. "Thank you. I would not see anyone suffer as my mother suffered. I only wish I could warn others of Gareth's cruel propensities too. I do not know if this is something that is passed from father to son, but Gareth does not even make a secret of his cruelty. He is a weak man who seeks to control those weaker than he. I wish I were in a position to warn others."

"As to that, I can make no promises. He has bought off the daughter of one of your father's tenants when he beat her so severely that she couldn't walk again, but

that is a confidence I cannot make public. Should I hear
that he is thinking of taking a wife, I will make it my
place to warn off her parents, but he will be an earl
someday. Not many will heed my warning. Perhaps he
will change. Stranger things have happened."

Pace's fingers squeezed her shoulder, and Dora covered his hand with hers. Pace could have developed into
a man even more violent than Gareth, but he had an
innate decency that Gareth would never have. Pace
would have destroyed himself faster than he would have
taken his violence out on those weaker than he. Dora
gave him a quick smile to tell him that.

She nearly missed what the solicitor said while she
stared into the loving depths of her husband's eyes. Only
when Pace's eyes grew wide and he tore his gaze away
from her to look over her shoulder at their guest did
she return her attention to the conversation.

Harriet snorted and pounded her cane on the floor in
some demonstration of glee. Josie came back downstairs
and stood in the doorway, smiling, as she glanced in
Dora's direction. When Dora returned a blank gaze,
Josie huffed into the room, forcing Sir Archibald to rise.

"She didn't even hear you, Archie! You just gave her
more money than this town is worth, and she wasn't
even listening. I swear, it would be easier if you just
took the money and dumped it into the ocean. It would
do just about as much good."

Dora turned back to the red-faced solicitor. He pulled
at his tight collar and looked down at Josie as if she were
a banquet for a starving man. Josie didn't even notice.

"Perhaps you'd better repeat what you just said, sir,"
Pace said politely. "Something about Dora's grandmother?"

Sir Archibald cleared his throat and tore his gaze away
from the woman hanging on to his coat arm as they
reseated themselves. "Your maternal grandmother
changed her will after your mother's death, Lady Alexandra. She despised Lord Beaumont and blamed him for
everything, despite his proclaimed innocence. She chose
to believe our one witness to the contrary, and even
donated large sums to the Society of Friends in later
years. She was convinced you were alive and well some-

where, and she left her entire estate to you, should you be found. The balance was to go to various charities as well as the Society should you not be found by the date of your twenty-fifth birthday. It is yours now. I've arranged for the transfer of funds."

Dora stared at him blankly. Pace spoke for her.

"I thought there was some objection to me as a suitable husband."

The solicitor beamed. "After hearing you speak so eloquently that day in the courtroom, I notified the trustees that you were more than suitable. I've since sent ample evidence verifying it. They are satisfied."

Still, Dora didn't speak. Pace squeezed her shoulder and sought the catch in this unexpected prize. "Under Kentucky law, Dora's husband has complete control over her assets. I'm sure your trustees will wish to reconsider."

That brought Dora to herself. She stamped one small shoe and glared over her shoulder at her husband. "Don't be ridiculous, Payson Nicholls. What would I do with a fortune? You may have it if you like. If we're to have half a dozen children, you will need it."

All heads swerved to stare at the demure young woman sitting with hands crossed in her lap. Pace spoke for them all, with a nervous catch in his throat. "Half a dozen children?"

Catching her skirts, Dora stood up and started out of the room with a regal tread that would have suited a queen. She didn't even turn her head as she replied, "One in the cradle and one on the way seems a good start as far as I am concerned. I'll check on Amy while I'm upstairs." This time, she did stop and turn around, her gaze going directly to her dumbstruck husband. "And you'll need to provide for Amy too. Charlie would have wanted it that way."

The riotous laughter outside seemed to echo the merriment in the room as Pace sank, speechless, to the chair his wife had just vacated.

Dora might not say much, but when she did, she certainly made her presence felt.

Pace stared at the ceiling overhead where his wife's

footsteps could be heard. With a curse, he said adamantly, "I will not name any son of mine Charlie."

Josie laughed and offered a wager to the opposite effect. While Harriet and Sir Archibald agreed on sums in Pace's favor, Pace rose from his chair like a man struck from too many directions at once.

He left a roomful of approving smiles behind him as he started toward the stairs, his speed increasing with each step closer to the woman above. They waited anxiously, expectantly, and were rewarded for their patience by the sudden hoarse creak of a bed.

As the little audience below hastily said embarrassed farewells, laughter drifted through the halls and down the stairs—carefree laughter that hadn't been heard in years.

The harps of heaven couldn't have made a sweeter sound.

Author's Note

Since this is a romance, I make no apology for not depicting the actual horrors of child abuse. I do apologize, however, if anyone reads this and believes that abused children can overcome their devastating emotional scars simply through their own motivation. Miracles can happen, but generally it requires the intervention of a third party.

Instead of offering actual scenes of abuse, I have attempted to portray the results of abuse through my characters. Children who suffer rejection from their families are frequently hostile and aggressive, emotionally unstable, lack self-esteem, and have a negative view of the world. Neglect often results in antisocial behavior, indulgence in drugs or alcohol, and inappropriate behavior such as fighting and recklessness. Often, a child who has never been praised for good behavior but is constantly punished for perceived faults will think the attention he receives for misbehaving is reason to continue the bad behavior.

With that kind of background, it is no wonder that abused children often grow into adults who cannot deal with life in any normal fashion. Girls, in particular, seek approval. As women, they continue seeking the approval of the kind of men who most resemble the parent who rejected them, thus inviting further abuse. Boys, being more aggressive, tend to take the opposite route. As men, their behavior is hostile, and they seek the kind of women who lack the self-esteem to fight back, women often like their mothers.

My characters may overcome these handicaps through their own strength of character and with the help of outside forces, but in reality, abused children, abused spouses, and their abusers need the kind of counseling the 1860s couldn't provide.

WE NEED YOUR HELP
To continue to bring you quality romance
that meets your personal expectations,
we at TOPAZ books want to hear from you.
Help us by filling out this questionnaire, and in exchange
we will give you a **free gift** as a token of our gratitude.

- Is this the first TOPAZ book you've purchased? (circle one)

    YES   NO

    The title and author of this book is: _____

- If this was not the first TOPAZ book you've purchased, how many have you bought in the past year?

    a: 0 - 5   b 6 - 10   c: more than 10   d: more than 20

- How many romances in total did you buy in the past year?

    a: 0 - 5   b: 6 - 10   c: more than 10   d: more than 20 _____

- How would you rate your overall satisfaction with this book?

    a: Excellent   b: Good   c: Fair   d: Poor

- What was the main reason you bought this book?

    a: It is a TOPAZ novel, and I know that TOPAZ stands
       for quality romance fiction
    b: I liked the cover
    c: The story-line intrigued me
    d: I love this author
    e: I really liked the setting
    f: I love the cover models
    g: Other: _____

- Where did you buy this TOPAZ novel?

    a: Bookstore   b: Airport   c: Warehouse Club
    d: Department Store   e: Supermarket   f: Drugstore
    g: Other: _____

- Did you pay the full cover price for this TOPAZ novel? (circle one)

    YES   NO

    If you did not, what price did you pay? _____

- Who are your favorite TOPAZ authors? (Please list)

- How did you first hear about TOPAZ books?

    a: I saw the books in a bookstore
    b: I saw the TOPAZ Man on TV or at a signing
    c: A friend told me about TOPAZ
    d: I saw an advertisement in_____magazine
    e: Other: _____

- What type of romance do you generally prefer?

    a: Historical   b: Contemporary
    c: Romantic Suspense   d: Paranormal (time travel,
       futuristic, vampires, ghosts, warlocks, etc.)
    d: Regency   e: Other: _____

- What historical settings do you prefer?

    a: England   b: Regency England   c: Scotland
    e: Ireland   f: America   g: Western Americana
    h: American Indian   i: Other: _____

- What type of story do you prefer?

  a: Very sexy   b: Sweet, less explicit
  c: Light and humorous   d: More emotionally intense
  e: Dealing with darker issues f: Other

- What kind of covers do you prefer?

  a: Illustrating both hero and heroine   b: Hero alone
  c: No people (art only)   d: Other_____

- What other genres do you like to read (circle all that apply)

  Mystery   Medical Thrillers   Science Fiction
  Suspense   Fantasy   Self-help
  Classics   General Fiction   Legal Thrillers
  Historical Fiction

- Who is your favorite author, and why?_____
  _____

- What magazines do you like to read? (circle all that apply)

  a: *People*   b: *Time/Newsweek*
  c: *Entertainment Weekly*   d: *Romantic Times*
  e: *Star*   f: *National Enquirer*
  g: *Cosmopolitan*   h: *Woman's Day*
  i: *Ladies' Home Journal*   j: *Redbook*
  k: Other:_____

- In which region of the United States do you reside?

  a: Northeast   b: Midatlantic   c: South
  d: Midwest   e: Mountain   f: Southwest
  g: Pacific Coast

- What is your age group/sex?   a: Female   b: Male

  a: under 18   b: 19-25   c: 26-30   d: 31-35   e: 36-40
  f: 41-45   g: 46-50   h: 51-55   i: 56-60   j: Over 60

- What is your marital status?

  a: Married   b: Single   c: No longer married

- What is your current level of education?

  a: High school   b: College Degree
  c: Graduate Degree   d: Other: _____

- Do you receive the TOPAZ *Romantic Liaisons* newsletter, a quarterly
  newsletter with the latest information on Topaz books and authors?

  YES   NO

  If not, would you like to?   YES   NO

  Fill in the address where you would like your free gift to be sent:

  Name:_____

  Address:_____

  City:_____   Zip Code:_____

  You should receive your free gift in 6 to 8 weeks.
  Please send the completed survey to:

Penguin USA•Mass Market
Dept. TS
375 Hudson St.
New York, NY 10014